LITTLE WADE AND WATCHTOWER

ABIGAIL AND THE GREAT GANG TRAP

SEAN MARCH

Copyright © 2020 by Sean March

All rights reserved.

No part of this book may be reproduced in any form or by any electronic or mechanical means, including information storage and retrieval systems, without written permission from the author.

For Naomi

Dark, yet glittering
A deep lake reflecting night
You are two, vast skies.

CONTENTS

Preface	xi
Prologue	1
1. Dark City	3
2. Laughter and Fire	16
3. At Your Service	27
4. Walking Home	34
5. The Great Pyramid	47
6. Ahkwiyàn	62
7. Good Morning	76
8. Mouse	97
9. Official Business	111
10. Phantasmagoria	126
11. Gang War	142
12. Urban Legend	161
13. Precinct Zero	177
14. Favorite Words	187
15. The Wisdom of Minerva	203
16. Peekaboo	220
17. The Master Plan	230
18. Bootblacker	247
19. The Great Gang Trap	263
20. Scorpion	280
21. A Good Death	291
22. Evidence	300
23. Ride to the Rescue	318
24. Gobsmacked	334
25. Working Men	342
26. The Longest Shadow	352
Coming Soon!	365
Acknowledgments	367
About the Author	369

<u>New York City</u>
<u>November 17th</u>
<u>1899</u>

"Even in the grave, all is not lost."
- Edgar Allan Poe

PROLOGUE

There's a legend for children who are sad and who cry,
About a little boy ghost, dressed in black, who can fly,
About a great, metal giant who stands sky high.
They'll always help you and they'll never lie.

They're the perfect team. One strong. One witty.
They know life is hard. Growing up is not pretty,
Especially when you live in New York City,
Whose streets can be dangerous, grimy and gritty.

Is there shouting at home? Do your parents drink?
Do you know someone arrested and thrown in the clink?
Is your family so poor that it always needs money?
Is life so much work that it's no longer funny?

Did either one of your parents leave?
Did someone close to you die and you continue to grieve?
Are you disfigured, deformed, disabled or sick?
Do you feel like life played some horrible trick?

Are your parents working themselves to the bone?
Are you miserable, sad, and feel all alone?
Are you afraid that you'll never live out your dreams?
Are you losing hope? Have you run out of steam?

Do you feel threatened with violence or strife?
Do you ever think about ending your life?
Don't lose heart! Don't forget there are people who care!
The ghost and the giant will fight your despair.

They will come to you when you are in danger.
They'll show you that there is still kindness in strangers.
They'll show you that, even in your darkest hour,
Deep inside you lies incredible power!

There's a legend about heroes only children can see,
About a wise little boy whose advice costs no fee,
About a fire-faced soldier as tall as a tree.
They will never stop fighting to set all children free.

So whenever your life is full of pain,
Or things are so grim that you might go insane,
You need help, but to ask will make you feel shame,
Don't ever give up. Just whisper their names.

Little Wade and Watchtower have so much to give.
When they appear in your life, get ready to live!

1
DARK CITY

"Help me!" Abigail cried out to over a thousand people at once.

Not one of them answered. Soot-blackened buildings loomed all around her. Silent storefronts ignored her cries. She knew that numerous people in their shops and apartments could hear her screaming, but no one did anything to help.

Sprinting down the sidewalk, her red hair flowing behind her like flames, her heart thumping in her chest, Abigail ran for her life. Smog infested the night sky. She saw no stars, no moon. New York surrounded her, a dirty, black city lit only by fire. All along the dark city streets stood tall, thin, metal gaslight lampposts, hissing like snakes. They illuminated the entire area with flickering flames encased in glass. Thick fog drifted inland from the East River, and the fiery lamplights created round pools of smoky light on every corner.

Cracked, uneven cobblestone streets were pocked with slimy, disgusting puddles. Sludgy rivers of curdled water gushed and overflowed in gutters. Clouds of flies buzzed over heaps of stinking trash. Rats squealed at Abigail's feet. Behind her, she heard loud, violent footsteps swarming over the filthy pavement. She could smell the men coming for her, their sweaty hands and the alcohol on their hot, rotten breaths.

"*Help me! Please!*"

Crying out, looking around for help, she found no policemen with their conical caps and brass-buttoned uniforms. At this hour, the only people out and about were homeless vagrants and scavengers, or there were a few gentlemen in top hats and long coats, but Abigail knew they meant no good. They grinned at her malevolently. She recoiled from them and raced away. No matter how many times she turned and doubled back and rounded a corner, it all felt like another confusing twist in some dark, dismal maze.

"Whoa!"

Horses and carriages, speeding up and down the streets like chariots, nearly ran her over, almost crushing her. Stallions, snorting and snarling, *clop-clop-clopped* with their heavy, metal-shod hooves. Rearing up, they brought them down like hammers that struck the pavement and splashed puddles. Large wooden wheels clattered and whirled. Carriages, lit by glowing gas lamps, lurched to abrupt stops. Coachmen, wearing top hats and overcoats, sneered and snapped their whips, forcing Abigail to stumble backward. Horses neighed, surging forward, dragging the carriages into the fog, vanishing.

Where am I? I turned left back there. Should I have done that? Should I turn right? Turn back? Where do I go? I don't remember the way. I don't remember!

Tears streamed down her face. She just wanted to go home.

Why did we move here? Why? Why? Why?

She cried as she turned another corner and fled down another ugly avenue that she could neither remember nor recognize.

"To save money," her father had told her. "We need to save money."

Save money? Abigail thought. *Who is going to save me?*

Panicking, she heard the men laughing, still storming toward her.

"*Someone please help me!*"

Nothing.

Abigail's voice echoed up and down the gloomy street. Block after block, building after building, people slammed their windows and shut their doors with loud snaps and cracks, like whips. Then she heard something that gave her hope. It wasn't a policeman's whistle. It wasn't the loud, boisterous voices of a crowd that could surround and protect her. No, the sound that gave her hope turned out to be a harsh whisper, like a snake's hiss.

"Pssst! Over here!"

Whirling around, Abigail followed the sound with her eyes. *There!* She saw a young boy, about her age, dressed in a finely tailored suit. He seemed to appear suddenly from the shadowy alley.

"I can help you! Follow me!"

Panicking, Abigail followed him. She was not sure why, but she trusted him, even though Father had warned her about boys.

"They're all rotten," he had told her. "They're either members of a gang or they want to be or they're going to be. Be careful, sometimes the gangs use little boys as bait."

Not this boy, she convinced herself as she followed him down a labyrinth of dingy alleys. *He does not look like one of them. He does not look bad at all. Actually, he looks rather elegant.*

Indeed, this mysterious boy wore a long, flowing, black tailcoat, black trousers, and a round-collared, white shirt underneath an ornate vest. To Abigail, he looked clean, wealthy, well-educated, polite, and quite old-fashioned. In fact, this little boy dressed in the kind of suit someone would have worn many, many years ago. That was it! This little boy dressed very much like her grandfather (who was long dead), but that was not the strangest thing about him.

"We're almost there! Hurry!" Moving fast, the boy darted to the left. Abigail followed. She could still hear the Longshadows thundering after her, grunting and snarling, but the boy moved so confidently. He said, "Almost there!" which meant he had a plan.

Thank Heavens! Her heart swelled up, hopeful.

"Come along! Keep up! You can do it!"

Abigail picked up speed, rushing as fast as she could until the muscles in her legs burned. As she sprinted alongside him, she wondered, *Who is he, and what is he doing out here at this time of night?*

Abigail's red hair was a twisty mess, and sweat soaked her brow while the boy's raven hair was perfectly combed and parted, even though he was running right beside her. Come to think of it, the boy did not seem to sweat, nor was he out of breath, even though they were both exerting themselves, but even these facts were not the strangest things about him.

"Just a few more blocks. We can make it."

They turned a corner and stopped briefly.

"Catch your breath. You are quite safe. Please take a moment to compose yourself." The boy even spoke like someone from a much older time, incredibly formal, polished, very mature for his age. Still, even that was not the strangest thing about him.

As they paused under one of the gaslight streetlamps for a brief rest, under that pool of light, Abigail felt just a little bit warmer. Doubling over, panting, trying to catch her breath, Abigail glanced down at the sidewalk and caught a glimpse of the boy's feet.

He wore no shoes, only a pair of long, silken white socks covering his slender feet. Abigail found this extremely odd, of course, but what she thought was even odder was that the boy's socks were completely, pristinely white. How could this be? The boy, just like her, had been running through the grimy alleys of the Lower East Side. Her shoes were filthy, but yet his socks were...pure white? That did not make sense. Nothing about him made sense.

White socks, no shoes...and a suit like grandpa? she wondered. So strange, but neither his shoelessness nor the clean color of his socks was the strangest thing about him.

"Everything will be all right. I promise. My partner and I have successfully conducted ourselves in this manner thousands of times, quite literally. Thousands."

The boy smiled. At that moment, Abigail discovered the absolutely, positively, certifiably strangest thing about him.

There they stood, perfectly still, under the white-hot gaslight, whose flame flickered and crackled like a torch, so Abigail could finally see this young boy's face clearly. He was very handsome. He had pale skin, mysterious eyes, long lashes, and a pleasant, charming smile. All of the features on his face, his graceful eyebrows, his sharp, sloping nose, his prim, proper mouth, and delicate chin, all seemed to have been drawn with the finest ink pen. At that moment, Abigail noticed that the boy's skin looked slightly...blue?

"Your partner? Who are you? Where are we going?" Abigail asked between gulps of air. Then she whipped around when five Longshadows appeared around the corner, under another streetlamp, under their own pool of light. Spotting her, they pointed.

"No time! Follow me!"

Even though her muscles burned from running and her chest felt tight from breathing too hard, Abigail broke into a sprint again but slower this time. Behind her, she could hear the Longshadows stampeding after her. She could hear them coughing, wheezing, snorting. They were tired too, but she could hear the rage in their breaths.

"This way!" the young, slightly blue boy with white socks yelled as he raced down the dimly lit street. Abigail quickly glanced behind her at the Longshadows gaining on them both. She hoped this boy knew what he was doing.

"Head for that light!" The boy pointed. Abigail spotted it, one lonely gaslight lamppost standing in front of the entrance to a cavernous alley. Anxious, she questioned the boy's strategy.

This makes no sense. All of the streetlamps were built in straight lines, following the gas pipes underground. Father taught me that. What's this one doing all the way out here, by itself? Also, wouldn't heading for something so bright make it easier for us to be found?

Finally, the glare from the gaslight made the alley look even more menacing, like a black mouth ready to swallow her up. Abigail worried about all of these things, but she still followed the boy. She trusted him; she had to trust him. The boy stopped when they reached the lamp. He pointed into the shadows.

"In there!"

Stumbling, Abigail entered the alley, delving deeper and deeper into darkness.

"We're here!" He sounded so confident, triumphant even, but she could not see why. They had sprinted into a dingy, dirty alleyway tucked between two squat, iron-grey buildings. *This is safe? How?*

Abigail stopped and considered retracing her steps back the way that she had come. The only illumination emanated from the single gaslight. Everything else was plunged into blackness, and from where she stood in the alley, the lone streetlamp now seemed as if it were miles away.

"Go in, as far as you can. All the way!" The boy's voice now seemed to echo all around her. Following the sound, Abigail ran and ran and ran until she slammed into something rock hard. Clutching her nose and face, crying out in pain, Abigail stumbled backward. She felt blood on her palm, and she tasted her split lip. She reached out and touched a solid wall of rough brick and stone.

"It's a dead end. What do we do?" Abigail asked but received no answer. "Where did you go?"

The boy had disappeared.

Oh no! Abigail panicked. *Father was right. This boy was one of them. His clothes were a costume...his hair...everything. He's led me into a trap. He baited me, and I fell for it. I'm going to die. This is it. I'm going to die.*

Abigail retreated as far back into the alley as she could and tucked herself into a tight little ball. From her vantage point, she could see the single gaslight streetlamp standing there, hissing, blasting out light in all directions. She wished it would go away, or turn off, or even fade just a little, but the fiery radiance just seemed to keep spreading deeper into the alley. The fire's orange glow seemed to crawl toward her, like lava.

Please, don't see me. Please, don't see me. Please.

Trembling and exhausted from running, she panted. Her deep breaths stirred up all her emotions, and she started to cry. Then her eyes sprang open.

Wait! she told herself. *If the boy disappeared, there must be a secret way out.*

She quickly checked everywhere for a hatch, a secret door, a ladder. There must be something.

Nothing.

Devastated, tears welling up in her eyes, she whispered, "Please. Please don't let me die." She tried to summon up some courage, but then her skin crawled when the sidewalk shook. Five sets of footsteps, like the galloping of horses, thundered toward her location. She froze. Crouching in the dark, terrified, Abigail fixed her eyes on the single streetlamp at the edge of the alley. She whimpered in fear when five brutal, ugly men appeared in the light, spreading their shadows across the walls of the buildings like black slime. Abigail held her breath. The alley measured about thirty feet deep. If she kept perfectly still and silent, they might just keep going, a slim chance, but possible. "Please," she prayed.

The men all panted, coughed, and wheezed. They leaned against the lamppost to take a rest. The Longshadows all dressed the same. All the men wore the same scuffed up, cheap leather shoes, the same tall hats, and the same scrappy, dirty, black suits with faded vests. When they stood together, clustered tight, they all seemed to meld together into the same monstrous black mass. Their faces, however, were all different shapes and sizes, all hideous and terrifying. Abigail did not know their real names, but in her mind, she gave them all nicknames to match their appearances.

The first, Growler, the oldest, had wolfish grey hair and a matching beard, cold blue eyes, sharp white teeth, and powerful, sharp-nailed hands. Abigail spied the butt of a heavy pistol and the bone handle of a long hunting knife tucked under his jacket.

The second, Thumbsucker, stood very tall and lanky, with oversized feet and hands, chubby fingers and swollen, blunt thumbs. His wild, crazy, bulging eyes were too big for his skull, and his buck teeth were too big for his mouth. He giggled and laughed at things even when they were definitely not funny. Clumsy, oafish, stupid, and immature but immensely strong, Thumbsucker struck Abigail as the kind of person who liked to "play." Unfortunately, while "playing," he could easily, accidentally poke out one of your eyes, dislocate your shoulder or break your arm and simply shrug and say "oops." To crush skulls and bash in people's brains, he carried a long, blunt wooden club horribly decorated with chips, scratches, notches, cracks, and bloodstains.

The third, Yellowteeth, the stinkiest and dirtiest, had obviously not bathed in weeks. He reeked of filth, and food stuck in his teeth. When he smiled, even in the dim light, Abigail recoiled at the sight of his ugly, stained teeth, full of cavities and cracks. Yellowteeth carried a pistol under his jacket as well. Clenching his jaws like an angry dog, Yellowteeth slipped a pair of brass knuckles over his hands and flexed his fingers.

The fourth, Spitball, a thin man, the fastest and sneakiest, blinked his sly, cruel eyes and slunk around like a snake. From his mouth, he dribbled and drooled juicy droplets of white spittle all over his chin as if it were venom. He reeked of too much alcohol, which he sipped from a silver flask that he pulled from his jacket. Giggling, Spitball whipped out a straight razor, a long, sleek, sharp silver blade that he could use to slit open a warm throat.

Finally, in the center stood their leader, who frightened Abigail most of all. A vile, older man, fat and grotesque, like a wild boar, Pighead snarled and grunted. Barely visible beneath his hat, Pighead's scalp bristled with tufts of hair. He had a nose like a hog's snout, stunted and smushed up against his face, with snotty, snorting nostrils. Pighead's swollen hands were covered in ugly, hairy bumps; his fingers ended in long, dirty nails. His plump belly bulged out, and warts covered his fleshy face. Too fat and heavy for his stubby legs, Pighead limped. His forehead overflowed with sweat. Panting, he inflated and deflated like a balloon. He smelled awful, like dirty laundry.

The five Longshadows, catching their breath, chuckled.

"Why you gotta make us run?" Spitball heaved. Then all of the men quieted down as Pighead wiped his sweaty, slimy brow with a dirty handkerchief and stepped forward.

He stared into the alley and locked eyes with Abigail. "You're a swift one." Pighead wriggled his bumpy fingers. Then his evil eyes glinted, "But it's over now."

Abigail backed up against the wall. With no way out, the alley may as well have been a pit. Pighead smiled maliciously. Instantly, the five Longshadows clumped together, side by side, and built a barrier with their sweaty bodies. They began to close in on her, sealing the alley off from the rest of the world. Stalking toward Abigail, they blocked the streetlamp's fire like an eclipse. Abigail felt even more enshrouded than before. Sinking down to the ground, Abigail could not contain herself.ABigail could not contain herself. Tears flowed down her face. The five men crowded around her.

"*Please! Somebody help me!*"

"Nobody's coming." Pighead limped toward her, flexing his ugly hands. "Nobody cares."

Crying, Abigail pitifully slapped Spitball's hand away when he poked and prodded at her. All around her, the five Longshadows laughed at her and jeered.

"Aw, you want your daddy to save you?" Pighead grinned.

On reflex, she nodded, which only made them laugh more.

"Awwww!" Yellowteeth chuckled. He reached for her.

"Don't touch me!"

In response, he raised one of his brass-knuckled fists in front of her face. "Behave yourself!" Yellowteeth hissed. His putrid breath, stinking like beer and vomit, forced her to retch. Disgusted, Abigail raised both of her arms to protect herself and covered her nose and mouth.

Pighead pursed his lips and jammed two of his fat fingers into his mouth and then blew, letting out a high-pitched whistle. It nearly blew out Abigail's hearing. Wincing, she covered her ears with her hands. A second later, from a short distance away, another high-pitched whistle responded. Then five more Longshadows, wearing similar dark suits and hats, appeared at the mouth of the alley. Abigail shivered. The second wave of black-clad gangsters flowed toward her like an oil spill. They cornered her. She felt the air getting sucked out of the alley, leaving barely enough for her to breathe.

The leader of this second pack of Longshadows, who Abigail nicknamed One-Eye (because he wore an eyepatch over his scarred face), saluted Pighead and then joined him. Now there were ten members of the gang, lit from behind by the single gaslight, creating sinister silhouettes. The tallest of One-Eye's group, a mammoth man she nicknamed Big Chin, carried a bulky, burlap sack that writhed and wriggled around, making muffled noises.

"Didn't expect you to be so close by." Pighead sounded a little surprised. He gestured to Big Chin's bag. "Who did you snatch?"

"Shoeshine boy," One-Eye spat. "We spotted him two blocks from here. Little urchin seemed healthy enough. Figured we'd scoop him up for the Boss."

Pighead's eyes narrowed suspiciously. "What shoeshine boy? We didn't see anything."

"We followed him straight here. You didn't spot him?"

"No one got past us," Growler growled.

"Guess you're losing your touch. We tracked him running this way, bagged him up." Then One-Eye leaned forward to get a good look at Abigail. "Who's she?"

Abigail stared straight at him and whispered, "Please, don't let him take me." For a brief moment, she detected in One-Eye's face a flash of real remorse. Something told her he probably raised children of his own. He briefly hesitated, then he sighed bitterly.

"I'm sorry, little girl," One-Eye whispered. "There's nothing I can do for you."

Abigail's heart sank. Tears streamed down her face. In response, the men all laughed out loud, barking like a pack of dogs. Spitball spat, and a clump of phlegm and saliva plopped in front of her. Abigail recoiled from it as if flinching from acid. Her eyes searched all of the surrounding buildings. There were dozens of windows and fire escapes with iron ladders and stairways, but they were too high up for her to reach. She felt like an animal trapped in a cage.

"*Help me! Somebody, please help me!*" Abigail exclaimed.

Then the burlap sack suddenly sprang to life, and the little boy trapped inside began to shout as well. "*Help me! Please help me!*"

"Shut up!" Big Chin grunted and dropped the bag onto the cold, stone ground with a loud *whoomph*! The little boy's voice cut off.

"Please! Help! Help!" Abigail desperately hollered. Her voice echoed throughout the alley, reverberating up the walls of brick, stone masonry, and metal that sealed her in like a prison. Only one window stood open. A faint, flickering candle stood on the sill, illuminating the smeared glass. Abigail called up to it expectantly, hoping for a sign.

"Please!"

Then the candle winked out, and the window's shutters slammed shut with a loud crack that echoed throughout the alley until it faded away, leaving only a hopeless, dead silence.

"She's got a tough spirit, this one!" Pighead boasted.

All ten of the Longshadows, who had quieted down to let her scream, waited for a moment, then burst out laughing. Abigail frantically looked everywhere for help, but nothing happened. No one answered. All of the windows were closed, cold, and indifferent. Staring up at the starless sky, Abigail slid down the wall, collapsing to the ground. She clasped her hands together, and she prayed.

"That's enough of this nonsense," Pighead snorted. "Come along, girl!"

"No," Abigail spoke quietly, but firmly, staring straight up at Pighead's awful, ugly face.

"What did you say?" Pighead sucked in his bloated, fat cheeks, surprised.

"I won't let you take me alive. There's nothing I can do. There's nowhere I can go. There's no one to help me. My life is over, so you may as well end it now. It will only be worse if I go with you."

All of the Longshadows grunted in confusion. They certainly had not seen that coming. Surprised, the Longshadows stepped back and argued among themselves.

"Now what?"

"What do we do?"

"We can't just kill her!"

"She won't come quietly."

"Then knock her out!"

While they bickered, Abigail sat back and wiped her tears away. She was done crying, screaming, asking for help, and running. Now, she recollected all of the happiest moments of her life. She recalled walking in Central Park with her father, holding his hand, reaching her other hand out to touch all of the flowers, and remembered running her hands over every wooden object that her father ever carved for her. She pictured all of the shelves stuffed with her favorite books. Their printed words echoed in her mind, their crisp pages crackled against her fingertips, and the smell of dusty paper and dry ink tickled her nose. She remembered the taste of her mother's cooking and felt her mother's warm cheeks against her lips. Abigail's fingers tingled as she recalled racing them through her mother's red hair, and then she let out a peaceful sigh. *I'll be with Mama soon. I've lived a good life, and now it's come to an end.* Resigned, Abigail took one last look around the alley, the last place she would ever see.

Wait, what was that?

Narrowing her eyes, Abigail rose to her feet because she spied something at the edge of the alley. Pighead quickly slapped her across the face with his rough, sweaty hand. Abigail fell backward, clutching her mouth.

"You behave!" Pighead barked. "Now someone knock this brat out, and let's be off!"

The ten men loomed over her. Lit from behind by the fiery light at the mouth of the alley, they cast ten long shadows over Abigail. She could smell the beer and food on their breath and taste her own blood in her mouth. *There!* She caught it again in the corner of her eye.

Something very strange happened, something that neither Growler, nor Spitball, nor Pighead, nor Yellowteeth, nor Thumbsucker, nor One-Eye, nor Big Chin, nor the rest of their crew noticed, but Abigail did. Every few seconds, she looked past these awful men, all the way down to the alley's entrance, where the gaslight stood there shining like a lonely star in a night sky. She hoped to see someone, anyone, a kind passerby, or perhaps even a Metropolitan policeman, cross into the shining pool of light. Then she could cry out, and someone might come and save her.

No one came, but she did see something quite different.

Peering past the men, at the mouth of the alley and the single streetlamp, Abigail, unfortunately, did not see anyone step into the light. Instead, she saw the lamppost at the edge of the alley...move?

Did I just see that? I did!

She swore that the lamp had moved. She swore that it turned to look directly at her.

2

LAUGHTER AND FIRE

"I'll knock her out," Thumbsucker volunteered.

"*No!* Not you! You'll break her in half."

"Boss doesn't want her damaged."

It happened again. Thumbsucker stepped between Abigail and the streetlamp for a moment, blocking her view. When he shifted position, she could see it again. The lamppost moved at least five feet closer! Before, it had been standing on the edge of the sidewalk, right near the street. Now it stood at the mouth of the alley. The brightness and angle of the illumination had changed, but the Longshadows seemed not to notice.

"We need a Blackjack. That'll do it."

"Anyone got a Blackjack?"

"Who's got a Blackjack?"

"Blackjack?"

"Nobody brought a Blackjack?"

"I didn't. Did you?"

"Why would I carry one? I kill people. You can't kill people with a Blackjack."

"That's the point. That's why we need one."

"Here, I've got a dang Blackjack."

One Eye pulled out a soft pouch with a lump of metal in it that could knock someone out with one, blunt strike: a Blackjack.

"All right, get on with it. Knock the brat out. Let's move."

"No." Abigail shook her head. "No. *No!*"

One Eye seized her by the wrist. "I'm sorry, girl."

"Hey, where did all of this fog come from?"

Distracted by the moving lamp, Abigail turned her attention back to the alley, which had filled up with a dense, silvery mist. It began as just a few wisps of white vapor around her hands and feet and curling around the fire escapes. Quickly, it spread everywhere, all around them, tangling them all up like a spider's web, obscuring everyone's sight.

"Something's off," One Eye sounded worried.

"It's just fog from the river, from the wharf! It's nothing," Pighead blurted out. He sounded nervous.

"I've never seen it like this," Growler warned them. He pulled out his hunting knife, sensing something.

Abigail sensed it, too…something in the air, something hiding, watching, surrounding them. Then they all heard rustling coming from the burlap sack that Big Chin had slammed down onto the ground, the bag that contained the shoeshine boy. Before, the bag had been screaming and writhing around in the man's arms. From the moment it hit the ground, it had gone silent.

The bag started to wriggle on the ground like a worm. Startled, One Eye released Abigail. Then the sack sat up and started to laugh, a cruel, mocking laugh, the laugh of a child about to play a nasty prank.

"*Hahahahahahahahahahaha!*"

Abigail could perceive the outline of the boy's face and his wide-open mouth, even through the sack.

"*Hahahahahahahahahahaha!*"

"*Shut up!*" One Eye yelled at him.

The fog thickened.

The flame flickered.

"*Hahahahahahahahahahahaha!*"

"I said *shut up!*" One Eye roared and then gestured to Big Chin, who drew back his fist and prepared to smash the shoeshine boy across his face.

Abigail screamed, "*No! Don't!*"

Just as Big Chin punched the burlap sack, it completely disappeared.

Everybody froze.

"Did you all see that?" One Eye spoke first.

"What?" Abigail managed to whisper.

"Jeez." Spitball's eyes sprung open.

Growler did not say anything. Sniffing, clutching his hunting knife, he glanced around the alley like he was about to be attacked.

"Wha...?" Yellowteeth could barely form words.

Pighead glanced around. "Stand fast."

One Eye lunged forward and thrust his hands down to the ground. Feeling around the fog-blanketed stone floor of the alley, he picked up an empty burlap sack and felt inside. The streetlamp flickered.

"We followed the boy," One Eye spoke up, holding up the empty burlap sack. "We ran him down. We picked him up...wait. You!" He gestured to Big Chin. "You grabbed the boy, picked him up, and threw him in this bag?"

"Yup," Big Chin answered with his deep voice.

"When you carried it, this bag, did it feel heavy or light?"

Shrugging, Big Chin simply grunted. "Everything feels light to me."

"What's happening?" Thumbsucker spoke for everyone.

"We're leaving!" Pighead roared, trying to instill order. "Did you hear me?" Pighead insisted. "It's a trick. The fog, the flickering light... the boy slipped out and got away. Seize the girl. *Now!*"

In the dancing light of the fire, One Eye gazed fearfully at Abigail. All color drained from his face.

"I know what's happening. It's them. It's *them!* They've come for *her!*"

"Me?" Abigail shook her head, not understanding. The fog closed around all of them like fingers. The Longshadows murmured, frightened. They readied their weapons. Abigail, alarmed and even more confused, backed away slowly.

"We have to let her go!" One Eye warned Pighead. "Leave her!"

"No! *No!* She's *mine!*" Pighead roared, reached out, and seized Abigail by the arm.

"*No! Don't!*" Abigail protested, but just as Pighead pulled Abigail toward him, the glow from the lamppost abruptly winked out and vanished, plunging the foggy alley into darkness.

"They're here," One Eye whispered.

"Stand fast. Strike matches! Ignite a torch!" Growler commanded.

"I can't see nothin'," Spitball complained.

"Shut up, all of you! Let's feel our way out," Pighead snorted.

Then Abigail heard a sound.

What was that?

They *all* suddenly heard whirring, clicking, clanking, hissing, knocking, popping, grinding, the sounds of some mechanism powering up. Abigail flinched at the screeching clamor of steel bending and gears cranking. Abigail recognized the noise, very similar to one of the hulking machines her father worked on in the factory, but she sensed that there was something more. It sounded like something waking up and coming alive.

Peering into the misty darkness, Abigail swore she could see something enormous lurking in the black. *There!* She could barely make it out. High up, at least twelve feet off the ground, a low flame lit up. A flickering red and blue dot appeared in the black as if an angry cyclops had opened its single, piercing eye. Deep, monstrous breathing, metallic and hollow, like someone sucking air through a metal tube, resonated menacingly throughout the alley and chilled everyone to the bone. Hovering in midair, the red and blue dot, the burning eye, floated forward. As it did, heavy, thudding, booming footsteps shook the ground.

Yellowteeth screamed. Something yanked him deep into the fog, and he vanished. Terrified, Abigail broke away from the Longshadows and scampered backward until she felt the cold, wet brick and stone wall against her back. Frozen in fear, she did not move. Thumbsucker, roaring like an ogre, rushed toward the flickering red and blue eye and swung his hefty piece of wood. He struck something with a loud *crack*, and the club split and splintered against metal. "Muh...muh...monster?" Thumbsucker managed to squeeze out of his clumsy mouth before something punched him in the face, sending him flying backward. His skull knocked against the wall, and several of his bones cracked. Abigail cringed as Thumbsucker exhaled before falling unconscious and slumping to the ground.

"*What's happening?*" Pighead squealed.

"*We have to get out of here!*" One Eye called out.

Whoosh!

With a roaring rush, the gaslight flame reappeared, this time standing in the dead center of the alley.

"*What the heck is that?*" Spitball yelled.

"*Run!*"

Something lashed out and attacked, and the Longshadows all started screaming. All around Abigail, the dense fog obscured her sight. Lit up by the firelight, the murky, swirling mist glowed bright gold, orange, and red. Inside the luminous cloud, the remaining eight Longshadows were nothing but tiny silhouettes getting thrashed by something gigantic and powerful. Abigail saw what resembled a miniature sun floating and darting through the fog. Every time the fireball moved, another thudding impact detonated in the alley. Peering closer, she swore she saw an incredibly tall, thin man reach out with incredibly long arms and brutally assault the Longshadows. It was like watching a scarecrow slaughter squawking black birds.

"*Shoot it!*"

Bang! Bang! Two pistol shots flashed and cracked the air like thunderclaps. Two loud *clangs* and then a pair of *pew pew* sounds reverberated throughout the alley as two bullets ricocheted and bounced harmlessly against the walls, sparking against the brick and stone. Abigail jumped at a loud swatting sound, followed by a loud crack.

"*My hand!*" Pighead screamed in agony.

Abigail then turned just in time to spot a smoking pistol fly past her head and crash against the wall. Someone, or something, had slapped the weapon clean out of Pighead's grip. Petrified, Abigail shut her eyes tight. Her hands clasped in prayer, Abigail did not see what happened next, but she could hear, smell, feel everything. She felt an overwhelming source of heat against her skin, and she flinched with every impact, every agonizing cry.

"*Too strong!*" Big Chin, his jaw broken, blood filling his mouth, whimpered just before something knocked him out with a crushing impact.

"*Run! Run!*" Abigail heard boots scuttling away from her, Longshadows trying to flee, but then she felt two huge, booming footsteps chase after them. Abigail heard men whimper, and then metal gears grind and groan. Then she flinched at a deafening, clamping sound, like a claw pinching flesh and bone.

"*It's got me! It's got me! Aaaaahhh!*"

Wailing men flew through the air and collided against the walls of the alley. Their pathetic cries stopped with loud *whumps*!

"*Fight!*" Growler roared. "*Fight!*"

"*Kill it!*" Pighead squealed.

"*Stab it! Stab it!*"

"*It's too strong!*"

Even though Abigail covered her ears, the battle sounded as if she were inside a burning storm. Something titanic rumbled and roared like thunder as it moved through the alley. Her ears took in so many horrific sounds. Ribs and skulls cracked against metal. Metal clashed and clanged with even stronger metal, and Abigail felt drops of blood and sweat fling themselves against the walls and splatter like rain.

"*Help me!*"

"*Aaaaaahhhh!*"

She yelped as another man flew through the air and crashed against the fire escapes, which loomed over ten feet above the alley.

"*Aaaaaaaaahhhh!*" another one of the Longshadows screamed.

Snap! Another bone broke.

Through it all, Abigail, even covering her ears, could not block out the whirring, clicking, hissing, clanking, stomping, thudding, punching, and screaming, so much screaming. Then, after a few more *whumps* and *slaps* and *crunches* and *yelps* and *whimpers*, the alley fell quiet. The wispy fog stood perfectly still, like a web that seemed to snatch up all of the sounds and clutch them tightly.

Silence.

Complete silence.

Abigail slowly, nervously, opened her eyes. Looking around, her mouth dropped open. The fog gently wafted and lingered in the alley, and the golden gleam from the gaslight, blurry but still bright, hovered in place. Because of the glow, the silvery vapor did not feel like an icy, chilly mist. Instead, it felt warm, like steam. The whirring, hissing, clanking slowed and quieted down. Abigail heard the metallic breathing again. Peering through the haze, Abigail could not detect any of the men.

"*Gah!*" A trembling hand reached out.

Abigail flinched. Pighead crawled out of the fog toward her. His crushed hat lay next to him, so Abigail could see the top of his scalp, which was covered in chunky warts and thin, receding hair. His lumpy nose had burst open, and it gushed blood. He spat out two of his teeth from his swollen, bruised mouth. His bloated cheeks dripped blood, and his vile lips were split open. One of his eyes, horribly bruised, puffed up. Something had fractured his right arm. Folded backward, his bashed limb twitched at his side like a broken wing. The man she called Pighead, who once loomed over her like a terrible monster, now seemed like nothing more than a crushed bug.

"Gah...guh...bleh..." he uttered as he painfully inched toward her, reaching out with his shattered, left hand. Two of his fingers had been snapped and bent backward, and his mangled thumb swelled up bright red.

"...I'm...sorry."

Obscured by the fog, the golden light floated toward Pighead. As the shining beacon moved forward, the clicking and whirring grew louder and heavy footsteps thudded against stone. Pighead turned and faced the light, which illuminated his panicked, battered face.

Then something from inside the mist grabbed Pighead's outstretched leg.

"No...*No!*" he cried and whimpered.

Something snatched him back into the fog with such force that he practically flew off the ground, vanishing back into the murky clouds. Peering into the smoky haze, Abigail could make out the silhouette of an incredibly tall, thin man, wearing a top hat. This mysterious figure loomed over Pighead, who cowered on the ground and feebly held up his one functioning arm to defend himself.

"We...were...just doin' what we were told!"

The giant with the top hat stood over the criminal. Abigail narrowed her eyes. *Strange, the blaze seems to be radiating from...the tall man's...face?* Abigail could not perceive anything clearly, but the light illuminated enough for her to see this gigantic figure raise his arm and bring it down like a hammer on Pighead's ugly, bulbous face.

"No..."

Whump!

Pighead's whole body snapped back, and his skull cracked against the stony ground. One last gasp escaped from his body. Then the dark giant with the top hat and the glowing face turned toward Abigail.

"Oh, no."

The floating flame moved forward, whirring, clicking, hissing, grinding, and clanking. The towering, shadowy figure stomped toward Abigail, and the leaden footsteps crushed hats, knives, pistols, even stones beneath them.

"Don't hurt me," Abigail clasped her hands in prayer and shut her eyes. "Please, don't hurt me."

"Don't worry," someone whispered in her ear.

"*Ahh!*" she screamed. Startled, her eyes sprang open.

Right next to her, there he was. The mysterious, stylishly dressed, little, slightly blue boy stood there again.

"He's not going to hurt you. He's never hurt a child in his whole, entire life, and he's been around for quite some time."

Immediately, Abigail chastised him. "You? Where did you go? You led me into this?"

"Of course, I led you into this," the little, slightly blue boy stated matter-of-factly. "We engineered a trap for them."

"You used me as bait?" Abigail fumed.

"You were not the bait," the little, slightly blue boy spoke gently, trying to mollify her. "You were the spring, and you played your part brilliantly. Thanks to you, ten gangsters will never torment another child again, or at least not for several years. Well done."

The boy's compliment, combined with his refined, exquisite manners, made Abigail feel better for a brief moment. Nevertheless, she was, understandably, very upset, and she quickly puffed up and reddened again.

"Why? Why did you leave me?"

"Please, forgive my absence. We needed the Longshadows to think that you were alone, and for that ruse to work, *you* needed to believe it, too. Besides, I had to concentrate on the bag illusion, which proved to be quite intricate and involved. Simultaneously, the situation necessitated that I produce a convincing fog as well," the little, slightly blue boy apologized. "Terribly sorry, but as you can see...it all worked out quite swimmingly."

Abigail noticed that the fog disappeared just as quickly as it had materialized, and her vision was no longer obscured. All ten Longshadows lay busted, bent, bashed, bruised, beaten, and bloodily unconscious. These nasty, despicable men were all lying flopped on the ground, contorted in strange poses like badly treated dolls that had been torn up and thrown away. Their chests rising and falling, they were not dead, but when they woke up they would wish that they were. Abigail could see all of this, not only because the fog had lifted, but also because of the golden glow that radiated from a flickering fire. When she beheld the true source of the light, Abigail, gazing upward, stepped back in awe.

"Go on, please introduce yourself to the young lady."

Someone, or something, very tall and very heavy, stepped right in front of Abigail with another *boom*. Immediately, Abigail marveled at her mysterious rescuer's shoes, which were finely crafted, leather, with silver buckles, the kind her father could never afford. They were a gentleman's shoes, sturdy, but very fashionable, a little scuffed now from the battle, but nevertheless of superb quality. Intrigued, Abigail listened to the constant whirring, clicking, clanking, hissing, knocking, popping, grinding noises, the sounds of a machine. She felt warmth on her face, like daylight. Using her hand to partially shield her sight, as if blocking out the sun, Abigail stared up at the immense man standing before her.

She estimated he stood at least ten feet tall, no wait, more than that, twelve feet. Even though quite tall and thin, he had wide shoulders, a broad chest, and a formidable pair of long, gangly arms. He wore a distinguished suit, very finely tailored, with a brocade vest decorated with dozens of finely sewn silver gears. Unfortunately, this stylish outfit had suffered several rips and slashes from the gang's bullets and blades. Through these holes, Abigail perceived what could only be described as polished metal skin. *Polished metal skin?*

This Herculean man wore fine leather gloves over his brawny hands. His fingers flexed open and closed, squeaking like hinges. Abigail finally detected the source of the mechanical whirring, clicking, clanking, hissing, knocking, popping, grinding: the giant's limbs and joints. Abigail became confused. *Is this a man or a machine?* His chest rose and fell as if he were breathing.

Who is he? What is he? she thought. Questions flooded her mind. *Does he wear armor beneath his suit? Have I been rescued by a Medieval knight? Wait, why would a knight be dressed in a suit? Might he be wearing a helmet? I better get a look at his face.* She adjusted her gaze up, up, up. This man was so tall! Craning her neck, Abigail elevated her sight all the way past his shoulders, above his neck...and she gasped.

His face was...the top of a lamppost?

Indeed, this colossal steel Goliath had no eyes, no nose, no mouth, no cheeks, no chin. Instead, four panes of glass contained a flickering gas lamp that radiated a gorgeous, incendiary light and spread a glowing warmth. Fire was the massive man's only facial feature. Abigail found this mysterious, metallic giant's head to be entirely indistinguishable from the tops of the gaslights that lined the city streets and provided luminosity and heat. For Abigail, who gazed up at him in absolute wonder, this humanoid mechanism had a face like a star. The flame glittered, glinted, and shimmered through the glass. His chest did indeed rise and fall like someone breathing, and with every breath, his fiery face flickered and flashed.

Gas, Abigail observed. *He's powered by…gas.*

Abigail could not see the very top of this strange being's wondrously odd head because he wore an oversized, black top hat, the most finely crafted she had ever seen. Then, this fire-faced, unusual individual reached up to the brim of his hat and saluted Abigail as a gentleman would. Apparently, this magnificent, massive, mechanical man had manners.

The little, slightly blue boy then bowed gracefully toward Abigail. "Pleased to make your acquaintance. Allow us to introduce ourselves. I'm Little Wade," he gestured to his enormous, whirring, hissing, clanking companion, "…and this is Watchtower."

3

AT YOUR SERVICE

Still clicking and clanking, Watchtower gently, gingerly, reached into the front pocket of his suit and delicately pinched a handkerchief. Extracting it slowly from his pocket, he extended it to Abigail, who received it in her hands. The fabric felt soft, like a feather, and wonderfully soothed her skin as she wiped her face, cleaning up blood from her split lip, snot from her nose, and the streaked tears on her cheeks. The pain, the dirt, the blood, the salty drops all seemed to completely vanish as if they had never happened at all.

"It's made from clouds," Little Wade gestured to the cloth and remarked as if that were perfectly normal. Abigail took a moment to examine it. Then she took another moment to behold the little, slightly blue boy, and the magnificent, massive, mechanical man, both standing politely before her.

"You're safe now," Little Wade comforted her.

After so much tension, Abigail allowed all of her emotions to completely unwind. She burst into tears.

"Thank you," Abigail cried. "Oh, thank you so much!"

She bolted forward and embraced one of Watchtower's tree-trunk-like legs, encircling his limb with her arms. He did not object. Underneath his suit, Abigail felt hard, iron bars instead of bones, and powerful, coiled springs instead of muscles. Her fingertips touched sharp metal joints, and armor-plated, steel skin. He did not feel cold. He felt warm-blooded. Her ear pressed up against Watchtower's leg, Abigail could hear steam and hot liquid flowing through him. Reaching down, he ever so gently patted her head with his gloved hand. Abigail turned to face Little Wade, who stood close by. Wiping her tears, clutching the handkerchief in one hand, she whispered, "You saved my life." He could tell what she intended to do.

"I'm going to forewarn you," Little Wade began, "what worked on Watchtower will not work on—*wait!*"

Abigail rushed toward Little Wade to hug him.

"*Wait!*"

"Whoa!"

Splat!

Wet, surprised, and confused, Abigail quickly sprang up and turned around. She had passed straight through him and had fallen face-forward into one of the alley's many cold puddles. Looking more closely, she promptly gasped when she saw that Little Wade was not actually standing there at all.

"You're...you're floating!" she exclaimed, pointing to his shoeless, white-socked feet that hovered above the cold pavement.

"I wanted to inform you, but the opportunity failed to present itself in time."

"You're...levitating off the ground."

"Very observant."

"How can that be?"

"It's not that difficult when you don't possess a body to weigh you down."

"What...are you?"

"Guess."

"Wait...are you...are you a ghost?"

"I am indeed."

"A ghost?"

"Ghost, phantom, phantasm, specter, wraith, haunt, incorporeal being, what you will."

"You mean...you're dead?"

"Last time I checked."

"You're dead? Actually dead?"

"Yes, unfortunately, or fortunately, depending on the circumstances and one's point of view. I confess mine changes daily."

"I'm actually speaking to a ghost? This is not some trick?"

Amused, Little Wade smiled and turned to his humongous friend. "Demonstrate, please."

Watchtower swung one of his heavy, metal arms back and forth, which passed through Little Wade's floating body as if it were nothing. Every time Watchtower's hand struck, Little Wade's spectral form flickered just a little bit in the way a candle's flame does when caught in a gust of wind. After a few seconds, Watchtower ceased. Little Wade hovered there and crossed his arms.

"How...how is this possible?"

"No time to explain right now, but if you accompany us, I promise this will all make much more sense than it does at this moment."

"Who are you?" Abigail asked, but then quickly corrected herself. "I mean, I know who you are. You gave me your names, but...I suppose a better question is...*what* are you?"

"All you need to know right now is that we consider your safety not only our responsibility but also our proud occupation. Rest assured you're in the hands of professionals. Now, would you care to give us the pleasure of your name?"

"Oh, heavens, I am so sorry," Abigail chastised herself. "You saved my life, and I haven't even properly introduced myself. My father would be so disappointed. I am so sorry. I'm Abigail Reid."

"No need to apologize, Abigail Reid," Little Wade laughed. "One time, a little boy we rescued took one look at us and forgot his own name for five whole hours."

"I didn't mean to be rude," Abigail apologized. "It's so strange. At first, you both surprised me, obviously, so I forgot, but then once I spoke to you, it felt as if I had known you for quite a while, so I didn't think to mention it."

This seemed to please Little Wade. "Encouraging. Not everyone takes the sight of us so well as you."

"Well..." Abigail shrugged. "You're much better than the alternative." She gestured to the ten unconscious hoodlums.

"Do you recognize these men?" Little Wade, curious, inquired.

"Yes. This morning, I spotted them watching me walk to school. Do you know who they are?"

"Yes, we do. More importantly, we know their master all too well."

"Who leads this awful organization?"

"A complicated answer. We will speak of him later. Now's not the time."

"Why were they trying to kidnap me? Do you know?"

"We don't know...yet...but we intend to find out," Little Wade answered cautiously before he changed the subject. "What were you doing out so late? Your parents must be worried sick about you."

"My father's working now, unfortunately. He always works late."

Little Wade's eyes narrowed.

"He's working now, at this time of night? Who is he? What's his profession?"

"My father's name is Martin Reid. He works three jobs. He considers being a carpenter his primary vocation. He freelances. Wait, I suppose that would be his fourth job. To earn a stable income, he works two shifts at the docks and one at a factory."

"At the docks, he works as a stevedore?"

"I know he picks up and stacks lots of hefty boxes."

"A stevedore, they work at all hours. Do you work as well?"

"Yes. After school, I assist Mr. Kowalski."

"The local butcher?"

"Yes."

"That explains your lack of squeamishness at all of this blood," Little Wade observed. "So, what happened? Did you end up working late at the butcher shop?"

"After I finish my shift, I do my reading for school at the shop,"

Abigail explained. "Mr. Kowalski set up a desk for me in the back. Most of the time, I leave the shop much earlier and head home, but today I fell asleep doing my homework. I underestimated my level of exhaustion."

"So...who resides at your home now?"

"No one. I let myself in and out." Abigail produced a key from her coat pocket.

Little Wade and Watchtower glanced at each other. Saddened at first, Little Wade then lightened his mood. "Well, Abigail Reid, you've nothing to fear from us," Little Wade remarked. "You're lucky we were out on patrol when we were. Now, with your permission, we would like to escort you home. It's our business, but also our pleasure. May we chaperone you?"

"I would be delighted!"

Little Wade snapped his fingers. Prompted, Watchtower reached into his jacket pocket and pinched a small business card, which seemed to pop up as if it were spring-loaded. Kneeling, he extended his hand and offered it to Abigail. Encouraged, Abigail reached out, took the business card from Watchtower, and she held it in her hand. Studying it carefully, she jumped when she heard *tweeeeeeet!*

A loud whistle, followed by the rough footsteps of boots on cobblestones, interrupted them. In the distance, several gruff men called to each other. "*This way! Over here!*"

"About time," Little Wade muttered, a little frustrated. Floating upwards into the sky as if to get a better view, Little Wade called down, "It's the police! They're coming from the south. It's time to go. Come along!"

Watchtower stomped off down the alley. As he exited to the sidewalk, he reached up and grabbed a long overcoat hanging from one of the fire escapes. Abigail deduced that he had cast it aside before the fight. Draping the coat around himself, Watchtower beckoned to Abigail and then marched away, whirring, clinking, clanking, and thudding. Next to him, Little Wade sailed nimbly, effortlessly through the air. Abigail hesitated.

"Come along! They can't hurt you anymore!"

Gulping, stepping over the unconscious, broken, bloody bodies of the ten Longshadows who had chased and attacked her, Abigail followed Little Wade and Watchtower out of the alley. Then she turned left and took off as quickly as she could.

Little Wade, zigging and zagging through the air, flew a loop-de-loop around Watchtower with a loud *"Woooooooo!"* Following them, dashing down the block, leaving the alley far behind, Abigail, giddy with excitement, giggled. When she had placed enough distance between herself and the site of the battle, Abigail paused for a moment to examine the business card she cradled in her hand. It read:

"Little Wade and Watchtower," Abigail repeated to herself and smiled. Relieved and relaxed, she exhaled and followed the little, slightly blue boy ghost flying alongside his giant, fire-faced, mechanical friend. Turning another corner, she stopped and took in a sight that overwhelmed her.

Usually, whenever she traveled down the streets of New York City, she always felt so nervous. She rushed all the time, avoiding eye contact with people, focused entirely on where she needed to go. The sidewalks, alleys, avenues, and crossings always seemed so menacing, grimy, and gritty. As a result, she never truly got the chance to stop, look around, and appreciate how beautiful it could be.

Stretching out before her, as far as she could see in all directions, an intricate network of tall, gas streetlamps cast a warm, ethereal glow all along the sidewalks. Although she knew the flames were small, like candles encased in crystal, tonight they shone like a million miniature suns, bathing the city in gold. Above her, the beautiful night sky gleamed full of stars.

The night sky looks like a vast city, and the city at night looks like a starlit sky. They reflect each other, two cities full of stars, two skies. This once threatening, smoky city now seemed to contain a whole multitude of universes with infinite possibilities. For the first time at night in New York, Abigail did not feel alone, helpless, and afraid. Instead, she felt completely safe and secure, something she had not felt in a very, very long time.

"Come along, Abigail Reid! It's time to take you home," Little Wade called out to her, backflipping through the air. "We have so many things to show you! *Wooohooo!*" Little Wade's voice echoed up and down the mostly deserted street.

Watchtower turned back toward Abigail and gestured with his massive arm as if to say, "Come this way." Watchtower had no face, no mouth, no voice, no words, yet Abigail understood precisely what he meant. She knew that she could trust him, trust both of them, completely.

Then she glanced around and oriented herself. *We're currently...on Mott Street, and the river is...that way...which means that...wait...*

"Wait! My home's not that way!"

She pointed in the opposite direction.

"I never told you where I lived!" Abigail called after them.

"We know! We have *no idea* where we're going!" Little Wade comically called out to her as he flew around Watchtower. "You must show us the way! We're following you!"

Tucking the business card into her pocket, Abigail joined Little Wade and Watchtower, and they all ventured down the street together.

4

WALKING HOME

Within a few minutes, Little Wade, Watchtower, and Abigail crossed into a safer section of the Lower East Side. All around them, gaslights shone brightly, like diamonds. Abigail was amused to see Watchtower walk alongside them.

It's like looking at a statue of a dragon and then seeing a real, live dragon walk next to it.

Just a few minutes before, Abigail had feared for her life, but now, in the pleasant company of this incorporeal little boy and his formidable friend, she felt invincible.

"I have sooooo many questions!" Abigail bounced down the sidewalk.

"I am not surprised." Little Wade fluttered through the air like a bird. "We will answer them all," he assured her, "but first, we need to exit this particular neighborhood."

"You make a good point," Abigail conceded.

"Once we get you clear of the area, we will be happy to answer as best we can. In the meantime, may we trouble you for your address?"

"I live at the intersection of Cherry and Catherine," Abigail informed them.

"We know exactly where that is." Little Wade soared. Watchtower nodded and quickly adjusted his course. "During the chase, you overshot your turn by only two blocks."

"Really? It felt like so much more."

"When you're afraid and it's nighttime, things can seem far more confusing than they truly are."

"Indeed, I completely lost track of where I was. This whole neighborhood felt like a maze."

"Are you new to the city, Abigail?" Little Wade flew closer to her.

"How could you tell?"

"We've been doing this for decades. We glean much from our first impressions, and you do not seem like someone familiar with the city."

"I'm most certainly *not*," Abigail replied rather pointedly.

Little Wade slowed his flight and seemed to take special note of this. Abigail walked alongside Watchtower, who strolled quite quickly, considering his size, which had changed. He had shrunk! Earlier, in the alley, he had stood at least twelve feet tall, but now as he escorted her, he had somehow compacted himself down to around seven feet. Still very tall obviously, but now he could pass for a *very* above-average human. Even so, as they moved toward Bowery Street, a thoroughfare packed with people, carriages, omnibuses, and trolleys, even at this time of night, Abigail wondered, *Why is he heading toward a crowd?* As they approached Bowery Street, a gaggle of people appeared from around the corner.

"Oh no." Abigail glanced anxiously at Little Wade and Watchtower, who, needless to say, looked more than a little odd, yet these two unusual gentlemen nonchalantly headed straight for these ordinary citizens.

"We need to hide!" Abigail whispered urgently.

"No, we don't," Little Wade did not whisper. In fact, he spoke quite loudly. "Fear not. I choose who can see me."

Watchtower dimmed his flame and pulled up his overcoat collar so that it covered three sides of his head, further dimming his light, but he still had a glass face! He wore an oversized, very loud pocket watch that dangled like a medallion. Abigail gleaned that it masked his clicking, whirring, clanking, popping.

Nevertheless, she remained quite concerned. "What about him?"

Little Wade did not answer. He only smiled and winked, then lazily drifted forward, turning around to face her as he swam into the crowd, backstroking. Abigail watched as all of the citizens, all shapes and sizes with their coats, hats, canes, pocket watches, scarves, purses, bags, and other assorted paraphernalia, all passed through Little Wade harmlessly as if he were nothing but air.

"But what about him?" Abigail gestured to Watchtower, who lumbered toward them without stopping.

"What about him?" Little Wade did not seem to understand.

"They're going to see him!"

"I certainly hope so. If not, they should seek medical attention." Little Wade shrugged.

Without breaking his stride, Watchtower swung open his glass face and dropped powder into his flame. She smelled…cigar smoke…but why? Then, still walking, he shut his glass face and continued. He neither tried to hide nor duck into the shadows, nor anything of the sort. Instead, he simply nodded politely as he passed by several couples, a group of young men, and a large family, chivalrously acknowledging them all. Abigail quietly watched, mouth agape, as every single one of these perfectly normal people walked right past Watchtower, treating him as if he were just another gentleman.

"Good evening, sir."

"Evening."

"Buenas Noches."

"Good Night."

"Top o' the evening to ye."

"Shalom!"

"Bonsoir!"

At least two dozen people passed by.

"I love this city," Little Wade laughed. Still swimming through the air, he tilted his head back and listened to the bustle.

As they turned on Bowery Street, it happened again.

"Evening."

"Good evening."

"Hello."

"Hmph."

"Good evening, sir."

"My, you're a tall one."

"After you, sir."

"Well, hello there."

Then it happened again!

"Evening."

"Evening."

"Good evening, sir."

"Nice night, isn't it?"

"My, what a lovely little daughter you have," an older couple remarked, referring to Abigail.

"I'm not his daughter," Abigail spoke up.

"Oh, she's so precious. Good evening to you, sir."

One particular man, fat and jolly, smoking a cigar, saluted Watchtower, winking at him.

"A fellow aficionado! Good evening to you, sir!"

Abigail spent most of the walk down Bowery Street looking rather confused. Before she knew it, they turned another corner and were alone again. For a moment, they had that particular patch of sidewalk all to themselves. Abigail pulled away from Watchtower and crossed her arms.

"All right, how did you do that?"

Little Wade whispered "Mirror" to Watchtower, who immediately reached into his pocket and produced a small sailor's signal mirror, which glinted and glimmered in the simmering blaze that radiated from his face. Watchtower tossed it to Abigail as if it were a coin. Surprised, she barely caught it in her hands. It landed in her palms with a *ding*! Seeing her face reflected on its shiny surface, Abigail furrowed her brow.

"What do you want me to do with this?"

"Turn around. Hold up the mirror and look at Watchtower's

reflection. Please."

Abigail turned her back on them, held up the mirror, and, closing one eye, peered into the reflection. Behind her, she could see Watchtower in his perfectly respectable suit and shoes. Then something struck her. She noticed that the holes in his suit had...healed?

"Lower it," Little Wade instructed her. "Please."

Intrigued, Abigail lowered the mirror and tilted it upward. When she saw his face, she yelped. In the mirror, Watchtower's fire and glass face had vanished, replaced with the face of an older, long-haired, bespectacled, bearded man clutching a long, smoldering cigar between his clenched teeth. The cigar glowed and burned brightly, radiating and reflecting off a pair of shiny glass spectacles. The shimmering, polished lenses enhanced the red smolder from the cigar, making it brighter. Abigail shook her head in disbelief.

An illusion! Marvelous! Peering closer, she realized that the illusory cigar's red glowing tip plus the reflection from the glasses plausibly explained why his face gave off so much light. *Fascinating.* There was one limitation. Watchtower's false face did not move. His face held one pose: clenched teeth, angry, irritable, an important man you neither wished to interrupt nor offend. Whirling around, she asked excitedly, "How?"

"The milliner that created his hat wove illusion magic into the fabric. When Watchtower dons it, he can blend in." Again, Little Wade explained all of this as if it were perfectly commonplace.

Watchtower popped off his top hat and handed it to Abigail, exposing the very top of his lamppost head. Shaped like a pyramid, the top of his cranium sported a pointy spike on top. In addition, four curled, sharp pieces of metal jutted like horns from each of the four corners of his head. That, combined with his hissing, fiery face, and the shadows created by his blaze, made him look like a metal devil.

"He's fine, as long as no one asks him for a cigar," Abigail, awestruck, joked. She returned the signal mirror to Watchtower, who pocketed it.

Little Wade giggled. "True."

"His hat is...magical." Abigail examined it. It felt quite normal, soft. Beautifully tailored, it smelled like ink.

"Oh yes, and he utilizes many, many hats of many different styles, for all occasions." Little Wade circled his friend and marveled at him. "Each hat equals a different identity. Very useful."

Noise emanated from around the corner.

"Quick, hand it back!"

Abigail tossed the top hat back to Watchtower, who promptly donned it just as another group, this one with a slobbery dog, turned the corner.

"*Ruff! Ruff!*" The slobbery hound jumped up and affectionately climbed Watchtower's leg. In response, Watchtower gently petted it.

After a few moments, the dog, its master, and their friends went on their way, and the trio found itself relatively alone again.

"I want a magic hat. Can you make one for me?"

"Who else would you want to be other than yourself?" Little Wade responded.

Before Abigail could answer, she heard a very unexpected sound. Watchtower held up his right hand and tapped his fingers together with a loud *clickety-clackety-clack* sound for several seconds. Then Abigail heard a *ping*! A piece of paper popped up from Watchtower's breast pocket. He pinched it between two of his fingers and presented the folded piece of paper to Abigail. She received it, unfolded it, and read it.

HELLO. STOP. THIS IS HOW I TALK TO PEOPLE. STOP.

"A telegram!"

"That's right," Little Wade boasted. Watchtower's fingers *clickety-clackety-clacked* and his pocket *pinged* again. Once more, he pinched and presented a crisp letter.

MY FINGERS TAP OUT THE LETTERS IN MORSE CODE. STOP. MUCH LIKE A TELEGRAPH OR TYPEWRITER. STOP. I HAVE A WIRE THAT RUNS UP MY ARM TO MY POCKET. STOP. THAT IS WHERE THE RECEIVER TAPS IT OUT. STOP.

Watchtower tapped out another message, clicking his thumb and fingers together in a myriad of combinations. *Clickety-clackety-clack. Ping!*

He handed her another note.

I AM VERY PLEASED TO MEET YOU, ABIGAIL. STOP.

"I am very pleased to meet you, too." Abigail curtsied.

"Come along." Little Wade floated forward. "There's much more to show you."

Turning left, Little Wade, Watchtower, and Abigail found themselves on another quiet corner. Glancing left and right, Abigail could not see anyone coming.

"I think this location...will...work," Little Wade remarked. He stroked his little, slightly blue chin. Checking to make sure no one else approached, he hovered patiently. Watchtower also stood still, locked his legs in place, and settled into position with a *hiss, clank,* and *thump.*

"Well, let us make use of this moment of privacy," Little Wade began. "So, what would you like to know?"

"Watchtower, how were you able to hide? I ran right past you, but you were not you. You were an ordinary lamppost."

"He can hide in plain sight if he wants to," Little Wade beamed proudly. "Do you see his long black coat?"

"Yes."

"Do you notice that he wears it unbuttoned?"

"Yes. I can see that."

"Watchtower, demonstration!"

From his relaxed position, Watchtower sprang to life, perked up, and stood up straight. Then he buttoned up his overcoat. Instantly, Watchtower transformed into a skinny streetlight.

"What?" Abigail stood there flabbergasted. "How?"

"Well, he buttoned up," Little Wade explained as if it were perfectly obvious.

"Where did he go?"

Watchtower reappeared, reverting to his seven-foot-tall, broad-shouldered, metal-skinned, fire-faced self. His unbuttoned overcoat hung open.

"Pole!" yelled Little Wade.

Watchtower buttoned up and transformed.

"Coat!"

Unbuttoned, he reappeared.

"Pole!"

Back to a lamppost.

"Coat!"

Back to being Watchtower.

"Pole! Coat! Pole! Coat!"

Watchtower ended the demonstration with a bow. Abigail clapped.

"That's incredible!" Abigail marveled at it. "How does it work?"

Watchtower held open one half of his coat like a bird might present its wing. Gazing into it, Abigail observed that the fabric lining the inside of the coat pulsed and flowed, almost like black water.

"Well, the outside resembles his hat. It has illusions woven into it. The inside fabric can somehow access a small pocket parallel dimension," Little Wade explained half-heartedly. "I confess I don't fully understand it myself, but it appears to be reliable, and quite fashionable, too."

"What about you? Those people back there could neither see nor hear you. You get to decide?" Abigail inquired.

"Precisely, ghosts exist invisible and inaudible to people, unless they choose to reveal themselves. I decide who gets to see and hear me," Little Wade boasted.

Watchtower seemed to groan in disapproval.

"Well, most of the time, anyway."

There seemed to be something much more than what Little Wade was letting on, but Abigail decided not to press the issue. They continued walking. So many questions bounced around Abigail's head, but one above all needed to be answered right away. She held up their business card. "Your card says in business since eighteen thirty-one. Does that mean you've been a ghost since that year?"

"Correct."

"So, you're an almost seventy-year-old spirit!"

"Correct again."

"That explains your old-fashioned attire," Abigail realized.

"It does. Every phantom's form matches the appearance of the precise moment of his, or her, or its, death. I was wearing this exact outfit when I perished. I can alter my appearance if I wish, but I prefer to devote my energies elsewhere."

"My earlier remark…I didn't mean…old-fashioned in a bad…I mean you're very presentable, both of you."

"Thank you, Abigail. No offense taken."

"Is he as old as you?" She gestured to Watchtower, who strode confidently.

"Older," Little Wade zipped and zagged throughout the air. "Much, much older."

Before she could ask how much older, Abigail realized that Little Wade and Watchtower had walked her all the way home to Cherry and Catherine. They turned and crept down yet another stinking, mud-caked side street festooned with overhanging laundry lines that dangled precariously, all overburdened with drying clothes that were all permanently stained with grease and sweat. These crisscrossing laundry lines obscured the sky and seemed to ensnare everything in a monstrous spider's web. This created perfect opportunities for nasty men to set traps, so Little Wade and Watchtower kept alert.

Abigail watched out for thieves, scoundrels, and snatchers. She spotted several ruffians, Longshadows, members of other gangs, and lone operators. They slunk back into the night as Watchtower fearlessly stalked by, pulling her close to him. Abigail cringed, and she mourned the sight of starving children, practically skin and bones, lying on hot vents, struggling to keep warm. She repeatedly averted her gaze, shut her eyes and let Watchtower guide her as if she hoped all this was a nightmare that would vanish once she opened her eyes again.

"You're safe with us," Little Wade assured her.

"I know. I've never come home this late before. I don't know what

I would do if you weren't here. I suppose I would just run as fast as I could, but I don't know if I would have made it."

At this time of night, the rag pickers were out in force. They were men and women dressed in ragged coats and pants that were full of patchwork spots sewn and sealed up with shreds from other jackets and pants. Wearing mismatched shoes and socks, these rag pickers scrounged and scoured for whatever scraps of trash they could find and piled their scavenges on their rickety, wooden carts. Occasionally they snapped or lashed out at each other and at thieves who tried to snatch something from their hauls. These rag pickers crouched in filth and, using their calloused hands, examined everything they found, sorting the garbage into piles. Abigail knew that, in the morning, they would try to sell whatever they could.

This is no place for a child, any child. How can people live like this? Abigail pondered this in her mind, then she concluded. *They don't, not really.*

"Here," Abigail informed Watchtower, who nodded and swung hard left. They turned a corner, away from any streetlights, and headed toward a cluster of squalid homes tucked away in a grubby alley.

"Is this where you live?" Little Wade asked rhetorically.

"Unfortunately." She sighed bitterly.

Like many destitute families, Abigail and her father lived with several other people, all crammed into a squat, two-story, decrepit row-house. The Lower East Side contained hundreds of these homes all mismatched, jumbled, and clustered too close together as if they were all keeping each other warm. This one had a pointy roof. A frail, faded, wooden building, the house had been built over fifty years before, back when the city was much smaller. Now old, dilapidated, and creaky, it should have fallen apart long ago. There were wet, rotten, brown patches all along the house's foundation, and several of the windows were cracked.

As tiny as the house appeared from outside, the house felt even smaller on the inside. All in all, five families crowded into Abigail's home. Two families, eight people in total including a screaming infant, filled up the first floor. Two more families, six people in total, roosted on the second floor. That left only one place for Abigail and her father to live—the attic. Luckily, because Abigail's father had repaired so much of the house to keep it from completely collapsing, they were given the attic all to themselves.

"Small definitely, but cheap," Abigail explained.

"In the winter," her father promised her, "we'll be warm because all of the heat from the stoves down on the first and second floors will rise, so we'll be lucky not to freeze. During the summer, we'll be able to open both windows, each one on a different side of the house, and create a tunnel of wind that will gust through the attic and cool us off."

The windows he referred to were quite impressive. They were both perfectly round, like portholes on the side of a ship. Spanning three feet in diameter, they contained four panes of glass, so they let a good deal of light in. Their design included hinges and locks, so they could swing open and shut like little doors.

"My father built and installed the windows himself," Abigail boasted proudly, which interested Little Wade. Evidently, her father possessed a real talent for carpentry. Little Wade also noted that the windows could function as a pair of emergency escape hatches.

Whenever Martin returned home very late from work, he scaled the side of the house. He accomplished this by grabbing onto carefully hidden pegs pounded into the outer walls, and then he could simply unlock the window and let himself in. Abigail, however, was forbidden from climbing up and down the side of the house.

"Too dangerous," her father warned her. This left her only one option. Unfortunately, whenever she returned home from either school or her job at Mr. Kowalski's, she let herself in through the front or back door. She tried to avoid the two loud, obnoxious, drunken, disorderly families that overcrowded the first floor and never properly cleaned up after themselves. At night, she would take extra special care to avoid waking the baby, whose screaming and bleating would wake up everyone else in the house.

To arrive at the second floor, Abigail had to ascend a creaky set of stairs. Once on the second floor, she had to bypass two nasty, miserly, nosy, gossipy, finicky, insufferable families. To make matters worse, all of the awful people stuffed into her house often quarreled with each other over noises and smells. So to finally get home, Abigail often endured sneaking up the endless steps through a house full of grunts, snores, and farts, climbing, climbing, climbing until she reached the wooden ladder that her father built that led up into the attic. "There's no door to our apartment," Abigail explained to her new friends. "There's only a hatch in the floor. Some of my schoolmates tease me about this, but most actually love the idea. They consider it quite endearingly odd."

"What about you?"

"Most of the time, I enjoy it, except now I dread it." Abigail pointed to the front door. "The moment I enter I will have to navigate through a crowded house full of sleeping, snarling people. Like a thief or assassin, I must tiptoe around people as if I were trying to stealth past room after room full of sleeping bears. One wrong step and everyone will wake up and roar. So right now I am mentally preparing myself to do just that."

In response, Little Wade smiled. "Not tonight." Then he nodded to his partner.

"It's too high." Abigail pointed to the window and then to Watchtower. "Not even he can reach that, even if he extends himself."

In response, Little Wade arched his eyebrows. "Are you sure?"

Watchtower, now seven feet tall, with sputters, whirls, clanks, clicks, and rumbles, cranked himself up with a *chank-chank-chank!* His arms and legs elongated with bangs and clangs, growing longer and longer as his metal frame extended and then locked into place. With each *clink, clank, shunk*, his shoulders, chest, and torso, unfolding and extending, doubled, then tripled in width. His magical suit grew naturally with him, so as his arms and legs shot out, his pants and sleeves simply wove extra fabric to cocoon them. Abigail noticed the suit also heavily muffled the sound. His fiery lamplight head, situated on top of his growing body, climbed higher and higher into the air until, within just a few seconds, the magnificent, mechanical man reared up to his maximum stature: twenty-one feet tall! When he finished, Watchtower, his face glowing brightly and casting a warm beam down onto Abigail, towered above her like a lighthouse by the sea.

"Won't he disturb the neighbors?" she inquired, glancing at the surrounding houses.

"I can conceal others as well." Little Wade waved his hands lazily. "No one can see us."

Watchtower, standing beside her two-story row house, carefully picked Abigail up and gently lifted her with his immense arms. She floated upward like a feather in the wind. Using her key, Abigail unlocked her round window like a door and swung it open. Watchtower delicately reached into Abigail's apartment and carefully placed her inside. Then he retracted his long arm back through the window. Little Wade simply levitated upward and prepared to pass through the wall like any sensible spirit would. Of course, like any gentleman, he did not presume to enter until she permitted him.

"Would you like to come in?" she asked.

Hovering by the window, he demurred, "Are you certain? I don't wish to impose."

"I would be delighted," Abigail assented and smiled, so Little Wade passed harmlessly through the wall and found himself inside Abigail's home. Martin Reid had not yet returned from work, so a soft silence filled the attic. Wasting no time, Abigail struck a match. She lit several candles, filling the room with a golden bubble that rose all the way to the ceiling, like a tasty warm loaf of bread inside an oven. Little Wade, who could see perfectly even in the dark (like any ghost could), nevertheless enjoyed watching the small flames illuminate the entire apartment. Little Wade had become accustomed to making other people gasp, but this time, he found himself saying, "Wow."

5
―――

THE GREAT PYRAMID

When they first set up their apartment, Martin Reid reserved only a tiny corner for himself. He took up enough space for a single bed, a squat nightstand, a lockbox to safely store money, and a wooden chest he built himself that contained all of his clothing. His toolbelt lay next to his bedside. Martin did not need much at all. That left the rest of the attic for Abigail.

A very talented professional carpenter, Martin, shortly after they moved in, crafted a wonderful wooden world for his imaginative daughter. Because the Reids lived in the attic under the slanted roof of the house, Abigail once remarked to her father that it felt "like we're living inside an Egyptian pyramid." So Martin, copying images from one of Abigail's books, beautifully engraved hundreds of hieroglyphics into the wooden rafters, the beams that crisscrossed the ceiling. He painted each engraving either red, white, yellow, green, or a bright, burning blue. There were images of gods, heroes on chariots, pharaohs and queens, gorgeous birds, crocodiles, animal-headed warriors, scarab beetles, and the eye of Ra. To enhance the effect, Martin also lavished much of the wood in gold paint to add luster, so in the candlelight, the ceiling glittered, gleamed, and seemed ten feet higher. Their small apartment felt ten times more spacious.

Five beautiful, shiny bookshelves overflowed with every possible book one could imagine. Martin had carved them with enormous care. Floating about the room, Little Wade examined Abigail's collection and observed there were little bookmarks stuffed into each one.

"I've read every volume at least once," Abigail remarked as she removed her dirty shoes and placed them in a corner so they would not track muck onto the smooth, sanded floor. "If you find a bookmark located somewhere in the middle, that means I am still in the process of re-reading it."

Impressed, Little Wade scanned the contents of her bookshelves with his sharp eyes and saw that they included many of the classics: TREASURE ISLAND, LITTLE WOMEN, HUCKLEBERRY FINN, TOM SAWYER, UNCLE TOM'S CABIN, GREEK MYTHOLOGY, OVID'S METAMORPHOSIS, THE KING JAMES BIBLE, DR. JEKYLL & MR. HYDE, GREAT EXPECTATIONS, OLIVER TWIST, DAVID COPPERFIELD, A TALE OF TWO CITIES, THE COMPLETE WORKS OF SHAKESPEARE, THE TIME MACHINE, THE ISLAND OF DR. MOREAU, ROBINSON CRUSOE, FRANKENSTEIN, DRACULA, 20000 LEAGUES UNDER THE SEA, THE MYSTERIOUS ISLAND, AROUND THE WORLD IN 80 DAYS, THE JUNGLE BOOK, THE ADVENTURES OF SHERLOCK HOLMES, THE LEGEND OF SLEEPY HOLLOW, MOBY DICK, and WAR OF THE WORLDS. There were many more, so many books! Where could she possibly find space to comfortably recline and read all of them? Then Little Wade found his answer.

Abigail slept in a soft hammock strung out between two heavy wooden posts that Martin carved into fat dwarves with swirling beards and broad smiles. It hung at the perfect angle for Abigail to lie comfortably and read by candlelight.

"Marvelous."

Then Abigail showed him a beautiful wooden dollhouse (castle actually) that her father had built for her. It could swing open and closed on a set of hinges. The house included a collection of incredibly detailed wooden figurines, but not dull everyday toys doing everyday things. Instead, Abigail possessed police dolls, pirate dolls, ancient Greek warrior dolls, and more. Little Wade marveled as Abigail demonstrated that the dollhouse (castle) contained several modular pieces that could be replaced. It could transform into a police station, pirate ship, ancient temple, medieval castle, fort, church, even a pyramid and tomb by adjusting and swapping out a few select pieces.

"Wonderful," Little Wade whispered to himself. Then he discovered something that truly excited him. Martin often challenged his precocious daughter to games of chess, and so he customized a set for them. All of the painted pieces, forged out of smooth wood, all took the form of epic fantasy characters. Bishops equaled sage, blue wizards, or evil, red warlocks. Little Wade admired the silver knights on horseback facing off against red armored knights riding wolves. Pawns equaled human foot soldiers in an assortment of poses on one side and vicious goblins on the other. Martin had transformed rooks into shining castles on one side and flaming catapults on the other. Finally, a plump, benevolent couple, a king and queen, ruled on one side. At the same time, an ugly pair of demonic-looking lizards, crowned with bones, terrorized the other.

"Exquisite," Little Wade remarked. "How often do you play?"

"Once a week. I usually win. I especially love the Queen. She's my favorite. Father calls it my lucky piece."

"That'll be useful," Little Wade whispered to himself, and then he quickly followed with an "Oh, nothing," when Abigail asked him what he meant.

"I'd offer you something to eat or drink, but you cannot ingest anything, can you?"

"We're quite satisfied. Thank you," Little Wade refused politely.

"Does Watchtower need anything? I feel terrible that he's just loitering outside doing nothing."

"Don't ever worry about him," Little Wade heartened her. "Right now, he's standing guard, ensuring that you now dwell in one of the safest places in the city. It's what he lives for. Watchtower never gets bored, and even if he did, believe me, his life, our life together, is never boring."

"Do you mind if I change? I'd like to get out of these boyish clothes."

"Would you like me to vacate the premises and give you privacy?"

"No, it's all right."

Abigail passed behind a curtain that Martin had hung near Abigail's bed, which served as a secluded place to change. Little Wade drifted away and kept his back turned to her as a gentleman should. Tucking herself behind the screen, Abigail removed all of her dirty clothes and quickly donned a soft, white cotton nightgown.

"Almost ready," she informed him. Behind the curtain, dipping her hands into a bowl of water and rubbing a bar of soap in her palms, Abigail washed her face and hands. Then Abigail squeezed toothpaste out of a collapsible tube and spread it onto her toothbrush. Looking into a small mirror, she began to brush her teeth. Little Wade, still looking away, respecting her privacy, continued to explore her wonderful apartment. He hovered above Abigail's father's bed.

"Does your father often work late?"

"Yes, I barely see him anymore." Abigail's mouth foamed as she brushed.

"He's safe to return home at this hour?"

Abigail spat foam into the bowl of soapy water so she could speak more clearly. "Oh yes, he walks home with several friends from work. They're all very strong like him. I'm not worried."

"Abigail, Watchtower and I were wondering. Before you were accosted by those awful men tonight, did they ever harass you before, perhaps while you walked to school?"

"My father and I recognized them as a threat almost immediately. Thankfully, I managed to avoid them in the morning."

"How did you manage that?"

"To walk to school, I dressed up as a bootblacker," Abigail replied as she emerged from behind the curtain.

"A shoeshine boy?"

"Yes. My father carved me a shine box. I carry my books, pencils, and school papers inside. No one can tell the difference. It's over by my bedside."

Little Wade darted over to her hammock. Joining him, Abigail, dressed in her white nightgown, reached into her own footlocker and produced a dirty set of boy's clothes and a wooden shoeshine box.

"That's very clever."

"My father did his job a little too well. My disguise turned out to be so convincing that dozens of men inundated me with requests to shine their shoes. I kept telling them no. I imagine I have established a reputation as the absolutely rudest bootblacker in the entire city."

Little Wade laughed, "I suppose you are."

"Dressed as a dirty boy, nobody pays you much mind."

"Hmm...but you didn't use the bootblacker disguise today. Why?"

"I didn't use the disguise this morning because my father had a later shift so he could walk me to school. We still tucked my hair under my cap and everything. As far as anyone knew, we were father and son. Still, the Longshadows figured me out. I think they had been watching me for quite some time. The leader of that bunch that you defeated somehow knew exactly where I would be. When I left Mr. Kowalski's, they closed in quite quickly. Do you think it was my hair that gave me away?"

"Definitely. We must assume that the Longshadows had targeted you specifically, and your locks are very distinct. We don't yet know why they wanted you, but we will find out. Those foot soldiers were undoubtedly told to seek out a girl with red hair. Your disguise probably frustrated their efforts for a while, but the Longshadows are clever. Following a hunch, one of the gang members probably followed you one morning and discerned your disguise. I imagine you doff it before you enter the school."

"Yes. I probably took off my cap and...out it came." She gestured to her spectacular hair.

"That's when they put two and two together. Your costume will no longer work, unfortunately."

"Speaking of which," Abigail wondered. "That shoeshine boy in the bag...not real at all...but it seemed real...another illusion...like the fog?"

"Yes, one of my many abilities," Little Wade replied, and then something occurred to him. "Speaking of illusions, Abigail, how long have you employed this particular masquerade?"

"About a month."

"You've lived in this city now...how long exactly?"

"Two months."

"So...how did you get to school before then?"

Abigail clammed up and avoided his gaze. Then she abruptly blurted out, "Um...my father walked me until he couldn't anymore."

Little Wade sensed that she concealed something. Taking note of it, he decided to change the subject to make her feel more comfortable.

"As I mentioned earlier, we gathered that you were new to the city. You did not seem familiar with the neighborhood. Where do you hail from, originally?"

"Upstate. Tarrytown. We used to live on a farm."

"Does your mother not reside here, too?" Little Wade asked that particular question in such a manner that it seemed he already knew the answer.

Abigail fell silent.

"When did she pass?"

"Six months ago."

Little Wade stopped floating and dropped like a stone to the floor. "We're dreadfully sorry for your loss, Abigail. Truly, please accept our deepest condolences."

"Thank you. It has...been very hard."

Abigail managed to avoid breaking down, but Little Wade could see that it was not easy.

"Your father moved you both here for work?"

"Yes, and my schooling. Opportunities dried up in the country. When my mother died, he needed a change, so...here we are."

"I suspect I already know what you will say, but...how do you like New York City so far?"

"Honestly, I'd like to go home. I don't like it here, at all. I haven't since I arrived, although, in the past several hours, it has become quite a bit more interesting."

"This city can be a marvelous place, Abigail."

"I wish I could believe that."

"I know it has been hard. You're a good person. You and your father are both good people. This city needs people like you. Watchtower and I are at your service, and I promise we'll turn you into a bona fide New Yorker yet. Oooohhhhh!"

A volume by Abigail's bedside caught Little Wade's attention, one she had perused very recently, a book with a Raven on the cover, and the letters EAP.

"You enjoy the works of Edgar Allan Poe?"

"Oh, very much." Abigail brightened up. "In fact, I'm quite sure he's my favorite."

"Interesting that you should say that. Many parents forbid children from reading his stories, dismissing them as too sinister and chilling for youth."

"They are, but I find them magnificent and incredibly imaginative. Do you enjoy Poe's work as well?"

"More than that, Edgar became a loyal friend of ours. I think it would make him very happy to hear you praise him."

"You knew Edgar Allan Poe?" Abigail's eyes lit up like stars.

"Oh yes," Little Wade answered. "He assisted us many times and played critical roles in solving several of our most difficult cases. Watchtower and I knew him as a brilliant, brilliant man, sad and troubled, but truly ingenious. We miss Edgar every day."

"I can't believe it. You really knew Edgar Allan Poe?"

"Indeed, one of our most powerful allies."

"Ally? Wait, Edgar Allan Poe led a double life as both an author and...what? Was he a detective? Was he a secret agent? Wait, was he a magician?"

"All three, actually," Little Wade answered as if it were perfectly normal.

"Well, I suppose he obviously must have investigated supernatural phenomena and dabbled in sorcery. Where else could he procure such incredible ideas for all of those stories!"

"Oh, I assure you, Abigail, his most amazing stories weren't written down," Little Wade grinned. "He lived them, and we were there, fighting beside him every step of the way."

"Edgar Allan Poe...wraiths...giant mechanical men..." Abigail finally permitted herself to get excited. She paced around her attic apartment. Nervous energy coursed through her entire body. "I've completely forgotten myself. Talking to you feels so natural, and yet I've just realized that I am having a conversation with a strange boy in my home. It's my first time by the way. To top it off, you're a phantom! I must document this." After racing around the apartment, plucking up a diary, a quill pen, and some ink, Abigail sat down at a small table and a pair of chairs that Martin had assembled.

"My mind overflows with so, so, so many questions. Do you mind?"

"Very well." Little Wade turned his attention to her. "We have some time."

"First, how did you die? How many other phantoms inhabit New York City? Does that make New York haunted? What similarities do you share with other wraiths and specters? What differences? Do all phantasms take the same form? What abilities do you and other incorporeal beings possess? If ghosts exist, does that mean that other strange things exist? Does that mean that ogres, goblins, orcs, demons, fairies, pixies, also exist? Please say yes, or maybe not. Not all of those should be real. Oh my, what about dragons? Are dragons real, too? I'm sorry. I'm asking too many questions. Focus, Abigail. Let's start with Watchtower."

Little Wade simply floated patiently while Abigail rattled off an endless series of energetic, interrogative remarks.

"How exactly do his magical clothes work? His shoes are quite stylish. Are they magical, too? What abilities do they possess? What about his gloves? How exactly does the magic cloth work? Who discovered it? Who invented it? Who is his tailor? Can any manner of eyeglass or spyglass pierce the illusion? Oh, I have a critical question regarding your secret identities. Has anyone ever spotted or exposed you to public knowledge? Should that occur, what would your response be? Or, if it has occurred, what did you do? Did Watchtower bop them on the head? Do you possess some sort of magic that eliminates memories? Oh, please don't eliminate or erase mine. Please don't."

"Well, if you must know—"

"Tell me about Watchtower! He's magnificent. Who built him? Where did he come from? How strong is he? How old? Earlier, you answered, 'older, much older,' which I could not help but notice." She playfully mimicked his voice. "You made him sound ancient. Is he ancient? Does Watchtower live alone, or with a family, friends? Do other mechanical people exist out there? Do they have their own world, a world that no one knows about? His flame...is that his soul?"

"Well—"

"Returning to you, can you confirm the existence of an afterlife? First off...angels, real or not? Do they exist? What about the rest of the afterlife's moral infrastructure? Do we get judged after we die? Is there some kind of sorting out process? Does it resemble Heaven and Hell, or perhaps the Egyptian afterlife? Does Osiris, the Judge of the Dead, weigh your soul against the Feather of Truth on a scale?" Abigail gestured to one of the hieroglyphics on the ceiling.

"Does divine justice exist? Does it take the form similar to what the Egyptians described, or perhaps the Greeks? In Greek mythology, there are three judges. They offer three options, Elysium, Asphodel Fields, or Tartarus. Is that how it works? No, no wait, that cannot be correct. At this point in time, it must follow a more advanced legal system with updated terminology and techniques. That would be quite fascinating, and logical, too."

Little Wade nearly spoke, but Abigail interrupted him.

"Then again, death is an ancient custom, the most ancient, so perhaps it might follow something more mythic. Still, the fact remains that we currently do not reside in Greece, nor Egypt. So does that mean that death and the afterlife follow the customs of perhaps the natives of this country? That would make sense since we are technically living in their territory. That's it, isn't it? Does the afterlife experience vary based on geography and culture?"

"Abigail—"

"That would be fascinating! Is the world of the afterlife divided into continents, countries, cities that mirror our own? If so, does that mean that when I die, depending on where I die, will that determine where and how I might cross over into the next world? Stop. I'm getting ahead of myself and getting too bogged down in details. Let me proceed logically. If ghosts exist, then some form of afterlife exists, and if that's true, that begs the question. Why do you, a kind, generous and pure soul, still exist here? Does that mean you chose to become a phantom, or were you sent back or held back? If so, why? Why do you linger here? Is there something you still need to complete?"

"Abigail—"

"If you're real and the afterlife exists, does that mean that Hell exists, too? Does that mean…the devil is real? Oh no, please tell me he isn't real, but he is, isn't he? He is. Oh no. That's terrible, but wait, then that means God must be real, too! My father takes us to church every Sunday. We read from the Bible together every week. He will be so pleased!"

"Abigail—"

"Wait, does this mean it's all true? I forgot to ask about genies before. Apologies. As someone who considers herself well-versed in world mythology, I consider that an unforgivable oversight. Do genies exist, even genies that come from lamps? Can they grant wishes? Can I get my wish granted? If so, I want my mother back. Might that be possible? Please tell me. My mother! Is she in Heaven? Please, say yes. Will I be able to see her again? Oh, please, I hope so! Please, say yes. Wait, back to the afterlife. If an afterlife exists, and a Heaven, does that mean I don't need to fear death? Will I go to Heaven? I think so. I think I'm a good person. I hope I've been a good person. Oh my, I suddenly feel terribly insecure about my moral choices! What about my father? I hope so. As I mentioned, he attends church every Sunday. He's such a good man. He's suffered such a hard life. Please say yes. Will he? Can we see my mother again? Can we, all three of us, be reunited and live together as a family again? Please say yes.'"

"I was murdered," Little Wade cut her off.

Silence hung in the room for a moment. The only sound anyone could hear was the flickering of the candles. Then Abigail, stunned, spoke first.

"What...what did you say?"

"Your first question...you asked specifically 'how did I die?' I was murdered, Abigail." He spoke in such a matter-of-fact way that it shocked her.

"Oh." Abigail did not ask another question for a while. "That was...foolish of me. All of this, all of this is so foolish. So utterly stupid. I am so terribly sorry."

"No need to apologize—"

"No! I do apologize for my selfishness. Here I am blabbering on about all of my questions and fascinations. Not once did it occur to me that your death may be a subject that required just the slightest bit of decorum."

"It's quite all right."

"No, I hope you will forgive me for my insensitivity. It's just...you saved my life. I'm still shaking from it, and you're a ghost and Watchtower...both of you are these amazing...things. This opens up whole other worlds and nearly infinite possibilities. It's greater than anything I could ever imagine, ever. I'm sorry. I just can't stop thinking and wondering. The whole world just opened up like a book, and I've only been experiencing page one. You've flipped the entire page!"

"Abigail Reid."

She stopped scribbling, stopped talking, and avoided his gaze.

"You're not asking the most important question."

She paused.

"No." Abigail became quite serious. "I don't want to."

"Go ahead and ask."

"Why were those men after me?"

"They wanted to bring you to their master."

"Why? What does he want with me?"

"We don't know."

"Their master, you know who he is, don't you?"

"Yes," Little Wade sounded especially sad and angry when he spoke. "Watchtower and I know exactly who he is, and we know he will strike again because he has targeted children before."

Abigail shuddered. Even in the warm comfort of her home with Little Wade accompanying her and Watchtower standing guard, she felt a deep chill, as if she were outside in the bitter cold without any protection at all.

"Why ask me these questions? Why tell me this? You're frightening me."

"Watchtower and I have been investigating a rash of kidnappings plaguing this area for the past several weeks. Indeed, we were on patrol investigating when we came across you in your predicament. So you see, we now find ourselves, partners, trying to solve the same mystery."

"Partners?"

"Yes."

"But how could I possibly help you?"

"You mentioned earlier that you play chess once a week, correct?"

"Yes, with my father. I beat him most of the time. How does a game of chess serve as an analogy to this situation? How does it assist you and Watchtower?"

"We all possess abilities and limitations, like chess pieces. Pawns, bishops, knights, rooks, queens, and kings, they all play key roles, but also suffer from constraints. Working together, however, they can accomplish great things. Humans can perform tasks that wraiths cannot and vice versa, so to answer your question, let me ask you one first, Abigail. What do you think you're capable of?"

This question struck her. She carefully considered her answer. "I don't know. I'm an excellent reader. I know that. I'm a decent enough butcher's assistant. I love my father very much. I hope I'm a good daughter. I'd like to think I proved myself often when I worked on the farm. Currently, Mrs. Whitlock, my teacher, refers to me as 'one of her finest students,' so that's something. Mrs. Whitlock says I write very well, but other than that...well, I don't know. I certainly don't know how I could possibly be of assistance to you. I don't know what I can do."

"We're going to find out, together, Abigail. Right now, undoubtedly, Watchtower and I must seem wondrous, and all-powerful."

"Indeed. You're both invincible."

Little Wade shook his head. "I'm not. Watchtower, neither. As superlative as we might seem, we also suffer from limitations. I'm just trying to prepare you before we begin."

"Begin what?"

"Formalizing our relationship. Abigail Reid, my business partner, Watchtower, and I would like to formally extend to you our services. We solve problems for children in this city. That's what we do, and we've been at it for decades. I mentioned that we might be partners in uncovering a mystery, and that's true. More to the point, we were wondering if you would be interested in becoming our latest client. We would be working for you. From this moment on, we will not do anything on your behalf without your say-so, unless we must intercede to save you from immediate danger."

"I would be delighted to hire you! How does this work? Whenever my father takes a job, there's usually a handshake or a contract."

"Well, a handshake is out of the question, obviously, but we can provide you with a contract tomorrow with all of the details."

"That sounds very official."

"Official indeed." Little Wade's tone became quite formal. "Understand this, Abigail. Once we enter into an agreement, Watchtower and I work for you, not the other way around."

"That's quite a lot of authority. I've never wielded that kind of power. My own phantom and mechanical man, it's quite overwhelming."

"So, do you wish to engage our services?"

Abigail proudly stood up straight. "Little Wade and Watchtower, consider yourselves hired."

Little Wade seemed genuinely happy.

"Excellent!"

A moment of awkward silence passed.

"That's it?"

"That's it. How do you feel?"

"I don't know. I've never hired anyone before. So...how exactly does this work? What happens now?"

"Well, as I mentioned earlier, Watchtower and I help children solve their problems. Right now, you fear to venture throughout your neighborhood, which has become perilous. The Longshadows have set their sights on you. They have endangered your travels out of this house, to school, to your job at the butcher's, and anywhere else in this immediate vicinity. Furthermore, your countermeasures, such as the disguise, while effective up until this point, can now be considered compromised and no longer protective. Watchtower and I intend to solve this problem for you. In fact, the timing has proven to be quite fortuitous. We were lucky to encounter you on Friday evening. Do you work on the weekends?"

"No. On Saturday I stay in all day, reading. Sunday we go to church, and then it's back to reading for me."

Little Wade absorbed this. "So that means we have two days, Saturday and Sunday, to clean up this neighborhood and neutralize the threat. This establishes our deadline as first thing Monday morning. Our goal is clear: for you to wake up that morning and return to school safely and without care."

"I feel better already."

"Well then, Watchtower and I do not require sleep, but you do. Over the next several hours, Watchtower and I will devise an action plan for your situation, and your father's as well."

"My father? You'll help him, too?"

"Yes, evidently, his current employment schedule prevents him from spending proper time with you. This must be remedied. With your permission, we would like to return to visit you tomorrow morning so we can brief you on our strategy. Will that be acceptable?"

"That would be lovely. We usually rise very early."

"Very well, in the meantime, however, you should get some rest. You've experienced a very eventful evening, so I will now bid you goodnight and take my leave of you."

"Wait, not so fast!"

"Is there still some way that we can be of assistance?"

"You saved my life. I know you work for me now. How can I pay you? How can I ever repay you for saving me?"

"Keep our secret," Little Wade answered her. "The fewer people that know about us, the better. I imagine it's fairly obvious as to why."

"The only fee is secrecy." Abigail held up their business card.

"You'll never owe us anything else."

"Oh! But what do I tell my father? I don't feel comfortable lying to him."

"Tell him that you were almost caught by the Longshadows, but strangers came to your aid. He wouldn't believe the rest anyway."

"I suppose that's what happened."

"Be prepared, though. Your father will be distraught, and he will bombard you with a multitude of questions."

"I won't know what to say."

"I will assist you tomorrow morning. Don't worry. We've handled similar situations many times before. In the meantime, you should get some rest, Abigail."

"I'm far too excited to sleep after everything that's happened."

"You'll need your energy tomorrow," he insisted.

"Well, if I am your client, then I should be a well-informed one. I obviously could rattle off a thousand questions. My curiosity overwhelms me; however, I recognize we are somewhat pressed for time, so I will focus on one specific category. Could you give me some sense of *your* capabilities?" Abigail prepared to write in her journal. "Can you tell me a little bit about ghosts?"

6

AHKWIYÀN

"First, the living vastly outnumber us," Little Wade began. "This city's population currently stands at around a million and a half citizens, give or take several thousand. The spectral population numbers only about one percent of that. Most people, when they die, cross over."

"They go to Heaven?"

"They go somewhere," Little Wade offered. "Most crossings that occurred in my presence all appeared to be quite serene and pleasant, so yes, most people travel somewhere very agreeable. This place possesses many names."

"Is that where my mother is? Do you think?"

"I am almost certain of it. If your mother did, in fact, transform into a specter, then I can ascertain that very quickly and report to you tomorrow morning."

"How will you accomplish that?"

"I will file an inquiry with the Registerium Mortuorum et Spirituum."

"The what, the what, and the what?"

"The world of the dead has been around for quite some time, Abigail. You would be pleased to know that, over the centuries, an army of very diligent spirits has organized it and kept it surprisingly neat and tidy. At this point, it has become quite a well-oiled machine with a well-established bureaucracy and efficient government, well... most of the time. To the point, every time a new ghost joins the ranks of the spirit world, the R.M.E.S. records it in its logs. Every spirit is accounted for...well...most are anyway. If your mother became a spirit at the time of her death, then the Registerium will most certainly possess a detailed record of it. I will happily visit their offices tonight. In my experience, their response time tends to be exemplary, so I can most certainly provide you with an answer by tomorrow morning. I think, however, that you should take comfort in the fact that she has most probably moved on to a better place."

"That's good news. I feel better already. In fact, I am rapidly becoming less afraid of death, but don't worry, I promise I won't be reckless," Abigail laughed, but then she stopped herself. "Wait! What happens to bad people?"

"Ah yes, well...Watchtower and I, during combat, have taken the lives of wicked men in the past, not by choice but by necessity, and we can confidently describe their crossings as...supremely horrible."

"Hell?" Abigail gulped.

"Wherever they go. It too possesses many names, but calling it Hell is accurate."

"I could regale you with more questions about the nature of the afterlife in general, but let us change the subject to one that is more upbeat—your fantastical powers!"

"Excellent, regarding my abilities, let us begin with the basics. Spirits cannot directly touch or affect the physical world," Little Wade explained. "It's quite impossible for most of us. We do not exist as physical matter anymore."

"Which explains why you do not get older."

"Death is one of the great forces in the universe, akin to gravity and time. Everything dies. People, animals, plants, even whole worlds, even stars. Death is the period at the end of every sentence in the great story of the universe. Death demarcates the border between this dimension and others. Ghosts live between dimensions. We exist partially outside of this world's space, and entirely out of its time. We are not unlike light or any other form of energy. Energy never ages, and neither do we, but, like energy, if we wish to interact with matter, then we must obey the laws of physics."

"So, you cannot touch or move anything."

"No. It's simply impossible, and most of us possess no desire to do so, and for good reasons. Some learn how to use energy to affect vibrations, which can manipulate matter. These rare phantoms become very powerful, but unfortunately, they often go quite mad."

"I've read of a few scattered incidents," Abigail recalled. "My father once brought home a collection of Penny Dreadfuls from a ship he unloaded that had docked from London. There were stories about poltergeists tossing around objects, wrecking whole houses."

"Yes, poltergeists have committed multiple incidents around the world, including here. A small minority, but, believe me, they were dealt with swiftly and terribly."

"By who?"

"You would call them angels."

"So angels *do* exist!"

"The term 'angels,' Abigail, merely describes a type of specter who is ancient, wise, cosmically powerful. They enforce our strict laws. They maintain order. Without them keeping supernatural affairs organized, the whole world would fly right off the rails. They patrol and protect something called the *Ahkwiyàn*."

"*Ahkwiyàn*," Abigail pronounced the word, which felt strange in her mouth. "What does it mean? I don't recognize the language."

"It's the language of the Lenape, the original native tribe that lived on this island. Literally, *Ahkwiyàn* means 'blanket,' but it has a more profound connotation, the safe illusion that covers this world, an understanding between the world of the living and the dead. We must remain hidden from you. The law states that the *Ahkwiyàn* must be maintained at all times, and the particular phantoms that enforce that harsh law, well…you would call them angels. We in the spiritual community call them Rattlers."

"Rattlers. Why?"

"Believe me, you don't want to know."

"Wait! Are you breaking any laws by revealing yourself to me? Now, I'm worried."

Little Wade shook his head. "We may reveal our existence to children because people tend not to believe children anyway. However, past a certain age, the law forbids us to initiate any direct communication."

"Why, because an adult might be considered more credible?"

"Theoretically, that's the reason, but in our experience when older people claim to see ghosts, they often find themselves declared by the authorities to be quite insane and can sometimes find themselves committed to the asylum."

"Well, I talk about my imaginary friends all the time, so you and Watchtower will fit right in. Wait, where are you going?"

Little Wade faded from view, becoming more and more transparent until he all but vanished.

"Nowhere. I'm merely showing you the basic concept of Fading. Every phantasm can do this."

Little Wade demonstrated, fading in and out, and went on. "I find it makes people uncomfortable if they can see through me. It makes every conversation extremely awkward. So I prefer to maintain a solid, opaque image. It's far more pleasant for everyone involved."

Fascinated, Abigail recollected her ordeal in the alley. "That fog you created...Mrs. Whitlock taught us that when water partially evaporates through condensation into a gaseous form in the air, *that* creates fog."

"Whereas mine isn't real at all," Little Wade added and then raised his hand. Fog instantly filled up the entire attic apartment. Impressed, Abigail waved her hand through the illusory mist. It rippled, curled and broke up as she slashed through it, but it quickly repaired itself. Then it melted away as quickly as it had appeared, receding like water.

"You're an illusionist," Abigail observed.

"Yes. We call this talent Dolosphera, the power to create sights and sounds that can seem all too real. We cannot create tastes or smells, however. Those require solid particulates in the air."

"Dolosphera...hmmm..." Abigail thought carefully. "I read that 'Dolos' was the Greek god of illusion, and 'sphera' is clearly a play upon the word 'sphere,' an object that is three dimensional. So... when you create an illusion...your power warps perception and tricks the mind because the images you create appear solid all the way around. Fascinating...but what about touch?"

"Another talent entirely, difficult to learn, called Somatophoria."

"Somatophoria?"

"Have you ever felt a shiver on your skin or up your spine when you feel fear, or perhaps a terrible feeling in the pit of your stomach?"

"Yes."

"Some ghosts can learn to stimulate the electrical impulses in the nerves beneath a person's skin and simulate the feeling of being touched."

"That's how you convinced Big Chin that he carried a boy in that sack."

"Big Chin?"

"My nickname for that especially large Longshadow in the alley."

"Oh, right, hmmm...charming." Little Wade chuckled. "Yes, quite so, I simply sat on Big Chin's shoulder, invisible, and stimulated his nerves. We also call it Tingling. It's difficult to do, and very painful for us."

"Oh, well, then you needn't demonstrate," Abigail demurred politely. "I don't want you to hurt yourself. What else can you do?"

Little Wade began to wave his arms around.

"I can also perform something called 'Polyplotting,' which comes in very handy."

"Hmm...I know 'poly' means 'many' in Latin. Wait! Does that mean that you can—"

Abigail immediately found herself surrounded by multiple, murmuring Little Wades, each one of which spoke, "Hello greetings this is Polyplotting hello there which means I can be in more than one place over here at the same time up above you down here can you see all of me?"

Placing her hands over her ears, Abigail called out. *"How many can you create?"*

"Depends. Some specters can create whole armies of themselves."

Abigail examined each of the Little Wades. They were all identical. They all spoke at the same time, which she found incredibly confusing.

"We can speak all at once and say the same thing!" all of the Little Wades bellowed like a chorus.

"Or we can all speak...," one Little Wade began.

"Differently...," a second Little Wade kept going.

"Saying different things...," a third Little Wade continued. They all spoke on top of each other. Within less than a second, all of the voices blurred together. They all digressed. One spoke about the weather. Another complained about how much he missed food. A third droned on and on about how different wrenches worked when repairing Watchtower. Abigail could not make out anything else. The chattering Little Wades sounded like a loud, honking gaggle of geese.

"How can you control them all?" still cupping her ears, she yelled.

"Well, someone calculated that a phantom well trained in Polyplotting can summon and effectively puppeteer one doppelgänger per two years of that particular spirit's total time as an incorporeal being."

Abigail quickly calculated.

"Wait, I just realized something. Your card says that you've been in business since eighteen thirty-one."

"Correct. Born in eighteen eighteen. I died at thirteen years of age."

"So...you're just over eighty years old!" Abigail's eyes nearly popped out of her head. "Yet, you do not age."

"Frozen outside of time."

"Could you look like an old man?" Abigail, curious, teased him.

"Yes. I can alter my morphology. 'Multiproteus' is the technical term."

"Named after 'Proteus,' the Greek god who can turn into anything he wanted. That should be easy for me to remember."

"We just call it 'Sembling' for simplicity's sake, as in resembling, assembling, reassembling, disassembling, or dissembling, but it requires effort." Many of the Little Wade Polyplots transformed. They displayed an incredible variety of outfits and ages, ranging from infancy to six years old to crinkly eighty. One even transformed into a rhinoceros, another a monkey, another a dog. Then they all reverted to his regular appearance, a handsome, slightly-blue-skinned boy. "When I perished, I wore these clothes, so I keep this as my default image, no additional effort required."

Abigail counted each of the images carefully and realized that not a single one of the Little Wade Polyplots wore shoes.

"You died with no shoes on?"

"Yes."

"How...how did you die?" Abigail inquired, curious about his slightly blue skin.

All of the Little Wades, including the original, hesitated, gazing off in many directions, avoiding the question.

"It's quite a tragic story," Little Wade warned her. "Are you sure you wish to hear it?"

"I'm sorry. How rude of me. Forget that I asked. I mean...if you want to tell me, please do, but I understand if you don't." Abigail quickly changed the subject. "Let's talk about something else. So... over sixty years as a ghost! No wonder you comport yourself the way that you do, so knowledgeable, so patient, so mature! You've refined your manners after decades of practice. Most boys my age possess one-quarter of the vocabulary of a frog. It's mostly grunts, chuckles, and snarls with them."

"Give them time. They'll grow some brains."

"I sincerely hope so. I long for good conversations. This ranks as the best one I've had in quite some time. Eighteen thirty-one...over sixty years as a ghost. Wait, so getting back to Polyplotting, if I am doing the math correctly...that means you can create up to thirty copies of yourself at one time?"

"*Yes.*" All of the Little Wades bellowed in unison, a thunderous roar. Abigail jumped. The flock of Little Wades swirled around Abigail like snow in the wind.

"How independent can they be?"

The Little Wade Polyplots began to flit and drift and swoop and soar about the room. Many even passed through the walls and ceiling and looped around the house.

"They're all as intelligent as I am, convenient when I scout neighborhoods looking for children to protect. I can fan out and cover a wide area. That's how I found you. I am currently capable of covering several city blocks, but the farther any one of my Polyplots ranges from me, the thinner, frailer, clumsier (and frankly dumber) it becomes. I prefer to keep it to a dozen with myself as the thirteenth. Otherwise, it becomes quite confusing ordering them all around."

"Like herding cats," she teased him.

"Indeed." Then he clapped, and all of the other Little Wades vanished. Abigail stood alone with just the one. The room grew darker. A shadowy illusion encircled all her candles' flames, gripping them like black fists, strangling and stifling their light. At first, Abigail felt nervous, but then Little Wade, floating above her, glowed gently, bathing the entire attic in a cool, pale blue, like moonlight.

"Apologies about the darkness. I simply needed a greater contrast. This is Spectromeda." Little Wade glowed brightly. "The spontaneous, inter-dimensional production and manipulation of actual, real light and energy. No illusion, Abigail. Anyone can see this."

"Now you're just showing off," Abigail chided him.

"Not exactly, well, maybe a little, but I do wish to make a point," Little Wade stopped glowing. He banished his shadowy illusion from the candles, returning the attic to its previous warm, orange atmosphere. "I imagine, having seen all of this, you must be wondering what you can trust."

"Indeed, I'm not sure I can tell what's real anymore."

"You did very well tonight, Abigail," Little Wade complimented her. "Despite your predicament with the Longshadows and your understandable fear, Watchtower and I believe that you handled yourself with great poise. The bootblacker disguise you conjured up shows incredible resourcefulness."

"I suppose living in the Lower East Side teaches you a thing or two about how to avoid danger. It's been a very sharp adjustment."

"True," Little Wade concurred, "but in the Lower East Side and other neighborhoods like the Five Points, evil rampages very much out in the open. The gangs look and dress like gangs, brutes have blood on their clothes, and murderers have blood in their eyes. Thieves may lurk and hide, but take one glance at them and you know what they are. It's like growing up in a zoo, a zoo without cages or bars, perhaps. Nevertheless, you can tell who the animals are. Tigers look like tigers, wolves like wolves."

Little Wade drifted closer to her.

"You must understand, however, that, in *other* places in this city, sometimes evil lurks in places that don't look evil at all. On the contrary, they look beautiful, shiny, clean. The people speak incredibly politely, smell like perfume, wear fancy clothes, live sumptuous lifestyles, ride in beautiful carriages. These monsters pose a far greater danger," Little Wade warned her, "because these forces lurk behind the gangs and control the creatures in the gutter. They, the truly powerful, decide how this city gets built, who rises, who falls, who disappears, never to be seen again."

"I understand all of this," Abigail sounded impatient.

"I know you understand," Little Wade added, "but you do not possess enough experience. Make one wrong turn, and your life could change forever. Do you agree?"

"So I'm caught in a paradox. Being inexperienced makes me vulnerable, but accruing more experience puts me in danger, so what am I to do?"

"You must develop your instincts like a dog utilizes a shrewd sense of smell, or a bird naturally understands how the wind works or a cat manages to land on its feet."

"Where do I begin?"

Little Wade smiled slyly.

"Have you ever played the game peekaboo?"

"Of course, everyone has."

Little Wade covered his face with his hands.

He vanished.

"Try to find me." His sweet voice echoed throughout the attic.

Pausing a moment, Abigail stood perfectly still, swiveling her head, peering around the attic apartment lit only by a few candles. She spun around slowly, tracing the edges of the glowing, orange light. She guessed that Little Wade would choose a tucked-away spot where the candle's radiance could not reach. She pointed.

Little Wade reappeared all the way across the room, startling her.

"Not even close. Try again."

He closed his hands over his face and vanished again.

Abigail, flustered, and frustrated, scanned the apartment once more. She got down on her hands and knees. She stood up again. Then she extended her hand and pointed.

Little Wade reappeared once more. Although she missed again, she did come closer, only about ten feet off this time.

"Not quite."

His hands closed over his face. "Peekaboo." He vanished again.

She studied the apartment. She tried again.

He opened his hands and reappeared, this time only three feet from her guess.

"Better."

He closed his hands over his face again, vanishing once more.

This time Abigail tried something different. *Don't use your eyes. You can't see him. Try to think as he thinks. Where would he be?* Then she opened her eyes again, opened her hands, spread out her fingers, and she inhaled a deep breath through her nose as if she were trying to sniff him out. Narrowing her eyes, she placed her hands over her stomach. She could feel it, something deep in her gut. She pointed to another area in her apartment.

He reappeared again, his hands open. This time she missed him by less than the length of one foot.

"Very good." He sounded impressed.

He closed his hands again over his face, vanishing.

She chose again, very quickly this time. She did not think but simply acted. This time she nailed down his location perfectly.

"Excellent."

One more time. She whirled around and pointed up to the triangular ceiling, and he reappeared, perched on one of the rafters. His eyes glinted like a cat's eyes. "Perfect!"

Abigail blew on her fingertip as if blowing smoke off a gun. "I enjoyed that. So much fun."

Laughing, Little Wade switched position, teleporting throughout the room over and over until he hovered level with Abigail's eye. "Welcome to the wonderful world of Warping." He teleported again.

"Warping. Very efficient. I wish I could to that. You would make a marvelous mailman."

"So, what happened there, that last time when you found me? Something changed."

"I stripped away all of my senses, and I followed a deep feeling inside myself. I waited for it to pull me, a little tug, gentle, like a needle in a compass, an electromagnetic feeling, invisible, but...solid. I would point in a direction, and something in me wobbled back and forth. Does that make sense?"

"That's exactly what I hoped you would say," Little Wade complimented her. "Just because you cannot see something with your eyes does not mean you cannot see it. Children possess powerful instincts, Abigail, deep, keen, perceptive senses that can pierce through many of the illusions and lies this world can conjure. Unfortunately, many children lose these senses when they become adults."

"Why do we lose them? I've been told we're all supposed to get smarter as we grow up."

"People young and old get lost out there in the city, Abigail. They get buried alive with jobs, responsibilities, worries, fears. You can only use your deepest senses when you know who you truly are. People forget who they are because they forget who they were and who they wanted to be."

"Well, I don't want to forget. Ever. Show me how I can use these senses."

Little Wade pointed at something very unusual and wholly unexpected.

"Do you know what that is?" Little Wade pointed to her belly button.

"Are you pointing at my belly button?"

"Yes."

"Why are you pointing at my belly button?"

"Do you know what it's for?"

"Not really. My school library contains several medical volumes, but I found them to be a little boring. I think it has something to do with detaching from the mother."

"It's an eye," Little Wade told her.

Looking down at her belly button, Abigail could not help but say, "Ew...gross." She recoiled.

"Not a literal eye," Little Wade corrected himself. "It's a metaphor."

"Metaphor for what?"

"Tell me, have you ever looked at someone and felt something in your stomach, something warning you?"

"Yes, many times," Abigail admitted. "I feel almost sick. My father calls it 'going with his gut' and often trusts it."

"Your father's lesson will save your life. Whenever you look at something, or someone, and feel something wrong, ugly, churning in your guts, at that moment you are seeing with your stomach."

"Seeing with my stomach," Abigail repeated as she poked her belly button. It tickled. She giggled. "I like that. Does it matter if I have an innie or an outie?"

"It works the same either way, sort of like having brown eyes or blue eyes. They both function equally."

"I have an innie." Abigail poked at her belly. "Do you have an innie or an outie?"

"I can't see my belly button anymore." Little Wade shrugged. "I am restricted to this permanent form, clothes and all, but in life, I had an innie."

"Can you still see things and people with your stomach?"

"Oh yes, Abigail, I see much more now." Little Wade's voice fell quiet. "I see much more than you can possibly imagine."

He sounded very ominous. Abigail, a little nervous, asked, "Why are you telling me all of this?"

"Because we are going to show you many things. Starting tomorrow."

"What time?"

"Well, Abigail. We serve you. You decide. Watchtower and I consider ourselves professionals and also gentlemen. We would never presume to know what you want. As our client, you set the terms."

"I usually rise around seven in the morning."

"Seven it is, then. In the meantime, Abigail, please think about how else we may be of service to you," Little Wade requested. "Now, we have definitely lingered too long. It's time we took our leave of you."

Little Wade ventured toward the window.

"Wait, where are you going now?"

"Out on patrol, of course."

"All night long?" Abigail sounded concerned.

"I'm a phantom, and Watchtower's a mechanical man. Neither one of us needs to eat, drink, or sleep. We're always on the move, day and night."

"Will you be rescuing anyone else tonight?"

"If we find any more children in need, we will help them the same as we did you."

As Little Wade drifted toward her window, Abigail blurted out, "I don't want you to go! Can't you stay a little longer?"

"I'm afraid not, Abigail. More importantly, after we provide our services to you and solve your problems, then we will move on so we can assist someone else."

"What? I just met you! Don't say goodbye already. That's terrible."

"I'm merely trying to set expectations," Little Wade answered sadly. "Good night, Abigail."

"What happens tomorrow? Can you give me at least some insight into your plan?"

"We intend to prove to you that this metropolis, despite its flaws, is indeed destined to become the greatest city in the whole world."

Little Wade smiled just before he vanished through the wall, but not before uttering one last phrase.

"Welcome to New York."

Immediately, Abigail rushed over to her window, opened it, and leaned outside to see if Watchtower still stood in the alley, but he had vanished. She could not see Little Wade anywhere.

At first, she felt a pang of sadness. She already missed her two new friends, the most wonderful new friends ever, and now they were gone, but then she perked up when she remembered.

"Tomorrow. Seven AM. Sharp."

Abigail, dressed for bed, blew out all of the candles except for one and leaped into her hammock, which captured and cradled her like a pair of soft, gloved hands. She felt as if she floated through the air in Watchtower's supernaturally strong grip. Curling up under her blanket, Abigail gazed into the flickering flame of her last candle. When she shut her eyes, she could still feel the heat of the fire gently against her skin. It banished all of her fears and potential nightmares. In fact, she slept better that night than ever before.

Tomorrow, however, would be something else entirely.

7

GOOD MORNING

"Pssssst."

Abigail awoke, slowly opening her eyes. Swinging in her hammock, still tucked beneath her blankets, she adjusted herself. Blinking several times, she checked the spent candle that stood on her nightstand, which had been reduced to a smeared pool of wax with a burned-out wick at its center.

"Pssssst."

Sitting up and looking around, Abigail glanced around. Daylight streamed through her window. Her father, lying in his small, cramped, single bed, snored loudly in the corner of their attic apartment. She deduced that he had returned home late last night, long after she had fallen asleep. His trunk-like legs jutted out over the edge of the small bed frame. He still wore his boots. Abigail shook her head sadly. Father always forgot to take them off before flopping into bed and falling asleep instantly. That meant he wore his boots on his feet all day and all night without giving them a moment to breathe. That meant when he removed them inside the apartment, they would release an explosive cloud of foul odor. Abigail practiced holding her breath for a moment. She anticipated that in a few minutes, when her father awoke, she would need to stop breathing altogether if she wanted to avoid the horrible, noxious smell of her father's sweaty, stinky feet.

"Psssst!"

Then Little Wade's head popped up through the floor.

"There you are," Abigail whispered back. "Good morning."

Her father snorted and rolled over.

"Good morning. Did you sleep well?" Little Wade, floating up through the floor, whispered. "No nightmares?"

"On the contrary. I feared I dreamed everything that happened last night."

"Good to hear. Nightmares can be quite common after such a traumatic experience. Let's begin with some good news. I checked the Registerium and found no record of your mother's transformation into a ghost."

"So, she's..." Abigail pointed up toward the sky.

"She crossed over and rests completely at peace."

"Thank you." Abigail wiped tears from her eyes. "Thank you for that."

Little Wade pointed to the window.

"It's a new day, a new world, and we are at your service."

"Wonderful," Abigail sat up, excited.

Snort! Grrrrrrr! Martin shifted in his bed.

"He's about to wake up. It's time to coordinate what you are going to tell him."

"I am struggling for the right words. I don't feel comfortable lying to my father. Am I allowed to mention you and Watchtower at all, if only as a legend?"

"The less your father knows about us, the better. We must conceal our existence from people as much as possible. Can you imagine what people would do to Watchtower if they found out about him?"

"That's a good point, but surely you have adult allies, don't you?"

"Yes, we do, but most of them began as children we assisted."

"Most, so there are exceptions? My father could be one. I know him to be a very trustworthy man. He would never tell a soul about you two."

"Unfortunately, I must refuse this request. We cannot allow a special dispensation for your father, Abigail. Almost every single client asks us that same question. Our answer must always be the same. Only you can know about us. You must keep our secret."

"Even from him?"

Snort! Grrrrrrr!

"Even from him. He won't understand. Look at it this way. You are protecting him. The less he knows about us, the safer he will be. Trust me."

"I must tell him something."

"I agree, but you must be careful. If you simply blurt out that you were attacked last night, he might keel over from a heart attack."

"I can't just lie to him."

"I agree, but you also cannot tell him the whole truth."

"Well, what do we do? I imagine you possess a great deal of experience in matters such as these."

"Indeed. We need to concoct a credible cover story that combines the necessary, mostly true elements, but spares the phantasmic, fantastical, and mechanical man bits."

"Very well. What do you suggest?"

"Trim down the scale of the encounter. Instead of ten, say you were accosted by two, maybe three. Instead of a ghost and giant, say—"

Snort! Gah!

"I'll prompt you," Little Wade whispered and retreated. "Try to treat today as a perfectly normal morning."

"Normal..." Abigail repeated the word, although she hardly recognized the word anymore.

They both quieted down. Rumbling and grumbling, Martin Reid, Abigail's father, slowly opened his eyes. Rising out of his crude, wooden bed, which creaked and squeaked and scraped against the floor, Martin stood up straight. His booted feet boomed against the wooden floor. His joints cracked and popped as he stretched and adjusted himself. Cracking his knuckles and coughing, Martin slowly stood up, careful not to bang his head against the ceiling. He yawned loudly, reached out, grabbed a cup of water from off his nightstand, and splashed his face. Then, shaking his face like a dog, he sprayed water droplets everywhere and opened his eyes wide, blinking several times.

"Abigail," Martin Reid spoke in a deep, gruff voice. "You awake?"

"Yes, Papa," Abigail called out from under her covers.

"Come have breakfast," Martin grunted. Then he squatted, reached under his bed and retrieved a tightly tied parcel. While Little Wade remained by her window, Abigail rolled out of bed, yawned and stretched, and then stomped over to the small table and chairs. Little Wade took a hard look at Martin Reid.

In his youth, he had been a handsome, dashing young man, but now years of excessive hard work, sadness, and too much drink had taken their toll on him. Martin had sad blue eyes, rough hands, and a short, bristly beard, rough like sandpaper. Although a large, powerful man with broad shoulders, a barrel chest, and thickly muscled arms, he moved slowly, gently around Abigail like a bear would around its little cub. Although he possessed tremendous strength and stamina, Martin, exhausted, limped from a recent injury. He seemed like a man who worked too hard for too little; however, the instant Martin saw Abigail, a bright, gentle smile bloomed on his face. They embraced each other fiercely.

"Good morning," he whispered into her hair.

"Morning," she whispered into his shirt.

"I went to Mr. Haskel's at the crack of dawn. You know what that means?"

"Haskel's?" Abigail's mouth watered.

"I brought your favorite."

Excited, Abigail did not say another word but plopped down into her seat. Sitting down and joining her at the table, Martin placed the parcel on the table. He tore it open with his big, beefy hands. Immediately, the fresh, luscious, succulent, smell of fried bacon, hot eggs, melted cheese, and toasted bread flooded the entire room. Abigail rolled her eyes in pleasure and dove her hands into the package, pulling out a sloppy breakfast sandwich. Laughing, she scarfed it down, munching hungrily, crunching the crispy bacon, lapping up the golden cheese and eggs. The flavors flowed like hot honey into her mouth. "Mmmmmmmm…"

Martin also placed a glass bottle of milk on the table with a *clonk*. "Drink your milk. It's good for you." Abigail gulped it down and licked the sides of her mouth. Martin ate as well, more slowly, but smacking his fingers, relishing every bite.

"Did you enjoy school yesterday? What did you learn?"

"Wonderful day. In history, Mrs. Whitlock taught us about the Ming Dynasty. In English, we read about the Trojan War. In science, she showed us how our plants, the ones we potted and placed on the windowsill, use sunlight to feed themselves. It's called photosynthesis. In math, we learned how to multiply fractions, convert decimals and calculate percentages."

"Hrmmm," Martin grunted as he ate. "That does sound interesting. That's good, and Mr. Kowalski? Were you helpful to him?"

"Yes, Father."

"Did he offer you anything from his shop?"

"Yes, he told me that this afternoon he'll provide us with six chicken legs. Seared. You can pick them up later."

"I'll pick them up after work, so that means you'll have something to eat tonight. Good. Did you read?"

"Always."

"What did you read?"

"A ghost story."

"A ghost story?"

"Yes, it's a story about a boy named Little Wade."

Little Wade's eyes sprung open, and he darted forward. Abigail winked at him.

"He died, murdered many years ago, and he's been a spirit for a long time, here in New York City."

"That sounds like a somber tale," Martin grumbled. "Why would you want to read such a sad story?"

"Well, despite his tragic backstory, Little Wade is a very good boy. Being a wraith grants him many powers and abilities, and he uses them to help children in need. He rescues them, and then he guides them out of trouble."

Martin stopped eating and perked up. "Sort of like an angel?"

"Yes, very much like that."

Martin became intrigued.

"So...what happened in the story?"

"Well, there's a young girl...quite similar to me."

"What...perfect?" Martin teased her.

"She's a redhead with freckles, and she loves to read. One night, Little Wade saves her and teaches her how to be brave. He introduces her to New York City, which turns out to be not so terrible after all."

Martin seemed genuinely moved.

"That...actually sounds like a good story."

"It is. In fact, it's such a good story, and I find the character to be so well written that it almost feels like Little Wade...actually exists."

"Hrm..."

"So, I hope you don't mind if from time to time I refer to him as... if he were a real friend of mine. I might even talk to him."

Martin furrowed his brow.

"Aren't you a little old for imaginary friends?"

"I just really loved the story. Little Wade has become very special to me."

Martin spoke carefully, like an ogre trying to handle something tiny and very delicate.

"Don't misunderstand. Your mother and I thought it incredibly charming when you were much smaller, and you spoke to your toys, and you told us about the spirits that you met out in the forest and the fields. We laughed for hours. I remember the gnomes that I carved for you. You gave them names and families and whole histories. Your mother and I loved it when you would talk to your books, and then you would open and close them as if they were moving their mouths and speaking. We loved every minute of it. We were thrilled that you possessed such an amazing imagination and such a sharp mind."

He sighed.

"But...you're older now...and I need you to understand that those things do not exist...and I need you to....I know it's been hard since you've moved here...but...I need you to try to give this a chance...and not...I need you to face reality."

Deflated, and hurt, Abigail protested. "Little Wade helped me."

"Little Wade isn't real." Martin sounded flustered and frustrated, but then he pulled back. "I'm glad you're reading stories you like. You're a bright girl, and it sounds like your school has exceeded my hopes and provided everything I hoped it would, the education you deserve. I just need you—"

"I understand."

They continued eating.

Over her father's shoulder, Abigail spied Little Wade floating, shaking his head silently as if to say, "Be very, very careful."

"Papa...there's something I need to tell you."

"What is it?" Martin ate his meal without looking up.

"Last night, I fell asleep at Mr. Kowalski's, so I came home very late."

Martin stopped eating and perked up again.

"While I made my way home, some of the Longshadows tried to snatch me."

Little Wade smacked his own forehead.

"What? Are you all right?" Martin immediately bolted up from his chair and crossed over to her, examining her. "Are you all right? They didn't hurt you, did they?"

"It's all right. I'm all right. They didn't catch me. Well, obviously, since I'm here."

"Thank Heavens you're all right!" Martin exclaimed.

"I'm safe, Father. I made it home."

"Abigail, I told you that you must be very careful," Martin warned her, reaching out and gripping her shoulders. "This neighborhood is not safe after sunset. The Longshadows! Abigail, I warned you to get off the streets as quickly as possible."

"I know, Papa."

"Then do what I tell you and *listen to me!*" Martin nearly knocked

over the table and then began pacing around the apartment, his boots knocking against the floor, his strong hands shaking. "The blasted Longshadows. They're everywhere. Abigail, we talked about this. We planned for this. When I tell you to do something, you need to listen to me!"

"I did listen!" Abigail shouted back. "I did everything you ordered me to do. I followed the plan, but I fell asleep at Mr. Kowalski's because schoolwork, homework, and real work exhausted me. I ran home as quickly as I could. For weeks, I even disguised myself the way we agreed, but they still knew who I was. I did everything you told me to do, and I still found myself in danger. You're the one who's not listening!"

Martin did not know what to say.

"I hate this city!" Abigail yelled. "I hate it! I hate it so much. I want to go home."

"Abby, we must accept that this is home now."

"No, it's not. This will never be home."

"We came here for you, for your education!"

"Well, I almost died. I certainly got an education last night!"

Martin almost tripped over himself.

"How...how did you get home?"

"I'm trying to tell you. You didn't let me finish."

Both Little Wade and Martin Reid stopped, completely surprised.

Stumped, Martin did not know what to say. He stood there, shaking, uncertain. He then stepped forward and embraced Abigail fiercely, hugging her like a bear.

"Thank Heavens you're all right. Oh, Thank Heavens."

Abigail embraced him back. She cried on his shoulder, finally releasing all of the tension from the following night.

"I'm sorry. I'm sorry I yelled at you." Martin stroked his daughter's cheek.

"I'm sorry I yelled at you, too. I was just so scared, so terrified. Nothing like that ever happened in Tarrytown. Nothing."

"I know." Martin gritted his teeth, frustrated. He wanted to hit something but could not.

"I'm all right, though." Abigail smiled and wiped her eyes. "I'm here!"

Martin lowered himself back down onto his seat.

"I'm sorry. Please...please tell me what happened."

"I knew I was late, so I ran all the way home, and then the Longshadows came after me."

"How many?"

"Ten."

"*Ten?*"

"Too many," Little Wade interjected. "I advised you to say two, maybe three. Now he's going to completely lose it."

Martin rose from the table again and began to pace around the apartment.

"There he goes." Little Wade pointed at Martin. "I told you so."

"Ten Longshadows. They're everywhere! I wanted to find a place close to your school. This was the best I could find. I can't...I can't afford anywhere else. I...wait...Abigail, how did you get home?"

"They tried to corner me, but I escaped."

"How?"

"I...uh...received...assistance?"

"Careful," Little Wade warned her.

"Who? Who helped you? Did the police help you?"

"No, not the police. Well, the police did come eventually, after I was already quite safe. All of the men were arrested."

"So if the police didn't help you, then who did?"

"Some...people came to my aid."

"Who?"

"Strangers."

"Strangers? Who?"

"I don't know. They were just passing through. One of them stood quite tall, so he scared the Longshadows away."

"One of them stood tall?"

"Yes, gigantic."

"A man?"

"Careful," Little Wade cautioned.

Abigail glared at Little Wade. "Yes, a completely normal man, just very, very toweringly tall."

"How could one tall man scare off ten Longshadows?"

"A good point," Little Wade interjected.

"He was walking a dog," Abigail blurted out.

"A dog?" Martin asked.

"A dog?" Little Wade repeated.

"Yes, a great humongous dog named...Watchtower. Watchtower barked loudly and scared the Longshadows away. He also gnashed his teeth and growled."

"The tall man named his dog Watchtower?"

"Yes."

Martin paused for a moment. "That's a good name for a dog, actually."

"I think so, too." Abigail giggled and shot a knowing glance at Little Wade.

"Wait! You said 'they'? What about the other one?"

"The other one?" Abigail stalled nervously, still making this up.

"Yes, you said a tall man, Watchtower the humongous hound, and another one."

"Oh...uh...right...I did...his son."

"Son?"

"Son?" Little Wade repeated.

"Yes, at first the tall man and his beastly hound intimidated me, but when I saw the little boy, the man's son, I knew I could trust them. That's it. A tall gentleman and his son and their dog, walking late at night, rescued me."

"We should thank them. Did you get their names?"

"Uh..." Abigail hesitated. Her story had outrun her imagination.

"Lamplight," Little Wade whispered.

"Lamplight," Abigail repeated, then glanced at him, confused.

"Lamplight?" Martin furrowed his brow, also confused. "Their name is Lamplight?"

"Yes, father and son. George...and Edgar Lamplight. They are the Lamplight family."

"So the Lamplights were out walking their dog," Martin repeated, then shrugged. "Dogs do need to be walked at all hours. That sometimes happens, especially with the larger breeds. What kind of dog?"

"What...kind...of...dog...uh...?" Abigail sounded it out, shooting a desperate glance toward Little Wade.

"Irish Wolfhound," Little Wade told her.

"Irish Wolfhound," Abigail repeated.

"Irish Wolfhound, eh?" Martin nodded. "That'll do it. Those things are monstrous. That's a good dog, big, strong. I...always wanted one."

Little Wade snickered. Abigail smiled and winked at him. Martin Reid felt better.

"Thank Heavens for the kindness of strangers." Martin breathed a deep sigh of relief. "I should have been there."

"You needed to work. You cannot control your schedule."

"That's no excuse. I'm supposed to take care of you. Last night I failed. I know it's been difficult for you. I arranged the best possible school I could for you. Mrs. Whitlock blessed us with her generosity. I found the closest possible place for us to live."

"I know, and you did right by me. It's an amazing school, and you've made this place as special as it could possibly be."

"Your job at Mr. Kowalski's, it helps us eat."

"I know. I don't blame you, Papa."

"I blame myself for this!" Martin hung his head, ashamed. "I work three jobs, and I still can't provide for you. If I could, you wouldn't need to work for Mr. Kowalski. You should've been at home reading, safe. None of this should have happened."

"You mustn't be too hard on yourself. I made it home safely."

"You got lucky! We got lucky! We won't get lucky again. That does it. From now on, I walk with you to school every morning, and I take you home every evening."

"Father, that's not possible. What about your work?"

"I'll find something else to do. I'll quit one of my jobs. I must. None of this means anything if you're not safe and happy. I do all of this for you. You're my life, Abigail, my whole life."

Moved by her father's words, Abigail now comforted him, "Papa, I'm all right."

"No, it's not all right, Abigail. I promised your mother that I would protect you. I can't do that if you're fleeing gangsters at night. It's not safe."

"You have an idea," Little Wade spoke in Abigail's ear.

"I have an idea?" Abigail repeated.

"You do?" Martin asked.

"I...do?" Abigail glanced at Little Wade, then she quickly corrected herself. "I mean, yes, I do."

"Well," Martin grunted, "let's hear it."

Little Wade raised his arms and conjured up a detailed image of her neighborhood, an elaborate three-dimensional model of the entire area.

"Wow," Abigail blurted out.

"What?" Martin wondered, bewildered. He could not see the image at all.

Little Wade waved his hands around like a magician, and bright, colorful lines streaked down several streets and avenues, different colors linking different landmarks. Blue. Red. Yellow. Green. Orange. A tiny Abigail skipped throughout the neighborhood, following the colored lines.

Abigail tried to decipher Little Wade's elaborate imagery.

"I was...thinking that this neighborhood contains colored lines... around this neighborhood...each line has a different color...and I... while skipping...would...stop skipping...and stop...at places...and people...people...who live in the neighborhood...today to see...if perhaps if I can...stop...by...and they could...become bright spots on a line...if I am skipping...and I need to stop...somewhere...I can become a great big bright dot, too...if a situation like that should ever happen...again?"

Little Wade gave her a thumbs up.

"I don't understand," Martin grunted.

"I don't, either," Abigail confessed, frustrating Little Wade.

He started to conjure images again. Then Abigail snapped her fingers.

"Oh! I get it! I see it now." She still stared at the elaborate floating map with colored lines and little moving people, but her father could not see it at all. He saw his daughter gazing intently at a table full of breakfast, so he stared at her as if she were bonkers.

Abigail, keenly aware of this, blushed.

"I mean...I meant to say that I utilize established routes that I take to school, to church, to work at Mr. Kowalski's, to the park, to the local stores, and back again. Perhaps I could find people and places along each one of these routes that can help me if I ever need them to do so."

Little Wade clapped and backflipped through the air.

"What, like stops on a delivery route?" Martin clarified her statement.

"Yes, like that. Well, last night, for example, I passed by several doors on my way home. If even a single one of them had sheltered me, even if only for a few minutes, then the entire crisis would have been averted. They closed their doors on me last night, but maybe if they knew who I was...they might help when the time comes." She aimed these remarks at Little Wade and her father simultaneously, talking to both of them at once. Little Wade applauded.

"That's quite sensible." Martin calmed down. "Better than that, it's an excellent idea, but I should go with you when you talk to people. Unfortunately, I am obligated to work again today."

"No, I want to do this on my own."

"After what happened last night and what happened a month ago? Remember, what happened to *her* happened during the day. No, I won't allow you to be out there by yourself."

Little Wade stopped in midair, and his eyes narrowed. Focusing on Abigail, he observed her become very nervous all of a sudden.

"Father, I—."

"No, you stay here today. Then when I return, together we'll figure out what to do. That's final."

"We'll lose a whole day where we could be solving the problem."

"Then we'll do it tomorrow."

"Tomorrow's Sabbath. Many businesses will be closed. We'll lose too many chances to talk to people."

"We can talk to people at church tomorrow."

"Yes, but if we do that after I talk to people today, it's more efficient."

"No. I don't want you going out there alone."

"It's broad daylight! I won't be alone out there."

"I can't believe this. You were attacked last night, and now you want to go back out there?"

"I can do this."

"*I said no!*" Martin roared, loud enough to make even Little Wade flinch.

Abigail, however, did not.

"Father, I cannot stay cooped up in here permanently. I must return to school first thing Monday morning. I need to solve this problem. It will be all right. The Longshadows can't operate during the day as freely as they can at night. I can investigate on my own. It's simply knocking on doors and talking to people in broad daylight. Coppers patrol the neighborhood. I can find one if need be."

Martin scratched his stubbly beard and grunted. He sat in silence for a second.

"Father..."

"I'm thinking," he growled in response.

A moment passed.

Little Wade and Abigail waited until she spoke up.

"Father?"

"Still thinking," he grunted again.

Another moment passed.

"I'm sorry." He shook his head. "No."

"Papa..."

"No, no, I'm sorry, Abigail. I can't allow that. I just need some time to think. I can't do that and work and worry about you out there. Not now."

"Father, please."

"What if it doesn't work?" he shot back at her, silencing her. "What if you spend all day out there in broad daylight, ask around, beg, plead, and no one agrees to help you? What then? Did you knock on doors last night?"

"Yes."

"Did anyone shelter you?"

"No."

"So aside from the Lamplights and Watchtower, who miraculously appeared at just the right time, no one else assisted you last night. Do you really think today will be any different?"

"I...had not considered that," Abigail confessed.

"It's time for me to go to work. We'll discuss this later."

Martin ducked behind his own curtain, dressed hastily in some new work clothes, and snatched up his tool belt, gloves.

"When will you be back?" Abigail asked sadly.

"I've got to work all day," he gruffly informed her. "Then I've got to be at the docks by sundown. I'll be home...I don't know when...when the job's done."

"Will we be able to read together tonight? That's my favorite time."

"I don't know. I'll try."

Martin saw the frown on his daughter's face; Little Wade could see the frustration on Martin's.

"We need the money."

"I know."

Martin hesitated. "Will you be all right, Abigail?"

"I wish I hadn't said anything. Now you're going to worry all day."

"I know it's been difficult. This isn't at all like Tarrytown, but all of the work, all of the factories, docks, workshops...they're located here in the city."

"I know it's not your fault. It's just...the way life is now," she muttered bitterly.

Deeply wounded by that comment, Martin Reid sighed sadly.

"Tomorrow, I'll get you some new clothes. Will you like that?"

"I don't need any more clothes. I'd like to see you more."

Offended, a pained look on his face. Martin snatched up the last of his things and made his way over to the hatch.

"I told you, I'll do what I can. I don't control when I work."

Martin opened the hatch. The hinges squealed.

Abigail turned her back to him. "You should go. You're going to be late."

Hurt, Martin sadly climbed down the hatch.

"I love you, Mouse."

"I love you, too, Papa."

Martin climbed down the hatch and shut it behind him.

The moment the hatch locked with a loud clasp, Abigail turned and glared at Little Wade.

"Do you want to explain all of that?"

"What?" Little Wade replied innocently.

"All that business with the floating, glowing map?"

"Spectacular, wasn't it?" Little Wade beamed.

"No," Abigail cut him off coldly. "It's not."

"You seemed excited by it just a moment ago. What changed?"

Abigail, rather sullenly, retreated from him. "For a moment, my heart swelled up, hopeful, but it's not going to work." Frustrated, Abigail returned to the table and cleaned up the plates, scraping up the last crumbs of food, scavenging as much as she could, and putting it in her mouth. "Time to go downstairs and get these washed. Can't wait to go out with you and meet all of the residents of the Lower East Side. I wonder if my neighbors will be as charming as my housemates. As you have probably gathered, we get along sooooo well." Sarcasm dripped from her words.

Little Wade floated next to her. "You think I would waste your time?"

"We can try it, but no one will raise a finger to help me."

"How do you know?"

"Because they didn't last night. Why should today be any different?"

"Most people reveal themselves to be fundamentally decent, Abigail," Little Wade promised.

Abigail stewed in silence.

"You don't believe me." Little Wade stopped floating around and hovered perfectly still.

"I'm sorry. I simply don't believe that," Abigail contradicted him. "Most people are not good. If that is true, then where were they last night? I ran through crowded streets yelling for help, but no one helped. I banged on every door I could find. Not one of them opened. No one cared. When I finally found myself in the alley, there were windows open. People witnessed my predicament. They just shut me out and left me alone. Nobody did anything."

"Nobody?" Little Wade challenged her.

"A phantom and a magical, mechanical, fire-faced, metal man saved me, not a real person. It's a miracle I didn't die or worse. I don't think you realize how special you are, but most people fall far short of being special. You needn't worry about getting hurt or dying anymore. Watchtower can more than match anyone or anything that crosses him. Most people reveal themselves to be stupid, selfish, scared creatures, not wondrous at all. They're not good. They only care about themselves."

Abigail placed the dirty dishes right next to the hatch so hard that she nearly cracked them.

"I hate this city. I hate what it's doing to my father and what it almost did to me."

"Are you quite finished?" Little Wade interrupted curtly, harshly.

"Pardon?"

"Do you intend to feel sorry for yourself all weekend?" Little Wade challenged her.

"Did I say something out of turn?"

"On the contrary, you proved my point."

"How?"

Little Wade gently drifted further into the room, and then he conjured up his floating map once again.

"Tell me, Abigail, when you were being chased through the myriad avenues, alleys, and thoroughfares of the Lower East Side, do you think it reasonable to assume that the Longshadows often operate in that particular area?"

"Obviously, we're in their territory. Everybody knows that."

"Then may we safely assume that every person you encountered last night could also tell a tale of at least one unpleasant encounter with the Longshadows at some instance in their recent lives? May we assume they all suffered some form of traumatizing harassment?"

"I see your point."

"Not yet, you don't. Were the Longshadows armed with knives or guns?"

"Yes. Both."

"Do you think the Longshadows train so they know how to use them?"

"Probably."

"Do you think any of those regular people you passed by…do you think they carry weapons and often train for battle?"

"Unlikely…all right, I understand why no one leaped to my defense, but that still doesn't explain why people could not simply open the door for me or help hide me."

"Did your father warn you that the Longshadows use innocent-looking little boys as bait for their traps?"

"Yes, I suspected you were one of them right after you vanished in the alley."

"So if you believed that I could be one of them, tell me, how were you dressed when you were fleeing, screaming, and shouting?"

"Like a little boy," she mumbled.

"I'm sorry…I could not hear that."

"I wore boy's clothing."

"You mean like possible Longshadows bait?"

Abigail vented, frustrated. "My bright red hair burst out from under my cap and streamed behind me. I revealed myself to be conspicuously female. Do you honestly believe that those people lumped me in the same category as those gangsters?"

"I am saying that those ordinary citizens simply did not know. Gangs like the Longshadows poison people's trust in one another.

They divide and conquer. If you show up on a person's doorstep, screaming, at night, then you will force them into a corner. These bystanders must make critical decisions in that instant, decisions that affect their families, their own helpless children."

"Wasn't I a helpless child, too? None of them did anything to help me."

"Yes, they did."

"What? Who?"

"Who do you think contacted the police?"

"No one. The gunfire and commotion from Watchtower's attack caused so much noise they came running."

Little Wade shook his head.

"True, but they still appeared quite quickly and in force, which means they were somehow directed toward your location. Besides, gathering a group of officers takes several minutes. Remember, a considerable length of time elapsed before Watchtower and I made our fateful move."

"Which means someone notified the police the instant the Longshadows cornered me in that alley. So who called for them? Was it you?"

"How could I?" Little Wade laughed. "What could Watchtower possibly say to a copper?"

"Wait, if the police headed straight for the alley, that means that someone in one of those surrounding buildings…somehow contacted the police? How?"

"Remember, I can be in more than one place at any moment. I Polyplotted into each one of the apartments. I witnessed over a dozen families, frightened. They wanted to help you, but some of them were elderly and infirm. Many of them were families with small children. They were all afraid. They all hesitated to intervene for the exact same reason. They became convinced that someone else would do it."

"So no one did. Exactly my point."

"Not true. One person did."

"Who?"

"The woman with the candle in her window, the one who shut her shutters with a loud crack. She snuck out the instant you were cornered."

"I lost all hope at that moment."

Little Wade conjured up an image of an older woman, a seamstress with worn hands.

"She hesitated at first because she had two of her grandchildren in her home. She shut her window, trying to protect them, but then this frail, frightened, old woman reconsidered and exited her apartment. Even though she suffered from a bad leg, she climbed down the stairs as quickly as she could, crept past the alley, and limped as fast as she could down the street. She accosted a nearby officer, who called the rest. She nearly gave herself a heart attack doing it. Decency always appears in the most unexpected places. A surprise is one of the most beautiful things that can bloom in this world."

Little Wade's images faded, and Abigail slowly sat down, humbled.

"She risked her own life, and the lives of her grandchildren, for me. I thought she had abandoned me."

"I see you are not yet convinced," Little Wade added gently.

"I suppose you're right," Abigail conceded. "There will always be exceptions, but I find it difficult to think that way when, at a moment when I needed people, so many others disappointed me."

"Stop thinking about yourself. They didn't disappoint you, Abigail. You cannot blame ordinary people for being ordinary, especially when they find themselves under extraordinary pressure. They didn't do anything wrong. You can't expect them to save you. You were caught in a nearly impossible position, but so were they. If you want people's assistance, you need to help them help you."

"*So what should I do?*" Abigail angrily stormed toward him. "I dress like a girl, that makes me a target. I dress like a boy, and they won't trust me. Enlighten me. *What am I supposed to do?*"

"The question is, what do you do now?"

"Well, clearly I have no idea," Abigail shrugged and went back to being sullen. "Clearly you do. So let's have it."

Abigail sat down and crossed her arms, brooding.

"Abigail, before we begin," Little Wade spoke delicately, "you became very angry with me all of a sudden. I sense that something else troubles you, and during the conversation with your father, he mentioned someone else, a 'her.' Who is she?"

Abigail exhaled a sharp, painful breath. Tears formed in her eyes.

"I've hurt you. I'm sorry," Little Wade apologized.

"No," she shook her head. Her eyes filled with tears. "You've done nothing wrong. I'm just thinking about Brooke."

"Tell me. Please."

Sniffling, wiping her nose, Abigail began.

8

MOUSE

"When my father and I first moved here just a few months ago, we had nothing. I had gotten accepted at Mrs. Whitlock's school, and my father managed to find this place, but we had no idea how we were going to make it work. This city overwhelmed us, but on my first day of school, I made a new friend: Brooke Adams. Her father, George Adams, worked as a laborer and shipwright. He helped us get settled, meet people, and he helped my father find jobs. Mr. Adams also introduced us to Mr. Kowalski so he could take me on as an apprentice. George Adams had also lost his wife, so we were very much the same. We felt blessed to meet such wonderful people in a city like this."

Little Wade listened intently.

Abigail continued. "At first, Mr. Adams and Brooke picked me up and we all walked to school together every morning. His jobs, both his day and evening shifts, started later, offering him a window of opportunity in the morning and the afternoon. So every day, he escorted us back and forth to and from school. Brooke held his right hand. I held his left. Mr. Adams, big and strong like my father, intimidated most people, so no one bothered us.

"One day, I remember a pair of Longshadows stepped up and

blocked our path. Brooke and I flinched, but Mr. Adams, completely unafraid, didn't hesitate. He roared at the brutes, commanding them to step out of the way, or he'd deck them both. I don't think the Longshadows expected that at all. I watched them creep away like cowards, but I'll never forget the look in their sharp, wicked eyes, like the gazes of a pair of serpents. They smiled as if they knew something we didn't."

"When did it happen?" Little Wade inquired gently.

"One month ago yesterday. I felt sick, so my father let me stay home. Brooke and her father went on without me. On that gloomy, overcast morning, they were on their way to school. Brooke held her father's hand. Then, a crowd overtook them, and they got separated. The chaos distracted Mr. Adams for one split second, and when he turned around, Brooke had vanished."

"Taken."

Abigail, in response, simply nodded.

"No one ever found her?"

"No." Abigail shook her head.

"What happened to Mr. Adams?"

"He went mad with grief. He loved Brooke more than anything else in the whole world. After she disappeared, he tried to take his own life," Abigail spoke quietly. "They threw him into Bellevue Hospital, in the ward where they put the insane. Now he won't talk to anyone."

"So you've been masquerading as a boy for this entire month, just to get to school."

"Yes. I know I'm not the only one."

"Shameful. I'm so sorry, Abigail." Little Wade drifted closer to her. "Why did you not mention this to us last night?"

"I wanted to, but I hesitated because...last night you and Watchtower excited and dazzled me. You two were just so miraculous. Last night, anything seemed possible, but we're back in the real world today. I thought I would wait until today to tell you, anyway. When my father just mentioned her again, reality came crashing back. It's horrible. I'm afraid I only offer bad news."

Little Wade's eyes narrowed. "Were you afraid that we would think less of you?"

"Yes."

"Do you feel responsible for her kidnapping, Abigail?"

She nodded sadly.

"That's it, isn't it? You did not mention it because you feel ashamed. You actually think the fault is yours?"

"Mr. Adams extended a generous hand to help my father and me. He walked me to school, protected me when the Longshadows threatened us. If I had been there that day, perhaps things may have turned out differently."

"Yes, two kidnappings and two fathers might be mourning instead of just one."

"It's impossible not to blame myself, at least a little."

"That's positively preposterous!" Little Wade shot back, flustered. "Blame the Longshadows entirely, Abigail, not yourself. You've no reason to feel guilty at all."

"Yes, I do. Brooke disappeared a month ago, and it already seems like the entire city has forgotten about her, even me. Now I feel guilty that I did not mention her sooner. You inquired about it last night. I wanted to say something then, but I just couldn't. I'm sorry."

"Do not chastise yourself too much, Abigail. Nothing pleased me more than to see you smile last night and forget your troubles, if only for a moment. I just don't want you to ever lose hope. If you decide to give up, then Watchtower and I will be forced to reckon with our failure."

"I know you're right," Abigail admitted, drying her eyes. "I know it's not reasonable to ask too much of people, especially when there's a real threat, but asking me to believe in people now is…well…it's asking too much of me."

Little Wade nodded thoughtfully, but then he narrowed his eyes as if planning something.

"Why does your father call you Mouse?"

"He's always called me that." Abigail blushed. "Ever since I was little, I mean even more little than I am now, I feared everything. I would tuck myself up into a little ball and hide under things whenever anyone new came to visit us at our house."

Abigail moved over to her father's nightstand and a framed portrait of the three of them, Martin, Sarah (Abigail's mother), and a tiny, baby Abigail. Next to it stood another framed picture, this one a drawing of a small farmhouse. It read T*ARRYTOWN* on the bottom.

"Everything looms larger when fear takes hold of you," Abigail began, "and most things are bigger than children. I am still small, so when something, anything terrifies me, it overwhelms."

Little Wade attempted to interject.

"I know you say fear creates illusions," Abigail cut him off gently, "but it feels so real. Out in the country, my father ordered me: 'don't go into the forest, it's dangerous.' Well, my father, a big, strong man, can take on anything. So if he warns me, that means whatever's out there must be as strong as him, or stronger, so I became frightened of the forest and all of the trees, which loomed fifty feet over me. They were all bunched up against each other, blocking the sunlight, creating humongous shadows, like a monstrous, rustling mouth just waiting to swallow me up. Forests became even worse at night. Every sound, every cracking branch, or rustling leaf made me jump because I wondered what caused it. What could be moving out there? So at night, I often ran home, but my home could be scary, too."

Abigail continued. She showed Little Wade the rounded edge of the wooden table.

"I banged my head on the corner of a cabinet years ago. It left a nasty scar, right here." She pointed to her forehead. "So I became aware of how many sharp corners there were in my house, on tables, on chairs, on stairs, on furniture. I realized how many shadowy, ominous places exist even in my own home, my closet, my cellar, my...attic."

Abigail picked up one of her father's wonderful wooden carvings, a dog.

"Even animals terrify me." Abigail moved about the room, frustrated with herself. "Even a dog can be frightful. Normally most dogs display nothing but warm affection, but I've experienced a dog baring

its teeth at me. We often forget dogs have fangs, long and sharp, sometimes rotten and yellow, and the dog's pink gums clutch the teeth like swords just waiting to tear flesh. I still recall that dog's growl, rumbling like a horrible beast, its breath stinking of food, of torn flesh. I thought I was next."

She picked up another wooden figure, a horse.

"Even a big, friendly animal like a horse can be terrifying, too. Out in the country, we used horses often, but I never got accustomed to it. The mare I often worked with, Brenda, towered above me. At any moment, she could crush my foot under one of her massive metal hooves or, worse, rear up on her hind legs and slam down on me and crush my skull like an eggshell. I feared to walk anywhere near Brenda because she might kick me in the forehead. One day, while working out in the field with my father, I found myself standing behind Brenda, and I startled her. She suddenly twitched and almost lashed out. I feared the last thing I would see before I died would be a horse's butt."

Little Wade burst out laughing.

"I tried riding Brenda. I wanted to make my father proud, but I panicked, bouncing up and down on the saddle with this large animal thundering beneath me. The ground, which seemed fifty feet away, moved so fast, like a blurring, spinning, buzzsaw, and I prayed that I wouldn't fall and get ripped in half."

"Abigail," Little Wade gently interjected.

"Yes?" she blurted out impatiently.

"You used to ride horses without fear, and pet dogs. You used to play hide and seek, run out in the fields. Didn't you? Even when you were little, you liked being a mouse, hiding and sneaking around. You stated emphatically that you've always been this frightened, but that's not true, is it? You haven't always been this terrified."

She shook her head.

"Have you felt this way ever since your mother died?"

"Please don't ask me that."

"How did she die, Abigail?"

"Please...I don't want to talk about that."

"Very well." Little Wade turned his back and floated away toward the window.

"I don't know. We don't know. One day, I remember, she fainted in the field."

Little Wade stopped and turned.

Abigail continued. "At first, we thought she might have been with child. She wanted another baby, a little brother or sister for me, but we quickly learned something horrible gripped her. Feverish, sweating, her skin slick and sticky at the same time, she couldn't rise out of bed. Her lips cracked and dried up. We tried everything. Nothing worked. We called every doctor. No one had any answers. We replaced everything in the house. My father burned all of our linens, and I knitted everything new. My father burned all of the furniture in the house and carved all new furniture. Nothing worked. Then one day, she couldn't breathe, no matter how hard she tried. She burned up with a fever, and she could not breathe, as if she were dying in a fire, dying from the smoke. Then one day, she just did not wake up from her sleep. One of the doctors, the smartest one, a man from here in the city, informed us that something small killed her, something we could not even see. 'Germs,' he told us. So then I became afraid not only of the things bigger than me but smaller, too."

"You became afraid not only of things you could see but hidden things as well."

Abigail acknowledged this. "People frighten me now most of all," Abigail confessed. "You always wonder what people are hiding, in their pockets, behind their backs, behind their eyes. I realize now that people, with all of their hidden dangers, behave more like diseases than they do animals."

"Moving here did not help any of this, I imagine."

Abigail shook her head. "Cities are the worst. They contain more sharp corners and sinister shadows than any home. They swarm with dogs and horses by the thousands, and tall trees, and even taller buildings. Finally, there are all the people...too many people. Cities teem with diseases, too. I've fallen ill twice since I got here, and my father has suffered from a few ailments as well. I've seen children in alleys with sores on their faces and hobbled feet and flaking skin. So many, too many, too much."

"You feel like a little mouse in all of this." Little Wade observed.

"Yes. I feel like a little mouse in a world built for cats."

"Thank you for sharing all of this with me, Abigail." Little Wade spoke very sincerely. "Anything Watchtower and I learn about you, any information you volunteer, assists us in better understanding you. You are our client. We intend to deliver our utmost efforts."

"What do I do?"

"Well, to start, you need to change the way that you look at things."

"How? Did I utter anything untrue?"

"Oh, it's all true, but something else is true, too."

"What's that?"

"Lie down on the floor. Please."

"Pardon?"

"Lie down on the floor, on your back, and look up. Please."

"Why?"

"Indulge me." Little Wade smiled. "Please."

Abigail did.

"World looks very different from down here, doesn't it?" Little Wade perched on one of the rafters above her.

"Are you making a point about perception?"

"Let us examine your father for a moment, a man of considerable and admirable size and strength, but do you think your father notices everything that you notice?"

"Certainly not."

"Because you're small, and weak, and afraid, does your weakness not sharpen your eyes? Do you not see and notice more things than a big, strong person would? Don't the lions and bears and tigers and hawks and great big people move through this world more blindly than you do?"

"I've never regarded my small stature in that way before, as an advantage, I mean. That's interesting. Please, go on."

"That's why Watchtower and I function so well as a team. He's so indomitable, hardly anything can hurt him, but I'm the one who sees things he cannot. He barrels through things. He's the arms, shoulders, hands, and feet, but I'm the eyes and ears. We need and complement each other. You need to think the same way. Imagine what a mouse sees that the rest of us cannot see. Imagine what a mouse knows. Imagine how much wiser a mouse must be than any other creature, precisely because of its weakness and vulnerability. There's a kind of wisdom that only a small person can have, and wisdom, Abigail, wisdom becomes power. This city will always be too vast for you, Abigail, no matter how tall, how strong you grow up to be. This world will always make you feel tiny, so you might as well enjoy being a mouse and let it hone your wits. Too much to ask?"

"No, I suppose not." She lifted herself off the floor.

Then she took a moment and stared at her round window. Daylight streamed through it. It seemed like a portal to a whole other world. Abigail stood there quietly.

"Abigail?"

"I'm thinking..."

Little Wade politely waited for a moment.

"Um...Abigail?"

"Still..."

Little Wade politely waited for another moment, then re-engaged.

"You do realize you're doing exactly what your father—"

"Yes," she cut him off gruffly.

"Very well." Little Wade retreated and politely waited.

After a moment, Abigail slapped her knees.

"All right, I'll give this a try," she agreed.

"*Excellent!* Now our project begins!"

"What sort of project, exactly, have you designed?"

Little Wade smiled and conjured up an even bigger, more detailed image of her neighborhood. It filled up her entire apartment. Abigail watched as the colored lines marking her routes changed. Perking up, Abigail watched as the lines redrew themselves. They no longer streaked down the streets, alleys, and avenues of her neighborhood.

Instead, they punched through buildings and entire city blocks, creating a labyrinth.

"It's like a symphony of light. What are you showing me?"

Little Wade smiled, "Abigail Reid, may I present The Secret Passage of Hope." Little Wade manipulated the map; the lines disappeared, but seven points lit up and stood out from the rest of the image. "You have one clear problem, Abigail. Time. Please look closely." Little Wade gestured to his spectacularly vast, floating illusion.

"Magnificently detailed!" Abigail remarked as the three-dimensional map swirled all around her. "You've recreated my entire neighborhood."

"Precisely," Little Wade remarked. Floating beside her, he pointed to several different buildings.

"First, here stands your home, on Cherry and Catherine. See?" *Blink!* A point sparkled at her intersection.

Then Little Wade pointed to another location several blocks away. "Here stands Mr. Kowalski's, where you sometimes work after school, at the intersection of Allen and Canal." *Blink!* Another point sparkled.

Then Little Wade pointed to a third location on the map, again, several blocks away. "Mrs. Whitlock's Grammar School on Essex." *Blink!* "The general store where everyone runs errands on Bowery Street." *Blink!* "Here stands the park where you like to play with your friends, here on Grand and Division." *Blink!*

"How did you know that?"

"All local children play there. Watchtower and I keep a very close eye on it. It's under our protection."

"It's just an old, condemned building. It's not really a park."

"Not yet," Little Wade winked. "Now, is...this the church where you attend every Sunday?" *Blink!* Another spot appeared.

"No, we attend Saint Augustine's Episcopal."

Little Wade adjusted his illusion, switching the dot to a church on Henry Street. *Blink!*

"I imagine you frequent Mr. Laird's Bookshop," Little Wade guessed.

"Almost every day," Abigail exclaimed. "I spend hours there!"

Little Wade added another spot to the map. "Here it is, also on Division, not far from you." *Blink!*

"You're missing one." Abigail blushed.

"Oh?" Little Wade studied his map.

"Mr. Magruder's Toy Store," Abigail confessed. "I adore that place."

Little Wade laughed. "Forgive the oversight. He keeps his store here on Clinton." *Blink!*

"Your problem can be summed up in one word: inefficiency," Little Wade explained as he glided effortlessly above her. Abigail watched as a brightly colored line began at her home and traced its way to Mrs. Whitlock's school, and then to Mr. Kowalski's, and then Church, the General Store, the Bookstore, the Toy Store and the Park.

"You take the long way around to move from one of these locations to the other, and you do so at hours close to sunrise or sunset. There are long shadows (no pun intended) in the nooks and crannies of every corner and crevice of every building and every street."

"During the winter, it will be even worse, even more tenebrous," Abigail realized with a shiver. "So, what do I do?"

"We," Little Wade corrected her, making her feel better instantly.

"You mentioned a secret passage? Wait! You're going to reveal its existence and show me where it is, aren't you? Ooooh, does it run underneath the city?"

"No, you're not going to *find* the Secret Passage of Hope. You're going to *build* it, and we're going to help you accomplish that today."

"Build it? How? Do you intend to have us dig beneath the street? Even with Watchtower assisting, and probably doing most of the work to be honest, that will take weeks."

Laughing, Little Wade looped around her.

"We're not going to construct The Secret Passage of Hope out of stones, but out of people."

"I'm afraid I don't understand."

He traced her path through the map.

"How long does it take you to walk to school?"

"I would approximate about twenty, thirty minutes if large crowds block my way. My first class begins promptly at 8:30. I leave here just before eight, and I usually arrive with some time to spare."

"So definitely twenty minutes. What about Mrs. Whitlock's School to Mr. Kowalski's butchery?"

"My classes end around three-thirty. I usually arrive at Mr. Kowalski's at fifteen minutes to four."

"So your walk to Mr. Kowalski's lasts between twelve to fifteen minutes at least, and from the butchery to back home?"

"I usually leave around eight o'clock, and arrive at home at around eight-fifteen, sometimes a little earlier, ten after, but last night those ten minutes felt like an eternity."

"Much can happen in what seems to be a short amount of time, especially when the sun goes down."

"To and from home, the general store and Mr. Laird's Books aren't so bad. Walking to the park from school eats up ten minutes."

"From the school," Little Wade pointed out, "but to get from the park back to your home devours fifteen."

Little Wade circled Abigail and his seemingly endless floating magical map. "So we have established, Abigail, that spending too much time traveling, given the Longshadows' predatory presence, endangers your safety. Therefore, we need to cut down the number of minutes you spend out in the open. Now just imagine if you could pass through these buildings here, here, here, here, here, and here."

Following Little Wade's words, the lines redrew themselves. Changing course, they passed through several buildings.

"Shortcuts!"

"Precisely, a network of shortcuts that slashes the duration of your trips at least in half and supplies you with multiple safe points at the same time."

"A Secret Passage of Hope," Abigail whispered, marveling at the glowing map hovering over her head. "So I need to convince people to let me pass through their homes or businesses in the morning and evening?"

"Precisely."

"How many?" she sounded discouraged.

"We will start with nine."

"Only nine?" Abigail gestured to the glowing map. "But I count over two dozen points where I need to cross and pass through, at least that many. I'll need a variety of paths to keep the Longshadows or any other gangs guessing."

"You grew up in a small town in the country, correct?" Little Wade asked rhetorically.

"Yes. Everyone knew each other, and everyone helped each other."

"Well, think of New York City as dozens of small towns all crammed together. People forget that. We're going to remind them. The Lower East Side contains many communities, all living next to each other: Italians, French, Jewish, Chinese, Irish, Spanish, Africans, Haitians, Indians, Arabs, and more!" Little Wade conjured up illusions to represent each of the groups. Abigail, encircled by a crowd of boisterous, imaginary people, laughed out loud. Little Wade inserted them into his detailed, three-dimensional map, lighting up diverse points throughout the neighborhood. "They all live in tightly knit communities, Abigail, tied together by language, family, religion. If you impress and form alliances with the leaders in these circles, then whole networks open up to you. Your secret passage will be..." Hovering above Abigail, illuminating the roof of her apartment like a second sky, the map sparkled with a constellation of possible paths.

"Everywhere," she whispered.

"Watchtower and I possess key contacts in each of these communities, children that we helped long ago. Now, as adults, they serve in positions of authority and influence and are raising children of their own. We can open the door for you. Together, we will find out what they need, and you can help each other. Accomplishing this will cover a majority of our map."

Little Wade gestured to his floating model of the neighborhood. "Then, once we have established those contacts, we will have a clear idea of where else and who else we will need to add. Filling these assorted gaps in the passage should not be too difficult. I estimate we will need an additional dozen, a manageable number."

"I also know a few people from church," Abigail realized. "There's Mr. Kowalski. He's Polish. Mr. and Mrs. Matsoukis, they're Greek. Mr. Duvalier, he's French. Then there's Mr. Milosz. He's from Bohemia. They all helped my father and me settle in. So far, we haven't requested anything from them. I can speak to them after services tomorrow. Maybe they could help, too."

"Excellent, between the three of us, we can do this!"

"What if they say no?" Abigail was visibly worried.

"Who is 'they'?"

"Anyone. What do we do if people decline to assist me?"

"Many will refuse for a variety of reasons, fear, self-interest, or they just can't spare the time or resources, but as you can see...you possess several options," Little Wade pointed out. "Even if more than a few say no, we can still make it work."

"But what if they *all* refuse? I don't mean your contacts. I mean the people I will have to convince on my own."

"They won't all refuse. Remember what I told you."

"Most people reveal themselves to be good."

"They do. They will."

"So I just ask?"

"You'd be surprised what you find in this city if you just ask. Worst case, you learn something you did not know before, even if someone says no."

Encouraged, Abigail considered this. "You make a compelling case," she complimented him. "Now that I think about it...why would they refuse me?" Abigail wondered, rather innocently. "I'm not asking for very much."

"They don't know you, Abigail. You're still a stranger to them. They might think you'll start asking for more, so it's really quite simple. The people that own these businesses or reside in these homes will not help unless you do something for them, so you must be prepared to offer something in trade. Quid pro quo, Abigail. Something for something."

"Helping a young child get to school every day isn't enough? I won't need more than a few minutes of their time. How tight-fisted are people?"

"I'm just trying to set your expectations, Abigail. If you set proper expectations, you lower the chances that you will waste your time, something we currently do not possess in excess supply."

"You say something to offer or trade, like what?" Abigail sounded nervous.

"I expect that it will vary depending on each person or place of business. Everyone wants or needs something. We will find out, but only if we ask." Rising up from his position, Little Wade rose upward and bowed. "Now, come along. You hired us to provide a service, and we intend to do so. It's time to explore your neighborhood. Somewhere out there, your secret passage awaits!"

"Now, I'm terribly excited and curious."

"That's very good to hear," Little Wade gestured outside, "but first, you must open your window."

"Why? Would you like some fresh air? Wait, you don't breathe anymore."

"Just do it, please."

Abigail did. The circular window swung open. A folded paper in the shape of a bird whizzed through and landed on the floor.

9

OFFICIAL BUSINESS

Curious, Abigail stooped down, picked up the impeccably crafted paper bird, and carefully unfolded it. An avid reader, Abigail quickly scanned through the document, which she instantly recognized as a legal contract. She recalled looking over her father's agreements for work, and the legal deed to their farm. Like any child, she found them infinitely boring to read. Still, they did teach her several new words like Affidavit, Appeal, Contingent, Creditor, De Facto, Heretofore, and Warrant, and this particular document fascinated her. Reading out loud, she sounded out the words. "Little Wade and Watchtower, protectors of New York's Children. Contract for Services. *Oh!*" Here she was, receiving a legal document from a phantom and a mechanical man. She could not wait to read every last detail.

"You hold in your hand a copy of our standard agreement for our clients," Little Wade informed her. "I apologize that we could not get this to you sooner, but we prioritized ensuring your safety."

"It's quite all right." Abigail continued to examine the document. "Without your help, I'd be done for."

"Consider our rescue last night an act of happenstance and friendship, and as an opportunity for us to prove ourselves to you;

however, if we're going to proceed over the next few days, we will require your consent."

"Consent?"

"Parents order children around most of the time. Do this. Do that. Don't do this. Don't do that. For the most part, it makes sense to listen because, for the most part, you can A) trust that they want what's best for you and B) that, being older, they know better than you do."

"Not always," Abigail replied.

"Exactly. Parents are not infallible. As a child, you forget all too easily that you possess the right to *choose*, to influence what happens to you. Which brings us to our case here. You must understand, Abigail, that Watchtower and I cannot order you around or simply tell you what to do or what *not* to do. We will always ask you. You must *consent*. You're a person, Abigail. You're a little person, but you're a person, and a person has rights. No one can ever force you to say yes to anything, not even us. You can always say no. Remember that."

"I will."

"Shall we get started?"

Abigail spread the elaborate legal document across the table, then she placed books as paperweights on the corners, so it lay stretched out across the surface. Little Wade sat opposite her.

"So to begin, we require no payment for our services, so do not concern yourself with that. We only ask that you keep our existence and activities concealed."

"The only fee is secrecy," Abigail repeated the slogan from the business card.

"If people knew about Watchtower, the authorities would put him in a zoo, or worse, take him apart until nothing remained. We've experienced many close calls, but...so far, we've managed to escape custody."

"Your secret is safe with me, I assure you."

Abigail examined the paper, which felt smooth and glimmered like pressed gold. The dark blue ink popped off the page, the letters were neatly typed up, and the unmistakable logo of Little Wade and Watchtower gave her great comfort.

"It looks very professional," Abigail laughed. "Did you prepare this yourself?"

"I did. Well, Watchtower typed it up, but yes. When I was alive, my parents hoped that I would grow up to become an attorney. Obviously, I don't think they ever envisioned this." He gestured to himself. "I suppose this is the closest I am ever going to get to fulfilling their wishes."

"Well, I consider your conduct and competence marvelous and very professional. I think you're doing splendidly so far."

Excited, Abigail read the contract over very carefully.

Little Wade and Watchtower, Co.
Protectors of New York City's Children
Contract for Services

On the date of **November 18, 1899** in the City of New York, **Abigail Reid** (hereafter referred to as the Client), age **13**, daughter of **Martin Reid**, hereby enters into a services agreement with Little Wade and Watchtower, Co., who hereby promise in good faith to provide services to the Client for the express purposes of:

First and foremost, the immediate physical protection from, and long-term removal of, dangerous gang elements infesting the Client's neighborhood that may pose a threat to her safety. Chaperoning will be provided.

Second, facilitation of the construction of the Secret Passage of Hope, a network of contacts and shortcuts to her place of education, places of recreation, place of employment, places of errands, and finally domicile, so that the Client may pass freely and safely to and from home without fear of harassment, harangue or capture.

"First, Little Wade and Watchtower (we) agree to provide you with a protective escort for the next several days, accompanying you wherever you go. Do you consent?"

"Most certainly. I feel safer with you both. Why would anyone say no to that? You're delightful company."

"In our experience, it never hurts to ask."

"Well, I consent, enthusiastically." Abigail grinned.

Little Wade continued, "Do you consent to Little Wade and Watchtower using physical force to protect you, your loved ones, or any other bystanders?"

"Haven't you already?"

"Remember, Abigail, we work for you now. Yes, or no?"

"Very well. Yes, but not lethally, if possible. I don't want you killing anyone on my account."

"Very well. Most clients prefer that option. Take a look at the next section, please."

She did.

```
Third, the facilitation of improved employment
prospects for Client's father, Martin Reid, so
that his earnings, hours, and quality of life may
improve so as to facilitate a higher quality
relationship with his beloved daughter, the
Client.
```

"You're going to help my father, too?"

"If you recall, I promised to help him last night."

"I do, but you already gave me your promise. Why the need to set it down here?"

"Always get important, professional promises in writing, Abigail, always. If a gentleman considers himself as good as his word, then he shall have no problem writing it down and being bound to it."

"That's sensible...but wait...how do you know what to do? I haven't told you anything about him."

"You told us plenty. We already know exactly where he works and how much he earns."

"How? Even I don't know that."

"We possess significant resources within this city," Little Wade explained rather professionally. "Last night, while you slept, Watchtower and I devised a plan to secure your father new employment better suited for his skills, in addition to some extra income. That way, he can spend more time with you."

"I...don't know what to say," Abigail replied, deeply moved.

"Say yes."

"*Yes!*" she did, enthusiastically.

Fourth, Little Wade and Watchtower agree to provide the following: facilitation of dramatically improved long-term prospects for the Client, in the form of contacts, acquaintances, sponsors, benefactors, allies and friends, that will assist Client educationally, financially, socially, medically, scientifically, legally, emotionally, spiritually, psychologically, logistically and perhaps even militarily for the foreseeable future should the need ever arise.

"I don't quite follow this."

"Watchtower and I have many friends, rich friends, poor friends, friends in the police department, friends who work all over the city, lawyers, doctors, laborers, business people, friends in high places, low places, sideways places, upside-down places, mysterious, otherworldly places. By the time this weekend is over and our services completed, those friends will be your friends, too."

"All of this sounds wonderful, and I'm deeply grateful for all of this...but..."

"What?"

"Militarily?"

"Just covering all possible bases. You never know when war comes knocking. Rest assured, by the time Watchtower and I bid you goodbye so you can go back to your normal life, you will never truly be alone again."

"Right now, I don't want to think about saying goodbye. Can we not speak of it?"

"Very well."

> Fifth, the rigorous education and training of the Client for the express purposes of increasing the Client's overall worldly wisdom, situational awareness, practical skill sets and talent for adaptability (hereafter all clustered together and referred to as "Street Smarts"), to improve Client's long-term prospects for survival and success in the Greater New York City Metropolitan Area.

"Hmmm...what sort of training and education?"

"Well, for example, we may devise scenarios or practice sessions that, while innocuous, allow you to experience situations similar to what you faced last night. They will be safe, but...designed to teach you...so if you find yourself in danger again, you will be better prepared to react. We teach you *our* way, so you do not learn the *hard* way."

"Will it be scary?"

"Yes. I'm afraid so. Quite frightful."

She gulped. "But, it's perfectly safe?"

"I don't know about perfectly. That's not the right question."

"What should I ask?"

"Try asking this. Out of the six thousand five hundred and thirty-one clients that we served before you...has any client ever been injured or been dissatisfied with this part of the service?"

"A good question indeed, and the answer?"

"Yes. Five."

"Five?"

"Yes, and they all occurred long ago and under rather ridiculous circumstances."

"Five out of six thousand five hundred and thirty-one?"

"Five out of six thousand five hundred and thirty-one."

"My, you have amassed a sterling record. What were the complaints, if I may ask?"

"Three told us it was too scary, while two thought it not scary enough."

"Not scary enough?"

"Yes, two claimed that they wished the training had better prepared them. Since then, we've ensured the training makes...quite an impact."

Abigail shifted nervously in her chair.

"Do you trust us, Abigail?"

"Shouldn't I? You seem so trustworthy, and you saved my life. We haven't known each other long, but I've already grown quite fond of you both."

"Don't use your emotions," Little Wade pointed out. "Consider the evidence. Six thousand five hundred and thirty-one satisfied customers, only five complaints. Make your judgment based on the evidence, Abigail."

"I do like those odds."

"Do you consent?"

"Yes, I do, on one condition."

"Yes?"

"Please warn me ahead of time, before you intend to frighten me."

"Very well." Little Wade smiled rather wickedly. "I'm warning you *now*."

Gulping, Abigail read on.

```
Sixth, Little Wade and Watchtower agree to
provide for the administration of any necessary
medical attention for the immediate redress,
respite, repair, and recovery from any injuries,
physical or mental, suffered by the Client during
the fulfillment of any of the services enumerated
in this contract.
```

Abigail furrowed her brow.

"Is something wrong?" Little Wade asked.

"What does this say exactly?" She sounded nervous.

"If you sustain any injury, will you allow us to administer medical attention to you?"

"How will that work? I imagine you won't be able to do much, being constrained in your incorporeal form."

"I observe and guide. Watchtower operates."

"You observe?"

Little Wade lowered his face to the table. His face melted into it. Then he retracted it.

"I can dip inside bodies and examine internal injuries and guide Watchtower's hands. I have refined my skills in anatomy over sixty years of study and intensive observation. I've participated in countless surgeries, and my senses are quite remarkable, particularly my sight."

"Is Watchtower skilled in this regard?"

"He is, most certainly. He can suture wounds, reset broken limbs, clear airways, and dislodge items from children's stomachs and throats. He has done so on multiple occasions."

"Oh, dear...reset broken bones...sutured wounds?"

"Some of our clients find themselves in mortal danger, as you did last night."

"But they were all right; the children were all right?"

"Oh yes, only a few fatalities."

Abigail stopped.

Dead silence filled the entire room.

"Wait...you mean...you've lost clients?"

"Unfortunately, yes...yes, we have." He sadly shut his eyes.

"How many?"

"Fifty-four," Little Wade replied ominously.

"*Fifty-four!*" Abigail exclaimed. "Fifty-four of your clients died during your service?"

"Yes. We did everything we could for them, but children can be fragile and their enemies...our enemies can be relentless."

Abigail rose out of her chair. Her hands, sweaty and clammy, shook. Her nerves sizzled beneath her skin, and her stomach churned.

"I'm suddenly feeling very uncertain and uncomfortable with all of this."

"I apologize, Abigail, sincerely, but if you ask me a question, I'm going to tell you the truth."

"Last night, in the alley, I could have been killed!"

"Possibly, yes. You were in a perilous situation, but you performed admirably. Exceptionally well, in fact."

"That's because you...saved me. I had absolute confidence in you. I followed you down the street and simply did everything you advised me to do."

"Yes, and it worked. We brought you home safely."

"Yes, but it could have failed. You could have been wrong. What if you had miscalculated the number of gang members, or your trap did not work, or..."

"Abigail, please." Little Wade sounded almost irritated. "There exists no perfectly non-treacherous environment in the world. Anywhere you go, there will always be some form of danger or another. What do you want me to say? Do you want me to say that nothing can possibly go wrong? Do you want me to assure you that we can provide zero probability of danger, disaster, or even disappointment? That would be dishonest."

"I just want to feel safe, but I now don't feel safe, even here."

"There exists only one safe space, Abigail, and it's located inside your skull." Little Wade pointed to her head. "You will find sanctuary only in your own mind. The sooner you realize that, the better."

A moment passed.

Tears slid down Abigail's face.

"I know you're telling me the truth," Abigail admitted. "It's just... when we lived in the country, my mother was still with us. I loved my life on the farm. We did not have much, but we needed nothing more. We had each other. I was happy. We were happy. I did not want things to change, but they always do...don't they?"

"I'm afraid so."

"Look at me, complaining to a murdered young boy. You must think me spoiled."

"No, Abigail, I don't. You're just afraid. It's perfectly all right to be afraid, but just make sure that you don't underestimate yourself. You've suffered. You've lived out in the country, on a farm, which can be a rough existence. You watched your mother die. Your best friend vanished, kidnapped by the gang that then tried to kidnap you."

"I wish none of it had ever happened. Look what it's done to me."

"Wishing something away won't solve your problem, will it?" Little Wade shot back.

Another moment passed.

"There's no such thing as wishes." Little Wade muttered bitterly. "You wondered last night if genies exist. Unfortunately, they are not real and never have been. There isn't a creature in this world or any other who can snap its fingers and change reality. This is a world full of wonder, but it's also dangerous, and you must fight to seize your rightful place in it. We can help. I am sorry, but I never told you that we were perfect or infallible. No one is, but we do consider ourselves to be your best chance."

Absorbing this, Abigail slowly made her way back to her seat.

"Chance...you say fifty-four...out of...how many cases again?"

"Including you?"

"Yes."

"Six thousand, five hundred, and thirty-two."

"What percent is that? Let me see." Abigail scribbled. "Six thousand, five hundred and thirty-two...fifty-four...fifty-four divided by six thousand, five hundred and thirty-two is...I need some paper. Where did I put my things?"

After a brief search, Abigail found a pad of paper and pencil, seized them both, and began to scribble.

"So...I'm looking for the percentage..." Abigail talked to herself. "There's the part, the whole, and the percent. Fifty-four represents the part. Six thousand, five hundred and thirty-two is the whole. What I don't know...I need to find the percent. So, if I set up a proportion here..."

Abigail scribbled. "Fifty-four divided by six thousand, five hundred and thirty-two is...quite a small number with several decimal places. She wrote out each one. Then I take that number times one hundred and round up."

She finished. "Point eight three percent," Abigail announced triumphantly.

"Correct." Little Wade applauded her.

"That's extremely low." Abigail felt better. "I've less than a one-percent chance of suffering injury or death in your care."

"Numbers do not lie, and neither do we."

Then Abigail sank into her chair, deflated. "The fifty-four you lost...they were your friends."

Little Wade frowned. "We remember all of them, their names, faces, smiles, and we remember their dreams. We remember not only who they were, but who they wanted to be. Not a day goes by that we do not think of them."

"Who could defeat you and Watchtower?"

"This city contains thousands of threats to children, not only the Longshadows. Most of the time, we win, but sometimes we lose. Sometimes, your enemy turns out to be stronger, faster, or even wiser than you expected. Sometimes your enemy can get the better of you. No one can guarantee victory, ever, and anyone who promises you that or promises you perfection quite frankly lies through their teeth to you. We do many things, Abigail, but we do not lie to children."

Gulping, Abigail brooded over this for a moment.

"Then I see no reason why I shouldn't consent to section six. We are entirely in agreement."

```
Heretofore agreed to on November 18, 1899 and
binding for the foreseeable future considering
that both Little Wade and Watchtower are effec-
tively ageless and nearly indestructible and,
therefore, could be considered technically
immortal.

Signed and Sealed (Client):
```

"Are you not satisfied?" Little Wade sounded very concerned.

"No, it's lovely, all of this." Abigail held the contract in her hands. "I am deeply honored, but...I don't see anything in here about finding and rescuing Brooke."

"No, I suppose not. Watchtower typed this up last night while you were asleep. We were simply working with the information that we possessed at the time."

"Can you help me find her, too?" Abigail requested.

"We would be honored to assist you in this matter. We will simply amend the document."

"It's not too much? I hate to ask. You've taken such trouble."

"Not at all. Simply go ahead and write it in now." Little Wade gestured to the bottom of the agreement, a clear space for her to write.

Abigail scribbled.

ADDITIONALLY, LITTLE WADE AND WATCHTOWER AGREE TO INVESTIGATE THE DISAPPEARANCE OF THE CLIENT'S CLOSE FRIEND AND CLASSMATE, MS. BROOKE ADAMS, WHO VANISHED ON ESSEX STREET ON THE DATE OCTOBER 17TH, 1899.

"Official enough?"

Little Wade examined it.

"Perfectly worded." Little Wade approved. "Now, if you wish... sign, and we are officially in business together."

Abigail signed the contract.

ABIGAIL SARAH REID, DAUGHTER OF MARTIN THOMAS REID AND SARAH HYLAND REID (DECEASED).

"Congratulations, Abigail Reid, on becoming client number six thousand, five hundred and thirty-two."

"That's a veritable legion of clients," Abigail calculated. "How many days does it take you and Watchtower to fulfill a contract? *Wait! No!* No, don't answer. Let me figure that out." Abigail calculated the average. "So...you've been in business since eighteen thirty-one?"

"Yes."

"It's eighteen ninety-nine now, so that's sixty-eight years...and that's three hundred sixty-five days in a year. Wait...are you telling me you've worked sixty-eight years straight? You've never taken a vacation or a holiday?"

"Never."

"Not even Christmas?"

"We work on Christmas."

"Halloween?"

"We're especially busy on Halloween."

"Thanksgiving?"

"Too many starving children."

"Are you telling me you...never...not a single day or night off? Either one of you?"

Little Wade shrugged his shoulders. "Leap Year, I suppose."

Abigail cocked her head to the side and shot him a skeptical glance.

"Wait, you work on Leap Year. You're just saying that to make my calculations easier."

"Maybe."

"All right. So let's just say for easy calculations' sake that you and Watchtower take one day off every four years." Scribbling on the paper, Abigail calculated. "So that's sixty-eight times three hundred and sixty-five divided by six thousand, five hundred and thirty-two, which gives me an average of about...let's see here...about 3.8 if I round up."

"That sounds about right, just over three days," Little Wade concurred. "Some clients take longer, some much shorter, but our usual services require about three days or so."

"So..." Abigail gently held her agreement in her hand. "So we still have...a few days together?"

"All weekend." Little Wade smiled.

"That's a relief. I don't want to say goodbye. Not yet."

"Oh, don't worry." Little Wade rose from his seated position. "The adventure is just beginning, and we have much to do."

"What's next? I'm excited." Then she studied the document. "What should I do with this?"

"You can leave it here. It will be safe."

"I'll hide it," Abigail glanced around her apartment. "You made it clear. No one can know you exist, not even my father. What if he sees this?"

Little Wade did not seem worried at all.

"Go ahead and tap it with your finger."

Abigail did so. The moment her fingertip tapped the paper, something extraordinary happened. The contract's very official, typed text slowly faded away. It vanished, replaced with a childlike drawing of a scribbled little boy with a blue face and dressed all in black with bright white socks. The little, blue, shoeless boy floated in midair next to a lanky giant with overly long skinny arms and legs, and an oversized top-of-lamppost head, and an extraordinarily oversized top hat. Someone had drawn Watchtower's fire and glass face as two lines containing a swirl of yellow and orange fire.

"Only you can see it. To anyone else, especially adults, it will look like that."

"Wonderful."

"Now it's official." Little Wade bowed. "We work for you."

Then his eyes seemed to sharpen. His sharp brows pointed down like daggers.

"What is the matter?"

"Watchtower and I fully intend to honor every last item listed in your contract, Abigail. We will help you build your Secret Passage of Hope. You will go to school on Monday freely and without fear, but—"

"Item one," Abigail interjected because she already knew what he would say next.

"Yes, before we build your passage, however, we must severely weaken the gang presence in this neighborhood."

"You mean the Longshadows? Did you not defeat them last night?"

Floating, his tailcoat billowing behind him, Little Wade shook his head.

"They lost ten men. At least one of the Longshadows we defeated last night has undoubtedly awakened by now and spoken to his fellows. Based on his report, the gang will retaliate. As we discussed last night, the gang was already tracking you."

"They must know where I live. Will they will send people here?"

"They already have. Look outside."

"Oh no!"

Abigail rushed to her open window. Across the alley, she spotted a pair of Longshadows crouching on a stoop, watching her house. They glared straight at her. One of them even waved.

Shrinking away from the window, Abigail was visibly frightened. "What do we do?"

"Don't worry, Abigail." Little Wade smiled. "We've been in this business over sixty years, and you're in the practiced hands of professionals."

Encouraged, relaxing, Abigail snapped her fingers. "You anticipated this move."

"Naturally."

"What is your plan?"

Little Wade drew close to her and winked.

"You've set another trap for them, haven't you?" Abigail nearly jumped.

"Not just any trap." Little Wade grinned wickedly. "We're going to set the Great Gang Trap, but we need your help to spring it! Do you consen—"

"*Yes!*"

"So, I guess you're not afraid anymore?"

"Well, I was afraid before, still am, but now I'm simply far too curious to say no."

"That's good, Abigail. The opposite of fear is not bravery, but curiosity. Bravery comes and goes, but curiosity always wins out. Now, Abigail, grab your father's lucky chess piece."

She did, clutching it tightly in her hand.

"It's a game of chess, and our board is the Lower East Side. Now, we make our first move."

10

PHANTASMAGORIA

"*Wahoo!*"

Many people smiled as Abigail rode piggyback on Watchtower, who carried her effortlessly as he took long strides down the sidewalks of the Lower East Side. He wore his trademark suit and top hat and his long, wondrous overcoat. The pockets were so voluminous that Abigail tucked her feet snugly inside. This supported most of her weight, but she wrapped her arms around his warm neck to stabilize herself. She felt quite comfortable and squealed with glee watching the crowds make way and part before them as they passed.

All around Abigail, the neighborhood was abuzz with a blur of activity. Horse-drawn carriages and omnibuses clattered and chattered about; steaming, metal trolleys scuttled down steel tracks like insects. Newsies called out the headlines. Sweepers clutched their brooms. Vendors displayed their carts. Messenger boys whizzed on bikes. Musicians, jugglers, hawkers, and peddlers filled up the sidewalks to the point of overflowing. Hundreds of pedestrians of all shapes and sizes, families, coppers, and crooks moved about. Finally, Longshadows intermingled with the crowds. Every few minutes, as Watchtower stomped forward, Abigail peeked behind her and spotted them. She informed Little Wade, who soared above the crowded metropolis, flipping and fluttering like a bird.

"They're following us."

"They won't dare attack you while you're with him."

"You're certain?"

"Would you?" Little Wade looped around her. "Enjoy the ride!"

Reassured, Abigail smiled, and she did enjoy the ride. Watchtower paid for an ice cream cone and plucked it up from a street vendor. He raised one of his arms and handed it to her. She eagerly seized it in her hand and lapped it up, trying not to smear herself too badly as Watchtower's elongated footsteps forced her to bounce up and down, up and down, up and down.

"It's like riding an elephant!" Abigail exclaimed brightly, "I mean...what I *imagine* riding an elephant must be like!"

"At full size, he can carry a dozen children at a time." Little Wade spun through the air like a dancer.

"Am I dressed properly for adventuring?" Abigail called out to him, gesturing to her clothes. "I changed rather rapidly."

"Do you feel like yourself?"

"It does feel good to wear what I want...and to not have to dress like a boy."

"Then that's all that matters," Little Wade swooped and climbed and dove. Abigail noticed that several Little Wades (Polyplots) swam through the flowing crowd like sharks, keeping a close eye on the Longshadows. Simultaneously, more duplicate Little Wades hovered high above, just over the rooftops, scanning the area as if they were hawks.

"Where are we going?" Abigail asked the real Little Wade, who flew closest to her.

"Would you like to know or be surprised?"

"Hmmm...let me think...I have decided. Surprised."

Little Wade, still flying loop-de-loops around her, flipped like an acrobat in slow motion. Watchtower continued to thunder forward, crossing yet another city block. Abigail's arms grew a little tired and slackened. Sensing this, Watchtower reached back with one arm, picked her up, and lifted her until she rode on his shoulders as if she were a tiny toddler. From this even more elevated position, she could see even further down the avenue, which stretched down endlessly like a vast river. The dense crowds encompassed her like flowing water. A thousand different hats and parasols swirled around her like foam. She felt like a sailor on the bow of a ship, slicing through it all.

"Is this what it feels like to be you?" Abigail marveled at how high up she was.

"One of the perks of being a ghost," he answered. Floating effortlessly above the rushing current of people, Little Wade spun around in the air. That moment of elation quickly passed when Abigail spied some of the Longshadows, who retreated and vanished, leaving only a handful to pursue them.

"Some of them have broken their pursuit. Why?"

"They're calling up reinforcements. No doubt, at least one of the Longshadows from last night cried and screamed about some sort of steel titan. Obviously, no one will believe that story, but now they've seen you with a very tall man that matches the description. They'll figure, 'It's not a monster. It's just a tall man.' So they'll make another try. I imagine they'll bring at least twenty this time around. They will plan to distract Watchtower long enough for at least one of them to snatch you. See, here they come."

Her legs looped around Watchtower's neck, Abigail bounced up and down. She turned and spotted more Longshadows creeping along after them, hiding in nooks, crannies, vanishing inside the crowd of citizens.

"You know, I don't find that at all reassuring," she called to Little Wade. In response, he looped back and forth rather lazily as they progressed toward their mysterious destination.

"Well, then you won't like what I'm about to say next, either."

"Well, now I'm too curious not to hear it, no matter how terrible it is."

Little Wade smiled mischievously. Watchtower turned a corner. The crowds thinned out. Abigail became aware of how much quieter it became.

"Let me begin with a question, Abigail. Why do the Longshadows skulk and creep after us, trying to be subtle?"

"I imagine they don't want us to spot them."

"Oh, they don't care if we see them. Those monsters are not hiding from us."

"To avoid the police?"

Little Wade shook his head again. "They've paid most of the police off."

"Then, who do they fear?"

"Didn't your father tell you?" Little Wade sounded disappointed. "The Longshadows are not the only gang in this city, and we're about to cross into another gang's territory, and, unfortunately, they are even more dangerous."

"A second gang? More dangerous?" Abigail's eyes opened wide.

"Here we are." Little Wade stopped, and so did Watchtower.

Abigail climbed down from Watchtower's back, adjusted her dress, and then beheld their destination, a blackened, charred, silent building. She knew exactly what it was, but that did not make her any less afraid of it. Father often warned her, "Don't go near that place," and now here they were.

The Orpheus Theater, once a grand hall of spectacles and shows, now a burned-out husk, towered before her. Still seared from the fire that had hollowed it out years before, it stood quietly, its doors and windows boarded up. A tattered old banner, for a show long since passed, fluttered in the cold breeze like the flag of some ghost ship. Peering closely, Abigail could make out what it used to say.

MADRIGAL THE MAGNIFICENT MAGICAL MAN.

"Here?"

"Well, we can't very well confront two gangs out in public. That would be rude and unmanageable."

"Two gangs?"

"Oh yes, the Longshadows won't miss the chance to take us under cover of a fearsome building such as this."

"Why are we fighting two gangs?"

"We're not. Item number one on your contract, Abigail. Last night,

Watchtower and I devised the best, most efficient way to dramatically decrease gang activity in your neighborhood. Step one is quite simple. We will manipulate the gangs into fighting each other."

"What will this accomplish?"

"Think for a moment, out loud so I can hear you. Please."

"Hmmm…the best way to get the gangs to stop harassing me is to distract them with something even more important."

"Go on."

"A battle against a rival gang is sure to fix their attention, which will buy us time to build my secret passage."

"Go on."

"Buying us time is only a temporary solution. The only way to remove the gang presence from the neighborhood is to arrest the leaders."

"Go on."

"The leaders are difficult to arrest because they hide behind their henchmen. Oh! So if you create a problem between two gangs, their leaders will have to step out into the open to resolve it, which makes them easier to apprehend."

"Correct."

"That's quite brilliant, actually."

"In business since eighteen thirty-one, we've learned a thing or two. Now, do you consent to the plan?"

"What if I don't? Do you have a backup?"

"We designed over a dozen."

"A dozen backup plans, for me?"

"I told you we work for you."

Abigail gestured to the Orpheus. "Is this your favorite option?"

"I confess that it is." He smiled.

"Then yes, I consent."

"Then let us begin!" Little Wade winked at her and passed through the double doors of the Orpheus.

Watchtower kneeled, placed his shoulder and hand against the doors and pushed. With a scattering of loud *cracks*, the sealed wooden doors splintered at the edges and swung open, releasing a noxious cloud of dust. Watchtower gestured for Abigail to venture inside. Holding her breath and tucking up her skirt, Abigail ducked into the dusty darkness, which smelled like ashes and death.

Immediately, she coughed and covered her nose and mouth. Their sudden entrance kicked up chalky debris that had lain dormant ever since the theater shut its doors permanently. As Watchtower entered and then shut the double doors behind him, he sent a gust of wind into the vast, expansive theater, disturbing it for the first time in years. Abigail, coughing and thumping herself in the chest, cleared her throat. Watchtower turned to her and sheepishly shrugged as if to say, "Sorry about that."

Reaching down and picking up a pair of old boards, Watchtower slotted them over the doorknobs. Then he produced a hammer from one of his pockets and nails from another, which seemed to pop up as if on a spring. He went about sealing the door, nailing the boards firmly into place. The loud *knock-knock-knocking* echoed throughout the deserted, decrepit building. Abigail took a moment to look around.

All around her, in the grave silence of the cavernous building, any noise was magnified ten times in her ears. Every bang, every snapping step, every crack and crackle, every metallic ping, echoed. Then, when Watchtower finished sealing the door, an eerie quiet filled the decaying Orpheus. All around Abigail, the floating dust seemed to whisper all around her, leaving barely spoken words hanging in the air.

The burned out building had been completely ransacked by the fire that destroyed it, and over the years, wear and tear had cracked the walls and ceiling. Now dozens of shafts of daylight crisscrossed each other, striking the soot and ash that swirled silently in the empty, desolate chamber. Touched by the rays, the clouds floated and drifted like phantoms. Abigail remembered that when light struck particles in the air it created something called the Tyndall Effect. Typically, whenever Abigail witnessed this phenomenon in her attic apartment, she referred to it as "fairy dust" or "stardust." It was like seeing tiny specks of life inside every beam of light, but inside this dank, rotten place, the effect felt much different. The shafts of light here were not gentle and warm, but sharp, clear, and cold.

"Who was Madrigal?" Abigail called out to Little Wade, who floated through the air.

"The greatest magician in the city," Little Wade answered sadly. "People came from all over the country, all over the world, to see him."

Looking around the destroyed theater, Abigail remembered when her father took her to a magic show. She recalled that the magician locked his assistant inside a box and then thrust several swords into it; each thrust made the audience gasp. All around Abigail, the crumbling theater seemed to seal her in. Gleaming streaks of daylight punctured through the cracked walls and ceilings like sharp, silver weapons, perforating the entire structure. The inside of this desolate building resembled a magician's box overstuffed with blades.

Then, as she stepped further in and beheld the full extent of the damage, she gasped. It was as if a fire-breathing dragon had rampaged through the Orpheus, gutting it, leaving nothing but devastation behind. Everything was charred black, burnt, melted, or otherwise disfigured and destroyed by flame. Superheated air had cooked all of the gilding and paint, peeling everything off like dead skin. Flames had clawed the walls, leaving deep scars. Abigail reached out and touched the remains of the seats, which were seared and mangled as if chewed up and spat out by some horrible, hot mouth. The grandiose stage, once an elevated wooden platform, had utterly collapsed and splintered into pieces, torn apart, bashed and flattened by an explosive fireball. Looking up, Abigail could see where wave after wave of flames had managed to scorch nearly every last inch of the building as if the fire had been fanned by enormous flapping wings. The Orpheus, its insides ripped out by an inferno, seemed like a charred skeleton, barely held together, barely able to stand. Gasping at the wreckage surrounding her, Abigail smelled mildew, fungus, and tar. She could taste the ash and rot. Floating dirt crawled into her mouth. She coughed again. Little Wade joined her.

"What happened here?"

Little Wade waved his arms around. Casting Dolosphera, he conjured a massive, intricate illusion and took Abigail back in time, recreating the night of the fire. Everything in the theatre that had been scorched or melted completely healed itself. Abigail gasped as clouds of ash and dust condensed and reformed into solid, carved wooden boards, banisters and railings that had been entirely devoured by the violent flames. All of the soot and ash stains that smeared the walls evaporated as shadows do before light, revealing the lavish décor. The smashed stage rebuilt itself into a magnificent proscenium platform, and plush purple and gold curtains reappeared and unfurled, cascading like waterfalls. Little Wade even restored the destroyed gaslight chandeliers that lay shattered on the floor. Resurrecting them and lighting them up like stars, Little Wade raised them upward, restoring them to their rightful place high up against the vaulted ceiling. Then he turned his attention to the audience. With a wave of his hand, he reconstructed the devastated balconies, mezzanines, and orchestra sections as if he were piecing together a scattered puzzle. He restored all of the seats and cushions and repopulated them with boisterous, chatty audience members, some of them children.

"It was a full house that night," Little Wade began, gesturing to the packed seats alive with excited whispers and laughter. "Madrigal the Magnificent was onstage performing his famous act." Clapping his hands, Little Wade conjured up a magician that wore a resplendent silvery-white robe and a tall, white top hat. A thirty-foot white screen rose up behind the magician and stretched all the way across the proscenium arch, creating a blank wall.

An enormous, boxy metal contraption that whirred, clicked, and chugged like a locomotive appeared and floated in midair above them both.

"Do you recognize that machine, Abigail?"

"Yes. That's a Magic Lantern," she replied. "I learned about it in school. It projects images by shining a spotlight through glass plates with images engraved onto them."

"Right you are," Little Wade mimed pushing the huge machine.

Abigail watched it float through the air, pass over Madrigal, and then disappear through the giant, white screen. Little Wade snapped his fingers and images appeared on the screen behind the magician.

"Mr. Todesco, the owner of the Orpheus, placed the machine backstage and projected images behind the performers to enhance the experience."

"I've read about this!" Abigail added. "You're talking about Phantasmagoria."

"Yes, unfortunately, a spectacle of this magnitude required a Magic Lantern of tremendous size which, in turn, required a very bright light. That meant that it needed a large flame that consumed a great deal of combustible fuel. This particular model was old and not properly maintained, and so—"

Boom!

Little Wade simulated the explosion and the inferno that erupted in the theater, but in slow motion, so the event moved at only a quarter speed. Red and golden flames slowly flowed through the air and up the walls like lava. A gargantuan cloud of black smoke encircled Abigail and the entire audience like the ringed top of a volcano. Bursting out from backstage, a massive fireball took form, melting the white screen as if it were no more than a sheet of ice. As Little Wade's infernal illusion expanded and consumed the Orpheus, row by row, seat by seat, curtain by curtain, plank by plank, the air blurred and everything seemed to float in heat. Abigail felt like she was inside the sun. Averting her eyes from the burning stage, she saw audience members fleeing in fear. Stumbling toward the doors, they coughed and suffered in the brutally hot smoke that swarmed throughout the air like a cloud of killer wasps, stinging eyes, noses, mouths, and every inch of skin.

"Did they escape? Please, please say yes."

Little Wade nodded. "Thankfully, the audience successfully escaped when the fire started. They simply threw open the doors and charged out, but not everyone managed to get out in time."

Little Wade clapped and abruptly ended the illusion. No trace remained, and they were back inside the gloomy remains of the

Orpheus. Peering into the musty darkness, she could see all the way backstage. Lying in the scorched, shattered remnants of the stage, the monstrous metal corpse of the projector that had ignited the inferno lay cold and silent.

"Abigail," Little Wade spoke, "may I ask something of you?"

"Yes," she replied. "What?"

"Please, try not to scream."

Three more wraiths materialized right in front of them. Emerging from the shadows, they floated forward into the beams of light. Unlike the quite presentable Little Wade, these specters were all horribly burned, murdered by fire. Little Wade conjured three moving images that introduced the three spirits by showing how each one had been created. Abigail witnessed their tragic fates as if they were happening right before her eyes in real time.

The instant the Magic Lantern projector exploded, it spat flames and rolled fireballs in every direction. Mr. Todesco, the owner of the Orpheus, heroically rushed toward it, hurling buckets of water onto it. The machine's metal skin hissed and steamed, but the fire would not go out. So, coughing and choking in the smoke, Mr. Todesco leaped onto the stage's monumental curtains, ripped them down and charged at the projector, tackling it and covering it with mounds of thick, heavy fabric, hoping to snuff out the flame. It failed. The fire consumed the curtains and killed him, and his spirit erupted from his body like steam rising from bubbling, boiling water.

In life, Mr. Todesco had been a portly, jolly man, bald with a large mustache, and every night he had watched the shows from backstage, managing everything while wearing an impeccable suit. Now, dead and floating like a balloon, Mr. Todesco's ghost frightened Abigail. Fragments of seared purple and gold curtains had grafted themselves onto what remained of his suit, creating a freakish outfit. A blast of steam from the machine had scalded most of his face and burst one of his eyeballs, leaving an empty socket. Flames had chewed up his legs and arms. His melted flesh clumped together like wax. Pools of squishy black tar collected in his mouth and blotted out his teeth. Abigail shivered at the sight of him.

Flanking Mr. Todesco, on his left, floated a woman who Abigail deduced must have perished from smoke inhalation. Watching the second moving image, Abigail saw that, when the fire started, Mr. Todesco's wife, Helena, quickly found herself trapped high above the stage in an area called "the flies," where curtains and pieces of scenery could be raised and lowered using winches and rope. When the Magic Lantern exploded, she had been crossing the rickety catwalk overhead. The detonation's force knocked her off her feet and stunned her. For the next several minutes, she swallowed all of the black smoke that erupted upward from the burning projector like ash rising from a volcano. Carried up by the superheated air, the black soot rapidly suffocated her. Helena's spirit climbed out of her blackened corpse, and Abigail watched Helena's limp remains roll off the catwalk, plunge into the flames, and promptly disintegrate. Because she took the form of the exact moment of her death, Helena was not burned at all, but instead smeared with carbon from head to toe; she floated like a shadow, entirely black except for her piercing blue eyes.

The third phantasm passed into the light, and Abigail nearly threw up in her mouth. On Mr. Todesco's right, the Magnificent Madrigal the Magical Man, or what the fire had left of him, hovered and billowed in the air. At first, Abigail averted her eyes, but then curiosity overwhelmed her and she looked at him.

When the projector exploded, Madrigal had been on stage. The resulting fireball melted through the screen and struck him from behind. At the moment of his infernal death, Madrigal was wearing his famous shimmering white robe laced with a silvery material, magnesium. It was gorgeous and amazingly dazzling, but also highly flammable. When the fire touched him, he ignited instantly and glowed white-hot like a piece of freshly forged metal. For an instant, the audience thought the fiery explosion was all part of the show. Oblivious at first to what was really happening, they clapped and cheered and roared with delight, even as Madrigal screamed in agony. Before Madrigal died, the last thing he heard was laughter and applause just before the fire gnawed his ears off, leaving melted, waxy stumps.

Abigail cringed at the sight of him. The fire had burned away most of his white top hat, leaving only a ragged ring fused and melted to his head like a seared, cracked crown. His shimmering magnesium robe burned away when the fireball struck him, vanishing in a hot flash. Unfortunately, the white screen behind him, before it completely disintegrated, melted and warped in the heat and then collapsed onto the stage, dripping down onto him like scalding wax, encasing him in a searing cocoon, drowning him in liquid fire.

So now, Madrigal the Magnificent Magical Man drifted throughout the Orpheus in a flowing, flaming white sheet that cascaded over his body and concealed all but his charred, clawlike hands and his red, disfigured face. The last shredded remains of his white, phosphorescent cloak, mixed with the seared, liquified white screen, rippled, flowed and warped, sculpting and re-sculpting itself. Madrigal had become a freakish spectacle, like an eternal white wax sculpture, continually melting and reforming in midair and melting again. When all three of these monstrous specters appeared, Abigail instinctively hid behind one of Watchtower's legs.

"Don't make any sudden movements," Little Wade whispered. Then he rose up into the air to meet them.

"We changed our minds," Mr. Todesco's voice rasped and growled. Black phlegm pooled in his mouth and flooded his teeth.

"You agreed last night to help us. Both the Longshadows and Wild Cards will be here soon. You approved our plan. We can spring our trap."

"We know they torment her, and we want to help children, but now you bring Longshadows here!" Helena croaked.

"We have nowhere else to go. You know we find it difficult to conceal our work, but we must act now. We cannot wait until nightfall."

"So now your partner will wreck this place, smash our home," Helena objected.

Watchtower pointed to himself as if to say, "Who...me?"

"I promise he will not. Remember what I told you. This incident will frighten people. People will stay away. Your legend will grow."

"Until they come to condemn this place and tear it down," Mr. Todesco replied.

"You know we can help you with that. When we spoke last night, we presented our proposal to you. We can help save this site. Watchtower and I will be happy to discuss that, but at this very moment, this young girl needs our help. That's all that matters."

"You ask much. We need to know. What do you offer in trade?"

Before Little Wade could answer, a voice cut into the conversation.

"He offers amusement," Madrigal, his white sheet flowing and billowing around him like a flaming cloud. "These evil men deserve pain and fear. They will suffer, and we will watch, or we can help if we like. Either way...this sounds like fun."

Mr. and Mrs. Todesco turned to Little Wade.

"Give us a moment."

"Not much time. Both gangs will be here soon."

"Understood," Mr. Todesco grumbled. "Plead your case with us... in private."

The four ghosts huddled together. Little Wade conversed with them. Abigail could hear them whispering to each other rather animatedly. A horribly burned little girl faded into view right next to Abigail, who jumped back and clutched Watchtower's hand. Floating in midair, the girl held an equally horribly burned puppy, which curled up in her tiny, seared arms. Together, the two of them resembled a discarded toy mangled by an animal. Their eyes and their sockets were completely blackened by ash. The young girl and the puppy both silently examined Abigail, looking her over with their sad, dead eyes.

"Olga, don't get too close!" Helena called out to the girl.

Abigail, slowly, reluctantly, approached Olga, who simply tilted her head to the side and studied Abigail, smiling with her smoke-stained teeth. Breaking their huddle, the three ghosts and Little Wade approached.

"Very well, Abigail Reid," Mr. Todesco gave his approval. "We will assist you. Spring your trap. Then leave us in peace."

"Thank you." Abigail bowed. "Thank you so much."

"Do not thank us. We do this because we owe Little Wade a debt. If it had been anyone else who requested our help on your behalf, you would already be running away."

In an instant, the Todescos vanished into thin air.

Olga and her puppy also vanished.

Only Madrigal stayed behind for a moment and winked. Then he vanished. Little Wade, Watchtower, and Abigail found themselves alone.

"Who were those phantoms?"

"Those were the Fire People, well...some of them anyway."

"Fire People? You mean spirits of people that burned to death?"

"Precisely. The Fire People control any location in the city that burned down and have dominion over any location where lives perished because of flame. Everyone respects their claim. You don't want to find yourself on their bad side, believe me."

"So phantoms can stake out territory," Abigail put it together. "So that explains hauntings and the like!"

"Correct. Without strict rules, there'd be chaos."

"How many Fire People exist in New York?"

"Too many."

"They remarked that they owed you. For what?"

Little Wade paused before he answered.

"Not all Fire People are good."

At that very moment, they heard knocking and voices at the door.

"They're here!" Abigail whispered.

Little Wade shot up higher into the air.

"We have work to do and not much time!"

Watchtower went to work, dusting off seats, arranging them in rows, lifting them up as if they were feathers. Then Watchtower, standing in front of the destroyed stage, pulled out an enormous white sheet. Cranking himself up to full height, Watchtower strung it up where the screen used to be. As the floorboards creaked beneath his weight, Watchtower stepped behind the sheet and carefully fastened it into position. Obscured by the makeshift screen, his flaming face burned brightly like the sun behind a thin layer of clouds.

"He's making it look like someone's been using the theater for recreation."

"Precisely. Watchtower will remain hidden in disguise while the Wild Cards and the Longshadows cancel each other out."

"Cancel each other out? You mean fight."

"Brawl, scuffle, skirmish, whatever word works, and our task is to ensure that no one dies. We want them all arrested."

Watchtower emerged from behind the screen and stomped back into the seating area, collapsing back to a smaller size with a *chank-chank-chank!* He seemed to be selecting his position very carefully, holding up his hands as if he were trying to frame a shot.

Casting Dolosphera, Little Wade blanketed absolutely everything with shadows. Day seemed to change to night. Little Wade's illusions enshrouded Abigail.

"Those spirits, did they leave?"

"No, they're hidden, waiting to play their part. You're going to love this."

Abigail followed Little Wade and tucked herself away into a corner concealed by darkness. Crouching in the shadows, with Little Wade floating next to her, she waited. After he finished setting up the theater, Watchtower stepped backward, away from the screen. Then he removed his own head. Holding his head in his hands, he removed the four glass panes that normally encased his flame, and then he swapped them with four plates that contained images engraved on them. Before he replaced his head back onto his body, Watchtower extracted a cylinder of a solid, yellowish-green substance from his pocket, installed it inside his new head, and then slotted the whole contraption back onto his neck and locked it tight. Then he replaced his top hat.

"I know what that cylinder is. I learned about it in science class. That's calcium oxide!" Abigail whispered and pointed. "You're making a limelight!" she exclaimed.

On cue, Watchtower's fiery face struck the cylinder, and a white-hot beam blasted forward from his face, projecting a slide image through the plate and onto the white screen. Abigail could smell the heated air.

"The Wild Cards," Abigail whispered to herself as she gazed up at the screen and saw a humongous cartoon of the gang wreaking havoc on the city.

Stepping backward slowly, focusing the image, Watchtower kneeled down and swept his overcoat over himself, and then he vanished. Only this time, he did not take the form of a lamppost, but of a bulky Magic Lantern projector.

"Another disguise!" Abigail marveled. "Now, I absolutely want one of those coats!"

Voices rumbled outside of the doors.

Little Wade whispered, "It's almost time to spring our trap!"

"Wait! What's my role in all of this?" she whispered.

"Come with me and find out." Little Wade levitated upward and pointed to a ladder. Abigail seized the rungs and began to climb.

The double doors burst open.

11

GANG WAR

Twenty Longshadows barged into the Orpheus. Their footsteps and voices echoed throughout the cavernous chamber lit by Watchtower's limelight and a beam of daylight streaming in from the breached doors. Abigail quietly climbed up the ladder and onto the second level, a blasted, burned-out mezzanine that overlooked the entire theater. Next to her, Little Wade floated quietly. Armed, wearing their scruffy black suits and hats, the Longshadows flooded into the abandoned wreckage of the Orpheus. Ducking down, out of sight, Abigail crept quietly alongside the remains of the balcony, careful not to creak or squeak too much.

"They're in here somewhere. Check everywhere!"

"Wow, they really set this place up."

"Yeah, it almost looks nice!"

"Shut up! Look around!"

"Boss, you sure we should be in here?"

"You know whose territory this is."

"Hurry up! We find them quickly, then it won't matter."

Dust filled up Abigail's nose. She desperately tried not to sneeze.

"We've got a score to settle," the Longshadow's leader (Abigail nicknamed him Mr. Gutter) uttered in his husky voice. "If the Wild Cards want to fight us today, let 'em try."

As if on cue, they all heard loud hooting and howling outside the building. A crowd of twenty men blocked up the doorway, creating a black, blob-like silhouette.

"You ready to play your part?" Little Wade whispered.

Nodding eagerly, she whispered back, "What do you want me to do?"

Twenty Wild Cards entered the Orpheus. Up until this moment, Abigail had only heard stories about them. Peering over the edge of the balcony, she got a good look.

While the Longshadows were all dressed in the same dirty, black suits, the Wild Cards were the exact opposite. Each gang member was an explosion of color, like a burst of confetti. They all wore odd patchwork suits that mixed reds and blues and yellows and greens in strange ways, like evil clowns. Some of their faces were even painted. While the Longshadows all wore the same type of hat, the Wild Cards wore a wide variety: short, tall, fat, thin, crooked, oversized, and damaged. Each man wore a wholly unique and bizarre hat decorated with several playing cards stuffed into the brim. Abigail, who was no stranger to card games, recognized some of the combinations as different winning hands at poker or gin rummy; however, many of them were just jumbles of cards that made no sense at all. As for the men, all of their bulging, bloodshot eyes darted around. They giggled, hooted, and emanated other odd noises. Their maniacal smiles frightened her.

"They're so...peculiar."

"Oh, they're all insane," Little Wade whispered. "The leader of the Wild Cards ran one of the city's biggest asylums. No one ever suspected that he secretly plotted to recruit a gang from all of the troubled boys the city sent him over the years."

"That's sinister."

"Yes. After we caught on to the conspiracy, Watchtower and I defeated the original doctor who created the gang. Unfortunately, you cannot keep a bad idea behind bars. His madness lives on. Years ago, a legion of rascals seized upon his vision and decided to run riot with it. You never know where the Wild Cards will show up. They take everyone by complete surprise."

"You say no one knows where they will show up, but you knew they'd come straight here," Abigail whispered.

Little Wade smiled wickedly. "Criminals are driven by fear, greed, or hate. The Wild Cards don't care about money, and they're not afraid of anyone, but they can't stand the Longshadows, so they wouldn't miss a chance to cross them."

Abigail wanted to continue the conversation, but Little Wade bolted away from her and swooped through the air, circling the two gangs like a crow. Abigail listened intently to the confrontation.

"Maybe you don't remember, but we rule this territory!" the leader of the Wild Cards shouted, his voice echoed. All around him, his team of colorful Wild Cards, like a pack of laughing hyenas, readied to fight. While the Longshadows carried the usual guns, knives, and clubs, the Wild Cards carried an odd assortment of freakish, improvised weapons that they had built themselves using random junk.

You never know what a Wild Card will do, Abigail reminded herself. *I must be careful.* She decided to nickname the Wild Cards leader Mr. Circus. He spoke up again.

"Our boss ordered us to leave this wreck alone and let it rot. He's trying to tear it down. Now we come in here, and we see that it's been set up to use. Look, the screen's up, seats set straight. How do you explain that?"

"We didn't do this," Mr. Gutter, the leader of the Longshadows, denied it.

"Oh, I suppose it just appeared by itself, like magic?" Mr. Circus sneered.

"The heck you talking about? *You* obviously set it up! Look at the screen. There's a slide of the Wild Cards, your gang, celebrating victory over us, the Longshadows."

"You sure?" Mr. Circus jeered and pointed.

Abigail glanced at the screen. At the same time, all of the Longshadows did, too. Like all of the rest, she had completely missed that Watchtower had switched the slide. Before, it showed the Wild Cards ruling the city, but now it showed the Longshadows celebrating victory...over the Wild Cards, a particularly embarrassing, humiliating cartoon.

"Wait...that wasn't there before," Mr. Gutter said.

"Sure," Mr. Circus retorted.

Then Watchtower switched the slide again, showing another Longshadows victory over the Wild Cards, this image even more demoralizing and humiliating than the last. It showed a gargantuan Longshadow terrorizing a bunch of tiny, bratty Wild Cards running around and crying like little children with no pants on. Abigail giggled. Whoever created the slides had done a masterful job drawing the cartoons.

"I think someone's playing a trick on us," Mr. Gutter tried to reason with him.

"We know all about your tricks," Mr. Circus coldly cut him off.

"Look, we're just after a little red-haired girl and her friend, a seven-foot-tall man. They came in here. You can't miss them. We'll just find them and be on our way."

"Oh...a giant? You're after a giant?" The Wild Cards laughed. "Tell me, did he travel with a spirit, a floating, shoeless boy?"

"They were just here."

"I suppose now you're gonna tell me that some kind of monster thwacked ten of your boys last night in an alley just a few blocks from here. Is that right?"

"I don't know what to say about that." Mr. Gutter stumbled over his words. "Did you see them come in here or not?"

"Tall fella? Seven feet? Eight with his top hat? Beanpole? Real strong? Doesn't say much?"

"That's the one! You know him?"

"We've seen him around. Sounds like we should hire him," Mr. Circus teased, and the Wild Cards all laughed.

"I don't consider this a joke. Several of our men were almost killed last night. We know that the girl and that man know something about it. I know you know what I'm talking about."

"What, you mean the ghost and the giant? Come on," Mr. Circus scoffed. "Yeah, we've heard stories. We've all seen things we can't explain, but the truth is...every gangster and goon in this city has been telling that story for over forty years."

"Don't you wonder if it's true?" Mr. Gutter pressed him.

"It's a legend. That's all. My father, grandfather, uncle, they were all there in eighteen fifty-seven, at the most epic gang war anyone's ever seen in this city. The Five Points turned into a war zone. Over a thousand gangsters poured out into the neighborhood. By the time the brawl ended, hundreds and hundreds of them lay broken, and that's not including the casualties, those who never got up. Police rounded 'em all up, and all of the wounded whimpered the same thing. They all claimed a ghost and a giant jumped into the middle of the fray and started tearing gangsters apart, and then they just disappeared. Over a dozen gangs went down that night, permanently, and, if I remember correctly, that's when the Longshadows first appeared."

"What...you think we're behind it?" Mr. Gutter asked.

On cue, Watchtower, still disguised as the Magic Lantern, clicked loudly, cycling another slide, this one displayed a titanic Longshadow stomping all over the other gangs. Abigail watched gleefully as murmurs and hisses spread throughout both groups.

"You Longshadows call yourselves tricksters and pride yourselves on your ability to seem more than you are. It makes sense that your gang would create a legend to scare your enemies and cover your tracks. That theory makes a heck of a lot more sense than a ghost and a giant being real," Mr. Circus taunted him.

"During that gang war, hundreds of people all said the same thing, but you don't think there's something to it?" Mr. Gutter retorted. "I'm telling you, someone's playing a trick on us."

"It's clever, really. I gotta hand it to you," Mr. Circus went on. "You're using the story to conceal your own operations. I think that there is no ghost and giant, just you and your Longshadows using tricks to seem scarier than you are, but we're not afraid of you."

"You're making a mistake," Mr. Gutter tried to reason with him again.

"No, you made one when you barged in here. Bunch of our boys got wrecked two weeks ago by the wharf, and now twelve good men lie wounded in the hospital. After they recover, they're going to jail. One of them told the same story: the ghost and the giant got them. Two weeks before that, the Squids lost twenty good men in one of their warehouses. Same story: the ghost and the giant. We know better. The Squids got ambushed, and so did our boys."

"Everybody's been attacked, the Dragons from Chinatown, the Pikes, the Black Roses, and a dozen other crews. Do you think we would declare war on the whole city? Come on! You Wild Cards can't be that crazy. Think!" Mr. Gutter's pleas fell on deaf ears.

"Everybody believes the Longshadows are just using the ghost and the giant as a cover story. Because we don't know for sure, we haven't retaliated, yet. Boss says we should try to keep the peace. Fine, fair enough; it doesn't make sense for us to make a move against another gang if we're not completely sure who attacked us. But now... here you are, right now, for real, no ghost, no giant, just you and more lies. No more stories. You're trespassing on our turf, and now it's gonna cost you!"

"All right, all right," Mr. Gutter, the leader of the Longshadows cut him off. "Look, we don't wanna fight. We'll get out of here, right now, but I'm telling you that somebody's—"

Creaaaakk...boom!

The whole theater instantly darkened. All the gangsters stopped talking. They turned around to look at the entrance at precisely the moment that Abigail finished pushing the double doors closed with all of her strength, slamming them shut. Sensing they were all looking at her, Abigail slowly turned around to face them all.

A moment of silence hung in the air.

Then a Wild Card yelled at her. "Who the heck are you?"

Abigail, utterly unsure of what to do, simply smiled and waved.

"It's her. That's her!" Mr. Gutter yelled.

The Longshadows rushed forward.

Unfortunately, when the Longshadows charged toward Abigail, the Wild Cards stepped between them and blocked their path, so the gangsters all crashed into each other.

"Get out of my way!" Mr. Gutter yelled. Then pushes became shoves, then punches, then vicious kicks, and that quickly sparked a thunderous brawl between the two gangs, a fight that swept through the old Orpheus like a second inferno.

While violence broke loose around them, Abigail quickly tucked herself away in a dark corner. Longshadows and Wild Cards, all heavily armed, ripped into each other, cracking each other's skulls and bones, swinging clubs, iron bars, fists, and heavy, rusted metal chains. They slashed and sliced at each other with knives and hatchets. Some forsook weapons altogether and resorted to using their hands, grappling and strangling each other or trying to gouge out one another's eyes.

Abigail smelled their sweat, blood, and the cheap cologne that the Wild Cards wore to cover up their stench. All around her, violence swirled, engulfing the Orpheus. Floorboards creaked; wood cracked and split and splintered; men grunted, snarled, screamed, and roared in anger or pain. Yet none of them detected Abigail at all.

I'm hidden, she thought, *but not that well-hidden.*

Then Little Wade appeared next to her and commented, "Quite exciting, isn't it?"

"Am I invisible?" Abigail felt compelled to ask as she examined her hands and feet, which she could see perfectly well.

"Currently, yes. I've masked you from sight. It's just another illusion, but it does require a great deal of concentration. I can't do very much else while I manage it."

One of the Longshadows, brutally fist-fighting with a Wild Card, knocked out three of his opponent's teeth with a bloody *crack*!

Trembling, Abigail answered, "Well, I more than appreciate it."

Chaos consumed everything around them. The Wild Cards and the Longshadows tore each other to pieces, bashing, bricking, punching, kicking, slashing, stabbing, tossing, throwing, hurling, and even biting each other.

"So...I'm wondering, Abigail...would you like to partake in an experiment?"

"What kind of experiment?"

"Well, I'd like for this to function as a bit of practice for you, if you wish."

"Practice? For what? For the complete collapse of civil society? For the apocalypse?"

"For the Great Gang Trap."

"You mean this isn't the Great Gang Trap?" Abigail gestured to the war raging all around them.

"Oh no," Little Wade grinned mischievously. "In our game of chess, this is our opening move. We use this to draw out the King, and then we checkmate. Now, do you consent?"

A Wild Card whacked a Longshadow over the head with a bizarre weapon made from chains and discarded bottles, knocking his victim unconscious.

"I suppose this is included in my contract," Abigail admitted. "Is this the training you mentioned earlier?"

"Indeed it is. It's entirely optional, but I think you will appreciate it."

A Wild Card swung a ragged, improvised flail, but missed his target; then a burly Longshadow punched him out.

"So, assuming I say yes, what exactly do you have in mind?"

"I suggest that I switch your invisibility on and off. This will grant you an opportunity to sample a few experiences of what it's like to confront these people, on your own, with only your wits."

"This is quite a hazardous environment," Abigail noted as she observed the ferocious melee. A bearlike member of the Longshadows, gripping a smaller, skinnier Wild Card, body-slammed him down on the floor with a loud *whumph!* The violent impact knocked all the air out of the Wild Card's lungs, but then another Wild Card brained another one of the Longshadows with an oversized mallet.

"I'll protect you. Seeing as how we are technically conducting an experiment, we will implement a few controls."

More screams and cries echoed throughout the Orpheus as two

Wild Cards and two Longshadows, wrestling each other, toppled over the side of a balcony and plunged to the floor below.

"We'll need a signal," Abigail offered. "How about this? Whenever I wish to vanish, I'll simply snap my fingers."

"That's perfect. We'll do that. Ready?"

Abigail flinched as she watched the men pummel each other, swearing she had never witnessed so much violence. Abigail cringed at the smells and the sounds: hard, wet thuds and slaps, like a butcher tenderizing bloody meat. Her stomach churned, queasy.

"You can say no," Little Wade offered, "if you're afraid."

"I'm less afraid than yesterday."

"Tomorrow, you'll be less afraid than today. Today you face your fears when your fears cannot see you. Soon, you will stare your worst fear straight in the eye. Then you'll know how much you've changed, how much stronger you've become. Do you consent to your training?"

"Snap, and I'll disappear?"

"Snap, and you'll disappear. That should give you ample opportunity to escape."

"So, you'll be concentrating on me the whole time?"

Little Wade shook his head, "No. I'm going to remain at your side. *He* will turn you invisible."

She looked up. Madrigal the Magnificent floated in midair. He held up his hands and gestured as if casting a spell on her.

"So, I just run around and…do what exactly?"

"Last night, the Fire People and some of our agents set three traps in here. I'm going to mark them now."

Little Wade snapped his fingers. Instantly, three objects began to glow: a lever connected to a set of old ropes and pulleys; a section of loose, weakened floorboards; and finally a heaping, very precarious pile of junk—an avalanche waiting to happen.

"We just need someone to trip them."

Abigail carefully studied all three traps.

"What do you say, Abigail?"

At that moment, Mr. Todesco, Helena, and Olga and her puppy all appeared around her.

"We will protect you."

At that moment, the battle reached a fever pitch. Abigail took a moment. All around her, the two gangs tore each other to pieces. Fists collided with jaws, skulls with clubs. Using a bizarre gauntlet spiked with lit matches, a Wild Card punched and burned another one of the Longshadows, who squealed in pain. At the same moment, another member of the Longshadows kicked a Wild Card in the face, breaking his jaw. She gulped.

"Ready?"

"I...did not dress for this."

"Yes, you did, Abigail. Encounters like these can happen anytime, anywhere, without warning. You're dressed perfectly. Ready?"

As the battle raged all around her, she focused on the first glowing trap. Summoning up her courage, Abigail snapped her fingers.

The First Trap

Sprinting forward, Abigail raced across the rotted, creaking mezzanine located on the second level of the Orpheus. From her position, she could see the entire battle. In the corner of her eye, she spied Madrigal the Magnificent. The ethereal magician focused his illusions on her like a spotlight. She could feel the air shimmer around her. No one could see her.

A Longshadow, wounded, rushed up the rickety stairs. Pursuing him, a Wild Card, carrying a homemade, bizarre, three-bladed hatchet, chased him down. They grappled and struggled, grunting and snarling. Heading toward her objective, the first trap, Abigail, invisible, rushed forward, ducking and dodging, avoiding them. As she slipped by them, the two men, wrestling, toppled over the side together. Screaming, they plunged several feet and smashed against the floor with a loud *bang* and *clang!* *Snapping* her fingers, reappearing, Abigail approached the mountainous pile of junk. She pushed on it, but the heap did not move an inch.

"It's too heavy."

"That one metal bar acts as a linchpin, holding it all together. Pull it out, and it crumbles."

Little Wade's illusions lit up a long iron rod embedded inside the junk pile.

"Look down," Little Wade, at her side, pointed to a hole in the rotten floor. "Wait for the target."

Abigail crouched down and peered through the hole. Beneath her, a crowd of five Longshadows and five Wild Cards pounded each other. Abigail gripped the iron bar.

"Wait." Little Wade held up his hand.

Two more Wild Cards joined in the fight, followed by two more Longshadows.

"Now!" Little Wade yelled.

Abigail yanked the iron bar out of position. It squealed, and then the pile of junk rumbled and thundered, pouring over the edge like a rockslide. Through the hole, the faces of the gangsters all blanched in terror. One of them uttered one squeak before—*krakaboom!* Dozens of heavy, blunt objects, old seat cushions, chunks of wood, a few iron bars, all rained down on the Wild Cards and Longshadows. A veritable avalanche of debris buried them, knocking them all unconscious. Dust erupted upward from the ground, culminating in a mushroom cloud right in front of Abigail, forcing her to cough.

"*There she is!*"

Whirling around, Abigail spotted Mr. Gutter climbing up the stairs. He stood between her and any escape.

"Attack," Little Wade advised her.

"What?" she asked, incredulous.

"Attack!"

Flanked by Little Wade, Abigail rushed toward Mr. Gutter, sprinting as fast as she could.

"All right, girl, if that's the way you wanna do it, fine!" Mr. Gutter, clutching a knife, charged at her.

Just as they were about to meet, Abigail *snapped* her fingers and vanished. Mr. Gutter, startled and befuddled, stumbled over himself and collapsed onto the floor right in front of an entirely invisible

Abigail, who marveled at the man's clumsiness. She seized a moment to breathe, but then two Wild Cards scrambled up the stairs. Mr. Gutter sprang up to fight them off. Abigail, unseen, snuck past them, rushed toward the stairs, and then hopped down as fast as she could. When she landed on the ground level, she took only two steps before she overheard intense screaming. Then Mr. Gutter and both Wild Cards plunged over the side of the mezzanine and crashed onto the floor right in front of her. Mr. Gutter, dazed but still awake, groaned. The Wild Cards lay unconscious. Then Abigail heard more screams; the terrified cries of grown men erupted and echoed throughout the Orpheus. The Fire People had made their move.

The Second Trap

Helena soared throughout the theater like a bird of prey, looping, diving, screeching, and terrorizing several of the gang members. Meanwhile, Mr. Todesco, floating next to Watchtower's limelight, created humongous shadow puppet creations that crawled and wriggled all over the walls like spiders. Abigail noticed that the Todescos were not frightening everybody, just a few key players, just enough to sow confusion through the raging fight. *Ghosts can choose who sees them,* she remembered. Abigail *snapped* her fingers once again, vanishing.

Invisible, Abigail skulked to another dark corner. All around her, the battle continued with no winner in sight. For every knockout scored by the Longshadows, the Wild Cards retaliated with a knockout of their own. Bones cracked, skin sliced, clothes ripped, lips split, eyes burst, blood spilled, jaws broke, teeth chipped, but nobody gained the upper hand.

"Which one?" Abigail whispered. She gestured to two more glowing traps. The first was a section of loose floorboards on the opposite mezzanine; the second was a lever on the far side of the orchestra seating section.

"That one." Little Wade pointed to the lever on the wall. "The mezzanine comes last, and then the grand finale. Ready?"

Nodding, still invisible, she crawled behind a section of seats as a Longshadow and a Wild Card pounded each other into pulp.

Rising up at the edge of the row, *snapping* her fingers, she reappeared.

"*There!*" someone yelled.

Two Longshadows climbed over the seats and stumbled toward her...right into the path of a pair of Wild Cards.

Snapping her fingers, she vanished again just at the right moment; the Wild Cards crashed against the Longshadows. Invisible, Abigail raced away. Then she stopped when she spotted one of the Longshadows and one of the Wild Cards embroiled in one-on-one combat. Both men clutched knives, but they were locked in a stalemate. Sweating, straining, each killer held his blade inches from the other's exposed throat. Not wanting to see either one win, Abigail decided to intervene. *Snapping* her fingers, she reappeared in front of the battling pair and interrupted them.

"You're going to kill each other!" she warned them. "Use your fists. Then you can both walk away."

Confused, the two men looked at her and then each other and then screamed when Olga and her puppy appeared before them and *screeeeeched*! Startled, the two gangsters tripped over each other and dropped their knives. Abigail quickly scooped the weapons up and tossed them into a corner where they could not possibly be found. Then she *snapped* her fingers and dematerialized again. Invisible, she witnessed both men stand up, look for their knives, realize they were gone, briefly say, "OK, let's do this," and then return to fighting, this time with their fists.

Satisfied, Abigail, still invisible, escorted by Little Wade, crept away until she reached the shining lever on the other side of the theater. Glowing and pulsing (because of Little Wade's illusion magic), the lever connected to a tight coil of rope.

Snap! She reappeared again.

"Pull it," Little Wade told her.

Abigail yanked the lever.

She watched as the tight, spooled rope *un*spooled and whirled around, unwinding at incredibly high speed. Then the rope completely uncoiled and released itself from the wheel, snapping and flying upward into the shadows above the stage. *What did I just do?* Abigail wondered, but then four Longshadows stepped up and cornered her. Her back against the wall, no idea what to do, Abigail hesitated.

"Stay." Little Wade, right at her side, whispered. "Wait."

Battered, bruised, sweaty, their clothes ripped and disheveled, their knuckles raw and their faces bleeding and puffy, the four Longshadows angrily stalked toward her.

"I don't know how you're doing that trick, little girl," one of the Longshadows muttered and grinned, exposing rotten teeth, "but you're gonna teach us before we're done with you."

Abigail stood against the wall and pretended to be afraid, which was not difficult at all. Her nerves jangled beneath her skin.

"Wait," Little Wade whispered. "Let me know when you see it."

"See what?" Abigail asked.

"Say what?" The Longshadows stopped, confused.

"What am I looking—?" Then Abigail's eyes opened wide.

Looking behind the group of four Longshadows standing in front of her, Abigail caught a glimpse of something. An enormous old chandelier made of metal and old, burned glass swung out of the darkness and toward them like an oversized mace and chain.

"Move to the side, please," Little Wade suggested.

Snap!

Abigail disappeared. She dove to the side, leaping out of the way just as the massive chandelier swung into the crowd of gangsters with an unbelievably loud *crash*! Knocking them over with a glorious impact, the chandelier buried itself in the wall, spraying old glass shards everywhere. All around it, the four Longshadows lay unconscious, completely blindsided.

Snap!

Abigail reappeared, about to gloat and cheer when she turned and saw a group of four Wild Cards. They had watched the trap from a safe distance. Cockily, they stepped toward her.

"Nice trick, but now it's—" *Crash!*

A second chandelier took them down and knocked them out just the same.

The Third Trap

"See it?" Little Wade whispered in her ear once again.

Crouched, hidden behind a pair of old seats, Abigail whispered back, "Yes. I see it."

After springing traps one and two, Abigail snuck halfway across the orchestra seating section. To cross to the other side and reach the set of stairs that led up to another mezzanine (and the glowing floorboards trap), Abigail needed to navigate a maze of broken seats. To accomplish that, she needed to zigzag past multiple brawls that whirled around like violent tornadoes. If she got too close, they might suck her in and thrash her. She planned to lure as many Longshadows and Wild Cards up to the balcony and then lead them over the floorboards. As far as plans went, it was simple, or at least it *sounded* simple.

"Ready?" Little Wade took his place at her side, and then he yelled, "*Go!*"

Abigail rushed into the fray, ducking, dodging, doubling back, and weaving in and out between fights. She allowed some gangsters to spot her, chase her, lose her, trip over themselves, and go back to fighting. Steadily, she made her way across the orchestra section, and then she sprinted toward the staircase leading up to the balcony on the opposite side. Before she climbed the staircase, however, she decided to have a little fun.

"*There! Grab her!*"

Snap!

Vanish.

A Wild Card tackled another one of the Longshadows.

Snap!

Reappear.

"*Get the girl!*"

Two Longshadows chased after Abigail, only to get tripped by a sneaky Wild Card hiding beneath the seats.

Snap!

Vanish.

Three Wild Cards, charging into battle, nearly ran over an invisible Abigail. Then two burly Longshadows seized them all and knocked their skulls together.

Snap!

Reappear.

"There she is!"

More Longshadows chased her.

Snap!

Vanish.

Confused, the gangsters continued to battle as the Fire People swooped and shrieked, terrifying several of the gangsters, preventing them from leaving the building. Any time that any ruffian tried to head for the double doors, Mr. Todesco, Helena, or Olga and her puppy melted through the wall or the floor and—

Raaaaaaahhhhhr!

Rolling, somersaulting, leaping and diving, Abigail crossed out of the battlefield. Finally, after weaving in and out of the fight, vanishing and reappearing, eluding capture, Abigail reached the second set of stairs. *Snapping* her fingers, she reappeared.

"Safe!" she shouted in triumph, but then, just as she commenced climbing up the stairs, she heard someone cry out.

"Get out of here!"

She turned. One of the Wild Cards, wounded, slumped against the wall, appealed to her. "You've got to get out of here!"

Surprised, Abigail did not know what to say.

"If they get ahold of you, they'll kill you! You must get out of here! *Get out of here!*" He pointed to the double doors.

Little Wade, darting around, scouting, assisting the Fire People, became distracted for a moment. Hesitating, Abigail stepped down from her position.

"No place for a child! *Get out of here!*" The Wild Card painfully clutched his bloody stomach. His face puffed red. His anguished blue eyes spouted tears. Suffering terribly, the young man whispered. "Leave now!"

Abigail got too close.

"Don't!" Little Wade whirled around and yelled, but it was too late.

The Wild Card grinned and snarled and reached for her, seizing her ankle, tripping her up.

"*Gotcha!*"

Abigail tried to snap, but the Wild Card seized her hands with his bloody fingers. Little Wade dove toward the young man and revealed himself.

He stuck his fingers into the corners of his mouth.

He stretched his mouth impossibly wide.

He extended his tongue impossibly long.

He grew his teeth into fangs.

Finally, from his grotesque mouth, he unleashed an inhuman *blalalalalalala* sound.

Screaming, the young man recoiled. Abigail kicked him in the face. His hands sprung loose of her, and Abigail quickly whirled around and scampered away. Her heart pounded in her chest. Terrified, Abigail raced up the stairs, banging her knee and her hands against the splintery wooden steps, drawing a bit of blood. Climbing up to the second level, she felt the vibrations of thundering footsteps behind her.

"*There she is! Get her!*"

A crowd of four Longshadows, followed by four Wild Cards, pursued Abigail up the stairs and across the crumbling mezzanine level. The gangsters snarled and growled like a pack of savage dogs, and their footsteps smacked loudly against the creaking wood.

"*Come here, girl!*" one of the Longshadows, an ugly man, growled. His head gashed open, his eye swollen, his lip split, his meaty hands raw and bleeding, he clutched a jagged knife and dashed after Abigail.

"Don't look back! Run!" Little Wade flew right beside her. Her swift steps creaked against the rotten, charred floor. Ahead of her, the glowing floorboards pulsed and shimmered. Beyond them, a glowing rope dangled from the ceiling like a vine.

Little Wade streaked next to her, keeping up. "Get ready to jump!" he exclaimed.

Behind her, the gangsters' boots rammed and slammed against broken wood. Abigail could feel their hands reaching out for her.

"*Now!*"

Abigail leaped off the edge of the balcony and reached for the glowing rope. She hurtled through the air, the floor twenty feet below her. Catching the rope, Abigail swung through the air like a clock pendulum, spinning around just in time to see the Longshadows and the Wild Cards reach the loose floorboards. The wooden planks gave way and collapsed under their combined weight with a loud *rumble*.

Swinging through the air, Abigail slid down the rope and lowered herself down onto the floor in front of the stage with a flourish. Stepping up onto a front-row seat, a perfect vantage point, she watched yet another avalanche, this time made of people. Eight men, four Wild Cards and four Longshadows, crumbled down to the first floor, crushing each other and knocking each other out. Abigail flinched as she heard several limbs crack and break, and more than a few skulls rap against hardwood. Another mushroom cloud of dust blew up from the dirty floor.

From where she stood, Abigail could survey the entire scene. In the beginning, there were twenty Longshadows versus twenty Wild Cards, forty in total. Now, after Abigail had sprung all three traps (and after the two gangs had thumped each other pretty hard), there were less than a dozen left. The remaining gangsters, exhausted and battered, still scrapped, each side stubbornly determined to win. Pinching her nose, Abigail noted that the air reeked; it smelled like a combination of a barn, a bar, and a sweaty gymnasium.

"Men are so gross." Abigail grimaced.

Mr. Circus, the leader of the Wild Cards, nastily flicked his knife back and forth at Mr. Gutter, the leader of the Longshadows. Mr. Gutter parried the blade away with his club and socked Mr. Circus in the face. Neither went down. Neither could score a winning blow. At this point, both gangs were just grinding each other down.

Then Mr. Todesco, Helena and Olga materialized once more, floating gently above Watchtower's Magic Lantern. His services no longer needed, the Magnificent Madrigal joined them, hovering in midair. Finally, Abigail watched as Little Wade floated up directly into the path of Watchtower's limelight.

"This must be the grand finale," she realized.

Nothing could prepare her for what happened next.

12

URBAN LEGEND

Before the grand finale, Abigail noticed something significant during the battle, but no one else did.

During all of the gangs' brawling, clashing and crashing, and all of Abigail's ducking, diving, evading, vanishing, and trapping, Watchtower dutifully played his part. He acted like a Magic Lantern, reloading and switching slides this entire time. No one noticed. Every few minutes, during the battle, he switched to a new slide and projected the image onto the screen, only instead of showing the Wild Cards or the Longshadows, these slides were quite different. They each displayed a different picture of Little Wade and Watchtower, each time striking a different, very humorous pose. Also, each slide contained different words emblazoned on them.

First Slide: "WE ARE REAL!"

During the battle, no one noticed.

Second Slide: "WE SET A TRAP FOR YOU!"

No one noticed.

Third Slide: "YOU ARE NOT EVEN LOOKING UP HERE!"

To his credit, one of the Longshadows actually stopped and pointed to the screen and called out, "Hey guys!" but then a Wild Card tackled him.

Fourth Slide: *"You are all such fools!"*

No one noticed any of the slides, and no one noticed when Little Wade floated up into Watchtower's limelight. He lit up another lever right next to Abigail's position. This lever, like the chandelier trap, connected to a set of ropes that led up and over the monumental white screen that Watchtower had mounted earlier.

"Pull it!" Little Wade yelled.

"It'll bring the screen down!"

"I know! Do it!"

She yanked the lever, and the ropes released, unspooled, and snapped out of position. The screen rippled and shook. Then Abigail heard the most unnerving sound, a deep moaning followed by a high-pitched wailing.

The sounds were coming from Little Wade.

"You shouldn't have come here!" Little Wade bellowed, not in his normal voice, but with a horrific snarl. Then he roared like some terrible monster from the deep. Little Wade's teeth vanished. His mouth became a toothless, gaping hole. *"Now you will suffer!"*

Abigail realized only Mr. Circus and Mr. Gutter could hear him. While the two gangs continued to scuffle, their leaders stopped fighting and immediately turned their attention to Little Wade. He floated in Watchtower's limelight, his tailcoat streaming behind him as if he were a majestic vampire.

"It's him. He's real," Mr. Gutter yelped.

"It's true?" Mr. Circus shook his head, flabbergasted.

"You should have believed in us!"

"I believed! I believed!" Mr. Gutter fell to his knees.

"Too late! Now you die!"

Then Little Wade convulsed in midair.

Abigail watched as Little Wade, the handsome, sophisticated, slightly blue boy, transformed into a gargantuan, slithering, floating monstrosity, with hundreds of eyes, tentacles, and tongues, all bursting with razor-sharp, spiky teeth. This monster, round like a planet, had mouths within mouths, eyes within eyes, tongues inside of hands and hands inside of eyes, teeth, and tongues. In short,

Abigail believed it to be the absolute ugliest, strangest, most disgusting thing she had ever seen in her life, and the sounds it made were even more disgusting.

"*Bllllaaaaaaaaaarrrrrrrghhhh!*" (or something like that).

Now everyone could see it, all of the gang members. They could not tell if they witnessed an image from the slide projector or if they beheld a figment of their imaginations. It did not matter. Two of the men peed themselves. All of the Longshadows and Wild Cards trembled in fear. The blood drained from their faces until they were as pale as paper. Their mouths dropped. Their eyes sprang open wide, and they tried to run away, screaming.

"*Aaaaaaaaaaahhhhhhhh!*"

"*I eat people!*" the monster roared, and it opened its gaping, worm-filled mouth and descended on the crowd of quivering gangsters. At that same moment, the screen fell forward, and the expansive white sheet rained down on top of the last Longshadows and Wild Cards as if the monstrous creature were swallowing them up.

"*Aaaaaaaaaaahhhhhhhhhh!*"

The plummeting sheet stifled all of the gangsters' screams as it cascaded over them, smothering them. Little Wade, in his monstrous form, slathering them in slimy saliva, crawled on top of them and spasmed and chomped as if he were devouring them. All of this occurred at the exact same moment that the sheet physically entangled them. The perfectly timed illusion forced the men to believe that they were actually being eaten alive. Even Abigail reacted to the terrifying image.

"*Aaaaaahh!*" Abigail screamed at the top of her lungs, followed by a quick "*Huh?*" when the monster vanished. Little Wade reappeared, floating through the air, laughing.

"It's all right. It's just me." Little Wade rolled through the air, snickering like a mischievous little goblin.

"What was that?" Abigail asked, incredulous, her emotions racing.

"Do you like it? I call it the 'Smorgasborg'!"

"The Smorgasborg? It's absolutely horrible!"

"Just a bit of Sembling," Little Wade explained. "Remember that I can look like anything I want. Watchtower and I invented it years ago," Little Wade chuckled. "As you can see, it contains a bit of everything, hence the name."

"Wait, isn't the real word 'smorgasbord' with a 'd' at the end?" Abigail corrected him.

"Yes, but Smorgasborg with a 'g' sounds better and more monstrous. Do you think the Longshadows and Wild Cards like it?"

Her heart bouncing up and down in her chest, Abigail barely suppressed a laugh as she watched the gangsters cower. Beneath the vast sheet, which blanketed nearly the entire seating section, the last Longshadows and Wild Cards screamed and cried for their mothers, floundering and stumbling. Whistling pleasantly and waving his hands around, Little Wade continued to cast Dolosphera. He convinced them they were trapped in the oozy jaws of a slimy, ectoplasmic monster.

Meanwhile, Mr. Gutter and Mr. Circus tripped and stumbled over each other as they tried to escape. When they turned around to run away, they found themselves assaulted by an impossibly bright, searing light and the unmistakable sound of hissing, whirring, clanking, popping, grinding. No more games. No more disguises. No more hiding. Watchtower cranked up to his full twenty-one-foot height, rising in front of them like a titanic monster.

Mr. Gutter just fainted and crumpled to the floor.

Mr. Circus remained standing. His jaw dropped open.

"I don't…believe it," the leader of the Wild Cards managed to eke out just before Little Wade appeared next to him.

"Believe it," Little Wade smiled, and then his face contorted into something macabre, and then he bellowed, "*Boo!*"

Then Watchtower punched Mr. Circus's lights out.

Abigail climbed down from her perch on the stage and conversed with Little Wade, who gently descended through the air. Watchtower took care of the last of the Longshadows and Wild Cards that still struggled beneath the white sheet. Whenever a moving lump appeared in the shifting, writhing fabric, he bonked it on the head, and it went down permanently.

Bonk!

Little Wade clapped, removing his shadow illusion; the oppressive blanket of darkness lifted, and shafts of daylight pierced through the walls and ceiling once again. All of the dusty sunbeams that illuminated the Orpheus returned like breaths of fresh air. Abigail stepped out into the light, dusted herself off, and caught her breath. Tired, she leaned against one of the rotting support columns.

Bonk!

"Are you all right?" Little Wade called out.

Watchtower could not reach one of the squirming white blobs with his extended hand, so he picked up a heavy slab of wood and used it as a very effective club.

Bonk!

"Yes, I'm all right."

"How do you feel?"

After a brief moment, she admitted, "I feel rather exhilarated, actually!"

Watchtower tried to reach another flailing, white blob, extending his arm. He tried once. He tried twice. He could not. So he picked up a seat with one hand, chucked it at his target, and knocked it out instantly.

Bonk!

"You did very well, Abigail."

"I enjoyed that immensely!" she admitted, but then added. "So, if I understand your plan correctly, word will get out about this. This will spark tensions between these two gangs. As a result, the Wild Cards and the Longshadows will be too busy with each other to bother with me."

"In addition, the conflict will spill out all across town, and then the police will swoop in and sweep them all up."

Taking a look around the battlefield, Abigail remarked. "This was quite grand, but you're telling me that the Great Gang Trap is going to be even bigger than this?"

"Oh, this is nothing compared to the Great Gang Trap."

"Nothing?"

"This spectacle serves only as a prelude. We're not only going to clean up your neighborhood, Abigail. We're going to clean up the entire city."

"How?"

"Do you want to know or be surprised? I promise, either way, you're going to love it."

Abigail thought for a moment. "Well, this surprise turned out to be very pleasant indeed, so I think I prefer for you to keep it a secret for a little while longer."

"You are the client. We are at your service."

Finally, Watchtower found the last two gangsters, their voices muffled, struggling beneath the sheet. He seized their heads and knocked their skulls together with a loud *crack*. They plopped to the floor, quite knocked out. Watchtower pinched the extensive sheet in his hands and then, in one swift, graceful motion, yanked it upward, fluffing it up until it filled the air like a huge cloud. As Watchtower lifted the fabric, Abigail could see all of the unconscious bodies of the Longshadows and Wild Cards littered beneath it. Like broken sticks, they lay scattered about. With his warm glow illuminating the theater, Watchtower loomed over all of them.

"Did any die?"

"No, knocked out, as promised in your contract. We avoid fatalities whenever possible."

Then Watchtower pulled the floating sheet toward himself, and it swirled inward, like a whirlpool. Magically, the sheet folded itself up in midair, collapsing into a small square of cloth that Watchtower folded once more and tucked into one of his long coat's deep pockets.

"Self-folding cloth. How marvelous!"

Dusting off his hands and nodding his head, Watchtower appeared satisfied. The battle had now officially concluded.

"Wait, you're not supposed to reveal yourselves. What will they say happened here?"

"Depends on who you ask." Little Wade's voice echoed as he

surveyed the scene. "Everyone witnessed something different, including you, and so everyone will tell a different story, but they will all conclude in the same manner. All anyone knows for certain is..."

"Two gangs walked into a theater..." Abigail began.

"And no one walked out." He grinned.

"You can be a very naughty boy, Little Wade."

"Sometimes." Smiling slyly, he descended toward Abigail. *"You can come out now!"* Little Wade called out. Abigail stepped back, surprised, as two people, not ghosts, but actual people materialized and stepped out from the shadows.

The first, a long-haired, bearded, Spanish gentleman, wore a top hat tipped with silver and a long tail coat, also tipped with silver. He clutched a cane that Abigail could tell definitely contained a sword and he wore goggles over his eyes so she could not fully see his face, but he appeared to be an incredibly handsome, graceful man.

The second, a woman, dressed as an Old West outlaw, wore a cowboy hat. A bandanna covered her nose, mouth, and chin, and goggles concealed her eyes. A hunting knife and a coil of rope were fastened to her belt and flanked by a pair of cracked leather holsters. Even though the mysterious gunslinger wore a long duster overcoat and carried a pair of revolvers, Abigail could tell by the grace in her stride and the swing of her hips that she was indeed a cowgirl and not a cowboy.

"Thank you for your help." Little Wade saluted them.

"Thank—" Abigail wanted to say something, but without a word, they saluted and then quickly exited the Orpheus through a side door, stepping out into the sunlight and vanishing.

"Wait...who were they?"

Little Wade shrugged. "I arranged for them to watch out for you."

"I was never in any real danger, was I?"

He shook his head and winked at her. "They were prepared to intercede at a moment's notice. That might not always be the case. Next time, however, I don't think your hands will shake as much."

"You're training me," Abigail observed.

"I am indeed."

"For what?"

"For life."

Abigail took a moment and gazed around the silent theater, ruined, but nevertheless majestic and grand.

"Is what you did...just now...is that allowed...for ghosts...to do that sort of thing?"

"Perfectly legal," Little Wade informed her as several of his Polyplots checked each one of the men to ensure they were still alive.

Stepping over another one of the unconscious gangsters, Abigail inquired, "Legal, you say? So this did not violate the Ahkwiyàn? Ooooh! May I read these laws? I would very much like to learn."

Little Wade, waving his hands around, conjured up a floating scroll that unfurled itself. On the glowing parchment, were several very official-looking paragraphs scrawled in very refined, cursive writing. Narrowing her eyes, stepping closer, Abigail read the scroll.

The Laws of Haunting

To begin, "Haunting" shall hereafter be defined as the act of a deceased, incorporeal being revealing itself to the mortal world for the primary purpose of eliciting a heightened, negative emotional response resulting in that mortal reflecting deeply on his or her own deepest fears and eventual mortality, and for the secondary purpose of ensuring that particular mortal never returns to visit a specific location nor interacts with that particular ghost, or if that mortal does return, quickly regrets it and then truly, never, ever returns.

First, you cannot Haunt without a proper license. If you do not possess a permit, please stop reading, and please cease your Haunting immediately.

Second, if you must Haunt, you must only do so indoors or, if outdoors, in a remote and difficult to reach area, or a dangerous and menacing one (or dangerous and menacing-looking). Under no circumstances may you Haunt a public, well-traveled, well-regarded, well-maintained, or well-groomed place.

Third, you must limit the number of people that witness you to a dozen or less at a time. If you reveal yourself to more than a dozen, please be prepared to provide proof of either Urban Legend (if you Haunt in a city) or Folk Tale (if you Haunt in the country) status.

Fourth, if you do choose to tingle or to pierce the Ahkwiyàn and reveal yourself for the purpose of Haunting, you must appear as something different to each individual witness, so that their stories will never match and no one will ever truly believe any of them.

Fifth, you cannot answer any direct questions or engage in any pleasant or informative conversations with the Living, and you cannot, under any circumstances, reveal any information about the world beyond. Please consult **Middlemitch's Guide to Providing Vague, Symbolic, and Evasive Answers to the Living** if you require guidance. Or say nothing. Nothing always works.

However, if you have been the victim of a crime (most likely murder seeing as how you are dead), or if you possess knowledge of a crime against another, and you wish to impart it for the sake of justice or perhaps mischief, you must provide only indirect information that requires the Living to use their wits to solve the crime. We do not wish to imbalance or disrupt the mechanisms of civilization. For further details, please consult **Davenger's Guide to Justice from Beyond the Grave**.

Sixth, while being a ghost does not obligate you to necessarily terrify people, you cannot make them laugh or feel pleasant in any way, or else they will seek to repeat the encounter because they enjoy your company. They should not enjoy your company. You are dead. They are alive. They should Live.

Seventh, you must provide a registered reason for choosing to Haunt a particular location. Please make sure to file your claim with the local Office of Spookery. It does not matter if you know or do not know where your local Office of Spookery is located. It knows where you are.

EIGHTH, ONLY PLACES AND CERTAIN OBJECTS MAY BE HAUNTED, BUT NEVER PEOPLE. WE ARE NOT DEMONS.

FOR A LIST OF APPROVED HAUNTED "ARTIFACTS," PLEASE CONSULT BALKANGEIST'S CHART OF TRANSPORTABLE AND TRANSFERABLE HAUNTINGS. YOU CAN ONLY HAUNT AN OBJECT IF YOU OWNED IT OR INTERACTED WITH IT OFTEN DURING YOUR LIFETIME (YES, THAT INCLUDES YOUR OWN BONES). ALSO, THE OBJECT MUST BE NON-PERISHABLE. YOU CANNOT HAUNT AN OBJECT THAT HAS ROTTED AWAY AND NO LONGER EXISTS. WE CANNOT BELIEVE WE HAVE TO WRITE THIS DOWN, BUT SOMEONE ACTUALLY TRIED IT. A STUPID GHOST TRIED TO HAUNT AN APPLE. IT WAS, STILL IS, AND ALWAYS WILL BE, EMBARRASSING.

SIGH...IF YOU ARE WONDERING, AND YOU SHOULD NOT BE, NO, UNDER NO CIRCUMSTANCES MAY YOU HAUNT A TOILET OR AN OUTHOUSE OR ANY PLACE WHERE PEOPLE GO TO RELIEVE THEMSELVES. WE CONSIDER IT SIMPLY, UTTERLY IMPROPER. ALL OF THE EXCEPTIONS TO THIS RULE HAVE ALREADY BEEN MADE AND THIS OFFICE DEEPLY REGRETS MAKING THEM AND WILL REGRET EACH AND EVERY ONE OF THEM FOREVER. THERE ARE ENOUGH HAUNTED TOILETS OUT THERE. WE NEED NO MORE.

NINTH, ONCE A GHOST CLAIMS TERRITORY TO HAUNT, THAT TERRITORY CANNOT BE TRESPASSED OR APPROPRIATED BY ANY OTHER WRAITH OR SPECTER. ANY TRESPASSING SPIRIT SHALL BE CONSIDERED A THREAT AND SHALL BE DEALT WITH BY THE APPROPRIATE AUTHORITIES. "AUTHORITIES" MEANS RATTLERS, WHICH ARE SUPREMELY REVOLTING AND TERRIFYING, SO PLEASE DO NOT DISTURB THEM OR GIVE THEM A REASON TO APPEAR. THEY ARE TRULY AWFUL IN EVERY CONCEIVABLE WAY.

FINALLY, IF YOU CAN ABIDE BY ALL OF THE RULES LISTED ABOVE, THEN WHILE IT IS CERTAINLY UNFORTUNATE THAT YOU ARE DEAD, PERHAPS YOU CAN FIND SOME MEANING IN SCARING AND UNSETTLING PEOPLE AND ADDING A LEVEL OF MYSTERY, MAGIC, AND MAYHEM TO PARTICULAR PLOTS OF REAL ESTATE.

HAPPY (MORE OR LESS) HAUNTING.

AS SINCERELY AS POSSIBLE GIVEN THE STAKES ARE TRULY LIFE AND DEATH, NEW YORK CITY'S NECROPOLITAN OFFICE OF SPIRITUAL, PHANTASMIC, INTERDIMENSIONAL NAVIGATION (OR NYC NO SPIN FOR SHORT)

"Fascinating!" Abigail remarked. "Necropolitan...do these laws only apply to the city?"

"Yes, Necronational laws represent a whole other level of bureaucracy."

Little Wade clapped, and the floating, glowing scroll rolled back up again with a loud, crisp *snap* and then vanished with a *poof!*

Abigail quickly counted the number of bodies, numbering forty in total. "Hmmm...there were forty men in here, a violation of the rules...but...you only revealed yourself fully to the last dozen, and during the battle...you and the Fire People only selectively manifested images to a few gangsters at a time, and you made sure everyone witnessed something different."

"Precisely."

"That Smorgasborg creature was quite imaginative. I wonder, do you transform into anything else?"

Little Wade grinned wickedly. "I thought you'd never ask."

Abigail suddenly heard whispers, growls, hisses, clacks, rattles, squishes, slurps and a variety of other icky sounds that gave her the willies. Glancing around the decrepit building, Abigail spotted a variety of bizarre creatures, each one more repulsive than the last, flitting and darting about in the most tenebrous corners of the theater. Slowly, twelve apparitions in total emerged from behind seats, pillars, shadowy nooks, piles of junk. Some were humanoid, but many were not. Startled, Abigail shifted her feet nervously, but then the pack of freakish phantasms bowed before her as if she were their queen.

"Hello there!" Abigail smiled brightly at this odd assortment of floating monstrosities. In response, some of them waved with their clawed hands or tentacled arms. "Pleased to meet all of you."

"These are my Haunters," Little Wade boasted proudly. "Sometimes it takes more than a flying little boy to scare the bejeebers out of a hardened criminal. That's where they come in. I often utilize these unpleasant incarnations to torment gangsters at night."

"Let me guess," Abigail said. "The following morning, your targets swear that their awful experiences were all just nightmares, so nobody believes them when they desperately appeal for help."

"For ghosts, the world of dreams is the perfect place to hide."

Abigail examined the Haunters. Because they kept to the shadows, she could not make them out clearly. She could tell, though, that some of the beasts possessed long, slimy tentacles, some venomous spikes, some jagged fangs, some all three. Even though she knew her hand would pass through their spectral forms, Abigail reached out and petted them affectionately. Each time she 'touched' a creature, it reverted to a standard, duplicate Little Wade (Polyplot). Giggling, Abigail pressed the Haunters like buttons, changing them until there were only Little Wades left.

"So...by varying your shape, you add another layer of security for yourself, another way to conceal your existence."

"Right you are. Over the years, Watchtower and I have found loopholes in the rules, which we've exploited to great effect, as you can see."

"Loopholes...that's a word I will need to remember and use in the future. So...how can you answer my direct questions, engage me in direct conversation, and be such pleasant company?"

"We appreciate the compliment, Abigail. My answer: I'm not haunting you. Watchtower and I and our activities fall under the jurisdiction of the Office of Spiritual Guidance, Supernatural Mentorship, Guardian Angelics, and Mysterious Heroics."

"Oh, I see, so the exact opposite of Haunting."

"Quite so. In fact, the office is located on the exact opposite side of the building."

"What building? Where?"

"In the City of the Dead. Where else would it be?"

Abigail's eyes widened. "There's a City of the Dead?"

"Oh yes, specifically a New York City of the Dead."

"Where?"

"All around us."

"Can you show me?"

"Eventually. First, we give thanks."

As if on cue, the Fire People materialized before them, floating gently as if underwater, their hair and clothes flowing and billowing.

"The police will be here very soon. Our theatrical spectacle has concluded," the Magnificent Madrigal boasted.

"I want to thank you so much for helping me." Abigail curtsied. "I won't ever forget your kindness. I will keep your secret."

"So much fun! We enjoyed ourselves tremendously," Mr. Todesco smiled.

"People will continue to believe that this place is haunted. They will leave us alone for a few more years. We can still call this place home," Helena added.

Finally, Olga and her puppy appeared before Abigail. She smiled and waved.

"I'm sorry for what happened to you." Abigail did not know what else to say. "I'm sorry for what happened *to all* of you."

"We were the first to die," Olga spoke and referred to herself and her puppy. "We were living on the street. Mr. and Mrs. Todesco took us in and let us stay here in the theater. They gave us a small room in the back. We were asleep when the machine exploded. The fire and the explosion struck at the same time and killed us instantly. We just never woke up. Sometimes, I still believe that this is all just a bad dream and that someday we'll open our eyes again. You get to wake up to a new day every day. You still get to dream. You still have your whole life ahead of you," Olga advised her. "Go out there and live it." The puppy barked (rather cutely).

"Thank you, dear friends." Little Wade bowed.

"Keep the people you love in your heart," Mr. Todesco whispered, "or they disappear. Remember that."

The Fire People vanished, leaving them alone. For a moment, Abigail stood there quietly, so quietly that Little Wade and Watchtower both glanced at each other, concerned.

"Are you all right?" Little Wade inquired politely.

"As bad as life can be, it can always be worse, and someone always suffers worse than you. These people all perished so unspeakably," Abigail whispered. "I sometimes forget to appreciate things. I get so bitter and angry sometimes because I'm poor, and my mother passed away, but that little girl never got to live at all, did she?"

"No, I'm afraid not."

"She's not alone. I'm sure we can find many more out there...like her," Abigail continued. "Correct?"

"Too many to count."

"Even with everything that's happened to me...I suppose I'm...lucky." The bitterness in Abigail's voice worried Little Wade.

"Don't be too hard on yourself," Little Wade consoled her. "Your problems still matter, Abigail. Everyone's problems matter."

"How do you choose who to help?" She turned to him and Watchtower. "How...with so many desperate people, why did you choose me?"

Little Wade and Watchtower shrugged their shoulders. "We know we cannot save everyone, Abigail. We do what we can to seek out children in need, but it usually ends up being wherever fate leads us. We just happened to be a few blocks away when we heard your cries for help."

"Those men that attacked me last night, the men in the alley," Abigail recalled, "a few of them knew who you were, and come to think of it...so did many of them." She gestured to the gang members splayed out all over the place.

"Well...we've...uh...we've sort of become a bit of a local legend." If Little Wade could blush, he would have.

Thinking back to the floating scroll, Abigail wondered. "Wait, have you two earned urban legend status?"

As if on cue, Little Wade and Watchtower both reached into their coat pockets and produced a pair of splendid badges and presented them to Abigail. Watchtower's, made of gold, gleamed. Little Wade's badge, an illusion, glowed.

"Conferred upon us in eighteen thirty-one, but only after we had successfully completed several cases. Their standards are quite stringent. They did not make it easy for us. We even had to take a written exam."

"Little Wade and Watchtower...urban legend, it must be nice to be feared and respected."

"It provides some advantages. Who knows? By the time this

weekend ends and Monday morning arrives, perhaps you will be, too."

"Hardly," she scoffed and blushed.

"Don't be so sure," Little Wade assured her. "You're capable of more than you know."

Rubbing her hand over her belly and wiping dried blood off her wrists, Abigail cursed. "I missed it. That young man almost got me. He acted so innocently. I...believed him. I failed to see him with my stomach. I should know better."

"Every eye blinks, Abigail," Little Wade counseled her. "We do not want you to become suspicious of all people. No one should live that way. With a little experience, you will learn to trust your gut."

One of the wounded men groaned.

"Let's be off." Little Wade gestured to Watchtower, who pried open the double doors with a loud, creaking *bang*. Daylight flooded in along with fresh air. Abigail breathed it in. The gritty, grimy streets of New York never smelled so good.

Then she heard shouting outside, and police whistles.

"The police! Here? Already?"

"This city contains many police precincts, Abigail," Little Wade explained. "Working in secret over the years, Watchtower and I recruited, trained, and installed officers in every single one of them. They were boys when we found them. They have become fine, fierce, dependable men. Even though our contacts all work for various police precincts, together they comprise a secret organization within the department, a *hidden* precinct if you will. While you were asleep last night, I sent word out to every one of our officers assigned to patrol the Lower East Side and entreated them to congregate at this establishment at...well...right about now."

"You called all of them...for me?" Abigail replied, deeply moved.

"Yes. These officers will be your allies, too. Prepare to meet Precinct Zero."

Abigail heard marching boots outside, like an army approaching.

"What a marvelous beginning to the day," Abigail noted as she exited.

Watchtower adjusted his hat and disguise, shrank, and collapsed down to his seven-foot "very above average size" mode. He locked his joints and gears into place, smoothed his suit, adjusted his overcoat, took a beat to collect himself, and then hunched his way out of the broken door, following Abigail and Little Wade.

13

PRECINCT ZERO

"*Tweeeeet!*" Loud police whistles split the air. Dozens of New York Metropolitan Police officers in their blue, brass-buttoned uniforms, conical caps, and glittering badges converged on the Orpheus Theater. They all carried billy clubs, and some carried shiny revolvers. While a veritable army of junior officers quickly bustled inside to arrest the gangs, a handful of senior officers remained on the sidewalk and saluted Abigail, Little Wade, and Watchtower.

"Gentlemen," Little Wade greeted them, and they all grunted in response. Abigail quickly surmised that the officers needed to conceal their knowledge of Little Wade. They could not acknowledge his existence, salute him, nor speak to him, so, to maintain the illusion, they simply grunted so that the bystanders who stood outside the theater would have no idea that the police communicated with an invisible, levitating boy. A grunt could mean anything.

While a multitude of citizens stood by and gawked at the site of Precinct Zero storming the theater, Little Wade introduced Abigail to the senior officers. He quickly rattled off the names of each of the men. Each one either tipped his hat or bowed or nodded or smiled at Abigail, but she promptly forgot their real names and, instead, as she did with the Longshadows the night before, assigned each one of them a special nickname that she felt described them better than any real name could. There were tall ones, short ones, fat ones, thin ones, scary ones, scarred ones, smiling ones, young and old. Their leader, a red-haired, red-bearded man she nicknamed Sergeant Blood, stepped forward.

"Guid mornin' Abigail Reid," Sergeant Blood acknowledged her gruffly in a nearly incomprehensible Scottish accent. He then handed her a map of the Lower East Side with bright lines drawn all over it.

"'Tis a schedule o' all o' oor roonds," Sergeant Blood informed her. *"That wey ye ken know wich o' us micht be oan th' strit near ye at ony given oor. We chaynge it up fae time tae time, tae keep th' gangs guessing, bit we'll juist gie ye th' newest copy whenever yi"ll need it."*

After briefly examining the schedule, she blinked several times.

"So I'll always know which coppers patrol nearest my location. Wait, what's this here?" Abigail observed what looked like garbled words or gibberish, or…wait. Scanning them, she recognized the names: NAUTILUS, NED LAND, NEMO, TRIPOD, PIP, SCROOGE, ICHABOD, among many others. "This is some kind of code."

Examining it further, Abigail grinned wickedly. "I recognize all of the literary references in this cipher. These all refer to the books I've read. You've chosen some very obscure ones. I understand them, but a gangster would not."

Little Wade smirked. "Last night, I memorized your bookshelf, right down to the specific editions. The only method by which the Longshadows, or any other gang, can decipher this code entails reading every book you've read, the exact editions on your shelf. Quite impossible."

"You've written the officers' names in code, using characters from books, as well as the scheduled times using chapter numbers. Oh! In case I misplace it!"

"We don't waant th' gangs knowing whit 'n' howfur we think."

"This will make my father feel so much better. Thank you!"

Sergeant Blood grunted in response. Then all of the senior officers of Precinct Zero stiffened up, smoothed their uniforms, and carefully formed into two lines, as if ready to salute someone or be inspected by their boss. One second later, a dark blue horse and carriage with the words NEW YORK POLICE DEPARTMENT emblazoned on its side pulled to a stop at their location. The horses snorted, grunted, and spat. Abigail noticed that the carriage's curtains were drawn entirely over all of the windows. She could not see inside. Sergeant Blood opened one of its doors, revealing darkness. Fidgeting for a moment, Abigail cast a sidelong glance to Watchtower, who, arms crossed, gestured toward the carriage as if to say, "Go on."

"Come along." Little Wade drifted forward. "She's waiting."

Abigail climbed inside the carriage and sat down. Inside, thick curtains blocked nearly all daylight and muffled the sounds from the street. Little Wade took his place at Abigail's side. Sergeant Blood shut the door behind them. Adjusting her eyes to the darkness, Abigail blinked. Across from her and Little Wade sat a woman dressed entirely in dark blue wearing a very high collar over her neck, a bonnet over her head, tinted goggles over her eyes and gloves over her hands. She sat with several thick files stacked on her lap that were all marked NEW YORK POLICE DEPARTMENT. Although Abigail could only see this woman's nose, mouth, and chin, she could tell that this woman was very pretty but also very, very pale. Abigail spotted a silver pistol tucked into the female officer's belt, a silver pocket watch that *click-click-clicked*, and finally a silver police badge pinned to her chest that dazzled like a brooch, even in the very faint light inside the enshrouded carriage.

"Abigail Reid, meet Night Owl Nell, one of our contacts in the New York Police Department. Nell works the night shift; more specifically, she works directly for the Commissioner. Her office is in police headquarters. From the very first night that she started, and every night after that, she completely organized, categorized, collated, and otherwise arranged all of the department's files. Each and every police report must go through her before it passes across anyone else's desk."

"So she's a nexus of information!"

"That's exactly what she is."

"How do you do, Abigail?" Night Owl Nell's voice sounded flat, almost monotone. Abigail could not even hear the question mark inflection in her voice.

"So pleased to meet you," Abigail responded politely.

All business, no-nonsense, no emotion, Night Owl Nell held up a police file and opened it, presenting it to them both.

"I pulled every record and dossier on the Brooke Adams case as well as any similar cases and collated them by several relevant criteria."

"Wait! How did you know to pull files on Brooke? I only told Little Wade about her earlier this morning."

"I told her," another Little Wade (Polyplot) abruptly melted through the wall and poked his head into the carriage and smiled.

"Oh, right!" Abigail shifted her glance to the Little Wade next to her and the Little Wade that phased through the wall. "You can be in more than one place at once. That's...very helpful."

"Will that be all?" Little Wade (Polyplot) asked the real Little Wade, who nodded.

"Yes, thank you. We'll need you to scout later on."

"My pleasure. Abigail, I'll see you again soon." Little Wade (Polyplot) winked at her and then vanished.

"I don't think I'll ever get used to that." Abigail shook her head and then collected herself. "I'm sorry, Nell. You were about to speak."

"No need to apologize. Little Wade informed me right after you told him, so I dove into our files, and I believe Brooke Adams, along with dozens of other children abducted over the past seven weeks, is being held somewhere within the city limits, most probably still in Manhattan."

"So they haven't been shipped away? We can still find her?"

"That's excellent news, Nell."

"It is, but right now, Abigail, I need more information, more data points to refine my search."

"How can I help?"

"Longshadows tend to work very quickly," Night Owl Nell continued in her precise monotone. "They spot something they want, and usually within twenty-four hours they strike. Abigail, just before they kidnapped Brooke, did she appear in public or display any extraordinary qualities? Did she do anything to attract attention?"

"Think carefully," Little Wade advised her.

Scratching her head, Abigail recollected carefully. "Let's see. That would be about a month ago…right before that…I think…oh, wait! Yes. She presented her models at a street fair."

Intrigued, Night Owl Nell cocked her head to the side. "Models."

"Yes, she and her father, working together, pieced together the most amazingly detailed model ships."

"What size models?"

"Oh, they varied. Some were itsy-bitsy, but some were at least this big." Abigail held up her hands to represent the size.

"Would you describe these models as very detailed?" Night Owl Nell inquired although Abigail could not hear the question mark in her voice.

"Oh, definitely. They were stunningly intricate, all of them. Brooke loved building models, her favorite activity in the whole world, especially because she spent such quality time with her father."

"Interesting," Night Owl Nell bit her lip; she appeared to be processing this information. "Small, delicate hands with fine motor skills."

"What do you think, Nell? I see your gears turning." Little Wade observed.

Pursing her lips, "Small hands," Nell whispered, and then she presented several more files.

"Fuyvush Rothman, a Jewish Boy from Hester street. Ramon Garcia, a Spanish boy who lived on Pearl. Li Jing, a young girl from Chinatown…now that I think about it, looking through the notes, they all worked jobs outside of school. Some of them worked full time…and all of their jobs required…small hands. Fuyvush, for example, polished the inside of glasses. Ramon helped his father string beads and gems for his family's jewelry shop, and Jing deboned small fish. At first, I suspected that they were being kidnapped for manual labor, perhaps in small spaces, tunnels perhaps, because of their diminutive statures, but..."

Night Owl Nell showed them a specific file marked H.P. on its cover.

"This one here, an outlier, did not match the others. Horace Pole is a very rotund, overweight boy, not suited for manual labor in small spaces at all. His parents described him as a gifted player of musical instruments. His friends often called him "Windbag" because he could sustain a note for several minutes. Playing musical instruments requires fine motor skills with one's hands. What about you, Abigail? What would you say makes you special?"

"Well, that's easy," she replied. "I read absolutely everything. Wait, now that I think about it, just before the Longshadows tried to kidnap me, I assisted a local businessman named Mr. Novak, a very nice man."

"Novak, the local cigar maker?" Night Owl Nell asked, or stated since Abigail could not hear the question mark.

"That's the one. Mr. Novak rolls cigars to sell. His entire extended family works for him, over a dozen people total. At first, I intended to help him and make a little money on the side, but I proved to be a very inefficient cigar roller. Then Mr. Novak learned that I could read, so—"

"You read out loud to the workers while they worked, to entertain them."

"Yes, and sometimes—"

"Mr. Novak requested that you read off instructions to them to make the process more efficient."

"How did you know that?" Abigail marveled at Night Owl Nell's ability to predict the future, or at least the future of Abigail's mouth.

"One of the Longshadows must have entered the cigar shop while you were doing this." Little Wade pieced it all together. "Then he must have reported you to his boss—a girl with red hair who knows how to read to workers. They would have snatched you right away, but it probably took them a little while to target you on the street because of your disguise, but once they figured out who you were, and where you were going to be, they struck."

"We still don't know why," Abigail lamented.

"Technical manuals," Night Owl Nell blurted out. Abigail could not tell if Night Owl Nell was excited or not because her voice remained completely flat and dull. "Abigail can read them out loud while the other children work with their hands. She can read the technical manuals and give the other workers instructions. With Abigail's help, the Longshadows could train dozens of children on the job while working them simultaneously. That would mean efficient, mass production of products that require small, delicate hands." She glanced at Little Wade. "You know what that means."

"Shock Troops," Little Wade hissed. "They're back."

An uncomfortable silence filled the darkened carriage. Abigail spoke up first. "Who are the Shock Troops?"

"The Longshadows work with many gangs," Night Owl Nell continued her odd habit of speaking in monotone. "Each gang specializes in some particular crime, robbery, narcotics, murder, smuggling, but Shock Troops possess expertise in something new."

"Electricity," Abigail guessed.

"New technology," Little Wade added.

"Oh, I know about that. Mrs. Whitlock, my teacher, she keeps us up to date on all of the latest scientific advancements. She even took us on a field trip to the Pearl Street Power Station. She showed us the transformers, generators, power coils, circuits, and electrical cables. I found the entire experience amazing...and very buzzy."

"So...what happens when technology gets more advanced?" Little Wade asked her.

"It shrinks," Abigail guessed. "Like the latest cameras for taking photographs. Cameras used to be bulky, boxy things that required tripods; however, in class, Mrs. Whitlock demonstrated a new box camera she could carry in her hand. So...if these Shock Troops seek to use children to help them build smaller and smaller technology, then that means they will force children to handle...very small electrical wires to build smaller circuits?"

"Well done, Abigail," he complimented her.

Night Owl Nell did not smile, "Now we know why they took Brooke Adams and all the rest. The Longshadows struck a deal with the Shock Troops, supplying them with small children with small hands to help them build smaller devices. Abigail, you've just broken this case wide open. You just refined our investigation, and you will very likely save those children's lives. I could not possibly be more excited or thrilled." Night Owl remarked without any emotion whatsoever, her voice as flat as a road.

Then something struck Abigail, and she became very worried. "But Mrs. Whitlock explained to me that the technology governing electricity debuted quite recently. Because it's new, engineers continue to discover flaws, problems, and dangers with wires and circuits. The children could be electrocuted. They could be hurt. They could...die."

"We're not going to let that happen." Little Wade promised Abigail.

Night Owl Nell flipped through her files again, revealing a detailed map.

"Shortly after they took over this neighborhood, the Longshadows established stash houses, hideouts and secret slave factories all over this city, but now we know to concentrate our search on those areas where electrical wiring has been installed. This narrows down our search to a handful of locations."

"Get the precinct on it!" Little Wade ordered Nell.

She replied with a completely monotone, "Right away."

Sergeant Blood knocked on the door. His voice boomed through the carriage walls.

"How's it gaun in thare? Ye saving th' world?"

Night Owl Nell yawned, but she did so very politely and discreetly.

"I know you've been up all night, and it's long past your bedtime, Nell. We sincerely appreciate you staying up."

"I'll just pretend that this a dream," she answered, her voice flat.

"We'll see you tonight, Nell. Thank you so much."

"Anything for you, Little Wade."

Little Wade melted through the walls of the carriage, leaving Abigail and Night Owl Nell alone. Just before Abigail opened the door to the carriage, they shared a moment of awkward silence. Because Nell wore tinted goggles that covered half of her face, Abigail could not tell if Nell stared straight ahead or at Abigail herself."

"You're wondering why I look like this." Night Owl Nell broke the silence. She tapped her goggles. "You're wondering why I keep myself in the dark."

"It's quite fashionable," Abigail complimented her, "but yes."

"I suffer from a rare condition. Sunlight hurts me, burns my skin. I can't go outside during the day, or if I do, I must be wrapped up like this, and I can only last for a short while."

"That's incredibly debilitating, and you're also a woman, too. Building your career, your life, it must have been very hard for you."

"Extremely."

"How…did you succeed against…all of those odds?"

"I took the job that no one wanted, worked hours no one wanted, assumed responsibilities no one wanted, and now I'm the one person they cannot live without."

"That's very impressive."

"What do you want to be when you grow up?"

"Oh, that's easy. I want to be a schoolteacher, like Mrs. Whitlock. She runs my school. She is so brilliant. I idolize her."

"That's a good profession." Night Owl Nell approved. "Women suffer setbacks and frustrations in any business, Abigail," Night Owl Nell advised her, "but don't ever lose heart. Don't ever give up. You can live out your dreams. Every step equals a step forward."

"I hope…one day, I can succeed like you."

"You can, Abigail, as long as you remember one thing."

Night Owl Nell reached into one of her pockets. She produced a silver coin and tossed it with a *ping* to Abigail, who caught it and then plucked it out of her palm. Pinching it between her two fingers, she examined the coin. On one side, it read:

AMISIT OCASIONEM INFIRMITATIS

"Opportunities lost because of weakness."

She flipped it over.

OCCASIONES PRO VIRIBUS NOVA INVENTA

"Opportunities for new strength discovered."

"Pick a flaw, any flaw, and you can flip that flaw over and reveal a strength, Abigail. My father, a chemist, could be absent-minded, sloppy, and disorganized. Still, he compensated for it by being an absolute genius in many ways. My mother could be very coldhearted and distant, but underneath that prickly layer, she possessed an incredibly strong, stable, consistent, and unwavering character and loyalty. On the other side of every weakness lies a strength. Keep that coin as a symbol to remind you, and if you ever find yourself in dire need of money, that coin is sterling silver," Night Owl Nell informed her, again monotone. "Trade it in at an official bank, and they will tell you that it equals ten dollars."

"Ten dollars!"

"I'm sorry I can't give you more, but Little Wade will furnish you with greater resources than I could ever provide."

"You've given me something even more precious, Nell. You've given me hope that I can find my friend again. Thank you."

"We'll see each other again soon, Abigail Reid."

Abigail got up to climb out of the carriage. When the door swung open, Night Owl Nell retracted herself to stay out of the sun as much as possible. Before she climbed out entirely, Abigail turned, careful to block as much of the daylight as she could.

"When I grow up, I hope I can inspire someone the way you have inspired me, and in such a wonderfully unique style too.... Except I prefer hats to bonnets. I find bonnets itchy, personally."

As she climbed out of the carriage, Abigail caught one last glimpse of Night Owl Nell's face, and she saw the hint of a tiny smile.

14

FAVORITE WORDS

As Night Owl Nell's carriage rolled away, *clop-clop-clopping*, Precinct Zero rolled up with several omnibuses to start loading the unconscious gang members. Little Wade, Watchtower, and Abigail, after bidding Sergeant Blood and his men goodbye, headed down the gritty, grimy streets of New York. Little Wade noticed a look of consternation on Abigail's face.

"What's wrong?"

"Nothing," Abigail grumbled. "It's just...the investigation...that all happened quite quickly."

"What did you expect? Did you think that Watchtower and I would lead you spelunking into tunnels so you could track the kidnappers yourself with a magnifying glass in your hand? Nonsense. When you need a matter investigated, and you need it done right, leave it to the professionals. As you can see, we saved a great deal of time."

"I suppose I'm just disappointed that no one cared enough to ask me these questions sooner. You've accomplished more in five minutes than the police have in over a month. Brooke could already be back home safe with her father. We could have resolved this long ago."

"We do what we can, when we can, as best as we can." Little Wade sensed her frustration, and he felt very frustrated himself. "We're on the case now, Abigail, and rest assured, we will not stop until we close it."

Abigail's eyes welled up, but she suppressed it. "All of those children...they must be so terrified. Brooke must be so frightened."

"Not for long," Little Wade assured her.

Watchtower, stopping for a moment, reached into one of his coat pockets. He handed Abigail a folded piece of paper. She unfolded it, revealing a charming, if a little rough, map of the Lower East Side. Abigail carefully examined the crude, hand-drawn map. It had clearly been created by more than one person, each contributor using different colors, techniques, styles. It contained all kinds of names for places like RASCAL'S ALLEY, MURDERER'S ROW, CREEPER CORNER, SCAVENGER STREET, KIDNAPPER'S CROSSING, NIGHTWALKER'S NEST, and WHERE CHILDREN DISAPPEAR. She also saw a phrase: WHERE IS NEW BANDIT'S ROOST?

"We call it the Map of Scratches," Little Wade explained. "It's been pieced together by many of our clients over the years. It tells you all of the secrets of the neighborhood and all of the places to avoid. Over the past decades, that parchment has passed through many hands. We hereby bequeath it to you."

"Oh my..." Abigail examined the map worriedly. "This neighborhood looks perilous and terrible."

"Look again." Little Wade crossed his arms while floating next to her.

Abigail peered closely once more at the Map of Scratches. She quickly discovered that it also contained very positive-sounding names like THE PECULIARLY POSITIVE SHOP, SAFE STREET, VERY SAFE STREET, HILARIOUS STREET, SOMETIMES SAFE STREET, THE MIRACULOUS MCANDREWS MILITARY MUSEUM (AND SAFETY ZONE), MR. KOSZURAS'S PROTECTIVE AREA, MRS. BUBULOV'S BUBBLING BAR (SORT OF) AND HAVEN FOR CHILDREN (DEFINITELY), among many, many others, and she blinked when she found the HAUNTED ORPHEUS THEATER (FRIENDLY GHOSTS...MOST OF THE TIME).

"Wait," she looked around and then back at the map, triangulating her position. "We're here...so...." She oriented herself again. "My home's location...is over...that way." She pointed. "It's not marked on the map."

Watchtower handed Abigail a pencil and then held out his palm. Using Watchtower's hard, metal hand as a desk, Abigail scribbled her home address onto the Map of Scratches. She also marked MAGRUDER'S TOY STORE, MR. LAIRD'S BOOKSHOP, MRS. WHITLOCK'S SCHOOL, and MR. KOWALSKI'S BUTCHER SHOP.

"This neighborhood and I may yet get along. It's starting to feel less and less like a maze," she remarked as she folded and flipped and manipulated the map several times as she absorbed its contents.

"Insert your own marks on any empty spaces in the map, Abigail. One by one, we will add the people and places that can offer you friendship and safety. We're about to add another."

As they strode along the sidewalks of the Lower East Side, Abigail relaxed and smiled. The day already seemed brighter. Little Wade flew circles around their location, twirling in the air like a bird. The night before, and indeed every day since she had moved to New York, the city always seemed grey, cold, and dead. Now, the whole city felt more...alive. Colors burst all around her. The neighborhood now seemed to be teeming with life. Well-dressed couples floated about the street like swans. Women whirled their parasols around like spinning water lilies. Children rushed about like puppies and cubs. Vendors, newsies, carriages, buggies, and a thousand people of all shapes and sizes bustled about like a dozen different animal species. Watchtower marched forward majestically like a giraffe. For every one of his long strides, Abigail made five small steps to keep up, giggling with each one. Maybe Little Wade had a point. Perhaps this city was not so terrible after all.

Watchtower stopped, and so did Little Wade.

"Ah, here we are."

In front of Abigail stood a storefront. An awning that hung above the front door read S.S. EXOTIC IMPORTS. In the window stood a porcelain statue of an elephant with over a dozen arms. Abigail recognized it as Ganesh, the great Hindu god. Next to Ganesh stood a

Buddha, next to the Buddha stood a Chinese dragon, and next to the dragon stood a beautiful statue of an angel. ALL WELCOME, a sign read.

"I've never noticed this shop before," Abigail remarked.

"You're going to discover that there's a great deal about your neighborhood that you did not know."

Little Wade swooped past Abigail and landed at the door.

"Coming?"

While Watchtower waited outside with his arms crossed, Abigail followed Little Wade into the store, opening the door with a loud *ding!* Inside, the shop contained just about anything anyone could ever think of. There were gorgeous wooden desks, chairs, tables, and shelves, all finely carved. Abigail passed shiny porcelain vases, jars, and urns, all decorated with brightly colored painted images from China. Polished cutlery and dishes glittered. Brilliantly carved and colored puppets, figurines, dolls, marionettes, and other toys decorated a section devoted to children.

Gorgeous, smooth tapestries tumbled down the walls like waterfalls of shimmering colors. One corner of the shop overflowed with blankets, cushions, and linens as puffy and soft as clouds. Abigail felt tempted to leap onto them and bounce up and down. Then there were whole beds and mattresses that were even more inviting. Intricate, plush carpets covered the floors. A hundred different kinds of lamps hung from a hundred different hooks on the ceiling at a hundred different levels, casting a hundred different luminescent colors throughout the store. The incandescent lights radiated perfumed smoke. In one corner of the store, a man wearing a turban sat cross-legged among a cluster of dozens of various musical instruments. This man quietly played the sitar while a cackling monkey climbed and leaped from object to object. Abigail also breezed past racks and racks of clothing of all styles from a dozen different cultures: India, China, Japan, and many more. There were shoes! So many shoes!

"Are we here to procure me some new clothes? Can we? Some of these shoes are dazzling!" She held up one particularly shiny pair and immediately began fantasizing.

Little Wade laughed at her enthusiasm, then smiled and shook his head.

"Not quite."

"I am pleased that you enjoy my wares," a voice boomed behind her. She turned around and dropped the shoes.

Abigail stared. Before her stood a tall man, not quite as tall as Watchtower, but still very tall. He wore a striking blue turban, which completely concealed his hair, and a dagger fastened the turban to his head like a silver clasp. He sported a magnificent mustache and beard, both dark brown tinged with silvery gray. A single scar streaked down his right cheek. Abigail recognized his magnificent clothing from one of her books. He wore a resplendent chola, a type of *bana* (robe) that warriors wear, coupled with a long, white *hajoori* (neckcloth) that tumbled down either side of his neck. On his feet, he wore leather *jutti* sandals.

"You're a Sikh," Abigail observed.

"Indeed, I am. My name is Saran Singh," he welcomed her with a deep, soothing voice. "I am very pleased to make your acquaintance, Abigail Reid." He also acknowledged Little Wade. "Good to see you again, old friend."

"You can see him?"

"Ever since I was a boy," Saran smiled. "I am at your service." Saran Singh bowed politely. "This shop remains open at all hours, both day and night. You will find it already on your Map of Scratches. You will always be safe here."

"I'm deeply grateful, Mr. Singh, but...you're not afraid of the Longshadows?"

"No," Saran answered her firmly, and then he nodded to Little Wade. "What you requested for her, it's here."

"Wait, something for me?" Abigail smiled brightly.

Saran Singh stepped over to a table. Something draped in purple cloth lay on its surface. Saran presented the bundle to Abigail, who felt something substantial and metal inside. Carefully unwrapping it,

Abigail peeled away the purple cloth to reveal a lustrous, metal pocket watch.

"Do you like it?" Little Wade sounded anxious.

"It's gorgeous," she marveled at it. "We haven't been able to afford a watch."

Saran Singh smiled gently. "There will be moments when your thoughts will be jumbled, possibly due to fear, confusion, stress, or surprise. When that happens, remember the watch. This watch organizes your time into a straight line, one second after the other. If you ever find yourself afraid or flustered, place your thoughts in order and think of them one at a time. Place your concerns in a straight line. You never have a million things to worry about, only a dozen at most."

"That's good advice. Thank you, Mr. Singh."

"Why don't you show Mr. Singh your lucky chess piece," Little Wade suggested.

Abigail pulled the queen out of her pocket and handed it to him. Saran Singh held it up, examining it as if it were a diamond. "Magnificent. May I borrow this for a short while? It's an excellent sample of your father's work."

"Is he going to help my father?" Abigail glanced excitedly at Little Wade.

"We will help each other," Saran Singh clarified. "Your father possesses immense talent, indeed mastery of his craft. I just need a little time to make the proper arrangements. In the meantime, I believe Little Wade has something to show you."

"Follow me please, Abigail," Little Wade drifted away, politely following a path that Abigail could easily navigate. They explored deeper into Saran Singh's wondrous, seemingly endless shop, filled with every possible object one could imagine. Venturing further and further in, Abigail found herself surrounded by glass.

She followed Little Wade into a separate room filled with glass boxes that contained all manner of creepy-crawly reptiles, amphibians, and insects, including snakes and spiders, swarms of ants, and wriggling frogs and anything that could quickly squirm out through a cage's bars. Abigail realized that, no matter how small some of these creatures were, if they got out, they could hurt and possibly kill people. While Saran Singh examined her father's work, Little Wade led Abigail on a little tour, navigating through the maze of terrariums.

"Tell me, Abigail, if you had to choose, what would be your favorite word in the whole world?"

As she tapped several of the glass boxes filled with critters and creatures, Abigail ruminated for a moment. "Hmm...I don't know. I think 'pickles.' Oh, wait, 'gobsmacked.' That's a word I've wanted to use for some time. I learned it last Thursday. That's it. 'Gobsmacked' is my favorite word."

Little Wade chuckled. "Charming."

"Why, do you have a favorite word?"

Little Wade smiled mischievously.

"Scorpion."

"That's because you're a boy," Abigail teased him.

"Oh no, let me show you."

He led her over to a desert terrarium, a glass box filled with sand, smooth stones, and cactus plants. On the side of the box, a label read HADRURUS SPADIX, DESERT, NORTH AMERICA.

Abigail pressed her nose against the glass wall.

"I don't see anything."

"Look, here it comes."

A tiny scorpion wriggled out of its little cave, scuttling on its legs, clicking its claws and snapping out with its pointed tail.

"Eeeew...," Abigail recoiled.

"Adorable, isn't it?" Little Wade admired it.

"I don't think so. It's an icky, ugly little thing." Then Abigail studied the label. "It says here that H. Spadix grows to be one of the most formidable scorpions, but it's tiny."

"It's not yet fully grown, Abigail. It's a child."

"On its own? That's dangerous. Does it not have parents?"

"Dead, I'm afraid. Nature can be unforgiving, Abigail, but we must learn to fend for ourselves. We can learn a lot from the small, unsightly things in this world."

"Ewwww...what can I learn from that...thing?"

"Think about it. Scorpions live their whole lives as small creatures. Even fully grown, this scorpion will only span about seven inches long. Most other creatures loom far larger and possess heavier, bulkier bodies. Scorpions must be afraid of almost everything, yet somehow they survive. Scorpions experience the world much like children do."

"I never thought of them that way before."

"Do you see that small metal hatch?" Little Wade gestured to one end of the terrarium and showed her a gate that led to an adjacent glass box.

"Yes."

"Go ahead and lift it."

She opened the gate, and two fully grown rats, black fur, pink tails, gleaming eyes, jagged teeth, slunk into the sandy glass box, licking their lips.

"Oh no," Abigail whispered. "Oh no, no, no."

Immediately, the rats both spotted the tiny scorpion, who tried to retreat toward its little cave, but it did not move quickly enough. Immediately, the rats lunged forward and encircled it, hissing and snapping their jaws. Encircled by the swirling rats, the little scorpion shrank into itself.

"No, no, no. Do something." Abigail pressed her hands against the glass.

"You just called it an icky, creepy little thing. Identify with it now, do you?" Little Wade challenged her.

"You made your point. Now, help it."

"No." Little Wade stood firm. "It's not my point to make."

One of the rats gnashed its teeth, forcing the little scorpion to flinch and retreat.

The second one snapped at one of its legs, clipping it.

The scorpion stumbled and fell.

"Please. I don't want it to die."

"Watch."

The rats, smooth and confident, moved toward the scorpion, but then something wondrous happened. Wounded, crippled, limping, the tiny scorpion, all tucked into itself, suddenly seemed to explode and triple in size. No longer afraid, but angry, the tiny scorpion raised its claws like a boxer raising his fists. It clicked loudly, and then it unfurled its tail, reared up on its legs, and lashed out with its sharp, poisonous stinger. *Bam!* It struck one of the rats directly on the nose. Squealing, whining, the rat winced and flinched and retreated. *Snap, snap, snap.* The tiny scorpion brandished its sharp claws at the rats, threatening to pluck out their eyes. The second rat snarled and charged, clamping its jaws on another of the scorpion's legs.

"No!" Abigail yelped.

Bam! Bam! The scorpion stung the second rat twice, directly on the nose and on the rodent's pink lip. Whimpering in agony, the second rat released the scorpion's leg and skittered away. The diminutive insect attacked, lunging forward, limping and injured, but it refused to give up. It spread its claws out wide like wings and whipped its tail around like lightning. Lurching forward one inch at a time, it forced the rats to scramble backward.

"It's...winning."

"No," Little Wade corrected her. "It won."

In one final push, the scorpion, clicking, darted forward and charged, imperfectly, scrappily, hobbling on its injured leg. Still, it did so with such spirit and ferocity that the rats, stung and frightened, tails tucked between their legs, retreated. Quivering blobs of black fur, they slunk out of the terrarium back through the door whence they came. Abigail slammed the gate shut. Then she immediately returned to her position and pressed her hands and face anxiously against the glass again. The little scorpion dropped its claws down into the sand and lowered its tail.

"It's so tired."

"It's tough."

Abigail shifted to the side and watched the rats in their own glass box, nursing their wounds.

"Will they die?"

"No. The scorpion's venom cannot kill or paralyze any organism, not yet anyway. Right now, the rats are burning and itching in pain. It will pass, but they've learned their lesson."

"I feel bad for them, too," Abigail confessed.

"That's because you're a good person."

"Why did you show me this?"

"Because nature and the world are neither good nor bad. Nature and the world will always be bigger than all of us. We're all little. Parents want to keep their children safe, but splashing around in a shallow, flat puddle or a pool will not prepare you to swim in the ocean. Baby birds, shortly after they hatch, get ejected out of the nest by their parents. They must learn to fly, or they die. Do you think that scorpion's mother taught it that life everywhere takes the form of a pleasant, soft, green grass field? No. This creature grew up properly prepared for a harsh environment. So did you. When you lived on the farm, did you slaughter animals for food?"

"Yes. My father often took me out hunting. I didn't enjoy it when he shot deer, but we ended up eating the whole thing. We wasted nothing. I understood why we needed to do it."

"You have a good, tender heart, Abigail. You're soft inside, but you need a tough shell to survive in this world, to protect yourself so you can grow."

Abigail returned to the little scorpion's terrarium.

"Scorpions can go for weeks without food, but they need water constantly. Those rats made the mistake of stepping between that creature's thirst and what it needed to survive." Little Wade gestured to a small, shimmering pool of water in the corner of the terrarium. Limping, the little scorpion scuttled over to it, dipped its small mandibles into the liquid and began to slurp, slurp, slurp. Abigail giggled. She found it cute, almost adorable, this tiny little thing gobbling up water.

"Will it heal?"

Little Wade shook his head.

"The leg will never fully grow back, but that's not the point. Something else will grow in its place."

"What?"

"Memory. When life tears away a piece of you, Abigail, a memory replaces it. Your mother died, and her memory took its place. One day, you will die, too. Your loss will leave a hole in this world, and the memory of you will take your place. Memories plug our wounds. That scorpion will never allow itself to be that vulnerable again. Next time, it will be even tougher to fight. I'll wager even three rats couldn't take it, and when it reaches full size, it won't be afraid of anything. So you see, Abigail, even the littlest thing can be brave if it needs to be."

"It's hard being brave all the time."

"What gave you the idea that you needed to be brave all the time? You don't have to do that."

"I don't?"

"No. Take a look at your new watch."

Abigail held it up. "It's beautiful. It feels very solid."

"Watchtower and I have gifted it to you," Little Wade began, "because your problem is not that you're afraid, Abigail. Your problem is that you're putting far too much pressure on yourself. No one will ever obligate you to be brave all the time. You only have a responsibility to be brave for exactly one second for every year old you are."

"Well...I'm thirteen years old, so only thirteen seconds?"

"That's it. Thirteen seconds on. Thirteen seconds off. Thirteen seconds brave and aware. Thirteen seconds afraid. Thirteen seconds on. Thirteen seconds rest. Like music."

"That doesn't seem like a lot."

"Most scary things happen quickly, but..."

"When they do happen, it feels like forever. I suppose that makes thirteen seconds plenty of time."

"That's why 'scorpion' is my favorite word. It reminds me that even the smallest of us can fight and scare things that are much bigger than we are."

Studying him for a moment, Abigail saw Little Wade in a different light. Even though he looked like a thirteen-year-old boy, at this moment Little Wade seemed very old and weary. His eyes looked sunken and sad. She felt deep sympathy for him.

"You feel overwhelmed too, don't you?"

"Every day," Little Wade confessed. "As capable as Watchtower and I can be, we have encountered an incredible amount of suffering and villainy in this city, so many disappointments, so many disillusioned children. We often feel well...much like our little friend here."

Taking another moment to watch the tiny scorpion still slurping water, Abigail added, "I suppose I was wrong to call that little scorpion repulsive. Now I think it's quite beautiful, in its own way."

"What sound does that watch make?"

Holding it up to her ear, she answered, "A clicking sound."

"What sound does a scorpion make?"

"Clicking."

"That's the true sound of bravery, Abigail. Courage does not take the form of a sword, nor a shield, nor a helmet, nor armor, nor a gun. Courage does not take the form of a weapon. Courage is a watch. Courage orders the mind. Courage means being calm, methodical, and consistent when chaos swirls around you. It keeps time and never falters. Turn the watch around, please."

She did. On the back of the watch, etched into the metal, she saw a symbol of a scorpion.

"Take this watch with you, Abigail. Remember, just because you're small does not mean that your enemies cannot be afraid of you. You can see what bigger creatures cannot, and then you can find a way to sting."

"I think that's a good lesson for both of us to remember."

"I could not agree more."

Abigail held the watch to her ear and shut her eyes. She listened to the rhythmic clicking. It soothed her. It soothed her because every stiff, loud click felt strong, unyielding, holding her up like her own bones. She felt incredibly comforted that one click promised that another one would come, and another, and another. The clicks came in precise, reliable intervals. They also never stopped. They seemed to march forward like soldiers, tireless, fearless, relentless. Then she heard much louder clicks, and clanks and whirs and pops and hisses, too. Opening her eyes, sensing someone behind her, she turned and saw Watchtower standing over her, tilting his top-hat-covered head to the side with a metallic whine.

"We do not want what happened to us to happen to anyone else. That's why we do what we do. I hope this lesson has been helpful, Abigail."

"It has, thank you."

"Now, with your consent, we would like to move on."

"I'd like to say goodbye before we go." Abigail took one last look at the little scorpion in the terrarium. The creature looked up at Abigail with its tiny eyes, studying her. Abigail swore that it waved at her with its little claw.

"What's going to happen to it?"

"Her. It's a female. Watchtower and I are going to adopt that little critter and give her a home in our office. It's the least we can do for the trouble we've put her through. We'll find her a suitable mate, and then she'll have children of her own. She'll be safe. We promise."

"Call her Pegleg," Abigail suggested. "Peggy can be her nickname."

"Peggy it is."

"Thank you, Peggy," Abigail whispered to the little scorpion. "You've taught me something I'll never forget."

"We've more to teach you, Abigail. The Great Gang Trap is coming, and when it does, you will need every second of your courage, or our plan will fail."

Following Little Wade and Watchtower, stepping out into the quiet alley behind Saran Singh's Exotic Imports and Exports, Abigail glanced around. At first, the three of them stood alone, but then Saran Singh excitedly joined them in the alley and pointed to one of its walls.

"To capture the best image, I will require that you stand close together," Saran Singh requested. He held up a small box covered in bright red leather. Abigail recognized it immediately.

"A camera!" Abigail marveled, and then she squealed in excitement. "Are we taking a photo together?"

"Indeed. We do this for all of our clients." Little Wade and Watchtower took position by a grey, brick wall. "Please, join us."

Excited, Abigail rushed toward the wall and quickly took position between Little Wade and Watchtower, who handed her a white placard that read:

A. REID
CLIENT
#6532

"Ready?" Little Wade flanked Abigail on her right. Watchtower stood on her left.

"Wait." Abigail adjusted her hair and smoothed her dress.

Barely able to contain her enthusiasm, Abigail struggled to stand perfectly still. Eagerly, she held up her client number and smiled one of the brightest smiles she had ever smiled in her whole life.

Click! Saran Singh snapped their picture.

"It will take some time to develop the film," Saran Singh apologized.

"Where will this image go? Can you provide me a copy?"

"Unfortunately not." Little Wade shook his head. "We cannot circulate photographic evidence of our existence. This picture will be framed and then hung on the wall in our office."

"You work out of an office?"

"Why wouldn't we? We consider ourselves legitimate professionals."

"Where do you work?"

"Our office is located at One Eighteen Moving Street," Little Wade offered in reply.

"Moving Street? What's Moving Street? I've never heard of it." Abigail unfolded and examined her Map of Scratches. "It doesn't appear on the map."

"It's a street that moves," Little Wade answered as if it were perfectly obvious. "It's never in the same place twice."

"It moves?"

"Quite efficiently."

"How is that possible?"

"I haven't the faintest idea." Little Wade shrugged. "To receive a proper explanation, you'd have to speak to the scientists that designed it. All I know, and all you need to know right now, is that Moving Street is a place where anything is possible. Anything."

"That sounds astonishing. Will we visit it? Please say yes!"

"Actually, we plan to take you there tomorrow."

Unbelievably excited, Abigail wanted to ask so many more questions. Before she could press him for more information, Saran Singh gently interrupted them by gesturing to the mouth of the alley.

"My shop cuts through the entire city block, Abigail. Step through it to the other side, and look where you are. I think you will be pleased."

"Thank you, Mr. Singh."

"Consider yourself welcome here, anytime, day or night. We never close, and we do not fear shadows here, of any length. Now, I must return to my business. Have a good day."

Saran Singh left them alone. Abigail gazed down the alley toward the street.

"Why did he say I would be pleased?"

"You don't know where you are, do you?" Little Wade grinned.

"I confess I don't." Abigail shook her head. "I just followed you."

"Well, consult your map."

Abigail checked her Map of Scratches and quickly oriented herself, finding Saran Singh's shop. Curious, she traced a line from her home address to Saran Singh's shop to...wait a moment! Abigail rushed down to the end of the alley and emerged onto the sidewalk. Immediately, crowds of people of all shapes and sizes mobbed her. Horses and carriages sped by, and Abigail took a moment to collect herself. Checking the map, she stood up on her tiptoes and peered through the crowd and across the hectic street. She smiled brightly because she recognized the storefront. Smiling, she turned to Little Wade and Watchtower.

"It's Mr. Laird's Bookshop! This marks the first stop on the first route, the perfect place to start!"

"We build the Secret Passage of Hope one contact at a time."

Little Wade drifted forward. Watchtower, strolling like a gentleman, joined Abigail. She took his hand. Gesturing to the bookshop, Little Wade floated through the crowd. Everything, people, horses, trolleys, passed through him harmlessly.

"Shall we pay a visit to your favorite place in the city?"

15

THE WISDOM OF MINERVA

Ding!

While Watchtower waited out front, Abigail and Little Wade entered Mr. Laird's Bookshop. Immediately, Abigail closed her eyes and breathed in deeply. She loved the smell of books. Opening her eyes, she spun around, smiled, and entered a maze of tall wooden bookcases. Shelves stretched up to the ceiling, overflowing with volumes. On the floor, there were books piled into pyramids and a few stacks that reached skyward like towers. Abigail loved the silences in bookstores, sacred like the inside of a library or church. It seemed appropriate to whisper.

"I spend hours in here. I'm certain Mr. Laird will help me."

"We will see." Little Wade sounded doubtful, which struck Abigail as odd. Expectantly, she glanced around the shop, looking for...there! An old man, white-haired, crookbacked, wearing a disheveled sweater and spectacles, emerged from behind one of the overstuffed bookcases. Clapping a book shut, blowing the dust off the cover, he coughed. Then Mr. Laird smiled brightly, recognizing the red-haired young lady who entered his store.

"Good morning, Abigail," Mr. Laird greeted her, his voice soft and frail.

"Good morning, Mr. Laird!" Abigail waved. She wanted to jump up and down with excitement; however, afraid she might topple some of the delicate piles of books, she refrained. Mr. Laird, stepping forward slowly, approached Abigail. He took every step very carefully, like a turtle, his hunched back overshadowing him like a shell. He peeked at the world through wonderfully round eyes under his spectacles, which hung on his long, beaklike nose.

"I've been waiting all morning for you," Mr. Laird smiled as he sat down at his desk near the front door.

"You have?" Abigail sat across from him excitedly.

"Indeed," he reached down, picked up a brown parcel marked **A. REID**, and placed it on the desk.

"For me?" Abigail squeaked, so loud Mr. Laird rubbed his ears.

"Yes, purchased early this morning by a Mr. Hector Excelsior Snodgrass, who left instructions that it be given to you. So, here it is."

Excitedly, Abigail seized the parcel and tore it open, revealing a magnificent, shiny book entitled: A YOUNG LADY'S GUIDE TO SURVIVING AND THRIVING ON THE STREETS OF NEW YORK CITY by Doctor and Captain Minerva Jonas.

"This is...perfect." Abigail flipped the book over and over in her hands. "Who's Minerva Jonas?"

"Oh, she's quite something," Mr. Laird explained. "According to the biography written inside, she used to live in this city as a young girl. Then she traveled to Europe and beyond, destined for great things. Ms. Jonas went on to become a scientist and a famous explorer, quite a fine illustrator, too, from what I could tell when I flipped through the pages before I wrapped it up. She traveled all over the world and embarked on many stupendous adventures. She wrote this book to advise young ladies, such as yourself. I guess Mr. Snodgrass wanted you to have it."

Abigail shot a glance over at Little Wade, who winked at her.

"It's been paid for, so off you go. Enjoy." Mr. Laird waved her away and began to work at his desk.

Stepping away from Mr. Laird, eagerly flipping through the pages,

Abigail whispered at Little Wade. "You bought this book for me, didn't you?"

"How can you tell?"

"Hector Excelsior Snodgrass? A positively ridiculous name! Obviously a pseudonym."

"Careful now," Little Wade cautioned her. "Don't insult the Snodgrasses of the world."

"All right, I won't. You're right. Snodgrass is a perfectly respectable name, but I'm right, aren't I? You bought this for me."

"Hector Snodgrass serves as a false identity that Watchtower and I employ from time to time whenever we conduct business with the world of the living."

Abigail tapped the cover of the book.

"Minerva Jonas, a former client, I presume?"

"Number one thousand two hundred and forty-seven." Little Wade beamed.

"I knew it!" Abigail uttered out loud, too loud, then quickly shushed herself. Diving back into the book, examining its table of contents, Abigail promptly discovered that it was divided into a series of lessons.

"Whenever you need excellent advice, crack open this book and let Minerva's wisdom guide and assist you." Little Wade gestured to the book. "Minerva used to be just like you, Abigail. When we first found her, she felt frightened and alone. Now, look at her."

Abigail found an illustration of Minerva Jonas. Tall, striking, her chin held high, Minerva wore a splendid uniform and stood on the bow of her very own ship. She wore a magnificent bicorne captain's hat, like the great naval commanders of old. Abigail noticed Minerva clutched a pocket watch in her hand.

"You gave her a watch too, like me."

"I taught her the same lesson. Her watch, however, bears the image of a fish, not a scorpion. Minerva used to be terrified of drowning and feared she could never hold her breath for long enough. Now, she sails openly on the sea."

"Do you think...that I could become like Minerva?" Abigail's tone was hopeful, but also nervous.

Little Wade smiled.

"If you remember only one thing that we ever teach you, Abigail, please remember this. When life is unfair, that is the perfect moment for you to do something unexpected. That is your chance to become someone extraordinary."

Deeply moved, Abigail examined the table of contents and then flipped to the beginning.

"Lesson #1," she read out loud. "Never forget the extraordinary women that lived and died before your time. They suffered more than you have and fought and sometimes died so you could appreciate whatever it is you possess now. Their spirits live on, and their combined wisdom speaks to you in books, in art and science. This is power passed down through generations. You are the latest in an army. Whenever you walk anywhere in any direction, march as if you fight for something, and will one day command."

Slapping the book shut, Abigail felt a swell of confidence. She turned to face Mr. Laird and strode up to him.

"Yes, Abigail," Mr. Laird acknowledged her, somewhat impatiently. "What else can I do for you this morning?"

His response struck her as odd. Just a moment ago, he had behaved very pleasantly. Nevertheless, Abigail persisted.

"Well, Mr. Laird, as you know, I walk throughout the neighborhood to get to school and to go to work and to visit the park and to come back again."

"Yes, and?"

"Well, as you know all too well, this neighborhood can sometimes be quite dangerous, especially at night. So I've been trying to establish a network of safe stops along my routes to and from school that I can duck into if there might be any problem..." Abigail let her voice trail off a bit, hoping that Mr. Laird might take the hint.

"Yes...and? Get on with it." He snorted rudely, which forced her to stumble through her words a bit.

"Well, I wondered if you could be one of those stops...perhaps in the evening, or afternoon if that's too much."

He huffed.

Nervously, Abigail qualified her statement. "It wouldn't require anything of you. You would just have to open your door, that is...if you happened to be here."

Immediately, Mr. Laird's smile vanished, and his face hardened. He shook his head firmly, and he retreated into himself like a turtle into its shell.

"Not a chance," Mr. Laird retorted. "I hoped you were going to buy something."

His reaction shocked Abigail.

"No? As in not at all?"

"I'm not going to stick my neck out for you. What happens out there in all that filth, I want no part of it! None of my business."

"But...I come here almost every day."

"Yes, you come in here every day, but you buy something one out of every thirty...if that. The one day you come in and pay, you matter, but as far as I'm concerned, the other twenty-nine you do not exist."

Hesitating, shaken, Abigail tried to reason with him.

"You were so cheerful just now when I bought a book from you."

"You didn't buy the book. Mr. Snodgrass, whoever he is, bought it for you. I'd like to see more of him. He paid me in fine, crisp bills."

"So, it's all about money with you."

"I'm not running a charity, girl. This business needs money to survive. If that will be all, I'm busy."

"But, Mr. Laird, the Longshadows almost took me last night while I ran home."

"All the more reason not to get involved. I don't want Longshadows and their ilk interested in my store. I'm lucky that most of them don't read or even think about books. That's the only reason I've managed to survive this long in this grimy neighborhood. Rent's cheap, though."

"Please, Mr. Laird, I need your help."

"Need? You think you're the only one who needs?" Mr. Laird

scolded her. "I tell you what I need, paying customers, not little girls that come in here and browse through this place as if it were some public library."

Abigail puffed up, and her cheeks burned bright red.

"Fine, if you won't help me, I will find someone who will!"

"Pay for another book, or be off with you," Mr. Laird sneered.

"I'm never coming back!"

"You'll come back." Mr. Laird smiled, and for the first time, Abigail realized how dirty his teeth were. "You love it here, and this bookstore's the only one in this neighborhood that will serve the likes of you. You'll come back."

Abigail stormed out of the bookshop. Little Wade followed her out. Whirling around, Abigail called out to Mr. Laird, who appeared at the doorway.

"How could you possibly be so mean? You own a bookstore?"

Sucking the tips of his fingers, the ratty old man practically spat out two words. "Paper cuts!" he barked at her just before he slammed the door in her face with a loud *thwack*! Stepping away from Mr. Laird's magical, musty bookshop, Abigail clutched A YOUNG LADY'S GUIDE TO SURVIVING AND THRIVING ON THE STREETS OF NEW YORK CITY. She stood there silently.

Tweeeeeet! They heard a loud police whistle.

A half-dozen police officers appeared from around the corner chasing a pair of Longshadows and a pair of Wild Cards.

"We were fighting each other!" one of the Longshadows yelled. "Why can't you just leave us alone!"

"Shut up! Keep running, and then we can go back to fighting once we've lost them!" one of the Wild Cards yelled in response.

Within a few moments, the Longshadows, Wild Cards, and police officers disappeared down the street.

"I suppose your plan is working," Abigail observed sullenly. "You told me this would happen. I just hope people aren't getting hurt."

"Only a few gang members that resist arrest. All aspects of our plan are coming together nicely."

"Not all," Abigail muttered bitterly and gestured to Mr. Laird's Bookshop.

"I'm sorry that did not work out." Little Wade consoled her while Watchtower stepped up next to her and placed his hand on her shoulder.

Holding the book tightly against her chest, Abigail shook her head, crying a little.

"I know you set my expectations," Abigail sniffled a little bit, "but nothing truly prepares you for the real thing. It...hurts."

"You believed you were on friendlier terms with him than you actually were."

Nodding sadly, Abigail agreed. "Yes. He always treated me so kindly whenever I visited the store, so polite, such a gentleman."

"Now you know..."

"He wants me to pay for books. He does not care about me, not really. I suppose I can consider that my first disappointment."

"There will be others, many others," Little Wade warned her. "Mr. Laird will not be the only one that will say no."

"I promise I will withstand those better than this one," she sniffled again.

"The first rejection always stings the most, but on the bright side, you will find that people will surprise you."

"He's right, you know. I'm still going to come to the bookshop and buy books. Mr. Laird may be a grouchy old man, but this is still my favorite shop."

"He will probably apologize the next time you come into his store," Little Wade counseled her. "He's no villain, just selfish and scared. Not an easy thing running a business in New York."

"He probably deals with all sorts of unpleasant people," Abigail added.

"You see, a little empathy softens the blow."

"Hmmm...still...I wish Mr. Laird had agreed."

"This will often happen in life, Abigail. The most obvious path will often be closed to you. The people you expect to help you won't, and the people you never thought would come through will. We work with what we have. Now, if you will permit us, Abigail, we would like to take you to a place where we know you will definitely be safe anytime. Would you like us to tell you about it, or would you like to be surprised?"

"No." She smiled. "I would like to be surprised."

"Very well then." Little Wade pointed west. "It's just two blocks that way. Onward."

As they headed toward the unknown location, Abigail read out loud from Minerva Jonas's manual. Because she firmly fixed her eyes on the pages, Abigail held Watchtower's hand with her left while balancing the book in her right hand, flipping the pages rather cleverly with her thumb like a very experienced reader. Little Wade, floating in front, would sometimes call out "left" or "right" as a signal to Abigail to move slightly to one side or another to step out of the way of someone walking in the opposite direction. This turned out to be very wise because very quickly, Abigail became completely engrossed, sucked into the world of Minerva Jonas's excellent advice.

"So, now that you know the first rule, can you tell me the second for surviving in New York City?" Little Wade inquired, guiding them down the crowded sidewalk. Watchtower slowly kept pace with Abigail.

"Oh, I am somewhere in the middle," Abigail laughed. "I find the book better balanced in my hand that way. I figured that because this book lacks any plot or story and instead contains a series of rules and advice, it does not matter where I start, only that I read the whole thing."

"Very well. Then, let us try Lesson Forty-Four." Little Wade continued forward, calling out, "Left!"

Shifting left, avoiding a mother with several small children following her like ducks, Abigail read out loud, "RULE NUMBER FORTY-FOUR. WHENEVER YOU ENTER SOMEPLACE NEW, MAKE SURE YOU CHECK ALL OF THE ENTRANCES AND EXITS, SO IF TROUBLE OCCURS YOU KNOW HOW TO GET OUT. IF YOU CANNOT DETECT ANY CLEAR EXIT AFTER YOU ENTER, THEN YOU MAY CONCLUDE MOST CERTAINLY—TRAP! IF YOU FIND YOURSELF IN AN

UNPLEASANT SITUATION, LOOK AROUND YOU, BE AWARE OF YOUR SURROUNDINGS. DON'T PANIC AND LOSE YOUR WITS. LOOK AROUND!"

"So, what do you think of Minerva Jonas?"

"I find her eminently sensible," Abigail complimented the volume. "She delivers very sage advice."

"Time for one more," Little Wade weaved in and out through the crowd, even though he could pass through them. It warmed Abigail's heart when she realized that he did it for her benefit so that she knew where and when to avoid crashing. Abigail dug back into the book, flipping the page.

"RULE FORTY-FIVE. WHEN YOU FEEL LOST IN THE DARK, BE LIKE THESEUS, THE ANCIENT GREEK HERO WHO CARRIED A BALL OF STRING INTO THE LABYRINTH WHEN HE FACED THE HORRIBLE MONSTER, THE MINOTAUR. WHENEVER YOU GO ANYWHERE, MAKE SURE YOU KEEP TRACK OF YOUR PATH SO YOU CAN RETRACE YOUR STEPS AND FIND YOUR WAY BACK AGAIN. ANYWHERE CAN FEEL LIKE A MAZE WHEN YOU FEEL AFRAID OR UNPREPARED, BUT IF YOU BRING A BALL OF STRING, EITHER LITERAL OR METAPHORICAL (I.E., IF YOU PLAN CAREFULLY AND KEEP YOUR WITS ABOUT YOU), THEN YOU CAN ESCAPE OR MASTER ANY LABYRINTH AND AVOID HAVING TO EXPERIENCE ANYTHING ON THE MONSTER'S TERMS. REMEMBER WHERE YOU CAME FROM. DON'T GET LOST. DON'T LOSE YOUR WITS. DON'T FORGET WHO YOU ARE."

"Oooohh, I've read all about Theseus!" Abigail bounced up and down as she walked, adjusting her tiny hand in Watchtower's oversized glove. "He wasn't the strongest of the ancient heroes, but the cleverest—his greatest weapon: his wit. Good advice for a young girl," Abigail noted, and then she slapped the book shut when Watchtower stopped. Little Wade paused as well, allowing a few people to pass through him.

"We're here."

Glancing around the intersection, Abigail scrunched up her nose, uncertain. "Where are we?" Then she felt a sudden chill when she recognized the location.

Little Wade presented the crowded intersection bustling with people. "The Longshadows snatched Brooke Adams right here."

"How...did you know?" Abigail gulped.

"Check your Map of Scratches, Abigail." Little Wade gestured to their surroundings. "Welcome to Kidnapper's Crossing."

While Watchtower and Abigail stood on the sidewalk, Little Wade floated into the middle of the crowded intersection, allowing pedestrians, horses, carriages, dogs, and trolleys to pass through him. Undisturbed, he raised his hands and began to conjure images.

"Did you walk to school every day along this side of the street?"

Abigail nodded. An illusion, indeed a perfect replica of her, red hair, freckles and all, appeared, holding hands with a ghostly image of a man.

"The Longshadows that first threatened you, accosted you, Brooke, and Mr. Adams right around here?"

He marked a spot with an illusion, reconstructing the scene.

"Yes. Mr. Adams took us this way to walk us to school faster. I suppose not all shortcuts lead to good places."

"It's a good spot here, a bottleneck. The crowd crushes together here at this corner. Very easy for a snatcher to strike."

Little Wade, sweeping his hands from left to right, conjured up a faint image of a young girl as well as replicas of several Longshadows.

"I do not know what Brooke Adams looks like, so I apologize for the crudity of my image of her. I merely use it as a placeholder. Observe."

Holding Watchtower's hand, Abigail peered into the crowd as Little Wade, manipulating his illusions like a puppeteer, recreated the scene of the crime, demonstrating the kidnappers' tactics.

"The Longshadows worked in a group, moving deliberately. The first, the Lookout, observed Mr. Adams and Brooke, giving the signal to strike. Mr. Adams did not hear the whistle because the noise of the city masked it."

One of the illusory Longshadows placed his fingers in his mouth and whistled.

"Two more Longshadows, known as Bustlers, caused a commotion, forcing the crowd to bunch up here…here…and here…you see?"

"Yes." Abigail observed the illusory crowd. "Mr. Adams told the police a chaotic throng of people overwhelmed him."

"The innocent crowd had no idea that they were being manipulated like a herd of sheep. Then a fourth member of the Longshadows, the Shiner, distracted Mr. Adams for a handful of seconds, leaving an opening for the fifth, the Seizer."

Abigail watched the recreated scene. The Seizer darted out through the crowd, snatched Brooke away from her father, and dragged her through the mass of people. Both Bustlers joined him, surrounding Brooke.

"Notice they quickly outnumbered her. Brooke, shocked, uncertain, did not know how to react. The Longshadows not only weaponize fear, but also confusion and hesitation."

"They trapped her in a maze of people," Abigail observed. "They gave her only one way out, their way."

"Yes. Brooke undoubtedly, eventually summoned up the will to scream and shout, but not until around this point." Little Wade focused his illusion on the far corner, an entrance to a menacing alley. "Before she could, however, they gagged her, tied her, bagged her."

Abigail, still holding Watchtower's hand, crossed over to the alley, where Little Wade darted ahead, scouting. Abigail watched him dive underneath the sidewalk and street, swimming through stone like water, searching for something until he shouted, "*Here!*"

Heading down the alley, Abigail and Watchtower discovered a rusted round sewer cover, a manhole. Watchtower reached down and plucked up the heavy metal object as if he were simply picking up a coin. The moment he lifted it and exposed an entrance to the sewer, Abigail immediately stepped back, repulsed by the nauseating stench.

"They used the sewers to spirit her away?"

"Yes, this is one of the city's most remarkable innovations. The authorities are currently planning to construct tunnels such as these under the entire city, and their plans are well underway. Watchtower and I still remember when citizens used to toss their waste out the window into ditches. Thankfully, the sewers allow all of that waste to flow beneath the city, out of sight, out of smell. Unfortunately, the Longshadows and other gangs now use it for nefarious purposes. This tunnel network, although still incomplete, stretches for miles."

"Another labyrinth," Abigail whispered to herself.

Little Wade nodded and then dove down into the stinking hole. From down in the pit, barely visible, Little Wade called up to Abigail and Watchtower.

"I'm going to delve down here and see how far this goes and where it comes out. I can't smell anything anymore, so it's no bother."

"While I will remain with you," another Little Wade (Polyplot) materialized next to Abigail.

Abigail, leaning over to look down into the disgusting tunnel, stifled her instinct to retch and called down to Little Wade, who glowed, illuminating the dismal darkness around him.

"While you are down there, search for power lines. Head toward the power station on Pearl. We can cross-reference where the sewer tunnels and electrical cables intersect," Abigail offered. "We can assume they took her somewhere in that area. If we share those findings with Precinct Zero, we'll connect another piece of the puzzle."

"Abigail Reid, that marvelous idea supersedes any of mine."

"Well, it's exactly what Theseus would do."

"Watchtower, please take care of our client while I'm gone. I'll be off."

"Will you be all right? I don't like the idea of you down there all by yourself."

"Oh, no need to concern yourself," Little Wade laughed. "I delve dangerously like this quite regularly. One of the perks of being already dead, very little can harm me. I'll see you both very soon."

Little Wade zipped down the tunnel, vanishing. Abigail turned to Watchtower.

"He will be all right, won't he?"

Watchtower placed a hand on Abigail's shoulder and nodded.

"It's just he used the precise words 'very little can harm me,' not 'nothing.' So, what could possibly harm a ghost?"

Watchtower clicked his fingers together with a *clickety-clackety-clack*.

Ping!

Another note popped up from his chest pocket. He handed her the note.

THERE IS MUCH YOU STILL DO NOT KNOW. STOP. DO NOT WORRY ABOUT HIM. STOP. WE HAVE BEEN DOING THIS FOR YEARS. STOP.

Comforted somewhat but still a little troubled, Abigail folded up the note and slipped it into her pocket. She did not want to litter.

"All right, shall we continue?" The Little Wade (Polyplot) politely gestured to the mouth of the alley. Abigail heard a terrible commotion, the sound of men grunting and yelling and then *tweeeet*, more police whistles.

"What is that?" Abigail rushed toward the sounds. Watchtower replaced the sewer cover with a loud *clang* and stomped after her.

When she emerged back out onto Kidnapper's Crossing, Abigail jumped when more Longshadows and Wild Cards, fighting viciously, burst out of a nearby building and spilled out onto the street. All around them, citizens reacted and backed away, clearing a path. Brawling and bashing each other, the Longshadows and Wild Cards disturbed the entire area, causing chaos within the crowd. Within just a few ticks of Abigail's watch, however, a squad of police officers quickly rushed out of the crowd and arrested the two gangs. One of the officers, an agent of Precinct Zero, turned and winked at Abigail, Little Wade (Polyplot), and Watchtower, eliciting an excited yelp from her.

"You told me this would happen. The fight from the theater spilled out across the city."

"The plan is working," Little Wade assured her. "For every scuffle like this that breaks out, the police will make more arrests."

"How do the police know where to find them?"

"Look up."

Abigail did and gasped. Dozens of Little Wade Polyplots soared above the neighborhood, circling like ravens.

"You can cover several city blocks." Abigail recalled her conversation last night. "You're always watching, aren't you?"

"Always."

"This is still not the Great Gang Trap, though?"

"Oh, no. We're just cranking up the spring. Soon...we will release it and inflict more damage to organized crime in one day than we have in years."

"I'm so tempted for you to reveal your plan, but I also soooooo want to be deliciously surprised when you do, so please keep me in suspense."

"Your wish is our command." Little Wade (Polyplot) bowed.

"So, are you the real Little Wade or...I don't know?"

"We're all the same," he answered, "but the center of our power is always closest to you."

As the police subdued the gang members, Abigail pondered their next move. "Where should we go now?"

"Check your map," Little Wade advised her.

Unfolding her map and quickly scanning it, Abigail traced a few possible paths.

"Why don't we focus on this section here, between Mr. Laird's Bookshop and the General Store on Bowery Street. I often take that route after shopping."

"Excellent idea," Little Wade assented, and they departed, leaving behind the gang members, the police, and Kidnapper's Crossing. Continuing toward Bowery Street, with Little Wade flying beside her, Abigail resumed leafing through Minerva Jonas's *A Young Lady's Guide for Surviving and Thriving on the Streets of New York City*. She began to read but then clapped the book shut.

"Something the matter?" Little Wade paused in midair.

"Well, before you showed me Kidnapper's Crossing, you told me you were taking me to a place where I would always be safe, so why show me one of the most dangerous places in the city? You don't lie to children, so if I assume you were telling the truth, then your remark did not make sense. For the past few minutes, I've been trying to figure it out, and I think I just did."

Watchtower stood by her. Little Wade drifted closer to her. "Go on."

Abigail considered her words carefully for a moment before she spoke.

"You showed me how the Longshadows kidnapped Brooke. You showed me their tactics. Now, whenever I walk these streets, I know what to spot. Now, whenever I find myself at that intersection or another one like it, I'm going to be much harder to snatch. I just watched five grown men kidnap one little girl. That's extremely cowardly. These men are neither monsters nor demons. They are... painfully ordinary. I see that you're trying to teach me to be more aware, but your real goal is demystification."

"Demystification?" Little Wade looked at her quizzically.

"Yes. You're doing this so that I see them as simply...people, so they don't loom as menacingly in my mind anymore. This leads me to a question. The actual, real number of full-fledged Longshadows... how many troops do they command on the streets?"

"I estimate their total membership at just over a hundred."

"Interesting. They seem to be infinite and everywhere, but that's precisely what they want me to believe, what they want us all to believe, isn't it?"

"Indeed. The Longshadows practice the art of 'projecting power,' creating the illusion that they're far more numerous and formidable than the reality. The original leader of the Longshadows began his career as a stage magician who perfected the art of shadow puppetry."

"You mean like Mr. Todesco, from the Orpheus?"

"Precisely, only Mr. Todesco used it to bring joy to people's lives; however, the original leader of the Longshadows used his skills for more nefarious purposes. He knew how to keep a multitude of people afraid and at the edge of their seats."

"So it's an optical illusion," Abigail continued. "Even the smallest object, presented next to a flame, can cast an outsized shadow on the wall. The Longshadows hold their territory by creating a great myth and mystery about themselves, but the more you truly know about them, the more human, more imperfect, but less powerful they become. If we can demystify them, we take away their power to intimidate the neighborhood."

"Abigail, you have encapsulated the situation perfectly."

They continued toward Bowery Street. Abigail skipped alongside Watchtower while burying herself in Minerva Jonas's book. Then, after a few more minutes of walking, Watchtower stopped. Abigail interrupted her reading and spotted the colorful awning of Mr. Magruder's Toy Emporium down the block. Her heart jumped a little bit. She assured herself that Mr. Magruder would be far kinder than Mr. Laird, or at least she hoped so.

"All right, let's look at your map," Little Wade hovered in place. Abigail unfolded her map and they examined it together while Watchtower shielded them from the passing crowds.

"I usually head straight to the General Store on Bowery Street, then I stop by Mr. Magruder's, then head to Mr. Laird's Bookshop, then head home, so we need to find people willing to help me on either side of Mr. Magruder's. Where should we begin?"

"There," Little Wade pointed to a series of storefronts that stretched down the block. "Watchtower and I know that the same family owns all of those different stores. If we speak to the owner, an old Italian man named Mateo Russo, we should be able to unlock all of those stores as possible safe havens for you."

"Mateo Russo?"

"Yes, a stubborn man, but also a grandfather who loves children, Russo currently finds himself in a very precarious situation with several problems that need solving. You can assist him, and then he will prove to be a valuable ally. He befriended Mr. Magruder years ago, and he should be visiting his shop right about now. You can speak to both of them at once."

"Let's hope this goes better than the last time."

"Chin up," Little Wade encouraged her. "Not everyone will say yes, but that means..."

"Not everyone will say no," Abigail finished his sentence.

"That's the spirit. All right, let's begin."

Eagerly, Abigail, holding Watchtower's hand, began to cross, but not before sensing that someone, or something, was watching her. Ignoring the feeling, dismissing it as just nerves, she continued. Stepping forward into the crowd, Abigail felt as if she were wading into a fast rushing river. She could feel Watchtower gripping her more tightly as the multitudinous horde of people overtook them, jostling them, pushing them, pulling them.

"Wait...something's wrong." Abigail adjusted her grip on Watchtower's hand. She felt a strong current pulling her away from him. Little Wade, his back to her, floated forward effortlessly. He did not notice her.

"Wait," she called out, but the overpowering noise of the mass of people drowned out her voice. She lost her grip on Watchtower's hand. *"Wait!"* Abigail cried out, then stumbled. Suddenly, she felt a cold, icy hand seize her wrist and pull her toward a shadowy cloak, enveloping her in blackness.

16

PEEKABOO

Opening her eyes, startled, Abigail awoke in a cramped, musty room, some kind of basement workshop. It smelled like rusted metal and rotten flowers. Abigail could taste iron in the air. Only a single, glowing red lantern illuminated the entire room. Little Wade and Watchtower were gone. *What happened?* Abigail glanced around the room. She still clutched Minerva Jonas's manual in her hand and immediately wanted to flip through it to find some way out of this, but the instant she cracked the book open, she realized that she was not alone in the room.

Shhhhhhh click! Shhhhhhh click! Shhhhhhh click! Abigail heard someone sharpening something. Turning around, peering into the faint, red light, she saw him. Dressed entirely in black, he wore a military uniform beneath a long overcoat. His boots were smeared with mud. His pants were coarse, durable, and full of pockets. He wore workman's gloves, rugged and tough, like what soldiers would wear in cold weather. A darkened metal breastplate that glimmered like an insect's shell encased his entire torso. He clicked, clinked, and clanked, not in a musical way like Watchtower, but like a man carrying hidden tools, like a thief. He crouched down in the dark, hunched over, like a rat feeding. *Shhhhhhh click Shhhhhhh click!* As this man moved closer to Abigail, she could smell dank water, filth, gun oil, and gunpowder. Then, as he inched into the light, she saw his head.

He did not wear a top hat like Watchtower, nor a tall, conical cap like a Precinct Zero officer, nor a fisherman's cap like her father wore when he worked. Instead, this mysterious figure wore a hood over his head, like the angel of death.

The metallic clicking paused. Slowly, the hooded apparition turned around, revealing his face. He wore a mask, a carved white pair of hands that covered his face as if to play peekaboo. Abigail saw no eyes, no nose, no mouth, just white hands concealing his entire face, and the fingers and knuckles were perfectly detailed as if someone had crafted them out of ivory.

In the red light, objects on his chest glinted. At first, Abigail mistook them for jewelry. Peering closer, she realized they were shotgun shells, tucked into a leather bandolier slung across his armored chest. Shifting position, he revealed the source of the clicking. He loaded a lever-action shotgun, the kind Abigail's father once owned on the farm, a heavy weapon with a barrel like a small cannon. One by one, he loaded buckshot shells into the metal magazine tube. He slid one last round into the weapon with a loud *shhhhhh click!* After he finished, he set the shotgun down on the floor with a *clank*. Abigail slowly backed away.

"Who are you?" she asked, trembling. "Where am I?"

The Man in the Peekaboo mask cocked his head to the side.

"What do you want?"

He spread out five fingers on one hand and set his fingertips down on the floor, and he arched his back and tensed up his legs as if preparing to pounce. With his other hand, he reached behind him to the small of his back, and he slowly pulled out a long, sharp tomahawk. He clutched it in his hand so tightly that it seemed as if it were part of him. Raven feathers dangled from the weapon.

"No, please, *don't!*"

The masked man lunged at Abigail. He raised his tomahawk. Screaming at the top of her lungs, Abigail turned and ran.

Sprinting after her, the Man in the Peekaboo Mask chased her, slashing at her with the tomahawk. Abigail frantically scrambled away, crying out for help. "*Watchtower! Help me!*"

Stumbling through the red-lit, shadowy room, she darted to the left and turned a corner—*crack*! The tomahawk's blade smashed into a section of the wall right next to her head. Crying out, Abigail stumbled backward, dropping her book. Screeching, the masked man leaped at her and swung again, barely missing her, sparking against the stone floor. Rushing away from the assailant, crying out for help, tears overflowing in her eyes, she turned left, right, right, left again, only to find herself back where she started. Glancing around frantically, she turned right again when she felt an icy grip on her wrist.

Yanking her toward him, the Man in the Peekaboo mask seized Abigail. His fingers felt as strong as a steel shackle. Screaming, Abigail shut her eyes. Clamping down on her wrist, the Man in the Peekaboo mask raised his feathered tomahawk with his other hand, and then he brought it down onto her forehead like a hammer.

Nothing happened. Abigail expected her skull to be split open and her brains splattered all over the floor. Neither occurred. Slowly, she opened her eyes. The Man in the Peekaboo mask froze in place, like a statue. Panting, her heart thumping in her chest, Abigail fell backward, amazed. Little Wade materialized out of thin air. The red lantern floated into the air and then became Watchtower's face as he reappeared. They both loomed over her. Her heart pounded, and she stared at them, surprised.

"What...where are we?" Abigail, still breathing frantically, demanded.

"Did you see the door behind you?" Little Wade, floating cross-legged, his tailcoat trailing in some imaginary wind, pointed at the wall. Abigail turned and immediately detected a red door.

"The door stood right behind you. You obviously felt threatened, frightened. Why didn't you escape? You froze in place, and then ran around completely chaotically, no plan, no method at all. If this had been a real attack, you'd be dead...or worse."

"Door? But there were so many twists and turns?"

"Were there? Take a moment. Look around."

Her heart pounding, her blood up, Abigail quickly sprang up and dusted herself off. Her face glowed red, and her eyebrows created a pair of knife edges. Stomping around, she examined her surroundings. Sure enough, what she had perceived as a complicated maze turned out to be nothing more than a pair of square stone columns.

"It seemed so much bigger, more intricate."

Little Wade appeared next to her. "It wasn't. Notice all of the doors?"

Abigail moved about the room and examined the walls of the chamber. Sure enough, there were doors there, too. Little Wade warped and appeared next to her again, startling her.

"You blew straight past them. You panicked, and you performed no better just now than you did last night, lost again. Now you're understanding the purpose of this lesson."

"You...kidnapped me? You...tricked me?"

"...and you utterly failed."

"You *tricked me!*"

Infuriated, Abigail lunged at him, forgetting his incorporeal form. When she passed straight through him and crashed to the floor, scuffing herself, she coughed and cursed.

"Are you quite finished?" Little Wade chastised her.

"How does this help me...to terrify me out of my wits with monsters? Why did you do this?"

"You signed the contract, Abigail. You agreed to be trained. Now pay attention." The sudden sharpness in his voice alarmed her. "It's to prove a point. There will always be unknown elements that attack without warning. Even after all we've taught you, you immediately collapsed back to your old, bad habits."

"Bad habits?"

"Did you check your surroundings when we crossed the street?"

"No, but I thought..."

"What, that I scouted ahead and found nothing? I warned you we were not infallible. Did you glance around for Longshadows or any areas where Longshadows might take advantage? A quick check, anything? Were you aware of your surroundings? Did you even do what Minerva Jonas advised you to do?"

"No."

"Or did you just expect Watchtower and me to do all of the work for you?"

Abigail stooped down and collected Minerva Jonas' manual from the floor. "I just felt safe with you. That's all."

"We will not always be around to protect you, Abigail. We need you to sharpen your senses. You must not take your safety for granted. You need not be paranoid nor nervous all the time, but neither should you lull yourself into complacency. Ever."

Calming herself, Abigail considered this.

"All right, you've made your point. I'm slightly less angry at you now, but honestly...what are the chances that I'm going to be attacked by a magical, masked assassin with a battle axe?"

"Tomahawk."

"I know it's a tomahawk, but you see my point."

"Don't be obstinate, Abigail, or so literal. At any moment, this world will throw something wholly unexpected at you, something different every time, a new threat. You must be ready no matter what comes your way."

"So you decided to teach me by attacking me with this ghastly thing?"

"It worked, did it not?"

"I did lose my composure, didn't I?" Abigail admitted. "I completely froze."

Sighing, Little Wade relented. "Watchtower and I have learned over the years that, to make our lessons stick, we need to make them...unpredictable."

"Well, mission accomplished," Abigail wiped her sweaty brow.

They laughed together.

"Where are we, anyway?" Abigail gestured to her dark, dusty surroundings. Watchtower adjusted his breathing, pumping more gas into his fiery face, illuminating the musty chamber. Red radiance spread everywhere.

"Inside Watchtower's coat," Little Wade explained. "On the street, when you broke away from him, he circled around and attacked you in your blind spot. He seized you, tucked you into his coat, and walked you back to the alley behind Saran Singh's shop. There, he currently stands masquerading as a lamppost in that alley. At this moment, we dwell inside a pocket space in a parallel dimension. You inquired earlier how Watchtower disguises himself as a streetlamp and then dramatically appears. Now you know."

Abigail pointed to the Man in the Peekaboo mask. "You did not select this apparition at random, did you?"

"You must know your enemy, Abigail. As fearsome as they may be, the Longshadows serve the forces of darkness as low-level brutes, thieves, murderers, but the real threat...is him."

Little Wade circled the illusion, which stood perfectly still, like a statue.

"We don't know who he is, or what he is, or where he came from. We have fought and nearly destroyed him many times, but ultimately failed. He has tormented us for decades. Kidnappers pray to him and worship him as some kind of...god. He considers every stolen child as a sacrifice to him. He created his own 'moving room' like this one, his own parallel, pocket dimension, and he can appear out of nowhere. When snatchers find themselves attacked or overwhelmed, they can summon him to assist them. When he appears, he often turns the tide of battle."

Circling the illusion, Abigail studied his face. "Why does he wear that mask?"

"Will you remember this moment?"

"How could I forget this?"

"Tell me, you played peekaboo when you were young, did you not?"

"Every day with my mother and father," Abigail answered nervously. "Why do you ask?"

"You enjoyed the game, correct? You consider playing the game a precious memory, yes?"

"I do. I was very young, but I definitely remember moments."

"So now, when you think of peekaboo, will you think of your mother and father, or will you think of him?"

"Oh."

"That's why he wears it, Abigail. The greatest thieves climb inside your mind. He seizes upon our most precious memories from our childhood and ruins them. The creators of peekaboo designed the game to teach a child that something, even though you cannot see it, still exists. The game shows you that when something disappears, it will come back. Your parents cover their faces and vanish, but then they reappear, and you squeal in delight. This becomes a lesson you carry with you. When your parents leave the room, you feel sad, but then they return. As time goes on, they leave the room or pass out of sight, you stop feeling sad or scared because you become more and more confident that they will reappear, just like in the game. The child learns that just because its mother or father vanished for a brief moment, they will come back, and the world will not fall apart. We learn that just because we become separated from things we love, that does not mean we have lost them. We learn to believe in things we cannot see because we contain them inside us."

"Peekaboo teaches us how to be brave, our first lessons in courage. I never realized that."

Little Wade gestured to the masked figure. "Precisely. He wants to make sure that you disappear and never come back, or that you come back forever changed, tainted, so you belong to him. His mask makes a mockery of a childhood tradition. All of the suffering and horrors he inflicts in this city, all of the lives he destroys, all of the families that he terrifies and tears to pieces, they all mean nothing to him. They are all simply sadistic pawns in a sick game of disappearing and reappearing children."

"This isn't just about my fear, but my father's fear as well. That's why he became so angry with me this morning," Abigail realized. "He's terrified to let me out again because he's afraid I'll disappear. When we were in the country, he would let me roam all around because he felt confident that I'd return. Now he fears I'll never come back. That's why he lashed out at me, why he tried to coop me up in the attic. I thought I understood his fear, but now I...I feel it. Parents must also learn to be brave. Parents worry every day and night for the rest of their lives."

"Every day, Abigail, you vanish, gone from your father's sight. Every day you must understand, he hopes, prays, that the same little girl that left him in the morning will come back, but he must accept that he cannot control everything that happens to you. Every time you reappear, you will be different. There will be many times when you will suffer, and your suffering will change you. When you return to your father he will blame himself because he could not be there for you. Every parent must painfully accept that reality. You must be strong not only for yourself but also for him."

Abigail held up her scorpion watch. "You and Watchtower want me to learn to become brave in those moments when I'm on my own. You want me to become independent, to keep my own time."

"Yes. If you want your father to set you free, then you need to show him that his love for you has made you strong. Whenever you reappear, show him that, even though life can treat you harshly, you will persevere and that he has not failed you."

Watchtower tossed a pair of small, white objects toward Abigail. They clattered and clacked and rolled across the floor until they rested against her foot. Reaching down, Abigail picked up a pair of white dice, but instead of black dots on their surfaces, they had little carved eyes, one, two, three, four, five, six, on each side. She shivered when she realized that the dice were carved from bone. Little Wade pointed and moved his finger like a pen, and a poem, written in floating fire, appeared next to her. Abigail read the words out loud.

> "Two eyes forward. One eye down.
> Six eyes above you like spikes on a crown.
> Three eyes left. Four eyes right.
> Five eyes behind you, day and night.
> Six of sixty, roll the dice.
> Six of sixty, save your life."

"Please, take out your watch."

Abigail did. It *click-click-clicked* in her hand.

"Take six seconds out of every minute to glance in six directions. Check your surroundings for threats. The dice serve to remind you. Whenever you travel anywhere, exploring, doing errands, but especially whenever you arrive somewhere new, roll the dice, Abigail, or else someone will roll *you*. Six seconds amounts to a small price to pay, a quick flick of the wrist or, in your case, six quick turns of the neck to ensure your safety."

Abigail clacked the dice together in her palm. "Why did you give me two?"

"Because you're going to keep one for yourself and give the other one to Brooke Adams when we rescue her."

"I just made the same mistake she made. She was not aware of her surroundings, and look what happened to her."

"Precisely. I apologize for the harshness of the lesson. Demonstration falls short. We wanted to plunge you into the same experience, so you remember how it feels. We need to burn these lessons into your memory, into your very muscles, so that when fearful moments come, and they will, you do not stumble back into confusion."

"You've lost clients in the past. You feel culpable for not training them better," Abigail observed. Her comment surprised Little Wade, who gasped, and then exhaled, shutting his eyes.

"Yes. Your perceptive instincts pierce me. Behind my irritation, what you hear in my voice...is guilt."

"I won't be like the others. I will figure this out. My mind races now. I think you're a wonderful teacher, a bit unorthodox, but...nevertheless effective."

"I am nothing, Abigail. Watchtower is nothing. We are nothing. Your enemy is your greatest teacher. Never forget that."

Abigail glared hard at the Man in the Peekaboo Mask.

"My enemy is my greatest teacher."

"It's impossible to never be afraid, Abigail, but it is possible to always be aware."

"Oh, I'm aware all right, but not afraid." Abigail clutched the dice in her hands. "I'm angry."

"In a few days, Watchtower and I will move on, and you will be on your own, Abigail," Little Wade admonished her. "Two days remain for your training, but unfortunately, as of right now, you are not yet ready to protect yourself."

"I'll do better next time. I promise. I'll be better prepared."

"There is good news and bad news."

"What's the bad news?"

"There exists only *one* person you can rely on one hundred percent, *you*."

"And the good news?"

"You can do a hundred different things to help yourself. When the Secret Passage of Hope is complete, that number will multiply to a thousand."

"So are we going to talk to Mateo Russo and Mr. Magruder?"

"No, Abigail. Not now. It's time to take you home."

17

THE MASTER PLAN

They reemerged in the alley behind Saran Singh's shop. Blinking, Abigail readjusted to the daylight. Watchtower draped his overcoat over himself and nodded at Little Wade, who guided them. It did not take them long to return to Abigail's house. Unfortunately, the entire time, Abigail, holding Watchtower's hand, wondered why they cut their exploration short. *Did I spoil the plan? What's going to happen now?* Little Wade drifted in front of them, gravely serious, brooding about something. Even Watchtower, who never uttered any words, seemed especially silent this time. Abigail decided to wait until they were indoors to ask since she would look like an absolute madwoman if they were to get into an argument out in the middle of the street.

I know I disappointed them, she chastised herself.

Within a few minutes, they arrived back at her house. Masked by Little Wade's illusions, Watchtower, at full height, picked Abigail up and raised her to her window, where she unlocked it. The instant she set foot inside, Abigail, after bottling everything up for blocks, blurted out, "I haven't ruined this, have I? If I have, I'm sorry. Please tell me. We're not done for the day, are we? Please, say no."

"On the contrary, we're just beginning." Little Wade melted

through her wall. "First, I regret to inform you that my excursion into the sewers yielded nothing."

"Nothing? Did my idea about following the electrical lines not lead anywhere useful?"

"Surprisingly, no. It was an excellent idea. I'm not sure why it did not work. I did as you advised, and I located a few hideouts, but they were empty. The Shock Troops had used them, but according to the evidence I found, they had vacated the premises several days ago. They must be lurking in another lair located somewhere in this city."

"Don't they require electricity for their plans? Why would they not be located near power lines? How can they do that?"

"An excellent question. I suspect we are about to find out."

"How?"

"Well, all this time, Watchtower and I have been waiting for a signal from our contacts at Precinct Zero. We just received it. It's time to implement the next, most important, and most dangerous, phase of our plan. That explains my serious demeanor."

Relieved, Abigail sat down on her hammock.

"Thank Heavens! I despaired for a moment. More adventures? Yes, please."

"You desire more danger in your life?"

"No...I mean...of course not, but...is it wrong to say that I'm terribly excited?"

"I suppose not," Little Wade laughed and swooped throughout her attic. "We must be careful, though. We set our plan in motion with the Orpheus Theater brawl, but our enemies have set their stratagems in motion, too."

"What is your plan, exactly?"

"Before I explain that, I wish to inform you of something."

Little Wade drifted toward the wall and gestured outside.

"Something just arrived for you."

"For me?" Abigail rushed over to her window and popped it open. Down below, she saw Watchtower. In his seven-foot form, he stood by her front door, striking the perfect balance between being menacing and gentlemanly. He held a sizable, brown parcel in his arms.

"Who sent it?"

"The Peculiarly Positive Shop. Who else?"

"The...what?" Abigail unfolded her Map of Scratches and very quickly found THE PECULIARLY POSITIVE SHOP marked on it. It was a wonderfully odd building situated in the center of her neighborhood. She wanted to visit it immediately, but then she turned her attention back to Watchtower and the package.

"Friends of yours?"

"You will find that the scientists and engineers of the Peculiarly Positive Shop will prove to be the most marvelous allies, Abigail. Before we continue adventuring, you will need—"

Smack! He heard the hatch behind him. Little Wade whirled around, realized Abigail was no longer in the room, detected the hatch on the floor had been opened, and heard the very loud *bump-bumpbumpitydumpbump* of her little feet descending the stairs at the speed of enthusiasm.

"—supplies." Little Wade finished his sentence (sort of).

After rushing all the way down and then all the way back up the stairs of her crowded house in record time, hefting the parcel, Abigail slammed down the package and caught her breath. Then she eagerly ripped off the brown wrapping, exposing a magnificent saddlebag, the kind that cowboys (or cowgirls) used on the frontier. Made of rugged, cracked brown leather, it struck Abigail as wonderfully crafted, but unassuming and nondescript. She could use it without drawing too much attention. It could be slung around a horse, but also around Abigail's shoulders like a backpack. Very quickly, Abigail emptied the contents of the saddlebag, discovering a variety of objects, each of which made her furrow her brow more and more. Finally, she found a letter addressed to her, which she tore open and read eagerly.

DEAR ABIGAIL REID,

SALUTATIONS! IT HAS RECENTLY COME TO OUR ATTENTION THROUGH A PAIR OF MUTUAL FRIENDS (HINT: ONE RESEMBLES AN ELEGANT, ELOQUENT, LEVITATING BOY AND THE OTHER A TITANIC, MECHANICAL

GENTLEMAN) THAT YOU SEEK ASSISTANCE NAVIGATING THE ENVIRONS OF NEW YORK CITY AND ACCLIMATING TO URBAN LIFE.

WE WOULD BE POSITIVELY DELIGHTED TO ASSIST YOU AND WISH TO EXTEND OUR WARMEST POSSIBLE WELCOME! (WELL, NOT OUR WARMEST AS TEMPERATURES IN OUR LABORATORIES CAN EXCEED OVER FIFTEEN HUNDRED DEGREES FAHRENHEIT, WHICH WOULD PROMPTLY MELT YOUR FLESH, BUT NO DOUBT YOU CAN ASCERTAIN AND EXTRAPOLATE OUR MEANING FROM OUR USE OF A WELL-WORN IDIOM).

ABIGAIL REID, WE SALUTE YOU!

ENCLOSED WITH THIS LETTER, PLEASE FIND SEVERAL ITEMS THAT YOU SHOULD (HOPEFULLY) FIND USEFUL DURING YOUR ENDEAVORS AND ESCAPADES.

1) THE INTREPID CAP: WE SPECIALLY DESIGNED THIS RUSSIAN-STYLE LEATHER CAP WITH DETACHABLE FUR AND FOLDING EAR FLAPS TO SHIELD YOUR PRECIOUS HEAD NOT ONLY FROM COLD WEATHER BUT ALSO EXCESSIVE NOISE AND SUDDEN, KINETIC IMPACTS. IT CONTAINS PLENTY OF PADDING TO PROTECT YOUR NOGGIN.

2) ADJUSTABLE BI-FOCAL GOGGLES: DESIGNED TO GREATLY ENHANCE AND MAGNIFY YOUR VISION, THIS UNIT CAN BE EASILY COMBINED WITH THE INTREPID CAP.

3) VULCANIZED RUBBER GLOVES: IF YOU MUST EVER TOUCH OR MANIPULATE ANYTHING SLIMY, SLUDGY, GREASY, DIRTY, FILTHY, FROTHY, INFECTED, INFESTED, OR (MOST IMPORTANTLY) ELECTRICAL, THESE GLOVES HELP INSULATE AGAINST SEPSIS, SHOCKS, AND CHEMICAL BURNS.

4) A RED-LEATHER-BOUND POCKET KODAK CAMERA: IF YOU EVER WISH TO SNAP PICTURES FOR EVIDENCE OR POSTERITY, USE THIS SIMPLE MECHANISM. SEND FILM ROLLS TO BE DEVELOPED AT ANY OF OUR LOCATIONS. YOU WILL FIND ADDRESSED AND STAMPED ENVELOPES INCLUDED WITH THE CAMERA.

NOTE: THE CAMERA COMES WITH SMALL POUCHES OF MAGICIAN'S FLASH POWDER IF YOU WISH TO TAKE PHOTOS IN THE DARK. JUST MAKE SURE YOU TIME IT CAREFULLY. THE POUCHES OF FLASH POWDER ARE WHITE WITH AN EYE EMBLAZONED ON THEM. IGNITE THEM WITH ANY SPARK OR FLAME AND POOF! BRIGHT FLASH!

5) A TUNING FORK: YOU NEVER KNOW WHEN YOU NEED A GOOD,

sharp fork, and this one also vibrates when you strike it and makes a fascinating diiiinnnngggg sound, which you will find quite interesting. It will benefit you in...unexpected ways.

6) A folding pocket knife: It never hurts to possess one.

7) A pair of clothespins: In case you must fasten anything to anything else, use these. They're also useful for pinching your nose if you find yourself in the presence of something particularly stinky. We included two because clothespins operate best in pairs, and clothespins should never be lonely.

8) Sergeant Slow Burn: This small, wooden statue shaped like a soldier contains a lighter embedded inside. Whenever you need a source of heat or luminosity or both, you can strike the lighter and fwoosh! Sergeant Slow Burn (carved of a unique wood that burns brightly but very slowly) will burst into flames and brighten up any darkness. You can hold him by gripping his legs like you would a torch, and the flame can be doused with a strong enough gust of air or by giving him a bath. Do not worry about hurting Sergeant Slow Burn. He considers himself a good soldier, and he signed up for this.

9) A deafening whistle: You never know when you might need to signal for help.

10) A small mirror: You never know when you might need to look around corners or look at yourself or signal for help without making a sound.

11) A small medical kit: This contains bandages to dress wounds, a suture kit to seal up very serious wounds, and small vials of alcohol that can disinfect them (painfully, unfortunately).

NOTE: The alcohol IS medicinal and absolutely NOT for drinking.

12) Marvin: Meet your pet rock. He weighs about one solid pound, and he may ideally serve as a paperweight, counterweight, or hammer/bludgeon. If you need to throw him, go right ahead. Marvin will always make his way back to you. We don't know how he manages this, but he does. It's rather miraculous.

You will find his name already painted on him so you can distinguish him from other, less extraordinary rocks.

13) All-Access, All-Hours, All-Tracks Ticket to New York's "El" Elevated Train Line: Just present this ticket to any conductor on any train, and you will be granted passage. This will prove very useful for rapid transit around the city.

14) A key: This unlocks your own personal Peculiarly Positive Shop locker that contains your very own bicycle. You will love it! Use it if you wish to zip around the city at higher speeds (but at greater risk).

15) Pencils and a journal: You never know when you might need to jot something down.

16) Finally, all of these items can be safely and conveniently transported via Wendy Lawson's Fabulous Saddlebag. This includes several additional pockets to house any interesting or useful objects that you may wish to add to your repertoire. While most of the pockets are composed of high-quality leather, a few contain metal mesh. We installed, in its own flap, a special section crafted from vulcanized rubber (similar to your gloves) to contain anything wet, slimy, or otherwise grotesque or unpleasant.

We sincerely hope that these seemingly random articles serve you well on your adventures. You can find Peculiarly Positive Shops located all around New York City. Additionally, you might be pleased to know they are A) open day or night, B) very heavily defended, C) ready to assist you at any moment, and D) will provide food and shelter whenever you require it. Add us to your Secret Passage of Hope. We are at your service!

Remember, even when life is difficult or disappointing...Stay Positive!

There are always people (and sympathetic beasts and machines) willing to help!

Signed (most Sincerely),

Professor Hectór Obradór, Proprietor, Peculiarly Positive
Shop #21
Lower East Side, Manhattan Island, New York City, Planet Earth, Dimension 6

"I don't know what to say," Abigail, moved nearly to tears, suppressed the impulse to hug Little Wade.

"No need to say anything. Only know you're not alone."

Marveling at her newfound equipment, Abigail added Precinct Zero's Coded Police Schedule, the Map of Scratches, Minerva Jonas's book, and the Bone Dice of Eyes to Wendy Lawson's saddlebag. Abigail briefly considered inserting Saran Singh's steel pocket watch, but then decided that she wanted to place it in the pocket over her heart instead. Then she fetched a ball of string from under her bed.

"Minerva Jonas wrote, 'Be like Theseus. He delved deep into the Labyrinth to hunt and defeat the Minotaur.' He carried a ball of string with him that he unspooled the deeper he descended into the maze so that he could make his way back out again." Abigail held up her ball of string. "Last night, this city seemed impossible to navigate. I swore that it would swallow me up. When you surprised me with Mr. Peekaboo, I was completely unprepared, thrown right back into confusion again, but Theseus prided himself on being prepared. He formulated a way out of the maze, and the ball of string helped him keep his wits about him. If I'm going to head out there again, I need to keep my wits about me. Saran Singh advised me to place my jumbled emotions and thoughts in a straight line. Here's my straight line, wrapped up in a ball. Besides, you never know when string might come in handy."

Abigail placed the ball of string into her saddlebag. In fact, she found that the bag contained a pocket ideally suited for it. It nestled itself snugly inside. Just then, a paper folded in the shape of a bird whizzed through the still open window and skidded onto the floor. Abigail gleefully picked it up and unfolded it.

YOU ARE BRAVER THAN YOU THINK. STOP. YOU CARE ABOUT OTHER PEOPLE. STOP. THE MOMENT WILL COME

WHEN YOU WILL CARE MORE ABOUT SOMEONE ELSE THAN YOU WILL ABOUT YOURSELF. STOP. IN THAT MOMENT, YOU WILL DISCOVER HOW BRAVE YOU CAN BE. STOP.

Pressing the note close to her heart, Abigail blushed and placed it in its own pocket in the saddlebag. She rushed over to the window, looked down and waved to Watchtower, who waved back. Turning back inside, Abigail pondered something.

"Why all of this?" Abigail hefted the saddlebag over her shoulder with a bit of a grunt. "What I mean is…I understand why you introduced me to Mr. Singh, the watch, the dice, and now the Peculiarly Positive Shop and gave me all of these gifts, but I confess I don't yet see…how it all fits together."

Smiling wickedly, Little Wade rubbed his palms together.

"This…is where things get very interesting. Now, I wish to reveal our plan."

Waving his hands, Little Wade cast Dolosphera and conjured up images of the battle at the Orpheus and the two skirmishes that she witnessed on the street during their exploration.

"That theater brawl served multiple purposes, Abigail," Little Wade explained. "Not only did we train you to face further danger, not only did we further damage the Longshadows, but we also incited conflict between them and their biggest rivals, the Wild Cards."

"Vicious brawls between them have broken out all over the city, but you already alerted the police long before it happened, so they were prepared to pounce."

"Precisely. As you saw twice already, right now, Wild Cards and Longshadows are scuffling and being rounded up all over town. Their leaders will be forced to emerge from hiding and will intervene."

"You said earlier that the Great Gang Trap would damage all of the gangs in the entire city, not just the Longshadows and Wild Cards. How does sparking a violent rivalry between two gangs accomplish this?"

"Because there is a deeper threat, Abigail, someone far more dangerous. If we want to keep you safe, we need to get him out of the way."

"Who?"

Little Wade created more illusions, vivid images of multiple gangs fighting, old newspaper clippings, a cloud of swirling violence.

"This city used to be far worse. Brutal street wars between various gangs raged all over New York City. Every neighborhood erupted into complete, bloody chaos. One gang would pick a fight with another, and it would unleash a cycle of vengeance with no end in sight. So many, many years ago, all of the leaders of the syndicates met in secret and came to an agreement. If any conflicts ever broke out between two criminal organizations, then they would contact a neutral third party to help them sort it out."

"A neutral third party? Who?"

Little Wade's mood darkened, and his voice became cold and harsh. "Now, whenever a quarrel erupts between gangs, they hire a man named Mr. Makepeace to settle the dispute by whatever means necessary."

"How does he do it?"

"That depends on the situation. The pact the gangs made grants Mr. Makepeace absolute power to resolve the conflict. Sometimes that means making the problem go away, and, in this case, the problem...is you."

"Oh my," Abigail sat down. "He's...he's coming for me..." Her voice trailed off.

"We're not going to wait around for that," Little Wade immediately assured her. "While you slept, Watchtower and I spent all of last night plotting and strategizing to intercept him before he inflicts any damage on you or anyone else. We've been after him for years."

"How will we manage to apprehend him?"

"That will be easy. Whenever criminals contact Mr. Makepeace, he always calls a meeting and summons all of the gangs. The leaders and several of their best lieutenants are obligated to attend. It's a tradition that has lasted for many, many years. Today will be no different."

Abigail sprang up, excited. "So we wait for the meeting, and then you, Watchtower, and Precinct Zero will swoop in and arrest them, all of them!"

"*That* will be the Great Gang Trap!"

Jumping up and down, she roared. "*Little Wade, your plan is genius!*"

"Are you ready for battle, Abigail?"

"*Yes! I'm ready for war!*"

"*That's the spirit!*" Little Wade clapped.

"Let's crush these scoundrels and...wait." Abigail stopped. "Not that I mind an adventure...but...why must I be there?"

"Because we are quite certain Brooke Adams will attend the meeting, too."

"Oh my, Brooke? You really think so? How do you know that? Why would she be there? Wait! Let me think...all gangs will be summoned, and that includes the Shock Troops!"

"Correct. Go on."

"They will be there at the meeting, too!"

"Correct. Go on."

"But why would Brooke be there?"

"Think."

"Mr. Makepeace plays a vital role in New York's criminal underworld."

"Correct. Go on."

"Father always told me: if you possess a skill, then people should pay you for it. Mr. Makepeace would never work for free. So, every gang must offer payment to Mr. Makepeace in exchange for his services. The Shock Troops...are building something...technology...using children...those children that Night Owl Nell mentioned earlier. The Shock Troops, as tribute, will offer a demonstration of their inventions!"

"Which requires..."

"Small hands. The smallest, delicate hands. That's it! They will bring Brooke, and possibly the other children as well!"

"Not only will we arrest all of the gang members, but we will also mount a rescue mission simultaneously. We could definitely use your assistance in this matter, but we will not proceed without your consent."

"Not only do I consent, I volunteer!" Abigail stomped her feet. "So...how do we ascertain the precise location of this very important meeting? How do we find Mr. Makepeace?"

"Quite easily, actually."

"Isn't he a master criminal?"

"Precisely. Mr. Makepeace always keeps a very regular schedule with very consistent stops around the city, a perfect, punctual reputation."

"So the gangs know exactly where to find him if they ever need to call on him." Abigail reasoned. "That's awfully considerate for a ruthless villain."

"It's horribly efficient, like clockwork. He's like a machine, and he's just as cold and indifferent. Speaking of which, please check your watch. May I trouble you for the time?"

"It's five minutes after noon."

"Perfect!" Little Wade somersaulted in midair. "Right on schedule. Mr. Makepeace gets his shoes shined at exactly the same spot every Saturday at the exact same time, without fail. He never misses an appointment, and he does not care who shines his shoes."

"He does not care?" Abigail's eyes narrowed.

"Oh no, he looks down on everyone. He considers most people beneath him, especially those who serve him, but today we're going to turn the tables."

"Do...you mind if I change out of this into something more adventurous?" Abigail gestured to the curtain strung up in the corner of her apartment.

"Not at all. Would you like me to leave?"

"No, but I would appreciate it if you could turn around."

"Very well."

Little Wade politely turned his back and drifted toward the far wall. Abigail stepped behind her curtain and changed. As he faced away from her, Little Wade, drifting slowly toward the circular window, continued speaking. "This is our plan. Watchtower and I have many contacts among the bootblackers. We have placed several of our shoeshine boys at that precise spot. One of them will shine Mr. Makepeace's shoes, but they will smear shoe polish on the soles, inking the bottoms of his feet."

"Go on." Abigail changed.

"Using your bifocal goggles, which will serve as binoculars, you (from a safe distance of course) will watch Mr. Makepeace leave. As he walks, he will leave tracks, and then you will follow (with Watchtower and I protecting you, of course). Together, we will pursue Mr. Makepeace to the rendezvous point. Precinct Zero will converge on our position, and then you (from a safe distance, of course), using your bifocal goggles, will identify Brooke Adams to confirm her presence. Then you will take cover, and we will spring the trap (while you watch from a safe distance, of course). Have I made myself clear, Abigail? Would you like me to repeat any aspect of—"

Plonk!

Little Wade whirled around when a shoeshine box dropped onto the floor. Stepping out from behind the curtain, Abigail, dressed as a shoeshine boy, presented herself.

"Why can't it be me? Why can't I shine Mr. Makepeace's shoes and follow him to the gathering?"

"Out of the question!" Little Wade shook his head furiously. "You wish to get that close to the man trying to kill you? Absolutely not. For us to let you...totally irresponsible."

"I want to help."

"Do you even know how to shine shoes?" Little Wade challenged her, gesturing to her shoeshine kit. "Is that not merely a disguise designed to hide your school supplies?"

She opened the box, revealing an actual brush and polish kit.

"Do you know how to use those?" Little Wade looked at her sideways, extremely skeptical.

"I learned the basics. How hard can it be?" Abigail shrugged. "Besides, won't you place shoeshine boys there to help guide me?"

"Our boys are already at the bench, working now, waiting for us."

"Perfect. They can help me if need be. I'm a quick learner." Abigail began packing and preparing.

Little Wade urgently whispered, "Abigail, Mr. Makepeace is a killer."

"Hmmm..." Abigail considered this. "This Mr. Makepeace...I assume that he pretends to be a gentleman, concealing his true criminal nature. Correct?"

"Yes, he considers himself a sophisticated man with refined tastes and manners."

"Then he wouldn't dare make a move on me in a public place," Abigail reasoned. "He must protect his sterling reputation, so even if he discovers who I am, he's not likely to try to murder me right there, in public."

"I will concede that. Good point."

"You wouldn't dare send me anywhere near danger without safeguards in place. I'm sure you will position those vanishing warriors nearby. Wait, you're invisible. Why don't you just sneak up on Mr. Makepeace, follow him to the meeting, and then have Watchtower... you know...gah...rahhh...bash...slam!" She mimicked Watchtower's fighting, even making the *chank-chank-chank* sounds of Watchtower's grinding gears.

After listening to her performance, incredibly amused, Little Wade answered, "Mr. Makepeace can see me."

"Wait...he can see you? I'm shocked. How is that possible?"

"Because he's a murderer."

"Murderers can see the dead?"

"Most of us go through life without hurting or killing anything, so we do not feel the touch of death until the end of our lives. On the other hand, every time someone commits a murder, death touches them, and that crime they committed tears a hole in the Ahkwiyàn, at least for them. Murderers can see the spirits of their victims; most cannot see other specters, only those they have created by the act of killing, but a criminal of Mr. Makepeace's caliber has committed so many homicides and torn so many holes in the Ahkwiyàn that... well...it doesn't exist for him anymore."

"What about animals? Predators? They kill constantly. Do they see dead spirits, too? Wait, if that were true, how would they ever differentiate between the living and the dead? There must be wraiths all around them."

"Most animals that die cross over, and as for the ghosts of animals…well…animals use senses other than sight and hearing to guide them through the world. They use their noses. Incorporeal beings do not give off any scent. So…there you are."

"Is that why so many ancient legends feature characters who commune with the dead…like Vikings, knights, Samurai and the like, because, during those times, there was more fighting, more killing, and so…more murderers?"

"That's exactly why. The world of the living and the dead used to exist much closer together. Thankfully, we have evolved to be more civilized…in some ways, at least. Mr. Makepeace is, in many ways, a creature from the Old World. He is the worst kind of predator. He kills for money, for power, and for sport."

"What about your illusions? Can they fool him, or can he see through them as well?"

"Yes, my illusions can still deceive him, but it requires tremendous effort. He has a particularly keen eye."

"Even if he can see you, can you not sneak up on him? You have proven yourself to be amazingly resourceful."

"Thank you for the compliment, Abigail, but unfortunately not. I personally cannot approach Mr. Makepeace because of Thrash."

"Who's Thrash?"

"His pet ghost who follows him wherever he goes."

"No! That's allowed?"

"It's not against the rules because it doesn't haunt Mr. Makepeace. Thrash protects him from…well…from me. Before he died, Thrash was a vicious hound used in fighting pits, abused by his former master. Mr. Makepeace found his ghost, trained him, and gave him a home. Now he's the ultimate watchdog, fierce and loyal. If I get too close, Thrash will sense me and warn him."

"So ghosts can sense the presence of other ghosts?"

"Yes. Sneaking past another phantom is very difficult. There are a few who can, but they are extraordinary and rare, and Thrash excels at detection and defense. If he spots me, I will be forced to fight him."

"Wraiths and specters can fight each other? That's a surprise. You didn't tell me that before."

"Yes...we can hurt each other," Little Wade warned her. "We can kill each other, too."

"How do you kill something that's already dead?"

"Energy can clash with energy, Abigail, and different energies can destroy each other. When ghosts battle, they can inflict horrible wounds. It's called Ryving."

"Ryving...that sounds...painful," Abigail's voice quavered.

"Phantasms can tear each other to pieces. Being ethereal, we can repair ourselves, but if an incorporeal being suffers too much damage, it loses cohesion, scatters, and fades...gone forever."

"You're talking about consciousness," Abigail guessed. "You told me last night that death was like gravity or time, and you explained that ghosts exist as pure energy. I did not quite understand exactly what type of energy, but now I think I am beginning to grasp it. Consciousness is another primal force in the universe. A person's unique spirit is another cosmic phenomenon."

"Precisely, Abigail. A ghost's source of power stems from one source: its mind. We are dead, but we are still conscious, our incorporeal forms held together by the sheer force of our thoughts, our reason, our imagination, our wits, and our will. We call this 'Thanity,' our name for what is essentially our soul."

"Thanity...hmmm..." Abigail thought carefully. "In Greek mythology, 'Thanatos' was the personification of death, and the particular name given to this magic is clearly a pun on the word 'sanity,' which leads me to believe that if a ghost loses its mind or sense of self..." Her voice trailed off.

"It ceases to exist. It scatters into the madness of pure, primordial chaos."

"Have you fought other phantoms before?"

"Yes. Many times."

"I won't ask if you've killed any...wait, I just sort of...did, didn't I?"

"It's all right, Abigail." Little Wade lowered his head, as if in mourning. No answer was his answer.

"A great battle approaches, doesn't it?" Abigail realized. "Not just for Watchtower, not just for Precinct Zero, but for you as well."

Sighing sadly, Little Wade admitted, "I'm afraid so."

Abigail felt a sudden chill when she realized something. "Mr. Makepeace, he killed one of your clients, didn't he?"

"Seven of our clients," Little Wade's voice seemed to drop on the floor like a lead weight.

"Seven?" Abigail could barely say the word. She sat down.

"He's one of the worst enemies we have ever fought. I am truly sorry to have involved you in all of this, but if we are to make your streets safer for you and all other children, we must face him. Watchtower and I always knew this day would come. I'm sorry that fate chose you."

"I just want to go to school. I didn't want any of this for anyone. Why did this have to happen?"

Little Wade sat down next to her.

"Abigail, are you certain you want to do this? Any of the other shoeshine boys, experienced agents of ours, can do it for you."

"Will you assign people to protect me, as you did in the theater?"

"Yes. Our finest operatives are moving into position as we speak."

Abigail considered this for a moment.

"Your shoeshine boys don't know Brooke. I do. It's better if I do it. I'm not only the right person for this assignment, I'm the only one."

"If anything happened to you—"

"This time you're going to beat him," Abigail gently interrupted him. "I can feel it."

"You were so frightened this morning. Now, look at you, ready to take on the world."

"Well, a combination of a bit of supernatural assistance, an exciting battle (that I survived), a fabulous book written by a role model, a first ally in the community, a surprise package from sympathetic scientists, and a renewed confidence in municipal organizations and law enforcement works wonders, apparently." Abigail sprang up and presented herself. "Now, how do I look?"

Little Wade studied her. "Convincing, almost, but a bit too clean."

Looking at herself in her new signal mirror, Abigail rubbed a mix of dust and ink on her face, creating streaks on her skin, smothering her freckled cheeks.

"Better." Little Wade approved.

"Now that I think about this...are we certain my disguise will work?" Abigail cautioned. "I'm not afraid...well...I am, actually, but this won't work if Mr. Makepeace recognizes me."

Absorbing this, Little Wade thought for a moment and then replied. "It's a good point, but remember, the Longshadows that spotted you had been watching you for days, perhaps even weeks. On the contrary, Mr. Makepeace has probably never, ever seen you. Additionally, we can reasonably assume that he does not possess any photographs of you. The Longshadows would have only provided a basic description of your face, your freckles, and your magnificent red hair, which we will tuck beneath your cap. So far, I believe we still possess the element of surprise."

While Little Wade spoke, Abigail moved around her apartment, carefully assembling her kit and slinging her new saddlebag over her shoulder. When she had finished, she turned, nervous but excited.

"I'm ready. Let's teach this villain a lesson he'll never forget."

18

BOOTBLACKER

Disguised, clutching her shoeshine box, Abigail strode quickly down the street. Her face streaked with soot and polish, her red hair tucked tightly beneath her dirty cap, she headed toward her rendezvous with Mr. Makepeace. She also slung Wendy Lawson's saddlebag over her shoulder and hefted it down city block after city block. It would take some getting used to, but Abigail felt a great deal of security carrying it. All around her, people hustled and bustled. She blended into the crowd, unnoticed. Those that did pay attention to her fell for her disguise, calling her "boy" more than once. *It's working*, she thought. *I can do this.*

For several blocks, she felt great comfort. Little Wade soared above and circled like a hawk, and Watchtower accompanied her. Up until yesterday, she hated this city and its cold, grey, grimy, stinking sidewalks. People buzzed around everywhere like swarms of insects, and the streets choked with noise and dirt, but now it felt cleaner somehow.

Before, the city seemed like something crumbling and falling apart. Now she felt as though she had entered inside the most marvelous clockwork machine. Everything and everyone seemed to click loudly around her as each individual slotted itself into place, and New York slowly pieced itself together, following some invisible, intricate, amazing design. She used to think that every messy corner seemed to overflow with noise. Now, she heard, felt something different. Women gossiped as they strolled; children and their parents jabbered; musicians belted out tunes; newsboys called out the latest headlines; dogs barked; cats meowed. Spinning carriage wheels *click-click-clicked*, and the horses' hooves *clop-clop-clopped*, and the trolleys *chug-chug-chugged*, and a multitude of bells and chimes *ding-ding-dinged*. There were whistles and instruments and so much singing, too. Abigail beheld this symphony of all of these different voices and sounds intersecting and interlocking with each other, like tiny little gears, whirling around and around.

She felt confident. Perhaps it was her new watch, beating inside her breast pocket like a stout, steel heart. Perhaps it was because she no longer felt alone in her search for Brooke. Instead, she became one of many pieces working together to resolve the situation. Little Wade's master plan slowly unfolded all around her, and Abigail knew that he and Watchtower had strategized everything in advance with her safety as their paramount concern. Perhaps that is why, even though she headed towards danger, Abigail Reid felt a profound sense of order in the universe again.

"Things happen for a reason," she spoke up. "That's what we all hope, isn't it?"

"Indeed, Abigail," Little Wade slowed down his flight and sailed next to her. "One very comforting thing about becoming a ghost, it instantly opened me up to new possibilities. When we first conversed in your apartment, you said it yourself. If spirits exist, then it may be reasonable to assume that Heaven must as well. If Heaven does, then perhaps all of this, everything that happens…is part of something bigger, something wondrous, and all of us play a part. Somewhere out there, somewhere along the line, all of this will make sense."

"I thought my life was broken, incomplete, unfinished, ruined," Abigail replied as they walked. "I have no mother, no money, no brothers or sisters. I see other families on the street and I envy them: both parents, two or three children, a cat or a dog, or both. I see that and sometimes I don't even consider myself a whole person. I'm like a toy that should be part of a set, but I have too many pieces missing."

"Do you still feel that way?" Little Wade asked.

"Now, however, I wonder if all of these broken edges that I have are more like the odd sides of a puzzle piece. Somewhere out there is a place where I fit, where *only* I fit, a role only I can play. Somewhere out there is the life that, in a strange way, I am supposed to have, a life where all of these parts of me, these fragments, somehow slot and lock together, connecting with something, all for a purpose. That's not too much to hope for, is it?"

"No, Abigail. In fact that's precisely what you should believe, because, in this city, you will have to fight for every inch of what you want, and wherever you wish to belong."

"I know now how life can fail. I don't know if it will work out for me, but because of both of you, living the life I want no longer feels impossible. Whatever happens, good or bad, I certainly feel less alone. Thank you for that."

"Watchtower and I would like to consider ourselves gentlemen. For us, being gentlemen means being honorable, honest, and kind. It means helping people whenever we can, however we can. A gentleman uses whatever power he has for good and asks for nothing in return. We accept your gratitude with utmost humility, Abigail. You are not the only one who is benefiting from this partnership. We may be improving your life, Abigail, but you are also most certainly dramatically enriching and enhancing our lives as well. Watchtower and I are proud to be at your service."

Watchtower stopped as if he could go no further, and then Little Wade leaned against him.

"We're here."

He pointed across the street to a corner where she saw a shoeshine bench with multiple elevated seats. A troop of poor, pale-skinned boys crouched at the feet of a line of wealthy, snobbish men who perched like vultures while the juvenile bootblackers polished their expensive leather shoes.

"He's on his way. What's the time?"

Abigail retrieved her watch. *Click-click-clicking*, it read twenty-seven minutes past noon.

"He will be here very soon. Exactly on time, as always."

"Wait, I've never seen Mr. Makepeace's face. How will I know him?"

"You will see him, Abigail," Little Wade assured her.

Abigail placed her hand over her belly button.

"You mean...see him with my stomach?"

"I believe sincerely that you're ready. As if sensing a predator, your body will spot him before your mind does. You will know him instantly, a profoundly evil soul, one of the worst men living."

"I'm ashamed to say it, but I'm afraid," Abigail confessed. "This will take longer than thirteen seconds."

"Yes, it will, but this time you will need to not only be brave, but also clever, curious, meek, deceitful, imaginative, and hopeful. Use that variety of emotions and thoughts to allow you to feel out the situation and adapt to it in the moment. The best way to avoid being afraid or worrying about being brave is to focus on being something else. You can do that, Abigail. You can do it all."

"You told me this morning that the true opposite of fear is curiosity."

"Indeed, would you consider yourself curious now?"

"Extremely."

"Then you are ready."

"Are your friends nearby?"

"Yes. Our best fighters, many of them. Very close."

"Where?"

"It's better that you don't know. One less lie to tell."

"That makes sense."

"You can change your mind. No shame in it."

"No, this is my fight. You and Watchtower cannot do everything for me. I need to fight for myself."

"Do you trust us?"

"Completely." Abigail struggled to control her breathing. "I just wish I trusted myself."

"Watchtower and I believe in you."

"Do you really?"

"Abigail, do you know why the queen is the most powerful piece on the chessboard?"

"She can move in any direction, straight or diagonal, as many spaces as she wants. Everybody knows that."

Little Wade shook his head. "That's true, but I find it fascinating that even though everyone knows how powerful the queen is, no one ever really sees her coming. All of the other pieces are constrained, and predictable; however..." Little Wade's voice trailed off deliberately.

"Although every player knows what the queen *can* do, nobody ever knows what she *will* do. Her choices matter the most. She is capable of the most surprise attacks."

"Now you're getting it. Now you're understanding who you really are. Compared to all of the other pieces, the queen possesses infinite potential, just like you. Now, make your move."

After winking at her, Little Wade vanished. Gulping, Abigail crossed the street. Quickly, nervously, she took her place, kneeling by three empty, elevated seats. Carefully unpacking her shoeshine kit, she struggled to steady her hands.

"Pssssst."

The other shoeshine boys saluted her. One of them extracted a piece of paper from his dirty jacket pocket. He unfolded it and held it up, revealing a child's drawing of a tiny floating boy and his beanpole fire-faced, top-hatted friend.

A contract!

Winking, this particular shoeshine boy stuffed the contract back into his pocket. She immediately breathed a sigh of relief. Her hands stopped shaking, and she kneeled down, ready to work.

A crowd of wealthy gentlemen approached the corner, whistling to the boys and snapping their fingers, signaling their intent. Smelling leather and dirty shoes, Abigail prepared herself. *Here they come. I can do this.*

Her first potential customer sat before her, thin and devastatingly handsome, with a sharp mustache and beard, brown eyes, and a roguish smile. He wore an elegant suit, and his long hair spilled down onto his shoulders. Silver spirals decorated his top hat, and he sipped from a silver flask and winked at her.

She felt nothing.

A second gentleman mounted the seats, this one far more powerfully built than the first man. He wore a grey suit and gloves, sported a neatly trimmed grey mustache, and wore a monocle over one eye. Beneath his homburg hat, his hair was cut very short, and he moved slowly, bluntly, almost as if he were dressed in heavy armor instead of cloth. Abigail suspected that this man had served in the military. He also wore a pocket watch. One of his legs made a hollow sound when he slotted both of his shoes into the shine ports, and his left arm did not move at all. *A false arm and a false leg, a wounded man, a former soldier.* Beneath his coat, she detected the glint of two guns.

Still, she felt nothing.

Then her stomach tightened up.

She felt a sinister chill all over her skin. To her right, a man climbed up onto the shoeshine chair like a spider. This man set down a leather bag with a strange symbol emblazoned on it. She did not see his face because just as she turned to look directly at him, he opened a newspaper and spread it so wide that it covered his entire torso and face. Abigail could only see the man's tall top hat, which bore the same strange symbol as his bag. This man, hidden behind his newspaper, slotted his shoes into place and waited. Abigail's stomach churned as if serpents slithered and writhed in her guts.

It was him.

Abigail, disguised, slowly approached the man. Clearing her throat, she lowered her voice as much as she could. "Shine your shoes, sir?"

"That's why I'm sitting here," a smooth, silky voice answered from behind the paper. As Mr. Makepeace adjusted it, turning a page, the periodical crinkled in his hands. Then he swiftly, sharply pulled his newspaper tight. It sounded like a bone snapping.

"Are you having a good day, sir?"

He sniffed. "It's about to get a great deal more exciting."

"Oh, why do you say that?"

"Why do you care so much about my business?"

"Sorry, sir." Abigail struggled to maintain her composure. "Just making conversation."

"Focus on your job, boy." Mr. Makepeace raised his shoe pointedly.

Abigail stooped down and began working. Next to her, the other shoeshine boys guided her. Setting out her polish and brush, Abigail dusted and wiped dirt off Mr. Makepeace's expensive shoes. Keeping her head down, she eyed the symbol on his leather case: the image of a Greek warrior battling a bull-headed monster. The Greek warrior clutched a dagger in one hand and a ball of string in the other. Both man and monster stood trapped inside a maze.

"Theseus and the Minotaur," Abigail blurted out.

"What did you say?" Mr. Makepeace shifted in his seat. His newspaper crackled.

"Uh...sorry, sir." Abigail panicked. "I just...saw the symbol on your case. It's Theseus and the Minotaur."

"You're an educated lad." Mr. Makepeace immediately sounded suspicious. "A little too educated for a shoeshine boy. How do you know it?"

Scrambling for an explanation, Abigail told the truth, sort of.

"Church. Father Browning teaches us to read. He read us the story last Sunday. It's why it comes to mind." Truthfully, Father Browning was the wonderful, knowledgeable priest in Tarrytown who first taught Abigail how to read, so she told a lie, but not a total lie.

"Hmmphhh...that's very godly of him," Mr. Makepeace commented.

"Yes, sir."

"Though, I hope he didn't raise your expectations too high," Mr. Makepeace added. "In my experience, some priests aren't so kind to children, and most simply aren't that smart."

"I suppose he just tried to help us find ways to pass the time."

Abigail kept her head down. "I'm sorry, sir. I'll just get back to work now."

After finishing dusting, she added the polish to his shoes, making sure she inked the soles so she could see his tracks when he walked away.

"So, we like the same story?" Mr. Makepeace, his face still hidden, spoke, startling Abigail, causing her to spill some inky polish on the sidewalk.

"Um...yes...yes, I suppose we do, sir."

"Hmph...I imagine that we like it for very different reasons."

Although she thought about staying silent, Abigail's curiosity got the better of her.

"Um...why do you like the story? If I may ask, sir."

"You first, boy."

"Well, I'm not very strong," Abigail answered carefully, trying to keep her voice low. "Many heroes pride themselves on their strength, but Theseus cannot compete with them; however, he's the cleverest. He descends into the labyrinth to kill the Minotaur that lives deep inside. The Minotaur is obviously much more powerful than he is, but he finds a way to win. He enters with a ball of string, a pouch full of sand, and a knife. He uses the string to make sure he can get out. He uses the sand to blind the Minotaur when they fight, and then he uses the knife to kill it. He uses his wits."

"So, it gives you hope?" Mr. Makepeace, still hidden, prodded her.

"I...suppose it does, sir."

Mr. Makepeace suddenly, sharply, almost violently folded the newspaper and leaned forward to look her straight in the eye, and Abigail saw his face for the first time.

Abigail's father once told her, "War is the monster with sad eyes." Mr. Makepeace had clearly seen so much violence and death that the darkness had sunken into him, pushing out his human insides, hollowing him out. He was a pale man, old, with a grey beard and mustache. She could see every line, wrinkle and scar etched onto his skin. His teeth were white, clean, and sharp, and his nose thin. His eyes struck Abigail as cold and empty. He seemed terribly mournful, not a man who enjoyed life. Even when his mouth smiled, his eyes did not.

"You like living in this city, boy?"

"I didn't at first, but I...uh...recently made new friends. It's hard... New York feels so big. I feel small, and I feel like I could get lost."

Mr. Makepeace tapped Abigail on the nose with his long finger.

"I know exactly how you feel. I get lost in this dirty city every day," Mr. Makepeace admitted. "You see...my favorite version of the story is slightly different. In my favorite version, Theseus delves deep into the maze, searching for the Minotaur. On his way, he finds other people, many other people, who have died in the maze, not because they were killed by the monster, but because they simply got lost and starved."

He leaned forward.

"In my favorite version, Theseus also encountered people who were trapped in the maze but were still alive. They managed to avoid the monster, but they had gotten lost, and they were lost for so very, very long, stuck in the maze, that they went mad."

"How...how did people survive in the maze for that long?"

"How else? They ate each other."

Abigail gasped.

"What a terrible version. Why tell me this?" Abigail did her best to try to sound like a toughened little boy.

"Where do you think you are?" Mr. Makepeace gestured to the city around them. "This city is a maze. It's a maze of buildings, of streets, of corners, of alleys, all carved into stone, all crisscrossing, twisting, turning. It's a maze of people, too. You know what's like to navigate through a crowd, everyone getting in each other's way. It's too easy to forget where you are. Even if you know where you're going, you're still outnumbered by people who don't know you, who will never know you, or care. Even in the middle of all these people, you're alone. You're nowhere."

Abigail briefly glanced around at the sea of people swirling all around them.

"We're all strangers to each other here. People get lost here every day, and no one remembers them or thinks about them. Look at all of these citizens, peacefully bustling about their lives. Do you know how many victims have died on these very streets?"

He pointed across to the opposite corner.

"Right over there, two young men were gunned down in cold blood, years ago. Over there..." He pointed to a different corner. "A young girl got snatched up, never to be seen again. Nobody remembers anymore. On this corner, where we sit now, a father of four children had his throat slit, and he bled out right where you spilled that little pool of polish, like an ink stain. Nobody remembers. Nobody cares anymore, but...I've learned...that's a good thing."

"How? That doesn't seem good at all."

"It's a good thing because a city only works if it's peaceful, boy. A city would never be peaceful if we all thought too much about everything that goes wrong. Peace requires that people forget. It needs people to move on. It needs people to feel *less* about things. People die and disappear in this city every day, and yet it just keeps moving along. Many of us go mad here, and some of us even eat each other, not literally, of course, but you get the idea."

"So you're saying...the maze...turns people into monsters?"

"I'm saying, boy, that in this city, there is no monster in the middle of the maze. The maze *is* the monster."

"I don't want to live in a city like that." Abigail's voice cracked. "Why must New York be like that?"

"You're still a child. You feel so strongly. That's your problem. You feel too much. One day, when you grow up, you'll learn the value of feeling less. The maze is a metaphor for all of life in this city. We all lose our way, and we all stumble around in the dark together. We all forget. That's how we get along. We build a maze, we all get lost in it, we all forget who we were, who we wanted to be, and then we...well, we just get used to it. We get used to each other."

"That...sounds...terrible." Abigail struggled to maintain her fake boy's voice.

"Terrible? Why?"

"That...sounds...so...cold."

"On the contrary," Mr. Makepeace replied. "It's actually quite warm."

"Warm? How?"

"Do you remember in the story of Theseus...do you remember who built the labyrinth?"

"The Evil King."

"Yes...the Evil King built the labyrinth. Do you remember why he built the labyrinth in the first place?"

"To offer sacrifices...to the beast."

"Good, and do you know what the king received in return for that sacrifice?"

"Peace."

"Exactly. Everyone always talks about the cost of war, but nobody ever talks about the cost of peace. Peace requires sacrifice. You see, peace is not just the absence of war, crime, and violence, boy. Peace is more than that. Peace is an energy source," Mr. Makepeace hissed.

"An energy source?" Abigail did not understand.

"Look around you, boy. Look at all of these people, working themselves to death, grinding like gears, like we're all inside some great big engine. Peace keeps this city running like clockwork. Peace keeps the people moving along and the machine of this city churning. Peace is an energy source like the gas that flows through the veins of this city, lighting it up, heating it when winter chills the streets."

Abigail pointed up to one of the gaslight lampposts on the corner. "You mean like...that gas?"

"Exactly, that gas is burned and destroyed to provide its light. Peace is like that light. For that light to exist, for...peace to exist in this city, something, or someone, always has to burn."

"Sacrifice." She gulped.

He grinned and nodded.

"So...peace is not cold at all. Peace is heat. It's...fire."

Mr. Makepeace glanced down at his shoes.

"Ah...my shoes look like roaches."

"I'm sorry, sir." Abigail's voice trembled.

"Not at all." Mr. Makepeace winked. "I admire roaches. They were here before we got here, and they will be here long after we're gone. They can crawl around in filth all day and all night and never be affected by it, never change. Roaches are survivors, unlike most of us. You did a fine job." Mr. Makepeace grinned and tapped his shoes together.

"Thank you, sir." Abigail just wanted him to leave.

Mr. Makepeace presented her with a coin.

"You're a smart boy with sharp eyes," Mr. Makepeace complimented her. Then he stuffed his newspaper into his leather bag. "Then again, children can see things that most people cannot."

Something appeared behind Mr. Makepeace, crawled up around the chair, and looped around his shoulders like some horrible serpent. Abigail gasped when she saw a horrific, spectral hound that had died after getting caught and tangled in vicious barbed wire that had strangled and shredded the poor animal at the same time.

Thrash.

Wire coiled around the beast's neck like a collar; his flesh was mangled, and his fur soaked and matted with blood. His snout was so damaged, his skin so flayed by the rusted, jagged metal, that Abigail could see sections of his skull underneath. Glaring directly at Abigail, the hound bared his bloody teeth.

"Children can see things other people can't." Mr. Makepeace winked at her. "Isn't that true, boy?"

Abigail let out a yelp and stumbled back.

Mr. Makepeace's arm shot out like a bullet and caught Abigail by the wrist. His hand clamped down like a metal shackle. He slowly reeled Abigail in and restored her to her original kneeling position. Thrash growled and grinned, glaring at her with his one functioning eye. The other eye socket was hollow, gouged out, with barbed wire covering it like a ragged eyepatch.

"Remember, boy, in this city, we're all lost."

His shoes shiny, like a pair of glistening black knives, Mr. Makepeace rose from his seat, plucked up his leather bag, and tipped his hat. Thrash, a dutiful dog, took his place at his master's side and then promptly vanished.

"Go in peace, boy. Stay warm."

Mr. Makepeace turned and walked away, quickly vanishing into a crowd of tall hats, parasols, horses, and carriages. Still shaking, Abigail seized her steel watch, which *click-click-clicked* in her hand. Steadying her heart rate, Abigail whispered to herself.

"Stick to the plan. Stick to the plan."

Examining the pavement beneath her, she tracked Mr. Makepeace's inky shoe polish footprints printed on the hard, grey sidewalk. Gulping nervously, she gathered up her things and followed him. Abigail, still dressed as a shoeshine boy, pursued Mr. Makepeace down the street. With every step, he stamped a clear footprint on the sidewalk. Carefully, she kept her distance.

"Is it working?" Abigail whispered to Little Wade, who materialized next to her.

"You performed brilliantly," he whispered back, even though he did not need to.

Watchtower joined them and offered his hand to Abigail, who took it. Sighing with relief, Abigail whispered, "I feel much better with the two of you here."

"We're not alone," Little Wade encouraged her. "Our agents gather to strike as we speak."

Where is he going? Abigail wondered, peering through the crowd at Mr. Makepeace, who moved surprisingly quickly. Before too long, the crowd began to thin out, but then it thickened again, this time with scavengers, rag pickers, and gang members. It was as if the city had disappeared and been replaced with dilapidated wooden buildings and creepy, splintery tenements not unlike her own home. Dozens of laundry lines, strung between the buildings and stretching across the streets, clouded the entire area like cobwebs. In the cold wind, everything creaked. Even the sky seemed gloomier. Abigail glanced around, repulsed. "Where has he taken us?"

"For years, there existed a street called Fifty-Nine and a Half Mulberry Bend. It became known as Bandit's Roost, the worst, most violent area of the city. Two years ago, the city finally destroyed it, razed it to the ground, and built a park in its place. We always knew that criminals secretly built a New Bandit's Roost somewhere hidden in the city. Now, thanks to you, Abigail, we've found it, hidden in plain sight."

Abigail nervously glanced around. Several gang members lurked about, leering at her. At first, they stared at Abigail, but one look at Watchtower and they scattered like rats.

"Quick! Over here!" Little Wade and Watchtower ducked into an alley. Abigail followed.

"What's wrong?"

Little Wade pressed himself up against the wall as if he were a real human boy trying to hide. Watchtower did the same, and Abigail found it amusing to see them both cowering the way that they did.

"We can't get too close, but we need to follow. I can't Polyplot and pursue him without Thrash seeing me, but you can help."

"Me? How? Oh, wait! I have just the thing!" Abigail pulled her Intrepid Cap out of her saddlebag and then attached the goggles. Abigail donned the Intrepid Cap and slipped the goggles over her eyes. Stepping to the edge of the alley, she stuck her head out and peered through the lenses. Scanning the crowd, she quickly spotted and focused on Mr. Makepeace. Carefully, she adjusted the knobs on the sides of her goggles and her vision magnified. Even though he stopped two blocks ahead of them, Mr. Makepeace loomed large, as if he were standing right next to her.

"I see him! These are remarkable!" Abigail forced herself to whisper, even though she was unbelievably excited.

"What's he doing, Abigail?" Little Wade, still hiding, wondered.

"He's entering a warehouse, two blocks down on the left."

Abigail readjusted her vision back to normal, but she kept her cap on, thinking that it might come in useful.

"All right, we're going to wait for a minute and then sneak in."

"Won't Thrash sense you?"

"It won't matter now. It's time to fight. Watchtower and I will take them down inside the warehouse. Precinct Zero will ride in like the cavalry."

"Something doesn't feel right. This feels too easy," Abigail warned them.

"I agree, but we must seize our chance, Abigail. Once we're inside, you must identify Brooke Adams, and then you hide somewhere safe. We will do the fighting. Are you ready?"

"Yes. I'm ready. Let's go find Brooke."

"We cannot act until we hear you say it."

Abigail balled up her hands into tight fists.

"I consent."

Abigail, Little Wade, and Watchtower covered the two city blocks very quickly and infiltrated the warehouse. Slowly, quietly, Abigail, still wearing her Intrepid Cap, carefully crept into the shadowy, dismal building, sneaking through an open window, careful to avoid creaking too much.

After melting through the wall, Little Wade slowly slithered through the air. Most impressively, Watchtower entered the warehouse through a carefully opened window, head and skinny arms first, followed by his elongated torso and then two long, beanpole legs. Then he slowly, quietly extended himself to his twelve-foot height. His costume muted the sound of his gears so much that Abigail could barely hear them. Then, moving very slowly, Watchtower spread his arms, legs, and even his fingers out wide, and he stalked forward like a massive, mechanical spider. Stepping ever so lightly and carefully, Watchtower hovered high above Abigail as she quietly crept through a dirty maze of barrels and crates.

Weaving in and out of the musty stacks, she swallowed a cloud of dust and nearly coughed. Little Wade and Watchtower froze. Abigail quickly stifled it and then held up her thumb as if to say, "I am all right." Then they all heard loud arguing, a cacophony of voices, all men. Abigail whispered to herself, "They're all here."

Listening carefully, Little Wade, Watchtower, and Abigail snuck deeper into the cavernous warehouse, following the sounds, which emanated from the next room, the loading dock. They found the perfect hiding place, an overlook that gave them a vantage point to gaze out over the entire chamber from above. Plucking Abigail up like a feather, Watchtower raised her up, set her down gently, then hunched over and skulked into attack position.

Crouching, hiding, Abigail briefly glanced over at Little Wade, who had ascended alongside her. He displayed an aggressive look in his eyes that she had not seen before. His eyebrows angled sharply downward like daggers. He peeled back his lips and bared his teeth with hatred and rage, and his hands began to flicker and burn. Then Abigail heard the guttural laughter of men, and she turned her attention to a crowd of torches and lanterns illuminating the faces of their targets.

The Great Gathering of Gangs had begun.

19

THE GREAT GANG TRAP

A menacing multitude of criminals formed a semicircle to face one person. When Mr. Makepeace stepped forward, they all acknowledged him.

The Longshadows had sent a pack of degenerate scum, led by a tall, skinny man that Abigail nicknamed Mr. Stretch.

The Wild Cards had sent a bizarre gaggle of whooping psychopaths, all grinning and giggling, led by a ginormously fat, crazy-looking man Abigail nicknamed Mr. Ball.

Then there were the other gangs.

The Smooth Boys dressed luxuriously in the finest clothing with roses pinned to their coats and hats. Representing the gang stood a group of dapper, young gentlemen led by an incredibly handsome young man that Abigail nicknamed Mr. Silver because of his watch, cane, and pistol, which all glinted in the firelight.

Peering more closely, she spotted several members of the Invisible Men. They were all of African or Haitian descent. Once they had been enslaved, quietly plotting against their masters, sneaking crimes under their noses. Now, free men, they worked as servants and laborers, making sure that everyone ignored them, at their peril. She nicknamed their leader Mr. Scars.

The Sewer Rats crawled up through a hole in the floor; several filthy boys and short, stocky men erupted up from the hole like black, sludgy water from a backed-up drain. They were led by a hunchbacked man Abigail called Mr. Crookback. Wincing, she could smell them even from all the way up where she hid and watched.

The Squids, a particularly brutish gang that terrorized the docks, brought their toughest enforcers, led by a tall, powerfully built man. Abigail nicknamed him Mr. Knots because he carried a thick, twisted rope. The Squids all bore ink tattoos of tentacles that snaked around their faces, necks, hands, and shoulders.

Los Seises (The Sixes), a Spanish gang with dice decorating their hats and coats, stepped forward, led by Mr. Twelve, who sported a pair of dice on his hat that showed both six sides up.

The Dragons, from Chinatown, all carrying colorful lanterns, showed up as well, led by Mr. Blueflame, whose blue lantern light glimmered and reflected off his spectacles.

The Black Roses, all of them pale-skinned like vampires, stepped forward, led by Mr. Skinner, nicknamed after the horrific-looking knife he clutched in his hand.

The Whistlers appeared out of nowhere, startling Abigail. They blew high-pitched, piercing notes from their lips, signaling their arrival, led by their boss, Mr. Flute.

The Pikes, a loud rabble of dirty men, all carrying crude weapons, barged in and roughly took their places, led by a red-faced, angry Irishman Abigail nicknamed Mr. Loud.

Taking the twelfth spot came the Hives. Legions of bugs crawled and wriggled all over their stinking clothes. They were led by Mr. Moth.

So many. Abigail worried. *I didn't know there would be so many.*

Then the semicircle parted, splitting into two fragments that moved aside, spreading out to make room for one, final group. All of the gangs seemed nervous.

Then one man stepped forward from the shadows, wearing a loud, clanking overcoat made of chain mail. He wore a top hat with wires snaking all over it and when he raised his head to reveal his face, Abigail gasped, as did the rest of the gangs. The man wore goggles, like Night Owl Nell, but his goggles, powered by an electric charge, caused the man's eyes to glow with white light, shining like two full moons.

Abigail nicknamed him Mr. Bright Eyes.

Behind him, two more men entered. She could not make them out at first, but they crackled and fizzled like their leader. Sparks flew from their clothes, and electricity snapped and buzzed between their fingers.

"Shock Troops," she whispered under her breath.

Following Mr. Bright Eyes, these sizzling, sparking Shock Troops pushed something on squeaking wheels. Whatever it was stood twenty feet tall, and the men strained with all their might to move it as it rumbled forth. *It must weigh a ton,* Abigail thought. *What could it be?* Mr. Bright Eyes took position next to the towering, wheeled object, which was concealed underneath a dirty cloth. After pushing it into the room, the two henchmen bowed and retreated, as if they were going to retrieve something else.

Peering deeper into the shadows, Abigail could make out two more figures who were dressed very, very oddly. They stepped into the circle of firelight and took their place next to Mr. Bright Eyes. They were the strangest men Abigail had ever seen.

Abigail called the first one Mr. Lens because he wore an oversized, spherical, deep-sea diving helmet with a round glass porthole where his face would be. The round glass resembled the circular windows in her apartment. Instead of showing the man's entire face, the glass porthole acted like a bizarre magnifying glass. When Mr. Lens spoke, his mouth magnified and took up the whole window. When he sniffed, his nose took up the entire lens. Whenever he wanted to get a good look at something, the round glass aperture turned into one gigantic, blinking eyeball.

Mr. Lens wore a bulky diving suit with leaden, clonking, metal boots on his feet and crude, metal gauntlets covering his hands. He hefted two enormous copper tanks of compressed air on his back. Even though she knew he was quite obviously evil, Abigail marveled at his technology. *If Mr. Lens were dropped underwater, even into the middle of the ocean, then he could probably survive for hours walking along the bottom. How bizarre. What is someone like him doing here?*

In his metal gauntlets, Mr. Lens carried a fearsome, oversized wooden crossbow made from fragments of a shipwreck. The weapon was still wet and slimy as if Mr. Lens had just emerged from beneath the waves. Crusty barnacles studded its surface and seaweed dripped from its lever, stirrup, string, and prod. Every time Mr. Lens took a step, every joint on him hissed and spewed white smoke. Over his shoulder, in a greasy leather quiver, he slung a cluster of harpoons carved out of whalebone.

Next to Mr. Lens stood a man dressed head to toe in cracked leather. His long coat, boots, top hat, gloves, everything about him bore the same color, a faded golden brown. He wore an especially strange mask that covered his entire head and sealed it tight. It had two round eyes made of glass. A long tube protruded from his nose and ran down his chest like an elephant trunk until it connected to a satchel that he wore slung on his side. Abigail considered nicknaming him Mr. Elephant, but he was neither large nor grey. So she decided to call him Mr. Goldsmoke because noxious, swirling yellow vapor emanated from every inch of his person.

Mr. Goldsmoke, in one of his hands, gripped a glass bottle filled with a glowing, smoking, golden liquid. In his other hand, he carried a leather case that clinked and clanked when he set it down on the floor. *He must be carrying more of those glowing, golden, glass bottles in there. Are they some kind of weapon?* Abigail wondered.

Abigail counted over a hundred gang members in the warehouse. They all gathered together to meet with Mr. Makepeace, who stood authoritatively before them, unflinching, unafraid, unmoved, and a little impatient. Imitating a judge in court, he cleared his throat, and then he rapped his cane down three times on the floor, unleashing a booming echo throughout the entire chamber.

"Gentlemen," Mr. Makepeace's smooth, calm voice filled the room as he addressed all of the gangs. "I hear that you're having quite a bit of trouble with a little girl." Mr. Makepeace could not resist mocking them a little bit.

"Don't look at us," the Smooth Boys' leader, Mr. Silver, snickered. "That's them." He pointed to the Longshadows and the Wild Cards, who blushed, embarrassed.

"My contacts in the police tell me that over fifty of you have been arrested all over town. Is that true?"

Both the Longshadows and Wild Cards spoke up, shouting, blaming, pointing fingers.

"Don't talk over each other!" Mr. Makepeace chastised them as if they were children. "Just say yes."

"Yes," Mr. Stretch and Mr. Ball sheepishly admitted.

"Good, now be quiet."

The rest of the gangs paid attention.

"I'll take care of this little red-haired rascal," Mr. Makepeace assured them all. "She'll be dead by dusk. The rest of you stay out of this. Our business continues as usual. Nothing changes."

"What about their territory?" the leader of the Pikes grunted.

"Nothing changes," Mr. Makepeace cut him off and glared at him.

"What, so they just get to make a mistake and not pay for it?" Mr. Skinner, leader of the Black Roses, huffed.

Mr. Twelve, the leader of Los Seises, spoke a mix of Spanish and English. "*Su territorio* should be ripe for us. If they can't hold it against a *chica*, then they don't deserve it."

The gangs all roared in approval, but Mr. Makepeace rapped his cane against the floor.

"If you all squabble over their territory, we'll be meeting like this every day for a month!" Mr. Makepeace shouted them down. *"Think!"*

Abigail observed all of the gangs very carefully. Although she knew they were obligated to attend this meeting, Abigail noticed something odd. *They all seem to have sent their largest, toughest warriors. Why?*

"What about her father?" the leader of the Squids snarled. "He works the docks. Do you want us to handle him?"

Abigail nearly jumped up. Little Wade calmed her.

"If I kill the girl, then he won't be a problem," Mr. Makepeace replied. "Leave him alone. If we kill his child, it'll break him, and he'll leave the city for sure. Maybe he'll even kill himself. The fewer corpses we produce, the easier it will be for our friends in the police department to sweep all of this under the rug, and we can all just get on with business."

"We should kill them all. Send a message!" Mr. Skinner riled up his followers.

"You know the rules!" Mr. Makepeace barked, silencing him. "You know who I can call if you cause trouble for me. Do you really want me to call...him?"

Every gang quieted down.

Abigail cast a glance at Little Wade. "Who is he talking about?"

Little Wade did not answer.

"Now, are we in agreement?" Mr. Makepeace demanded an answer from everyone in the room.

They all mumbled.

"I can't hear you."

"*Yes*," they all assented.

Satisfied, Mr. Makepeace set aside his cane and rubbed his hands together eagerly, like a little boy at Christmas.

"You know how this works. Tribute."

Little Wade leaned over and whispered in Abigail's ear.

"Here they come."

One by one, each of the gangs stepped forward and offered Mr. Makepeace something. Mostly, they offered money, but there were a few interesting items. A few provided slips of paper with important secrets written down on them. Looking them over, Mr. Makepeace smiled and then folded them up and tucked them into his pockets. Abigail noticed that Mr. Goldsmoke offered Mr. Makepeace the glass bottle with the glowing, golden liquid. Mr. Makepeace took it carefully and held it in his gloved hand, palming it as if he intended to use it.

Finally, Mr. Bright Eyes stepped forward. He snapped his fingers, sparking electricity, and Abigail watched as a group of children, all chained to each other, all wearing collars around their necks like dogs, stepped forward. There were five children, three boys, and two girls. The three boys, one stocky Spanish boy, one Jewish boy wearing a yarmulke and with payos in his hair, and one rotund, overweight boy, working together, carried a long pole with a bulb attached, a miniature lamppost.

"Fuyvush Rothman, Ramon Garcia, Horace Pole," Little Wade whispered. Abigail recognized the names of the children Night Owl Nell had mentioned during their meeting in her carriage. The first young girl, Chinese, carried a length of copper wire. "Li Jing."

Finally, the last child, another young girl, carried a metal, cube-shaped object. She was a slender girl with beautiful raven hair, piercing green eyes, and delicate hands. Although terrified, the dark-haired girl stepped forward gracefully. Abigail's eyes opened wide. She remembered her training and said nothing. She did not have to. She simply pointed at the young girl carrying the heavy, metal box.

Brooke Adams.

"It's a demonstration," Abigail whispered as she watched Brooke, Jing, Ramon, Fuyvush, and Horace assemble the device. The three boys set down the miniature lamppost. Jing strung a copper wire between the pole and the metal box. The last, and most dangerous task, fell to Brooke. Wearing vulcanized rubber gloves, Brooke took hold of Jing's wire. She carefully wrapped the copper wire tightly around the top of the metal box, creating a pair of copper coils. Sparking, the box hummed to life, and the electric cable shuddered and shook. It jolted Brooke, who snatched her hand away as if from a fire.

Blinking on, the electric lamppost flickered and then illuminated the entire chamber with a bright, shining light. It emitted a loud, humming, electrical sound. Everyone in the room *ooooohed* and *aaaahed*, astounded.

"It's a portable battery!" Abigail whispered.

"That's why we couldn't find them." Little Wade replied.

"Remarkable," Mr. Makepeace sounded genuinely surprised and impressed.

Mr. Bright Eyes snapped his fingers with another spark, and Jing stripped the wire from the miniature lamppost, killing the light. Jing handed the cable to Mr. Bright Eyes, who snatched it from her hands and then pushed her away with a spark. Then, his two servants pushed the mysterious, hulking object covered with a dirty cloth, rolling it forward. Then, peeling up the cloth, he forced Brooke to place the battery inside what looked to be some kind of small compartment in the colossal device. Mr. Bright Eyes forced Brooke to attach the battery to...whatever it was. He needed her tiny hands to connect everything properly. After she finished, he snapped his fingers with a spark and gestured rudely for her to step away. Brooke retreated. Releasing the cloth, letting it droop down again, Mr. Bright Eyes smiled and gestured to the hidden behemoth.

The children, still with their collars on, were led to a door at the back of the warehouse by the other two Shock Troops. Peering through her lenses, Abigail watched them vanish into a storage room.

"So, it will work?" Mr. Makepeace asked.

Mr. Bright Eyes, his goggles glowing, smiled and nodded.

"What's under the cloth?" Abigail whispered.

Little Wade, legitimately worried, shook his head. "I...I don't know."

Mr. Makepeace began to laugh.

"I am very pleased with this," Mr. Makepeace complimented the Shock Troops. "Thank you all for coming here today. Then he turned specifically to the Wild Cards and the Longshadows. "I know you gentlemen are not at fault for what's been happening lately. We all know who's truly responsible. They've been a nuisance for quite some time. Haven't they?"

Abigail's eyes sprang open. *Uh, oh.*

"Tell me, Abigail Reid," Mr. Makepeace called out, "did you really think I didn't recognize you at the shoeshine stand?"

Thrash materialized next to Mr. Makepeace and growled, glaring straight at Abigail with his one functional, gruesome eye.

Mr. Makepeace turned to look up directly at her. "You think you're the only ones who make plans? Why do you think we're all here?"

Little Wade began to glow.

"If you know we're here." Little Wade shouted as he revealed himself, "then you know how much trouble you're in."

When they saw Little Wade, some of the gang members howled and roared. Others seemed confused as if they could neither see nor hear anything.

"And...you know I don't work alone!" Little Wade's voice boomed.

Crash!

Watchtower burst into the chamber, smashing through the wall as if it were paper. *Crank-crank-cranking*, he drew himself up to his full twenty-one-foot height. Frightened, all of the gang members faltered. They huddled together, raising their weapons.

"New York Police Department!"

Behind Watchtower, who kicked up a cloud of dust, over fifty officers of Precinct Zero stormed in and massed at Watchtower's feet. Abigail held her breath as the two armies stood facing each other. Although the gang members outnumbered Precinct Zero two to one. Watchtower, standing on the police side, made it more than a fair fight.

Still clutching Mr. Goldsmoke's glowing glass bottle, Mr. Makepeace reached into his bag with his free hand and pulled out a pair of charred skulls that had melted and fused together in a raging fire. He held the skulls up, smiled, and sneered, "Rest in peace." Then he slammed them down on the floor with a loud *crack!* Two misshapen ghosts burst forward from the melted skulls, spewing upwards like a volcanic eruption until they coalesced into their hideous form. Joined at the skull, shoulder, torso, hip, and leg, the two ghastly specters, one man, one woman, had died together holding each other tightly in a white-hot fire that melted their flesh and bone, fusing them together forever into a bizarre, monstrous form.

Their skulls had melted into a grotesque double skull. Their faces conjoined into one revolting visage. Two jaws had melted into one oversized mouth, two noses into one three-nostrilled nose, two tongues into one seared, serpentine tongue, and four eyes into three cooked ones. The middle eye, bulging and double-sized, dripped fluid like a runny egg. His right leg and her left leg, intertwined and fused, transformed into a long, fleshy tail with a sharp, jagged stinger made from melted bone and toenails. Their two bodies floated in the air, parallel to each other like twins. Their free legs and arms spread out wide on either side. Unleashing a cloud of spectral black smoke that spread like wings, the Melted Skulls Ghost soared through the warehouse like the battered skeleton of a gigantic, deformed bat.

Thrash, Mr. Makepeace's ferocious phantom hound, transformed into a repulsive, serpentine form with a wolfish head spouting green flame. Facing them, Little Wade, glowing brightly, his eyes shimmering like stars, recited.

"In many forms, I've terrorized you for years.
Now, under one roof, behold all of your fears!"

Little Wade clapped his hands and split into thirteen duplicates of himself. Abigail watched as twelve of the Little Wade Polyplots each transformed into a unique, fantastical creature. Abigail recognized them immediately from the theater: the Haunters, the many terrible forms Little Wade had taken over the years to strike fear into the hearts of criminals. As each monster completed its metamorphosis, Little Wade called out their names one by one in rapid succession.

"Grabblygook!" A crooked, troll-like creature with slimy blobs for hands and wriggling fingers for teeth.

"Sniggerwing!" A laughing, impish devil with blurry, humming wings, large goggles, and a pair of smoking pistols.

"Phosphoroctopod!" A squid made out of lava with constantly bursting bubbles for eyes.

"Nastersnout!" A spiky-haired werewolf with wooden splinters for fur, wasp's eyes, and a long stinger for a nose.

"Trigglyverm!" An unnatural combination of a white rat, a centipede, and a squishy slug.

"Talonoculus!" A ruthless bird of prey covered in eyes instead of feathers.

"Weaponwood!" A longbow carrying, hooded ranger, only he was some kind of inhuman, wooden creature with twigs for fingers, branches for arms, and a hollow of a tree for his hood, a dark hole with no face inside.

"Nightmarker!" A dead, pale-skinned gangster carrying a butcher's cleaver in one hand and a sawed-off, double-barreled shotgun in the other.

"Slowbones!" An animated, fossilized skeleton of a tusked, apish ogre.

"Bloodygoobrius!" A giant, glass jar filled with red liquid and a freakish specimen floating in the fluid, banging on the glass, trying to escape.

"Zappathoth!" A jellyfish made out of storm clouds with tentacles made of lightning.

"Spellfire!" A dark wizard, bleeding from his mouth, clutching a burning book with both hands.

As for Little Wade himself, Abigail smiled when she saw his long black tailcoat morph into giant scorpion's tail. Black fire, in the shape of scorpion's claws, covered his fists like boxing gloves. Before this panoply of terrifying spirits, the gangs hesitated and cowered. Defiantly, Thrash and the Melted Skulls Ghost roared, but then Little Wade roared back. *"This is our city!"*

Tweeeeeeeeet! Sergeant Blood blew his whistle, signaling the attack. Watchtower, the officers of Precinct Zero, and the Great Gathering of Gangs charged toward each other and collided in the center of the room. Whirring, clicking, clanking loudly, his fiery face glowing brightly, Watchtower illuminated the entire warehouse like the sun. He stormed forward with long, booming strides. His footsteps cracked the floor.

Floating high above, pointing towards his enemies, Little Wade ordered his Haunters forward. They attacked Thrash and the Melted

Skulls Ghost, who also charged. The warring spirits collided and created a glowing maelstrom as they tore into each other. Roaring like thunder, all of the phantasms whirled around each other so fast that Abigail, watching them from her perch, felt as if she were inside a hurricane of light. Abigail pulled down the flaps on her Intrepid Cap to protect her ears from the horrible shrieking.

A terrible battle unfolded before Abigail's eyes. She saw Watchtower swing his metal arms from side to side. Barreling through the crowd of gangsters like a massive, rolling boulder, he knocked enemies aside like bowling pins. Several gangsters raised revolvers and fired at Watchtower, but the shots bounced pathetically off his armored skin. The officers of Precinct Zero, using Watchtower as cover, returned fire and then charged when they got close enough.

"This shouldn't take too long," Abigail boasted as she carefully concealed herself in her overlook behind one of the pillars. Watching through her bifocal goggles, she spied Mr. Makepeace, Mr. Bright Eyes, Mr. Goldsmoke, and Mr. Lens standing by the tall, mysterious object draped in cloth. Even as they beheld their fellow gangsters getting utterly smashed by Watchtower, they calmly stood their ground, waiting for Watchtower to come to them.

Why are they smiling?

Then the Hives struck. Foul men riddled with bugs, the Hives did something fiendishly clever. They tossed bottles filled with swirling insect swarms directly at Watchtower's head. Shattering, the glass bottles unleashed hundreds of flapping moths that quickly blanketed Watchtower's glass face. They were attracted to his flame! Blinded, Watchtower clawed at his face to drive them off, but he only crushed and smeared them against the panes.

Then the Whistlers ringed Watchtower and uttered piercing high-pitched noises that prevented Watchtower from hearing properly, so he flailed about blindly, clumsily, lumbering through the roaring, shouting mob. Lassoing him with thick ropes from the docks, the Squids and the Pikes, the strongest of the gangs, wrangled Watchtower while the Sewer Rats, scuttling at his feet, poured grease onto the floor under him to trip him up. When Watchtower stumbled close enough, Mr. Bright Eyes stripped the cloth from the mysterious object and unveiled a tall, dark, strange-looking...iron statue?

Watchtower, peeling away the moths for a moment, spotted Mr. Makepeace, Mr. Lens, Mr. Goldsmoke, and Mr. Bright Eyes. Long arms outstretched, he snapped the ropes that were binding him and thundered through the throng. Just as he was about to sweep his attack from side to side and wipe the four men out, Mr. Lens screamed. His horrible mouth took up the entire porthole on his face as he uttered three fateful words.

"Turn it on!"

Mr. Bright Eyes flicked a switch. Abigail heard fizzing, buzzing, and crackling. She felt a violent vibration in the room as the large metal object hummed to life. Her metal watch, trapped inside her breast pocket, pulled away from her and stretched the fabric of her clothes.

An electromagnet!

Watchtower stumbled forward, sucked toward the magnetic iron statue until he stuck to it with a loud *thunk*! Mr. Lens, wearing his heavy metal diving suit, pressed buttons on his heavy metal boots and activated rubber suction cups on the soles of his feet that fastened him to the floor. He stayed put.

All of the guns and knives flew through the air and stuck to the huge electromagnet as well. Only Mr. Makepeace managed to holster his pistol beneath his coat just in time so he could hold onto it. Some of the metal weapons whizzed through the air so quickly that Mr. Goldsmoke ducked to save himself from injury. Zooming in with her goggles, Abigail saw that Mr. Bright Eyes' chain mail coat was painted black, but it appeared to be composed of copper, which crackled with electricity but did not seem to be attracted to the magnet, which firmly trapped Watchtower.

For a moment, the entire mob stopped, dumbfounded. All of their guns and knives rattled, stuck to the electromagnet's vibrating, rough, iron surface.

"*No guns? Are you serious?*" Mr. Stretch, the Longshadows' leader, whined.

"*No knives?*" Mr. Skinner complained.

Even the officers of Precinct Zero grumbled, irritated that they too had lost their firearms.

Mr. Makepeace yelled at all of the gang members.

"Come on. You knew this was part of the plan. Punch it out! Punch it out! Let's get this over with!"

Frustrated, everyone grunted and sighed. "Oh, all right," many of the men muttered. "Fine," a few others huffed. Then the fighting resumed. Luckily, the officers of Precinct Zero had brought their wooden billy clubs and promptly pounded their gangster opponents. Without Watchtower's help, although they fought mightily, Precinct Zero quickly found itself badly outnumbered. As the coppers struggled to fight off the swarm, a handful of Precinct Zero officers bravely bashed through the crowd and rushed toward the electromagnet to save Watchtower.

In response, Mr. Goldsmoke reached into his leather bag and extracted not a glass bottle filled with liquid but a sealed, ceramic grenade with a ring-shaped pin on top. Gripping the pin with his gloved fingers, he yanked the ring out with such force that it struck a spark and lit a fuse. Then he hurled the smoldering grenade at the approaching police. It landed at their feet and ruptured, spewing forth a swirling, noxious yellow smoke. From a safe distance, Abigail watched several officers double over, retching, their eyes inflamed. Mr. Lens, in his diving suit, stepping slowly using his suction-cupped boots, waded through the yellow gas completely unaffected, as if he were exploring the depths of a poisonous, yellow sea. Watchtower pulled with all of his strength, but the electromagnet kept sucking him back down as if he were chained to a rock.

"Not so strong now!" Mr. Lens yelled at Watchtower. His ugly mouth filled up the entire porthole in his helmet. "Not so invincible." Mr. Lens loaded one of the whalebone harpoons into his crossbow and cranked it back with all of his strength, preparing to shoot.

In his hand, Mr. Makepeace clutched the glass jar filled with a smoky, golden liquid that Mr. Goldsmoke had given him. "Let's hobble him first," Mr. Makepeace sneered. Then he hurled the jar at

Watchtower's knee. It struck steel and shattered with a loud *hiss*. Acrid smoke erupted, and Abigail watched the golden liquid gnaw through Watchtower's clothing and melt through his metal skin.

Mr. Lens's mouth filled up the entire circular window on his face. "*Look! A soft spot.*" Then, his mouth became a huge eye. Aiming carefully, raising his crossbow, he fired a barbed whalebone spear at Watchtower, hitting him directly in his hissing wound. With a loud *shunk*, the jagged harpoon pierced Watchtower's armored skin and jammed into his joint. If Watchtower could scream, he would have. Abigail watched him struggle and squirm, still stuck. A rigid column of white steam burst out of Watchtower's knee like a broken bone, and machine oil spewed out of him like warm blood. Watchtower desperately tried to free himself from the electromagnet, but he could not move. Mr. Makepeace watched and smiled. Next to him, Mr. Bright Eyes giggled gleefully.

Why isn't Little Wade helping him? Abigail frantically searched for him and was shocked to see Little Wade and his Haunters struggling against the other two horrible wraiths. A wounded Thrash bit off Little Wade's scorpion tail. The Melted Skulls Ghost, severely wounded by Sniggerwing, Zappathoth, and Grabblygook, opened its disjointed mouth and retaliated, breathing spectral flame and eradicating all three Haunters with a single blast.

At the same moment, Mr. Lens, his eye dominating his face, reloaded another vicious-looking spear into his crossbow with a loud *click*. Abigail desperately tried to signal Little Wade for help, but all she could see were the spirits swirling around the ceiling, ripping each other to pieces. Precinct Zero fought bravely, but they were too outnumbered to reach Watchtower.

They advised me to wait here, Abigail told herself. She hesitated, breathing rapidly. Her hands twitched nervously. Then she felt her watch *clicking* by her heart, and she gritted her teeth. *I'm not going to stand by and do nothing.* Abigail pulled on her vulcanized rubber gloves, designed to protect her from shocks. It would take small hands to reach in, disconnect that battery, and shut off that electromagnet, and Abigail Reid possessed two of them.

Snapping her fingers, she became invisible in her mind. While the brutal battle surged all around her, Abigail Reid climbed down from her safe spot and raced forward. Sprinting into the chaos, Abigail headed straight for the electromagnet. She had thirteen seconds of bravery, and she was going to make them count.

One.

Reaching into his leather bag, Mr. Goldsmoke extracted and tossed two more glass vials of acid at Watchtower. They struck him in the chest, burning through his suit and his armor plating.

Two.

His eye dominating his face, Mr. Lens aimed and fired another harpoon and pierced Watchtower's chest with a loud *shunk!* As she approached, Abigail smelled the gas that erupted from the wound.

Three.

Mr. Lens's ugly nose dominated his face as he sniffed loudly and chuckled. "*Smells like death!*" His gas supply sputtering, Watchtower coughed and wheezed. Running out of breath, he stopped fighting. His flame flickered as gas leaked out of his lungs. More machine oil and steaming hot water gushed onto the floor as if an artery had been punctured.

Four.

Mr. Goldsmoke raised his arm to hurl another acid vial.

Five.

Wap!

Just before he hurled another acid vial at Watchtower, a rock struck Mr. Goldsmoke in the head, knocking him sideways. He dropped his acid vial right onto Mr. Lens, who yelped as the acid quickly melted through his diving suit.

Six.

Mr. Goldsmoke quickly fumbled through his bag, picked out a second glass bottle, this one filled with green liquid, and threw it at the squealing Mr. Lens.

Seven.

It shattered on the diving suit, quickly neutralizing the acid, creating a frothing foam and releasing a stinking green smoke.

At the same exact moment, Mr. Makepeace glanced down at the rock that skidded to his feet and saw that it had a name.

"Marvin?" Mr. Makepeace read the name out loud.

Eight.

A small pouch landed between all four men, a white pouch with an eye symbol on it.

Nine.

Then something fiery clattered across the floor and rolled toward the pouch. It was a small wooden soldier, on fire, whose outstretched, burning arm touched the white pouch.

Ten.

Whoosh!

The flash powder ignited, unleashing a bright, white burst.

Mr. Makepeace, Mr. Bright Eyes, Mr. Lens, and Mr. Goldsmoke all stumbled back.

Eleven.

Blinking, clearing his blurry vision, Mr. Makepeace spotted Abigail crouching behind the towering electromagnet. With her vulcanized rubber gloves, Abigail reached inside to disconnect the battery.

"Stop her!"

Twelve.

Stretching her arms inside the machine, Abigail felt around for the copper coil and wire. Electricity crackled through her fingers, hands, wrists, and forearms. Although the rubber protected her and blunted the shock, the high voltage still burned through Abigail's muscles and fried her nerves.

Thirteen.

Crying out, agony shredding her arm, Abigail gritted her teeth and stripped the wire from the battery. She felt the vibrations cease. The humming quieted down. She heard a sound, like a gigantic metal lock...unlocking.

20

SCORPION

Falling backward, her arms still aching, Abigail struck the cold floor with the back of her head. Thankfully, her Intrepid Cap protected her. Blinking, groaning, recovering, she gripped the big, boxy battery in her hands. Then, in the corner of her eye, she saw Mr. Makepeace, Mr. Bright Eyes, Mr. Lens (partially melted), and Mr. Goldsmoke. They all charged toward her, but just as they were about to reach her, Watchtower, free from the electromagnet, rose up and swatted them aside, scattering them in all directions. Then Abigail noticed that she lay next to a pile of revolvers and daggers, all of which had detached from the electromagnet.

"Uh oh," she uttered.

"*Guns!*" someone yelled.

"*Kniiiiiiiiiiiives!*" another yelled.

Everyone rushed toward the pile of weapons. Abigail scampered out of the way just in time. Watchtower picked up and slammed the enormous electromagnet down on the pile of revolvers and knives with a loud, metallic *crunch*! A few weapons scattered across the floor, but most were damaged beyond functioning.

"Oh come *on*!" one of the criminals whined, and then the gangs and Precinct Zero went back to fighting each other with fists and clubs.

Yanking the whalebone harpoons out of his knee and chest and snapping them like twigs, Watchtower struggled to stand. Severely wounded, his flame flickering, his body bleeding hot water and oil, he struggled to repair himself. His damaged joints spewed steam, and his chest heaved from a lack of gas. He reached under his torn clothing and turned several squeaking knobs, rerouting the gas, oil, water, and steam flows through his body, stopping his bleeding. Abigail heard gears grinding, metal clanking and shrieking, valves sputtering. Then she spied Mr. Goldsmoke and Mr. Lens, who had both reloaded. They ambushed him from behind.

"*Watch out!*" Abigail cried.

Just before Mr. Goldsmoke could throw another acid vial, Watchtower reached out his elongated left arm, seized Mr. Lens, gripped him around his ankles, and lifted him up.

"*This is going to hurt!*" Mr. Lens's mouth dominated his face just before Watchtower swung Mr. Lens around like a heavy metal mace, swatting gangsters left and right, blasting them into the air and scattering them like shards of shattered glass. Squealing in terror, Squids, Wild Cards, Longshadows, Pikes, and Sewer Rats flew throughout the warehouse and crashed into the walls, knocked unconscious. Precinct Zero cheered. Watchtower was back in the fight.

I...I can't believe I just did all of that. Abigail caught her breath, but her moment of respite was quickly interrupted. Still swinging a screaming Mr. Lens, Watchtower barely missed Mr. Goldsmoke. Clutching his leather bag full of chemical poisons, Mr. Goldsmoke stumbled in Abigail's direction. Precinct Zero, wounded and battered, rallied again and charged, swinging their trusty wooden clubs, knocking heads. Struggling to escape, Mr. Goldsmoke, panicking, turned toward the wall. As Precinct Zero officers closed in and tried to apprehend him, he tossed several glass vials against the brick surface, melting a hole through the wall within seconds.

"*Stop that man!*" Abigail pointed to him. Three officers from Precinct Zero charged him. One of the officers hurled his wooden club at Mr. Goldsmoke and struck him in the back. Dropping his leather bag, Mr. Goldsmoke turned around to see three officers converge on him. Frantically pulling out another one of his gas grenades, popping the pin, dropping it onto the floor, Mr. Goldsmoke vanished, spreading more sickly, yellow smoke. Although Abigail kept a safe distance, the foul stench of rotten eggs still repulsed her. Abigail recognized the smell from her chemistry class. *Sulfur.* The three officers caught in the cloud doubled over, vomiting. Their irritated, bloodshot eyes leaked tears; they flailed about helplessly in the smoke.

"Get out of the smoke! Follow my voice!" she called out to the officers. Stumbling out of the cloud and over to her, they collapsed, coughing. One of them almost tripped over Mr. Goldsmoke's leather bag. As the yellow smoke dissipated, Abigail saw that Mr. Goldsmoke had escaped through the hole in the wall. She turned her attention to the officers. Pulling out her medical kit, she distributed gauze and bandages to them.

"Are you all right?"

"Fine, ugh!" One spat yellow bile and held gauze up to a gash on his forehead that he had suffered during the melee.

"It...just makes...you sick," the second managed to reply, then vomited and wiped his mouth with a bandage.

"I think we're winning!" the third one, dressing a wound on his arm, called out and pointed behind her.

Abigail quickly glanced around the warehouse. She could see neither Mr. Bright Eyes nor Mr. Makepeace, but the tide of the battle had turned. Watchtower, still swinging Mr. Lens, waded into the violent mob, flattening gangsters, knocking them unconscious. Around him, Precinct Zero clobbered anyone who managed to dodge Watchtower's relentless assault.

Above her, the spirits continued to maul each other. Seared and scorched by Phosphoroctopod's lava tentacles, Thrash gained the upper hand and devoured the glowing squid. The Melted Skulls Ghost, also ravaged by Little Wade's magic, crashed into and shattered Slowbone. Commanding his Haunters, Little Wade, soaring throughout the room, kept his attention firmly fixed on the warring specters.

What else can I do? Abigail asked herself. Scanning the area, Abigail spied Sergeant Slow Burn on the floor, still on fire. Quickly recovering her small wooden statue and blowing him out, Abigail jumped when a rock, kicked around by the all of the shuffling feet, skidded right toward her and came to a stop by her ankle like a loyal pet.

Marvin.

Scooping up her rock, Abigail took six seconds and scanned the entire warehouse. Even under her capped ears, she heard shouting, roaring, *thuds, slaps, crunches,* and *loud bonks!* She smelled sweaty men, blood, gunpowder, the last traces of Sulfur, and gas. Watchtower, even coughing, short of breath and low on gas, still towered above everyone and tossed gangsters aside as if they were nothing.

Up above, the specters continued Ryving each other. Another of Little Wade's Haunters, the one called Nastersnout, finally succumbed to his wounds and disintegrated, but not before ripping off one of the Melted Skulls Ghost's wings. Trigglyverm, the rat-centipede-slug hybrid creature, encircled and squeezed Thrash's serpentine body and then bit him viciously, scoring a nasty hit before Thrash popped spikes out of his own spectral form. Impaled, Trigglyverm released Thrash and discombobulated. Thrash, weakened, visibly struggled to keep fighting.

Brooke and the others! Abigail's mind raced. *Where did they go? Where did the Shock Troops take them?* Then she spotted the back door. *On the other side, the children might still be there!* Stuffing Sergeant Slow Burn and Marvin back into her saddlebag, Abigail felt her *clicking* steel watch by her heart. *Thirteen seconds on. Thirteen seconds off.* She approached the door. Her hands trembling, she opened the door slowly and crept inside, hearing the screams and cries of children.

One.

Sneaking into a storage room filled with animal cages, Abigail stopped. *This must be where they have been holding the children hostage this whole time!* Mr. Bright Eyes towered in front of Fuyvush, Horace, Jing, and Ramon, intimidating them. His glowing goggles illuminated all of their terrified faces. He stood with his back to Abigail.

Two.

"You're not going anywhere!" Mr. Bright Eyes' voice boomed. Abigail caught a glimpse of Brooke cowering behind the other four children.

Three.

"*Back in your cages!*" Mr. Bright Eyes roared and lashed out, threatening them.

Four.

Frightened, the children whimpered and fell silent.

Five.

Abigail's hands trembled. Mr. Bright Eyes was the largest man she had ever seen, almost as tall as Watchtower's seven-foot form, and he probably weighed over two-hundred pounds. Watching helplessly as he stalked toward the children, Abigail clasped her shaking hands together.

Six.

Mr. Bright Eyes, with his long, crackling, chainmail coat, his goggles glowing brightly, dominated the room. Next to him, Abigail felt like a mouse. *Wait! Mouse! What does a mouse see?*

Seven.

Her whole body coursing with nervous energy, Abigail spotted… an opening.

Eight.

She skittered quickly toward Mr. Bright Eyes, who opened his hand. Electricity crackled between his metal-gloved fingertips. The children flinched. Abigail snuck up behind Mr. Bright Eyes, her soft footsteps drowned out by the children's cries and the *bangs, clanks,* and *crashes* of Watchtower's assault in the next room.

Nine.

Abigail crouched and then reached out with her tiny hands. She gripped Mr. Bright Eyes's ankles, creating little claws with her fingers.

Then she quickly looped them like hooks around the cold, heavy metal boots. "Scorpion!" she whispered.

"Wha..." was all Mr. Bright Eyes managed to mutter out of his mouth.

Ten.

Gritting her teeth, Abigail pulled his ankles with all of her strength. Her legs, back, neck, arms, hands all strained. Her muscles pulled taut and tense. Her fingers could not wholly encircle Mr. Bright Eyes's booted ankles, so her grip nearly slipped off. Her wrists ached. The exertion and the weight, so much weight, almost overwhelmed her.

Eleven.

Then Mr. Bright Eyes became weightless in her grip as he tripped and toppled forward like a stone tower. It took him by surprise and happened so fast that he did not have time to catch himself, and his long arms flailed out to his sides.

Twelve.

He fell face flat, bashing his nose and knocking his forehead against the cold, wet, stone floor with a loud *whump!* His goggles cracked, their light snuffed out.

Thirteen.

Abigail stepped forward, placed her booted foot on the prone, unconscious Mr. Bright Eyes's back, and stood straight up, regal, like a queen.

"Who are you?" the children asked.

Abigail removed her Intrepid Cap and unleashed her fiery, red hair. Horace, Fuyvush, Jing, and Ramon, stunned, struggled to speak to this complete stranger who had just saved them. Then Brooke burst forth from behind the group and threw her arms wide open. "*Abigail!*" Embracing fiercely, the two girls practically collided in front of the other children.

"Abigail, is that really you?" Although she was excited, Brooke's voice sounded odd, distant.

"I can hardly believe it myself, but yes," Abigail replied. Up close, she got a good look at Brooke. Her friend had changed. Still beautiful,

Brooke had lost all color in her skin and looked painfully thin. Her eyes were sunken and sadder, and her lips and fingers shivered as if she were freezing. When Abigail hugged Brooke, she felt only skin and bone. Brooke's skin felt cold and clammy. This only inflamed Abigail, who burned bright red.

"I feared you were gone forever." Abigail nearly teared up.

"Abigail...why are you here?" Brooke touched Abigail's face and hair as if she did not believe Abigail was real.

"I'm here to rescue you. Let's get those collars off. We're all getting out of here."

"You can't beat them." Brooke shook her head. "You can't. They're too strong and too many. They're everywhere, Abigail. They own everything. They control everything. Everything...hurts."

"Nonsense!" Abigail stooped down and fished a set of keys from Mr. Bright Eyes's belt. "They are most certainly not invincible. Exhibit A!" She pointed to the unconscious Mr. Bright Eyes. Through the door, they overheard the battle raging, screams, cries, shouts, and loud *bonks*.

"You brought the police?" Fuyvush gestured to the door and the noise outside.

"I'm here with Little Wade and Watchtower."

"Little Wade and Watchtower?" Horace's mouth dropped open.

"The ghost and giant?" Jing's mouth dropped open, too.

Ramon spoke a mix of English and Spanish. "*Espera, la leyenda es verdad*? They...they're real?"

"*Yes, we are!*" Little Wade yelled as he flew into the room, still battling the other specters with swirls of light. A second later, Abigail opened the door, and the children jumped when they beheld Watchtower marching through the room, swinging his immense arms back and forth, his body crawling with gangsters trying to slow him down.

"They're real!" Brooke exclaimed.

"We need you to clear us a path. Can you do it?" Abigail turned toward Little Wade and commanded him.

"We're on it. Well done, Abigail." Little Wade turned to the other children. "Hello, Brooke. Shalom, Fuyvush. Ni Hao, Jing. Hola,

Ramon. Greetings, Horace." Then Little Wade flew off. All of the children were too dumbstruck to reply.

"We can't stay here. It's not safe!" Abigail pointed to the side door of the warehouse. "There! That's our way out! We'll wait for the right moment."

"Abigail, does my father know I'm here?" Brooke asked, pulling Abigail's wrist.

Abigail hesitated. "Your...your father?"

"Yes...does he know? Did he come with you? Is he here?"

Using the keys, the children unlocked each other, dropping their collars to the floor with loud *clanks*. They handed the keys to Abigail, who unlocked Brooke's collar.

"Brooke, I won't lie to you. When you disappeared, your father went mad with grief. He's in Bellevue now, in the...ward for the mentally ill."

"Oh...no...he's...he's in the asylum?" Brooke nearly fainted. "I...put him in the madhouse?"

"You didn't do anything."

"This is my fault. I was stupid. I let them take me. He's there because of me."

"Listen to me!" Abigail gripped Brooke's frail shoulders. "This is not your fault, Brooke. We'll get you out of *here*, and we'll get him out of *there*! He thinks you're dead, but you're alive. We're going to take you home. You'll both get to live again! Are you with me?"

Brooke, crying, nodded. "This has been...so horrible."

"It's almost over, but right now I need you to fight." Abigail tossed Brooke's metal collar onto the floor and turned to the other children. "We're all scared, but we all need to fight. Ready?"

They were about to move when they heard whispering behind them. Whirling around, Abigail gasped. Mr. Bright Eyes, his nose bleeding, his lips split, lay injured on the floor. Sweaty, shivering, Mr. Bright Eyes, his broken goggles flickering and blinking on and off, rolled and curled up into a nearly fetal position. He clutched something in his hand and whispered frantically.

"What...is he...doing?" Brooke spoke first.

"It looks like he's...." Ramon did not know what to say.

"He's...praying," Fuyvush finished his sentence.

"For what?" Jing wondered.

"To who?" Horace added.

Abigail felt a chill.

"Oh, no."

Mr. Bright Eyes continued to pray, and then his goggles stopped flickering. Something in the room had changed. Abigail could feel it. It was as if some door...had unlocked.

"No," Abigail whispered. "No...no, no, no, no, no."

As she retreated from the praying Mr. Bright Eyes, her hand brushed against the wall, and she immediately felt something cold and wet. Recoiling, Abigail whirled around and screamed as a swirling, liquid black hole appeared in the wall, opening like some sinister, monstrous eye. Abigail tried to run, but the other children were too frightened to move.

"We must go. Now!" Abigail pleaded with the others, who stared at the liquifying wall.

"He's here!" Mr. Bright Eyes giggled maniacally.

Something moved inside the pulsing, black fluid portal. Then someone stepped out of it very slowly, revealing himself one piece at a time. A mud-smeared boot emerged first and planted itself on the floor, then another; two boots connected to two legs connected to a man dressed all in black, wearing a military uniform. His black-armored torso was connected to two arms and two hands, one clutching a tomahawk, and the other a lever-action shotgun. The hands were connected to arms that were connected to shoulders connected to a neck connected to a head enshrouded with a hood and a carved mask, a pair of hands covering his face, white hands, the color of bone.

Mr. Peekaboo stepped into the room, tucking his tomahawk into a loop on his belt and cycling the lever on his shotgun, loading it to fire. He stalked toward the children, forcing them out of the back room and into the warehouse. He reached out one hand toward Brooke. Retreating, Abigail and the others, terrified, backed up until *boom!*

Watchtower, twenty-one-feet tall, stepped between the children and Mr. Peekaboo. Gripping a flailing gangster in his hand, Watchtower tossed him away like some pesky rodent and turned his full attention to Mr. Peekaboo. While Precinct Zero battled the remaining gangsters, Little Wade's Haunters continued to grind down the evil spirits, and Abigail and the children observed and cheered, Watchtower and Mr. Peekaboo faced off.

Mr. Peekaboo attacked first. He fired and cycled his shotgun, unleashing two booming blasts that Watchtower blocked with his armored arms. Abigail could hear the shots denting steel. Then a third blast struck Watchtower directly in his glass face, cracking, but not breaking, the glass. The impact momentarily surprised and stunned Watchtower.

Seizing the moment, Mr. Peekaboo carefully aimed his shotgun and unleashed a fourth booming blast into Watchtower's badly damaged knee, completely destroying it, splattering machine oil and spraying metal gears all over the floor, forcing Watchtower to his knees. Cockily, Mr. Peekaboo approached Watchtower, preparing to fire again, this time at Watchtower's wounded, still smoldering chest area. Faster than anyone would expect, Watchtower, with a spring-loaded *boing*, shot out his hand, grabbed Mr. Peekaboo's shotgun, and crunched it like paper.

Mr. Peekaboo released his shotgun, drew his raven-feathered tomahawk, climbed up onto Watchtower's fist, and sprinted up Watchtower's arm. Leaping forward, he scrambled onto Watchtower's shoulders. Making his way to his opponent's head, he hacked at Watchtower's cracked glass face with his tomahawk, chipping a hole in it. Then Mr. Peekaboo yanked a shotgun shell from his bandolier and tossed it through the hole in the glass into Watchtower's flame. *Boom!* The shotgun round exploded inside Watchtower's glass head, shattering three of the glass panes, stunning him.

Tearing Mr. Peekaboo off his shoulder, Watchtower threw him against the far wall with an incredible impact. Mr. Peekaboo dropped his tomahawk, which clattered to the floor, and he struggled to get up. Charging, Watchtower threw a tremendously powerful punch that could obliterate the side of a building, but Mr. Peekaboo surprisingly sprang up from the floor and caught Watchtower's fist. Somehow, Mr. Peekaboo absorbed the impact like a pillow. He slid backward, but he did not fall. Watchtower stopped, confused.

Mr. Peekaboo, his legs tense, and his arms gripping Watchtower's metal limb with all of his superhuman strength, held fast, straining. Not to be outdone, Watchtower, advancing, pushed Mr. Peekaboo back up against the wall and then rotated his entire arm like a drill. Watchtower's shoulder *crank-crank-cranked* and his fist, gripped by both of Mr. Peekaboo's arms, swiveled until Watchtower's knuckles faced down and his palm faced up. Mr. Peekaboo, superhumanly strong, grappled and gripped Watchtower's metal fist as it turned, turned, turned until it stopped, and locked in place with a *chank*!

Watchtower's fist cranked open, blooming like a flower, revealing his open palm. Mr. Peekaboo desperately clung to his hold on Watchtower's hand. There was a small hatch on Watchtower's metal palm. It popped open, and a tiny hiss escaped. Abigail immediately smelled gas. Watchtower snapped his fingers, creating a spark, igniting the combustible vapor. A fireball erupted in Mr. Peekaboo's face, smothering him in flames. Mr. Peekaboo, from behind his mask, uttered the most chilling, awful scream, the sound of a thousand children crying. Watchtower seized the flaming Mr. Peekaboo and flung him back through the door to the storage room and back into his swirling, whirling liquid portal. Burning, flames crackling all over his uniform, Mr. Peekaboo disappeared, and the portal closed. His tomahawk remained on the floor.

Fuyvush, Horace, Ramon, and Jing cheered loudly.

Abigail raised her arms in triumph.

"*Abigail, look out!*" Brooke screamed.

Abigail turned just in time to see Mr. Makepeace aiming his revolver directly at her. Squeezing the trigger, Mr. Makepeace fired.

21

A GOOD DEATH

Standing outside of her own body, Abigail watched herself crumple to the ground and heard herself utter one last bloody gasp, "Mama," before she lay still, a red gunshot wound blooming on her chest like a rose. Brooke cried and fell to her knees. All of the other children screamed. Watching herself die, Abigail completely choked up, speechless. Mr. Makepeace, triumphantly holding the smoking revolver, stood twenty feet away from her.

What just happened? Abigail instinctively placed her hands over her chest and frantically felt for a wound. *Did he...did he just kill me? Have I become a...* Abigail's breathing accelerated, and a deep chill cascaded through her body as if ice water had been poured all over her. *No, no, no, no, please, no!*

"*Abigail!*" Brooke's agonized shriek split the air. For a brief moment, the entire battle ceased. Everybody stopped fighting. All of the shouting voices silenced. Even the ghosts paused in midair. A few of the gangsters and officers gasped. Brooke and all of the children wailed almost uncontrollably.

What is happening? Abigail waved her arms around frantically. *No one can see me. I'm right here. No one can see me! I'm dead. I'm a ghost. I'm dead!* Shaking her head, tears filling her eyes, Abigail slowly retreated from her corpse, which lay on the floor with a bloody hole through its heart. *No! I don't want to be a ghost. I don't want this. Please, no! This cannot be happening! No!*

Little Wade screamed Abigail's name just before Thrash attacked from behind and bit off his arm. Although he could not speak, Watchtower let out a low, mournful, moaning sound and reached out for Abigail's lifeless body, but a tsunami of gang members overtook him. The Dragons attacked first, hurling burning lanterns that burst and ignited Watchtower's suit. Within seconds, flames spread all over him. Then a pack of Wild Cards, hooting and hollering, hurled fireworks and sticks of dynamite at Watchtower. The instant the brightly colored bombs touched his flaming clothes, they detonated. *Bang! Crack! Pow!* Shooting colored sparks everywhere, the explosives pummeled Watchtower like sledgehammers, badly denting his armor and hobbling his joints. Shielding his cracked glass face with his hands, Watchtower, his leg crippled by Mr. Peekaboo's attacks, and his chest exposed and vulnerable, retreated as the onslaught drove him back and away from Abigail's corpse.

"Take him down!" Mr. Makepeace barked orders at the men, who redoubled their relentless assault. Swatting several men aside with his burning arms, Watchtower reached under his burning clothing, seized several valves, and twisted them until they burst. *Hisssss!* Watchtower expelled steam from several points on his body, dousing the flames. Heated by the fire, Watchtower's heavily damaged skin sizzled. Low on water and oil, his joints creaked and jerked crudely. He was back in the fight, but he moved clumsily. Sensing weakness, the gangsters raised their weapons and charged him, hoping to overtake him like a swarm of rats. With a loud *clang*, Watchtower toppled like a tree. All of the ruffians set upon him.

Oh no! Watchtower!

Brooke and the other children huddled around Abigail's body and wept. Abigail opened her mouth to scream and call out to her friends when she suddenly felt a sharp tingle encircle her wrist. She whirled around and saw Little Wade grabbing her, using Somatophoria to stimulate the nerves beneath her skin.

"You're not dead," Little Wade whispered and then pointed behind her. Abigail turned and saw the real Fuyvush, Ramon, Jing, Brooke and Horace all huddled together, quietly creeping toward the side door.

"Not dead?" Abigail whispered, and then she noticed a shimmering illusion surrounding them all like a crystal dome. The invisibility spell created a transparent barrier that concealed them; gazing through it as if through a window, Abigail saw the false Brooke, Fuyvush, Ramon, Jing and Horace all mourn Abigail's own fake corpse. Little Wade released Abigail's wrist and guided her to the others.

"What about Watchtower?" Abigail whispered.

"He knows," Little Wade replied. "You have to go, now!" He urged her to escape, but Abigail could not help but linger for a brief moment and watch.

With Watchtower distracted, Mr. Makepeace, smoking revolver in hand, a satisfied look on his face, took a moment to survey the scene of the battle. Outnumbered, the officers of Precinct Zero struggled valiantly against the gangs. Mr. Makepeace smiled as, one by one, the officers fell. It was only a matter of time. Above the battle, Mr. Makepeace observed amusedly as the Little Wade's Haunters, damaged and decimated, battled Thrash and the Melted Skulls Ghost. Spellfire, reading from his burning book, launched a fireball that struck Thrash, searing him, but then Thrash struck Spellfire with his barbed tail and popped him like a bubble. Bloodygoobrius, the hideous specimen inside the jar, burst from his confines and latched onto the Melted Skulls Ghost like a vile parasite, dissolving whatever it touched. Wailing in agony, the Melted Skulls Ghost howled and struck back, scraping, scratching, shredding Bloodygoobrius into smithereens. Finally, the last two Haunters, Nightmarker and Weaponwood, inflicted incredible amounts of damage onto their enemies before they themselves were torn apart. Mr. Makepeace smiled, satisfied with himself. All of the Haunters had been destroyed. Only Little Wade was left. "Two against one. I like those odds," he chuckled.

Abigail noticed the battle taking its toll on Little Wade, who visibly strained and struggled. Ryving drained him. Polyplotting and maintaining the illusions simultaneously had stretched him too thin, taxing his Thanity to its limit.

We'd better get out of here.

Just as Abigail arrived at the door with the others, Mr. Makepeace turned to the fake Fuyvush, Horace, Brooke, Jing, and Ramon, who kneeled in a circle and mourned the equally fake Abigail. Pantomiming being anguished and devastated, the illusions very convincingly wept and comforted each other. Smugly, Mr. Makepeace sauntered towards Abigail's counterfeit "body" until he stood over all of the fake "children," who cowered before him.

"You all feel too much, and now you all have seen too much. I'm sorry."

Mr. Makepeace raised his pistol and fired five more times, emptying his revolver at high speed.

"What?"

Nothing happened.

Even though he had fired bullets at point-blank range, the children did not fall and die. They just sat there, sobbing.

"Impossible."

Brooke and the other illusions suddenly froze in place, like statues.

Little Wade gasped in pain and exhaustion. "I can't hold it."

Time to go, now! Abigail pulled open the side door.

"He can't do that," Mr. Makepeace whispered in total surprise, staring at the images of the children, who stood perfectly still. "He can't do that. Not while he's fighting. He can't."

Abigail pulled open the side door. Little Wade faltered. His image flickered. All of the simulated children vanished before Mr. Makepeace's eyes. Abigail's lifeless body dematerialized. Mr. Makepeace aimed his revolver at…nothing. Then he spotted the side door opening. To him, it swung open as if moved by an invisible force. He stepped towards the door, passed through the illusion as if he had crossed through a curtain, and spotted the most certainly not dead

Abigail, Brooke, Jing, Horace, Ramon, and Fuyvush, all sneaking out the side door, ushered by a weakened Little Wade.

"No!" Infuriated, Mr. Makepeace frantically emptied the cylinder in his revolver, raining empty shell casings onto the floor. "No!"

Abigail, very much alive, panicked. "He's reloading! Move! Move!" She urged Fuyvush, Horace, Ramon, Jing, and Brooke out the door.

Stalking towards them, Mr. Makepeace pulled bullets out of his pocket and slotted them into his revolver. Little Wade, whirled around and looked Abigail straight in the eye. He gestured through the side door to the outside. Wincing in pain, fading in and out, Little Wade gasped. "I'm sorry, Abigail. I couldn't hold it all together. It's too much. Please, get out while you—*Aaaaaahhh!*"

Something stuck Little Wade from behind. A vicious stinger punctured him, burrowing through his body and blowing out his chest, spraying spectral plasma everywhere. Little Wade screamed in agony as the Melted Skulls Ghost lifted him as if he were stuck on a meathook. Abigail and the other children screamed, for real this time, as the Melted Skulls Ghost tore Little Wade into shreds.

Mr. Makepeace laughed. The Melted Skulls Ghost screeched. Thrash howled. Celebrating victory, Mr. Makepeace reloaded his pistol. The two abhorrent spirits flanked him on either side.

"Go ahead and try to run, Abigail, you and your friends." Mr. Makepeace slotted the final round into his revolver. "Let's see how far you get..." Mr. Makepeace's voice trailed off because he saw Abigail's eyes and mouth open wide. She was looking at something behind him.

Something enormous appeared behind Mr. Makepeace and his two monstrous phantoms. Emerging up through the floor, a gargantuan, globular, grotesque ghost rose up like the sun, and it very quickly filled up almost the entire warehouse; the ghastly beast unleashed a deep, guttural growl that rippled like thunder. Abigail recognized the monster immediately because she had seen it before.

"Smorgasborg," Abigail whispered.

"What?" all of the other children asked.

"What?" Mr. Makepeace looked at her strangely. Then he, Thrash, and the Melted Skulls Ghost whirled around and gasped.

"Impossible," Mr. Makepeace whispered.

"*Smorgasborg!*" Abigail cheered.

Towering before Mr. Makepeace, Little Wade, in his monstrous Smorgasborg form, unleashing and snaking a thousand titanic tentacles around the rafters, filled up the entire ceiling like a storm cloud. Then he catapulted himself forward and bristled with a thousand sharp spines. The Smorgasborg's almost unfathomable jaws opened wide just before the creature crashed into the Melted Skulls Ghost and Thrash, chomping them both like a shark. The three entangled spirits blew through Mr. Makepeace like a tornado. Even though they passed harmlessly through him, he stumbled, disoriented.

Even Abigail flinched. All around them, Thrash, the Melted Skulls Ghost, and the Smorgasborg battled like colossal monsters beneath the ocean, all whipping tentacles, jagged fins, gnashing teeth, bulging eyes, and glowing, green flesh. The Melted Skulls Ghost, swinging a razor-sharp, smoky wing, slashed and disemboweled the Smorgasborg, spewing ghostly guts across the ceiling. Still interlocked with one another, the three spirits vanished. Just as Mr. Makepeace collected himself, two gang members, battered and bloodied, raced past him.

"It didn't work. He's too strong. Run!"

Then Mr. Makepeace gasped when he heard the unmistakable sound of whirring, hissing, clanking, followed by booming steps. Watchtower, gangsters hanging from his body, his clothes charred, his metal skin pocked with dents and gashes, attacked Mr. Makepeace. Panicking, Mr. Makepeace emptied his revolver at Watchtower, but the shots only seemed to enrage the mechanical giant. Watchtower, his leg busted, unable to stand and walk properly, crawled along the floor toward Mr. Makepeace, picking up speed, thundering towards his enemy like a steam locomotive. Watchtower swung his arm at Mr. Makepeace, who barely dodged the attack and dropped his smoking gun. Just when he reached Mr. Makepeace, a dozen gang members swarmed Watchtower, battering him with whatever they could—stones, hammers, clubs, their fists. Although more of a nuisance than anything else, the gangsters distracted Watchtower enough to prevent him from maintaining his pursuit.

Frantically trying to escape, Mr. Makepeace reached down to the floor and scooped up Mr. Skinner's vicious-looking knife, which had avoided getting crushed by Watchtower earlier. Pointing it at Abigail, he hissed, "I'm going to cut out your heart." Then he raced toward the hole that Mr. Goldsmoke had melted through the wall.

"He's escaping!" Abigail cried. She broke away from the children and sprinted after him.

"Abigail, wait!" Brooke cried.

Mr. Makepeace rushed over to Mr. Goldsmoke's discarded leather bag filled with chemicals. Stooping down, he quickly rummaged through it.

"We can't let him get away!" Abigail chased him.

"*Abigail, watch out!*" Brooke screamed.

Something caught Abigail's leg, a hand with cold fingers and a grip of steel. Falling to the floor, she turned around. His right hand encircling her ankle, Mr. Peekaboo, smoldering, charred, but still alive, rose out of another liquid portal, this one on the floor. Screaming, Abigail tried to crawl away, only to slide backward. Helplessly, Abigail watched Mr. Makepeace exit through the smoldering hole in the wall.

All around her, the battle raged. Little Wade, still whipping and whirling and roaring in Smorgasborg form, struggled to fight off the other two horrible wraiths, who tore chunks out of him. Watchtower peeled the gangster scum off him. Grunts, screams and loud fisticuffs reverberated throughout the whole warehouse. Mr. Peekaboo, climbing toward her as if emerging from a swamp, clawed at Abigail and dragged her toward him like a crocodile trapping his prey.

Fuyvush, Ramon, Jing, and Horace all linked arms to form a human chain. Horace stood at one end and gripped a support pillar with one arm. Ramon, on the other end, grabbed and held one of Abigail's wrists. As Mr. Peekaboo sucked her toward him and the portal, Abigail ferociously kicked him in the face. Digging her boot into his mask, she struck what felt like solid bone.

"*Get off me!*"

No matter how hard Abigail fought, nothing seemed to stop him. All of the children pulled as hard as they could, but Mr. Peekaboo still overpowered them.

"*Pull!*" they all cried.

"He's so strong!" Horace cried, struggling to hold onto the pillar.

Mr. Peekaboo reached out his left hand and seized Abigail's other leg, doubling his strength. As her feet reached the portal's edge, the cold liquid chilling her heels and ankles, Abigail panicked. Frantically, she called for Little Wade and Watchtower, but they were embroiled in battles of their own.

"No! *No!*" Abigail fought.

"*Pull!*" all of the children yelled, but their grip was slipping.

Mr. Peekaboo prepared to yank Abigail into the portal when a shadow passed over him. Brooke leaped onto Mr. Peekaboo and cracked him over the head with the tomahawk he had left behind. Raising the weapon over her head, screaming, her face red, Brooke, chopping mercilessly, brought down the raven feathered blade onto his arms, shoulders, and his mask. Releasing Abigail, Mr. Peekaboo shielded himself from Brooke's vicious attacks. Abigail felt Jing, Ramon, Fuyvush, and Horace grab her shoulders and arms and pull her to safety.

"*Get them out of here, Abigail!*" Brooke ordered.

"*No!*" Abigail screamed. "*Brooke!*"

Mr. Peekaboo, much stronger than Brooke, disarmed and seized her. His hands crawled onto her shoulders like a pair of spiders. He dragged her down into the portal.

"You found me once! Find me again!" Brooke sank beneath the water.

"Brooke!"

"*Tell my father I'm alive. Tell him. Tell him I'll fight them. I'll fight them every day! Find me! Find me!*"

Mr. Peekaboo submerged and yanked Brooke into the portal until only her hand reached out to grasp at air. Abigail reached for Brooke's outstretched hand.

"Brooke! *Brooke!*"

The whirlpool sucked Brooke in and then vanished.

"*Brooke!*" Abigail screamed and struck the hard floor over and over in frustration. Unfortunately, any trace of Brooke or Mr. Peekaboo had disappeared, as if they had never been there at all.

"Brooke," Abigail ran her hands over the cold floor. "I was supposed to save *you*."

Surrounding her, Fuyvush, Horace, Jing, and Ramon consoled her. Abigail completely broke down into tears.

"We were so close," Abigail wept. "So...close."

For a moment, they all wept.

Then they all noticed how quiet it was.

Slam!

A member of Los Seises, bloodied and bruised, dropped in front of them. He gave them one last frightened look and whispered "*Mama Mia!*" just before Watchtower seized him by the ankles, lifted him, and then threw him across the warehouse. Hurtling through the air, the screaming gangster landed on a pile of a dozen other unconscious gang members. The impact knocked him out.

Looking around, all of the children saw that the dust kicked up by the battle was settling. Spirits no longer battled against the ceiling. Groaning and moaning echoed throughout the entire chamber. Dozens of wounded bodies lay strewn across the warehouse. Watchtower, grinding, clicking, clanking, limping, collapsed onto the floor with a loud, clattering *clang*! All of the gangsters were knocked out, wounded, or cowering in fear.

Hats. There were hats everywhere—so many hats.

Abigail blinked twice to take it all in. Too sweaty, too tired, she was also too sad to smile.

"We...we won."

22

EVIDENCE

Abigail watched Precinct Zero subdue and arrest the gang members, handcuffing them, chaining them together. Many of the police officers, she saw, were grievously wounded, but they did their jobs anyway; however, some were too weak to even stand. Every sound echoed in the cavernous warehouse. Abigail smelled sweat, dust, blood, oil, gas, ash, gunpowder, and sulfur.

Precinct Zero dragged an armored, unconscious, and very heavy Mr. Lens out the door. They arrested the Longshadows and Mr. Stretch, folding him into a pretzel shape and locking his arms and legs together. They wrangled the Wild Cards, cuffing them. They knocked out the very fat Mr. Ball, and then they rolled him right out of the warehouse. They detained the Sewer Rats and nabbed Mr. Crookback, seizing him by the legs before he could slip back down a jagged hole in the floor that led into the sewers. They tangled all of the Squids together, gagged and silenced the Whistlers, tackled the Pikes, snuffed out all of the Dragons' lanterns, chained all of the Black Roses, and led all of Los Seises out at gunpoint. The Smooth Boys politely surrendered. Abigail could see neither the Invisible Men nor the Hives anywhere. They had escaped during the chaos.

They were not the only ones; Mr. Bright Eyes and the Shock Troops had vanished, too.

When Mr. Goldsmoke escaped, his acid melted through the wall and left a disgusting, hissing hole behind. Dripping with sizzling acid, it reeked like rotten eggs. Abigail stared at it, remembering the snide look on Mr. Makepeace's face just before he absconded through the same exit.

"I tried to chase him, but I failed."

"Abigail. You saved us," Jing comforted her.

"Do not be too hard on yourself," Fuyvush added.

"I still let him get away."

"*No te preocupes*, Abigail. Mr. Makepeace will not get far," Ramon interjected.

"He implicated himself in numerous crimes today. The police will surely arrest him by the end of the day," Horace finished.

Taking a moment, Abigail glanced around. She could not see Little Wade anywhere. Then Fuyvush pointed to a dimly lit corner in the room.

"Look!"

Drawing her pocket knife, Abigail stepped in front of the other children. "Stay behind me." Together, they all stared into the dark corner. A growling erupted from the darkness, but then it degraded into a wounded whimpering. Something limping, injured, slowly emerged.

"It's...Thrash."

Abigail could not believe that she could get this close to him. Even though he did not possess a physical body, Thrash, nearly annihilated by Little Wade's powers during the battle, had transformed into a tiny little puppy, cowering in the corner. There was simply not enough of him left to be what he once was; all around him, fragments of his spectral form wafted through the air, and then they faded and dissipated, like dust. Abigail recalled what Little Wade had told her.

"Ryving," she whispered, pitying what she saw. Fuyvush, Horace, Jing, and Ramon kneeled down and delicately held out their hands to

Thrash, who slowly, very slowly, crawled toward them. No longer a vicious hound, Thrash, broken down and humbled by his battle with Little Wade, yelped.

Where is Little Wade? What happened to him?

While the other children gently played with Thrash, who warmed to their comfort, Abigail spotted the fused skulls lying on the floor. Swirling around the object, the Melted Skulls Ghost faded into view. The two fused wraiths were also horribly wounded, mauled by their battle with Little Wade. One half of the ghost had been almost completely erased, and the other half moaned, mourning the loss of its companion. The pulverized, monstrous specter slunk back toward the relic. Defeated, the Melted Skulls Ghost shrank, retreating into one of the skull eyes, and then the loathsome apparition vanished.

Stooping down, Abigail reached out to touch the skulls.

"*Stop!*" She heard a booming, chilling voice cry out from behind her. Whirling around, Abigail gasped. Someone entered the warehouse, stepping through the huge hole that Watchtower had made when he burst through the wall and into the room. At first, this stranger seemed like yet another tall man wearing a long coat and a top hat. Crossing the threshold into the light, he stepped forward and revealed himself to be very different indeed.

A Haitian man, brown-skinned with bright blue eyes, wearing a top hat decorated with bones and crosses, approached her and the melted skulls. He carried his own leather bag as Mr. Makepeace did, only this man's bag was covered with living spiders that scuttled back and forth, making Abigail quite nervous.

"Do not touch dat, girl," he whispered harshly. "Step a-waya."

Abigail backed away from the skulls, and the officers of Precinct Zero respectfully made way for him. They all called him "Baron."

"*Bonjour,* Abigail Reid!" The Baron smiled and revealed his teeth, some pearly white, some yellow, some grey, some made of shiny metal, some missing, all mismatched, like a poorly put together puzzle.

"I'm sorry. My curiosity got the better of me."

"Some 'tings bettah left untouched." He tipped his hat to her. As she watched, he crouched down and reached out with his very long arm. Bone bracelets on his wrist and bone rings around his fingers clacked loudly. The Baron carefully examined the skulls.

"Who were they?"

"Peepahl who could not let go of deyar pain. Poor souls," he whispered and then breathed on the skulls as if performing some kind of incantation.

"Some specters haunt places. They haunted...that?"

"Yes, 'tis called an anchor. Death eez an ocean, Abigail Reid, all around us. We all move deep undah eets waters. Ghosts do not fly. Dey swim like fish through deez vast waters of death, but without anchors to fix them in a proper place, dey drift far, far away, or sink down deep...to da abyss."

"Don't skulls...eventually decompose?"

The Baron presented the skulls to Abigail. Examining them more closely, she discovered that they were made of metal.

"Bones do not decompose naturally for quite sum tyme, but many yeerz ago, someone poured pure bronze all over deez skulls, so dat dey would never trooly rot away."

"Who would do such a thing?"

"Best you do not know."

The Baron carefully lifted the melted skulls, transferred them into his bag, gently secured them inside, and then his spiders sealed the bag with their silk. Thrash, enjoying the children's attention, responded to the Baron's whistles and fluttered over to him. The Baron opened his coat and revealed a deep pocket, also decorated with clacking, clattering bones, and Thrash slipped inside and made himself comfortable, like a pet.

"You...you collect them?"

"I take care of dem in my house," the Baron explained and wiped his brow.

"Your house must be the most haunted place in the whole city!"

"It iz an island in dis ocean. I help ghosts find peace."

"How can you do all of this?"

"Dere are da living, and dere are da dead. I walk in between."

"*Baron!*"

They both turned. Another strange man stepped into the room. Like the Baron, he stood very tall and thin. A Spanish man, he dressed very stylishly in a chestnut tailcoat and top hat decorated with copper gears. Like Night Owl Nell, he wore a magnificent set of goggles. Stepping forward, he leaned on a copper-colored cane, also decorated with gears.

"Professor Obradór." The Baron saluted him with the most profound respect.

Abigail recognized the name.

"We're ready," Professor Obradór called out to the Baron.

"Ready for what?" Abigail did not understand.

"Little Wade needs our help," the Baron answered, worried.

"Is...he all right?"

"It takes more dan dis to destroy him," the Baron answered, "but today's victory come at a cost." The Baron poured white powder into his hands. Then he stared up at the ceiling and the vast emptiness of the now nearly silent warehouse.

The Baron's voice boomed. "*Little Wade...Prince of Light. Heart of da city. Come forth!*" He blew a cloud of white dust toward the ceiling. It hung in the air. Staring into it, Abigail could see strange currents flowing in the air, almost like water. *He said Death is an ocean all around us.*

From his coat pocket, the Baron extracted a fishhook carved out of bone and connected it to a ball of twine. Whirling the hook, he whispered an unintelligible chant, uttering guttural sounds. Then with a loud roar, he hurled his bone fishhook up and into the cloud of white dust and then yanked down as if tearing down a curtain, suddenly revealing Little Wade, eyes closed, hovering in midair, adrift.

"*Dere he is!*" the Baron shouted and pointed.

Abigail cried out, "*Oh no!*"

Little Wade was badly maimed from his battle. His face horribly disfigured, his right arm ripped off, and his left leg gone below the knee, he floated down toward the floor like a falling leaf. His eyes were closed.

He looked dead.

"What happened to him?" Abigail desperately reached out to Little Wade, who drifted aimlessly. *Boom!* She jumped as the double doors to the loading dock burst open, and a spectacular trolley backed into the warehouse. Unlike most streetcars, which needed tracks to guide them, this trolley had wheels, like it could travel on any road, anywhere. Massive and composed entirely of metal and glass, this strange vehicle quickly expanded and extended with loud *chank-chank-chank* sounds similar to Watchtower. It also whirred, clicked, clanked, blew off hissing steam, and then settled into place with a loud *whump*. Abigail could make out four words emblazoned on its side: THE PECULIARLY POSITIVE SHOP.

With a loud *sproing*, the trolley hatched like a mechanical, clockwork egg, opening up a dozen different doors, hatches, gates, platforms, and it seemed as though an infinite number of mechanics climbed out of it, all dressed in greasy uniforms decorated with copper gears. The trolley contained a seemingly, endlessly complex automated workshop that unfolded, unfurled, unwound, and unwrapped itself, revealing an impressive laboratory, foundry, and arsenal, overstuffed with all kinds of elaborate gadgets, knickknacks, thingamajigs, and whatchamacallits.

"*Aquí! Bring it here!*" Professor Obradór beckoned to a small squadron of his mechanics, who quickly assembled an elaborate contraption—a tall, glass cylindrical tube capped with copper and brass, standing on a heavy metal plate.

"What a strange machine. What is that?" Abigail inquired.

"If it could speak, it would identify itself as a Plasma Coil!" Professor Obradór stepped forward, tipped his hat, and bowed. "And you must be the inimitable Abigail Reid, client number six thousand five hundred and thirty-two. *Buenos días!*" Professor Obradór spoke in a mix of English and Spanish.

"I received your package," Abigail saluted, "and put it to good use. Thank you."

"*De nada,* Abigail Reid. We are delighted to make your acquaintance—*Don't touch that!*" Professor Obradór suddenly called out.

Startled, Abigail whirled around and saw Horace and Ramon standing near the destroyed electromagnet. Pinching their noses, Horace and Ramon pointed to a grey, greasy slime leaking from it.

"It appears to be bleeding," Horace observed.

"It's sizzling, and it stinks," Ramon added.

"*Por favor, no se acerquen.* Please, don't go near that," Professor Obradór warned them. "Step away. *Lo siento.* Apologies, Abigail Reid, for that outburst. I was merely concerned for their safety and *seguridad*. I am *Profesór y Doctór Hectór Obradór*, and I am at your *servicio*."

"What's that liquid?" She pointed to the slime.

"As you now know, the Shock Troops have developed a portable battery, but what you don't know is what's inside. They use a lead acid solution to generate electricity."

"Lead acid? That sounds terribly toxic."

"It is. *Peligroso pero poderoso,* very dangerous and volatile, but very powerful. Not only does this particular emulsion generate an immense amount of voltage and amperes, but it can also be recharged after being used up."

"A rechargeable battery? That's astonishing."

"The first of its kind was developed in eighteen fifty-nine by a man named Gaston Planté. Forty years later, battery technology is still in its *infancia*, or so we thought, but the Shock Troops must have someone brilliant developing weapons for them. These particular batteries are a thousand times more powerful than anything Planté could have imagined. Though it may be crude, this *tecnología* is decades ahead of its time."

"So there's more than one battery inside that device. When Watchtower smashed it, he broke open the batteries, and now they're leaking acid."

"*Precisamente,* the battery that you saw demonstrated was one of a dozen. Eleven other batteries, just like that black box that you removed, were installed inside that giant magnet. The Shock Troops daisy-chained them together to create a supercharge. Activate one, and you activate them all. The *electricidad* multiplies, hence the immensely powerful *atración*. When you shut down that magnet, you turned the tide of the battle."

"I wasn't thinking, really," Abigail replied modestly. "I saw them do it, and so I thought I would simply undo what they did. It seemed to work."

"Well, we need it to work again," Professor Obradór informed her.

"Again? How? The magnet is destroyed."

Professor Obradór gestured to the plasma coil. "We brought an invention of our own, not quite as large, but vital. Do you wish to assist Little Wade?"

"Absolutely!"

"Then we need your help to make our *máquina* work."

"My help?" Abigail wondered. "How?"

One of the mechanics working by the plasma coil appeared to be pumping all the air out of the glass tube. When he finished, he nodded to Professor Obradór.

"For this to function, we require electrical power. *Normalmente*, we would simply draw the necessary voltage from the city's power grid. Unfortunately, there are not yet any electrical cables laid down in this particular part of *la ciudad*, but the Shock Troops brought their batteries, and we will use their weapon to help us. Thanks to you, there is one battery left. It should be *suficiente*. We need you to help us connect it to our coil and power it up. What do you say, *chicos*? Will you lend us your small hands?"

Abigail, Fuyvush, Horace, Ramon, and Jing sprang into action. They quickly set the battery next to the plasma coil. Abigail, wearing her rubber gloves, guided by the others, carefully attached the battery to the plasma coil, slowly looping the wires until the machine hummed to life.

"*Observen*. It's a vacuum tube," Professor Obradór explained. "We've sucked out all of the air, leaving the inside completely empty. Now, we're charging the plates with *electricidad* from the battery. Look! There!" As the battery buzzed, the glass tube filled with a glowing pink light. "Plasma!" Professor Obradór clapped. "*Bueno*, we've created a stable field. Bring him in!"

"Of course, Little Wade exists as pure energy, so you're going to use energy to heal him!" Abigail reasoned. "Professor, are you certain this will work?"

Professor Obradór smiled. "Positive."

Guided by the Baron, who whispered incantations, Little Wade's mangled form drifted into the glowing vacuum tube. The pulsing plasma enveloped his body, and he floated inside the cylinder as if he were a specimen in a glass jar. Abigail watched as Little Wade's phantasmic body slowly began to repair itself, knitting ghostly tissue and skin back together. His shorn leg began to grow back, and his missing arm slowly, painfully rebuilt itself and reattached to his shoulder.

Fuyvush, Horace, Jing, and Ramon all whispered, "Ooooooh."

Jolted by a sudden rush of energy, Little Wade's eyes fluttered open.

"Abigail!" Little Wade called out.

"I'm here," Abigail comforted him. "I'm all right. We won."

Little Wade, his handsome face ravaged by the battle, smiled weakly at her.

"You...surprised yourself," he whispered, and she tried not to cry. "You...bloomed."

Then Little Wade spasmed as his body continued to sew itself back together.

"Will he be all right?" Abigail asked Professor Obradór.

"After a battle, it usually takes him several hours to restore his form, but using this method and this *máquina*, he should be ready sooner."

"How soon?"

"We don't know, but it appears to be working quite well."

"You did...so well..." Little Wade, encased in glass, reached toward Abigail. If he could touch her cheek, he would have. "The others?"

"She saved us," Jing spoke for all of them.

"Mr. Peekaboo kidnapped Brooke. She sacrificed herself to save me." Abigail struggled not to cry. "Mr. Makepeace escaped as well."

"We will find her," Little Wade promised. "We have Mr. Makepeace on the run. The Great Gang Trap...it worked...because of you."

Abigail shrugged. "I guess I make good bait."

Little Wade leaned forward, almost touching the glass. "Remember the alley. You were not the bait, Abigail. You were...the mainspring."

She could tell that it hurt for him to speak.

"We're going to be all right," she comforted him. "You can rest now."

Little Wade drowsily shut his eyes.

Then someone grunted behind them.

"*A' richt, bairns,*" Sergeant Blood interrupted. "*We've awready sent word ahead tae yer parents. They're aff tae be ower th' moon whin thay hear you're a' richt, bit richt noo, it's time tae tak' ye tae th' station. Th' commissioner's gonna waant a word.*"

"Did anyone understand that?" Ramon asked.

"It's time for you to go," Abigail translated. "Your parents will be so happy. They'll get you anything you want, so you better start making a list."

"Thank you for saving us." Jing wiped away tears.

"Not all of you," Abigail lamented.

"We'll find Brooke," Fuyvush encouraged her.

Ramon finished, "*Juntos.* We'll do it together."

"Abigail, I mean no offense, but...what were you doing here?" Horace wondered.

"Yes, how did you get involved with all of...this?" Jing asked.

"Oh, I'm just trying to walk to school safely. The Longshadows tried to kidnap me last night. Little Wade and Watchtower stopped them. Together, we're building the Secret Passage of Hope."

"What's that?" Jing shook her head, not fully understanding.

In response, Abigail unfolded her Map of Scratches, presented it to the four children, and briefly explained Little Wade's plan.

"That sounds like a wonderful idea." Horace scratched his fat chin. "So you need people in the neighborhood to help you?"

"Precisely. We were in the process of going door to door and asking people for help...before all of this," Abigail replied.

"I'll ask my rabbi," Fuyvush promised her. "My community lives on Hester Street."

"I'll tell my grandfather," Jing chimed in. "He knows everyone in Chinatown. We will help you, too."

"I'll talk to my *abuelo*," Ramon added. "*Mi familia* works all over this neighborhood. *Te ayudaremos.*"

"I'll speak to my entire family," Horace finished. "We've lived here in this neighborhood for generations. We'd be delighted to assist."

Examining the Map of Scratches, they whispered to each other.

"Do you have a pencil in that bag?" Jing requested.

"You're missing quite a few things here." Fuyvush winked.

Reaching into her saddlebag, Abigail gave them one.

"Do you mind if we take a moment and do this?" Fuyvush asked Sergeant Blood.

"*You'll see her again soon enough, bit hrmmmph, how come nae?*" Sergeant Blood agreed.

Abigail watched as Fuyvush, Horace, Jing, and Ramon took turns excitedly scribbling on her Map of Scratches. Jing marked multiple locations on the map with Chinese characters and a smiling face. Fuyvush marked a whole section of the map in Hebrew letters. Horace very gracefully signed several areas in the neighborhood in the loveliest, most graceful handwriting. Ramon scribbled several pathways along many streets and avenues. He drew tiny images of horses and carriages that symbolized delivery routes that his family worked every day. He drew a trio of three different carts that could serve as "piggyback rides" for her. Ramon even drew smiling little pigs and labeled each of the three carts Chancho, Puerco, and Cerdo. Fuyvush, Jing, Ramon, and Horace, working together, built a whole network of secret passages. When they were done, they handed the Map of Scratches back to Abigail. Their contributions connected Abigail's home, Mr. Laird's Bookshop, Mrs. Whitlock's School, Magruder's Toy Shop, and her church. They also linked several parks she frequented. Finally, they included a few new locations that were circled.

"What are these circled spots?"

"Our homes," Jing spoke for them. "You are welcome anytime you like."

Moved nearly to tears, Abigail Reid barely eked out a whispery, "Thank you!"

All of the children embraced warmly. Some of them teared up. They all turned to watch Little Wade slowly healing inside the plasma cylinder, bathed in a pink glow, as if he floated in a womb, being reborn.

"I think he planned this all along," Abigail whispered, placing her hand against the glowing, curved glass, which felt warm. "He doesn't just want to help one child. He wants to help us all, and he accomplishes that task if we help each other. The Secret Passage of Hope... it's not just for me. It's for all of us. If we work together, we can all be safe."

Behind them, Sergeant Blood grunted.

"Time tae goo."

"I'll see you all very soon," Abigail promised as she embraced them one by one.

"What about you, Abigail? Do you need us to take you home?" Fuyvush offered.

"When they're fixed up, Little Wade and Watchtower will escort me home."

"No fair," Horace joked. "You get to do all the exciting stuff. No fair."

"Come alang," Sergeant Blood instructed. Abigail waved to the children as Sergeant Blood escorted them out of the warehouse to take them back to the police station, and then home.

Prang! Abigail jumped when she heard what sounded like bells behind her. Hot, steaming metal clanged onto the floor. Abigail whirled around. Mechanics from the Peculiarly Positive Shop huddled around the severely damaged Watchtower, who lay back, clicking, grinding, whirring, clanking, and falling apart. A mechanic, using oversized iron tongs, removed Watchtower's melted armored plating. Then he chucked it ten feet away, where it landed with a loud *hiss* and *splat*. Another mechanic, wearing a protective mask similar to Mr. Goldsmoke's, emerged from a hole in the floor, carrying a long, yellow hose. He yelled something muffled through his mask that sounded like *mphhh u gsshhhh loin!* Abigail translated his nonsensical grunts into, "I found a gas line!"

Watchtower reached out his arm and opened his hand. Abigail watched the small hatch on his palm spring open. The mechanic slotted the yellow hose inside, and a loud hiss sounded. Watchtower's flame roared, and his chest puffed up as if he were inhaling deeply. The head mechanic, a frail, grandfatherly old man, with tools dangling and jangling on his belt, waddled over, kneeled down, and cradled Watchtower's head in his arms like a father would an infant. His glass cracked and his hat torn and ruined, Watchtower nestled his head gently in the man's thin arms. "We'll get you fixed right up, boy. Don't you worry," the old mechanic comforted him. Professor Obradór, supervising them, took his place at Abigail's side.

"What happens if he runs out of gas?" Abigail asked Professor Obradór, not wanting to know the answer.

"His fire has been burning *constantemente* for a very, very, very long time, Abigail, but if anyone ever snuffs it out, then he dies."

Watchtower breathed in and out, keeping his flame alive. He lay perfectly still while the mechanics repaired his body. He did, however, manage to tap his fingers together, making a loud *clickety-clackety-clack* sound and then *ping!* A crumpled letter sprung up in Watchtower's torn breast pocket. Abigail pinched it, removed it herself, unfolded it, and read it.

YOU SAVED MY LIFE. STOP. THANK YOU. STOP.

"You saved mine first." Abigail tenderly squeezed his metal hand. Then she reached into her own pocket, pulled out the handkerchief that she had received from him the night before, and gently wiped his damaged, smeared glass. "You were right. Whatever I accomplished, I managed because I didn't think about myself at all. I only thought about helping you."

"Our *enemigos*, they're getting stronger and cleverer every time." Professor Obradór shook his head while the mechanics hacked, hammered, drilled, screwed and unscrewed, patched and repaired, all to restore Watchtower's damaged body. "I fear the next *batalla* will be even worse."

Before Abigail could respond, two people suddenly appeared right next to her, materializing out of thin air, forcing her to jump. She recognized them immediately— the mysterious gentleman and the cowgirl from the Orpheus Theater!

"*Buenos días*, Abigail Reid," the handsome, dashing, long-haired Spanish man introduced himself. "*Me llamo* Ezekiel Morales."

"Wait, I saw you at the Orpheus Theater, but also at the shoeshine bench!"

"*Por supuesto, para protegerte!*" Ezekiel winked. "We had orders to look out for you. You were very brave earlier when you spoke to Mr. Makepeace. He's never done that before with anyone. I think he was impressed with you, honestly, but I was there in case that monster tried anything."

"So vas I," a third man appeared, the stern, monocled, grey-suited military man with the artificial limbs, also from the shoeshine bench. "*Guddentag*, Abigail Reid. I am Mr. Otto Otto, or Otto Sqvared, eef you vish." Mr. Otto Otto (or Otto Squared) uttered in a German accent.

Ezekiel grandiosely gestured to the cowgirl, who gulped down the contents of a canteen, "And may we present Wendy Lawson."

"Wait! You loaned me your saddlebag!"

"'sright," Wendy Lawson smacked her lips and chuckled. "Only it ain't no loan, but a gift. It's all yers now. Yer puttin' it ta good yoos!"

"You were with me…the whole time…again?"

"Yup. We hadger back, course!" Wendy Lawson, the cowgirl, shrugged. "We wuzz even goin' ta save Watchtower, but then when you did what you did, we dun decided to let you go ahead and git it dun! Imagine that, Mr. Makepeace turned stoopid by a thirteen-year-old girl! Hehe!"

"We apologize about your friend, Brooke Adams," Ezekiel lamented.

Mr. Otto Squared wiped his brow and added, "Precinct Zero vas outnumbered. Vee ver compelled to join zha fight."

"Don't apologize. Without your help, the situation would have worsened considerably. I just wish I could have saved her."

"Don't punish yourself, Abigail. Thanks to you, we came very close. In fact, we're going after Brooke now," Ezekiel comforted her. "We just came to say *adiós*."

"So soon? You just got here...well, sort of."

"Vee vill hunt after da Shock Troops," Mr. Otto Squared barked. "Zhey vill not get fahr."

"They're about to pee their pants!" Wendy Lawson blurted out.

"Thank you all for watching out for me."

"It comes vith zha job." Mr. Otto Squared polished his monocle.

"If you don't mind my asking," Abigail wondered. "How can you all simply vanish and reappear— *Oh!*"

A fourth member of their group, this one obviously a ghost, materialized above them, floating cross-legged, wearing traditional Chinese clothing. In life, he had been a venerable, kind grandfather until someone shot him three times in the chest. Now here he was, floating above his three very alive companions.

"Ni hao," he clasped his hands and bowed. "I am Yu Jin. It is a pleasure to meet you."

"Three warriors and a ghost that can cast illusions to conceal all of you until you strike, I can see how that can come in handy. Where did Little Wade and Watchtower find all of you?"

"Wendy, Otto and I were all clients of Little Wade and Watchtower when we were children," Ezekiel answered, gesturing to his partners.

"Little Wade trained me after I was murdered," Yu Jin added.

"We've been fightin' fer children ever since," Wendy Lawson chuckled.

"We should go," Yu Jin interjected.

"So soon?" Abigail wanted to speak to them more.

"We have the Shock Troops' trail. We mustn't lose it," Ezekiel explained.

"Before we depart, vee have a geeft for you, Abigail Reid," Mr. Otto Squared smiled.

"Another gift? I'm acquiring quite a collection. Today's better than Christmas."

Ezekiel handed Abigail a compass, beautifully crafted, like her pocket watch.

"North, south, eest, vest, nevvah loos your vay aggen," Mr. Otto Squared puffed up with pride.

"Fue un placer meeting you, Abigail Reid." Ezekiel winked. *"Adiós!"*

Wendy Lawson tipped her hat before Yu Jin cast another illusion and they all vanished right in front of Abigail.

As the officers busied themselves with corralling all of the gang members out of the warehouse, Abigail explored. Very quickly, she located Mr. Goldsmoke's leather bag, the same bag that Mr. Makepeace rummaged through just before he escaped. Stooping down, using her vulcanized rubber gloves, she fished through it herself. Inside, she found more of his rotten egg "gold smoke" grenades as well as several more pairs of glass bottles, some with gold liquid, some with green, like the bottle Mr. Goldsmoke threw at Mr. Lens. She immediately noticed that one of the yellow bottles was missing.

Acid...and base. Green cancels out yellow. I do not have much use for the acid because I am not in the habit of melting people or destroying things. Abigail left it alone. *However, the green base, a liquid that could counter acid and prevent it from destroying...that could come in handy indeed.*

Carefully, Abigail removed one of the sulfur rotten egg gas grenades and one green liquid vial from the leather bag and carefully stuffed them into her saddlebag. Then she called out to one of the officers and pointed to the bag.

"I think you will want to collect this for evidence."

"We'll take it."

"I may have confiscated one of the greens and one of the grenades for myself, to fight evil, obviously. I hope you don't mind."

"As long as Little Wade and Watchtower don't mind, I think you've earned it," the officer complimented her. "Besides, there's plenty of evidence here. If we need anything more from you, we'll let you know."

Thanking her, the Precinct Zero officer carefully picked up Mr. Goldsmoke's bag and carried it out of the warehouse. Then a thought struck Abigail.

Wait! Abigail stopped. *Why did Mr. Makepeace rummage through that bag before he escaped? What did he want? He stole one of the acid bottles, but why?*

Sergeant Blood re-entered the warehouse from outside and called out, *"We've git maist o' thaim loaded!"*

There remained only one gangster left in the room, and he was screaming.

"Where's my knife?" Mr. Skinner, leader of the Black Roses, roared as a pair of Precinct Zero officers handcuffed and wrangled him toward the door. *"I want my knife!"*

"Ye can't hae it," Sergeant Blood barked at him.

"Where is it? You stole it from me!"

"I know where it went," Abigail interrupted their squabble.

"You know?" Mr. Skinner glared at her. "Where? Spit it out!"

"Mr. Makepeace snatched it before he escaped."

Although badly bruised from the fight, Mr. Skinner grinned gleefully.

"Good," he snickered. "A knife like that needs to be used. If he stole it, he intends to use it."

"A' richt, a' richt, c' moan ye!" Sergeant Blood pulled Mr. Skinner's long top hat over his face, muffling his voice, and then forcibly led him out of the building.

There were no gangsters left, and the wounded officers had all been evacuated, so the warehouse stood empty except for Watchtower, Little Wade healing in the plasma tube, and the Peculiarly Positive Shop scientists and mechanics helping them both. Abigail, surveying the entire area, realized that the Great Gang Trap had indeed succeeded. Nevertheless, she felt uneasy. *Something does not feel right. What could it be?* Noticing the anxious look on Abigail's face, Professor Obradór and the Baron immediately approached her.

"What troubles you, Abigail?"

"Something's wrong." She brooded and paced nervously. "This

feels too easy. Mr. Makepeace smiled before he escaped. He seized some chemicals from Mr. Goldsmoke's bag, and he snatched Mr. Skinner's knife. He told me he'd cut out my heart."

"He always says things like that," Professor Obradór huffed. "A proper, ruthless *villano*, I must admit."

"Wait..." she realized. "He knew my name."

"It iz hizz bizness to know tings." The Baron shrugged.

"He knows my name, where I live. He must know everything about me...that means...He promised he would cut out my heart."

"Oh no!" Professor Obradór gasped.

"My father!" Abigail exclaimed. "He's going to kill my father!"

23

RIDE TO THE RESCUE

Bursting out of the warehouse, Abigail raced as fast as she could out to the street. She did not see Mr. Makepeace anywhere. Officers of Precinct Zero loaded the gang members into numerous police omnibus carriages drawn by powerful horses. *He's an old man.* Abigail's mind raced. *He can only move so fast, but he's had such a head start!* She panicked. *He might already be there. It might already be too late!* Latching onto Sergeant Blood, she pleaded.

"Sergeant, can you spare a horse? I can ride it!"

"A'm *sorry.*" He shook his head. "*We need a' o' thaim fur th' carriages, fur th' inmates 'n' fur th' wounded. We can't spare ony.*"

"Mr. Makepeace intends to kill my father. I must warn him!"

"*It's tae dangerous tae gow alone. Some o' us we'll gang wi' ye!*"

Some of the gang members seized the moment to try to wriggle away, forcing the officers to react.

"*Just give us a moment.*" Sergeant Blood urged her as he subdued one of the smelly Sewer Rats.

"Please, I need a horse!" Abigail begged him. "I can ride."

"Take this one! His name's Barney!" Another one of the Precinct Zero officers called out. He led a large, saddled stallion toward her.

Just before he handed the reins to Abigail, a brawl broke out as the gangsters tried to escape. Immediately, the Precinct Zero officers retaliated and began to force the hoodlums into the omnibuses. The scuffle, however, startled Barney, who overreacted. Rearing up and neighing loudly, flailing his front legs around, the enormous horse towered over Abigail. Her eyes widened. She froze in place. Barney brought down his front hooves on the stone street like a pair of sledgehammers, then he reared up again. Terrified, Abigail slowed her breath and focused on the reins swinging from side to side.

I can ride. Abigail steadied herself. *I've done it before. Barney won't hurt me. I can ride! I can ride!* Lunging forward, she shot out her arm, took hold of the reins and quickly calmed Barney, stroking his mane. Then Abigail gracefully slid her foot into the stirrup, pulled herself up, and leaped onto his back. Groaning a bit under her saddlebag's weight, she swung her legs over the saddle and fixed herself into place. Tightening the reins, she took control of Barney. He stopped rearing and spinning, and Abigail pointed him in the right direction. All around them, Sergeant Blood and Precinct Zero stuffed the last of the gangsters into the Omnibus carriages.

"I must go. Now!" Abigail prepared to ride off.

"*Abigail, Mr. Makepeace will kill you. Wait!*" Sergeant Blood warned her.

"There's no time!" Abigail shouted.

She spurred Barney and charged down the street. Astride a galloping Barney, Abigail rode as fast as he could through New Bandit's Roost. Most of its residents skulked away, hiding inside the decrepit buildings. Still, there were more than a few creepy men who clawed at her, even stepped in front of her.

"*Get away from me!*" Abigail roared.

She directed Barney to step on one ruffian's foot, blew past another one, and she slapped away the hand of a third. *Nothing will stop me!* she swore to herself. Although filled with dread, Abigail clutched her metal watch, which *click-click-clicked*, and continued onward, blocking out every other sound. *I must reach him!* she repeated, but the moment she arrived at a major intersection, she stopped. Pulling back on the reins, glancing in all four directions, she panicked.

Where do I go? she chastised herself for not tracing her path or marking the map or even looking at signs when she had followed Mr. Makepeace earlier. She had failed to be like Theseus with his string. Guiding Barney, she whirled around, surrounded by trolleys, carriages, and over a thousand people. *I...I don't know where I am. Where? She glanced around frantically. Where do I go? Wait...wait. Where was Father working again? He told me the address! I don't...I don't know this place...I don't remember! I don't remember!*

Then Abigail slowed her breathing and calmed herself. Clutching her steel watch, she felt it *click-click-clicking*. Closing her eyes, she gathered all of her chaotic, disorganized, fearful emotions, and she marshaled them until they fell into formation and began to march forward. Slipping the watch into the pocket over her heart, she remembered what Saran Singh taught her. "*Place your concerns in order, in a straight line, and think of them one at a time.*"

Reaching into her pocket, she pulled out and unfolded the Map of Scratches and held it up to the sun. *First, I should check for landmarks,* Abigail reasoned, and then she glanced around, spotted two church spires and several stores she recognized. Biting her lip, calculating, she turned her attention back to the map and found her exact intersection. *So if I'm right here...what is the location of Father's job site?*

She did not remember, but she *did* remember Minerva Jonas's manual. Pulling the manual out of her saddlebag, Abigail quickly flipped through the very helpful table of contents. Within seconds, she found a chapter mark that read WHEN YOU CANNOT REMEMBER SOMETHING AND YOU NEED TO IN A HURRY! RULE 126. PAGE 144.

Abigail quickly found page 144 and beheld an illustration of a little girl in a diving suit marked *memory* at the bottom of an ocean, looking up toward the surface. The diving suit was weighted down. She read the text. "RULE NUMBER ONE HUNDRED AND TWENTY-SIX: IF YOU'RE TRYING TO REMEMBER SOMETHING WHEN YOU'RE IN A HURRY OR FLUSTERED, ELIMINATE WRONG ANSWERS FIRST. DROP THEM LIKE DEAD WEIGHT. IT WILL HELP YOUR MEMORY FLOAT UPWARD TO THE SURFACE."

Slapping her book shut and stuffing it back into her bag, Abigail checked the map and began to eliminate whole areas that she knew were irrelevant. "No...no...not here...no...no...no...no...wait...somewhere around here...wait...I remember...I *remember*. Division...Division...and...Pike. *Division and Pike!*" She quickly traced a route with her small pencil.

"I have to head five blocks that way to get to this intersection, and then it's a clear path. Straight. Left. Two Blocks. Right. Two Blocks. Left one block. Right!"

Folding up her map, she glanced up to the sky, hoping for a sign from Little Wade.

Nothing.

The sky was empty. Abigail was alone.

Her heart sank. Little Wade could fly ahead and spot Mr. Makepeace easily. He could even find a way to warn her father somehow, but now it was all up to her. Impatient, Barney huffed and grunted.

"I can do this," she whispered to herself, reached into her pocket and gripped her watch tightly. It beat in her hand like a steel heart. "I can do this. I must warn Father. I can do this! *I can!*"

Spurring Barney, she took off toward her destination, racing as fast as she could, her red hair flowing behind her like fire. Five city blocks later, Abigail quickly hit a wall of trolleys, omnibuses, carriages, and overflowing masses of people blocking her route. Barney had taken her this far, but if she wanted to continue, she would be forced to do so alone. Glancing around, she spotted a uniformed copper with a conical cap and a brass-buttoned uniform.

"*Officer!*" Abigail shouted. He responded, startled. Abigail dismounted and presented Barney's reins. "I need you to take this horse. It belongs to the New York Police Department." She pointed to an insignia emblazoned on Barney's saddle. "I did not steal it. They loaned it to me. I must save my father from assassination, but I am compelled to continue on foot. Please tell your fellow officers to converge on a construction site at Division and Pike!"

Before the surprised officer could even respond, she slapped the reins into his hands. "He responds to Barney. Thank you!" Leaving the befuddled officer and the horse behind, Abigail vanished into the crowd.

"Straight. Left. Two Blocks. Right. Two Blocks. Left. One Block. Right," she repeated to herself over and over as she dashed down the congested avenue.

Abigail navigated an elaborate maze of people, objects, and vehicles that seemed to move against her. Avoiding horses, carriages, and trolleys, she splashed through slimy puddles, ducking and dodging through hundreds of New Yorkers. Every step forward forced her to take two or three steps sideways, then forward, then sideways, then back, but then forward and sideways again. Then she found a diagonal and sliced across, making some progress, but her father felt a thousand miles away. *No, that's wrong!* Abigail remembered the route she had traced on her map. She had only a few more blocks to go.

She ran until her legs felt heavy, her lungs burned, and sweat completely masked her face. The worn-out soles of her boots nearly broke off from slapping against the stone street. Out of breath, her damp hair matted, Abigail doubled over and coughed, trying to catch her breath.

"I'm...so tired." Every disgusting odor that infested the city jumped up into her nose at the same time. She smelled horse manure, grease, shoe polish, ash, fire, dogs, rotting food, expensive perfumes, hundreds of unwashed, dirty men. All of these stenches exploded in her nostrils, forcing her to breathe in and out through her mouth. Gasping, she pumped polluted city air into her lungs.

Just a little farther, she told herself. *I can do it. I can do it. I must!* Catching her breath, Abigail stood up straight and wiped the sweat from her forehead. *Keep moving. Come on! Come on!* Summoning as much strength as she possibly could, Abigail pushed forward again. As she raced down the block, her tiny boots pounding against the sidewalk, she turned, turned, then turned again, moving toward her objective. Abigail heard dozens of loud men's voices and sawing, banging, scraping, hammering and nailing, and she smelled sawdust in the air. Her heart beat faster. She picked up speed, charging forward toward the corner, where she turned. She arrived at a colossal construction site swarming with men. Clouds of sawdust and cement choked the air as an army of workmen built an entire row of buildings, all three times as high as her own home.

I made it! Her body surged with energy, but then she frowned. There were literally hundreds of men scrambling all over the massive construction site like insects. Abigail searched for a foreman, a boss, anyone who could help her. A big, burly man brushed past her while carrying a long, heavy beam of wood.

"Pardon me!" she accosted the worker. "I'm looking for Martin Reid."

"Girl, we've got over a hundred men on this site. I don't know half their names."

"What about the foreman for this site. Where can I find him?"

"I don't know his name either, or where he is. Off with you."

He passed by her rudely. Frantic at first, Abigail remembered Little Wade's advice. *"The only person you can rely on one hundred percent is you. You can do a hundred different things to help yourself."*

"Fine," she huffed, "I'll do it myself. Think, think, think, Abigail."

Gripping her watch, *click-click-click*, she organized her thoughts again. *Could Mr. Makepeace infiltrate the workers himself?* she wondered, then quickly banished that notion. *No...no...he's dressed like a gentleman, and he's also old. That means he intends to use stealth to attack, and he's planning to escape in such a way that he won't be seen out in public. That can help me find him, but* first *I must locate my father!*

Rummaging through her saddlebag, Abigail pulled out the Intrepid Cap. Slipping it over her hair, strapping it on snugly, she slotted the bifocal goggles over her eyes. Blinking, finding her focus, she adjusted the knobs on the sides carefully, zooming in and out, scanning the sprawling construction site. *Father, where are you?* Hurriedly, her eyes swept over the entire site, over hundreds of sweaty workers, cursing at every crowd of men or cloud of dust that blocked her view. Peering closely, she checked every face.

No. No. No. Not there. Not him. Too tall. Too short. No beard. Not him. No. No. Where would he be? She began to panic. Mr. Makepeace could strike at any moment. She felt her steel watch *click-click-clicking*. *I'm running out of time.*

She calmed herself down.

Think! Would Mr. Makepeace wait until later? No, he would do it now, *but how?* Abigail scanned for her father using the goggles. *He would not attack him out in the open. That would get him arrested, even if he used a rifle or a gun from a distance. It's too public. No. No. He would want to make it look like a horrible accident.*

Abigail continued to search for her father, scouting the entire construction site. *Accident...falling, making the building or something heavy fall on my father. Fall!* Adjusting her goggles, Abigail zoomed in on the highest level of the construction site, several stories tall, easily the most hazardous place to work.

Father possesses amazing carpentry skills combined with years of experience. They would entrust him with a hard job, an important job, a dangerous job. There! She spotted her father working all the way at the top of the construction site. He balanced on one of the beams while he hammered several pegs into place. He wiped the sweat from his brow.

Is Mr. Makepeace up there? She panned from left to right. *No, Mr. Makepeace would not climb up there. Too dangerous. Too much trouble. He would be...down low.*

Abigail zoomed in on each and every level of the buildings, but she still did not spot him. *Too many people. Anything he tried...someone could stop him. Lower. He would need to go...* She zoomed in all the way and focused on the foundation of the buildings, where wooden supports for the construction frame stuck out from—

Underground! He's going to try to bring the whole frame of the building down! He's going to use some of Mr. Goldsmoke's acid! That's why he was rummaging through the bag earlier!

She quickly panned back up to her father. Martin had very sensibly tied himself to the post where he worked diligently. If he were to slip or trip, then the rope would catch him, but if the entire building came down, it would be hard for him to untie the rope and escape in time. As Abigail carefully peered through her lenses, she realized that all someone needed to do would be to destabilize the frame. Then the building would collapse, and her father would plunge to his death! She spotted the one building support that Mr. Makepeace would need to damage. *He's underground. How do I descend? How did he descend underground?*

She smelled it first before she glanced down and saw it—a half-open manhole cover that led down into the sewers and stared up at Abigail like a horrible, metal eye. Mr. Makepeace had managed to slide the very heavy manhole cover open about halfway, enough to squeeze through and climb down an iron ladder. Even smaller, Abigail slipped through easily. Descending into the sewers, Abigail climbed down the ladder into a long drainage tunnel. Immediately, the awful, noxious smell overwhelmed her, worse than any pigsty or cow barn she had ever scrubbed while working on the farm in Tarrytown. The acrid stench of stale urine irritated her nose. She winced when her boots plopped down into the filthy stream of sickening, sludgy water that slicked the floor and trickled down the tunnel. Reaching into her satchel, she removed her ball of string.

"Theseus in the Labyrinth," Abigail whispered to herself. "Always know your way back."

She tied one end of the ball of string to the ladder. Then she cupped the ball in her hand and let it unravel as she proceeded forward. Heading deeper into the putrid smell, she crept away from the daylight pouring through the half-open manhole. Within a minute, she reached a crossroads with three possible choices. Pulling out her compass, peering very closely at it in the painfully dim light, Abigail watched the needle wiggle and whirl until it settled. She calculated her orientation carefully.

Above ground, the river is straight ahead down Pike. That's south, and the foundation beneath Father was...southwest of my position. Southwest in this case...is right. Turning and entering the tunnel on the right, Abigail stepped forward and the last remaining light disappeared. As she crept further and further into the labyrinth, as the ball of string slowly unwound in her hand, Abigail's mind raced.

Little Wade told me that the city is laying sewers beneath every area of the city. *The construction site's foundations must include pipes that connect to the sewers. The architects would make sure to install all of that infrastructure first, before building anything on top of it, so that means there must be some kind of basement level full of support pillars for the building's foundation. Mr. Makepeace must be looking for a place where the sewers and the foundation meet.*

Abigail, in total darkness, reached into her saddlebag and felt around for a wooden doll with an outstretched hand. Removing Sergeant Slow Burn, holding him up like a torch and then flicking the lighter with her thumb, Abigail ignited a fire and illuminated the endless tunnels that stretched into nothingness.

"Thank you, Sergeant Slow Burn," Abigail whispered. "You are definitely earning your stripes today."

Holding Sergeant Slow Burn like a torch, Abigail picked up her pace. As she hurried deeper into the squalid sewer, her boots splashing in the foul water, she continued to unspool the ball of string. After less than a minute, shining her flame ahead of her, she quickly located a heavy metal door. It was ajar. *Found it. He's already inside. I hope I'm not too late.* After calculating the number of steps to the door, Abigail doused Sergeant Slow Burn's flame by dipping him into the trickling stream on the floor, extinguishing the flame with a loud *hiss. Sorry, Sergeant. Not the cleanest bath, I know.*

Stuffing the wet wooden statue into one of the rubber-lined pockets of her saddlebag, Abigail proceeded forward, counting her steps as she approached the metal door. Running her right hand along the slimy sewer wall, Abigail felt for it, felt for it, felt for it. *Found it!* Locating the handle and the lock with her fingers, she felt for the keyhole and felt something metal jammed into it. *A lockpick!* Taking a moment, Abigail tied the other end of the string to the handle on the door.

Then, gritting her teeth, hoping the hinges did not squeak, Abigail slowly opened the door and slipped inside. Thankfully, although heavy, the door swung open smoothly and without making any noise. Sighing with relief, Abigail crossed into the basement level of the construction site. Above her, through the creaking wooden ceiling, she could hear the thunderous sounds of tools hammering, sawing, and thwacking and workmen's boots stomping around. The wooden construction frame dominated the room. Metal pipes, recently installed, snaked through the rafters. Builders had not yet erected the cement and concrete support pillars. The entire edifice above them still rested on a fragile, wooden base.

Still wearing the Intrepid Cap, Abigail adjusted her lenses, focusing until she spotted a faint flame. Gulping, she headed straight for it, careful to count her steps exactly. In one hand, Mr. Makepeace clutched a lantern, the source of the light. He reached into his coat pocket and pulled out something made of glass. Abigail recognized it from the battle, one of Mr. Goldsmoke's acid vials, the ones that ate through Watchtower's plate armor. Mr. Makepeace prepared to throw it onto one of the wooden support beams holding up the building. Abigail saw that, if he succeeded, he could bring it all crashing down.

"*Stop!*" Abigail yelled.

Mr. Makepeace whirled around. Approaching him, Abigail stepped into the light. She stuck her hand inside her saddlebag, prepared to fish something out of it in a hurry.

"My, your father raised you to be a stubborn one," Mr. Makepeace teased her.

"I won't let you hurt anyone else."

"You're too late. I'll drop this and scurry down these tunnels before anyone knows what happened." He grinned.

If he throws the acid, I can't throw the base from here. I have to get closer. I must find a way to make him leave.

"You know I planned to kill you in that warehouse and then leave your father alone, but you forced me to improvise. Sloppy, but it will be effective. I'm sorry, girl," Mr. Makepeace sighed bitterly. "I bear you no ill will, nor your father, but, like you, I am bound by a contract. It's my job. It's how this awful city works."

"This city doesn't need to be awful."

"Oh, come now, girl. You hate this city as much as I do."

"I don't hate it. It just frightens me, but I don't want to be afraid anymore."

"You've got spirit. It's going to be a shame to kill you and your father, Abigail Reid."

"You knew that was me at the shoeshine stand. Why did you talk to me?"

"I've been doing this for so long, I don't know. I suppose I just wanted you to know why you needed to die."

"None of this needs to happen. You're not required to do this."

"I've been given orders, Abigail. Consider yourself lucky. Little Wade and Watchtower got to you first. They got to you early. Someone else, someone very different from them, got to me early, too, and I can't say no to him. No one can."

"Who are you talking about?"

"Who do you think built this city?" Mr. Makepeace smiled sadly. "They call this the Empire City, but nobody ever asks who the emperor is. That's how he likes it. No one sees him, but he sees all of us. We're all living in his vision. He wants his towers, his riches, and his magnificent metropolis, all of it a monument to him. Nothing can tear his creation down. Today, we're just going to bring down a little piece." Mr. Makepeace held up the bottle of acid. "Don't worry. In less than a week, another building will rise up in place of this one, and no one will ever know or remember that any of us were ever here. None of us matter, only him."

Alone, Abigail trembled with fear. She hoped Little Wade and Watchtower were on their way. Would they arrive just in time? She did not know. Sweat slicked her palms. Her skin tingled. Her breath jittered, but then she felt her sturdy steel watch *click-click-click* in her pocket, and she stood up straight and composed herself.

Only thirteen seconds. That's all I need.

One.

Steeling herself, Abigail pulled something out of her saddlebag.

Two.

Mr. Makepeace dashed the acid vial against a wooden support beam; the glass broke with a *hiss*.

Three.

The acid began to chew through the wooden supports of the building.

Four.

Abigail held up one of Mr. Goldsmoke's grenades.

"Gold..."

Five.

Abigail smiled. "...smoke."

Six.

Mr. Makepeace's eyes widened.

Seven.

He drew Mr. Skinner's long knife from his coat and held up the lantern. Lit by the flickering fire, the blade gleamed.

Eight.

"Wait!" Mr. Makepeace yelled.

Nine.

Pinching her nose with a clothespin, Abigail gulped as much air as she could and then clamped her mouth shut.

Ten.

Hissing, the acid chewed through the wood.

Mr. Makepeace, knife in hand, rushed toward her, charging like a bull.

Eleven.

Holding her breath, Abigail pulled the ring out of Mr. Goldsmoke's grenade.

Twelve.

Mr. Makepeace raised his knife to slash Abigail.

Thirteen.

Whoosh! Bursting open, Mr. Goldsmoke's grenade ruptured and released the sulfur gas trapped inside. A thick, noxious yellow cloud erupted from the weapon and quickly filled up the basement. Abigail shut her eyes as the world disappeared.

Letting go of the grenade and diving to the side, Abigail dropped to the ground as she felt Mr. Makepeace blow past her, slashing the air viciously with his knife. Her eyes shut, she could hear him coughing and cursing as the sulfur burned his throat and eyes. She felt his knife whip and whizz through the swirling gas, barely missing her. Abigail heard the metal door swing open as Mr. Makepeace stumbled out of the room, banging his foot against one of the sharp corners of the door. Howling in pain, he desperately, blindly tried to guide himself out, flailing around. His steel blade scraped and sparked against the gritty walls of the tunnel. Abigail heard Mr. Makepeace scramble through the clouds of yellow smoke, gagging, spitting. Then he limped away, his shoes splashing in the swampy water on the sewer floor.

He must be heading back toward the manhole.

Reaching into her pocket, Abigail gripped her watch, which *click-click-clicked* steadily even as her heart pounded in her chest, and her mind raced in a million different directions. Calming herself, still holding her breath, her nose pinched, her eyes shut, Abigail reached into her satchel and gripped the glass bottle with the green liquid, the base.

Readying to throw the bottle, she listened carefully for the sound of acid gnawing through the wood. Aiming as best she could, she hurled her glass bottle toward the sound. It shattered and *hissed*. Whirling around, Abigail retraced her steps, counting backward. Clutching her watch, which beat vigorously, she reached out with her other hand, spreading all her five fingers out...feeling for it...there! Locating the door, she found and gripped the string. Using it to guide herself out of the basement and back into the sewer, Abigail took off and raced down the tunnel.

Click-click-click.

Behind Abigail, acid sizzled, the wood creaked and splintered as the foundation began to give way. Above her, through the sewer's stony ceiling, she could hear men crying out. *"It's coming down! Run!"*

Please, let my father be all right. Please, don't let anyone get hurt!

Turning left, following her string, Abigail pursued Mr. Makepeace with her eyes closed, her shoes splashing through the gunky, chunky water on the sewer floor.

Click-click-click.

Abigail headed toward the hollow metal sounds of Mr. Makepeace climbing up the ladder. She heard him cough and push the half-open manhole cover aside with a loud *rumble* and *clang!* Mr. Makepeace gasped for breath outside.

Her lungs swelled up inside her chest like balloons. Abigail, her eyes still closed, her nose pinched, moved through the toxic gas. She could feel it tingle against her skin. *Click-click-click.* Guiding herself along with the string, Abigail ran down the tunnel, back toward the manhole. Above her, through the ceiling, she heard the building shake.

Click-click-click. Following the string, sprinting, Abigail could feel her air running out. Behind her, she heard wooden beams collapse with a thudding crash. *Please, don't let it come down.* Letting go of the string, still clutching her *click-click-clicking* watch, she could feel air flowing upward toward an opening above her: the manhole! Reaching out with her eyes still shut, she felt frantically for it. *There!*

Pocketing her watch, Abigail gripped the crude iron ladder that led up to the surface. She quickly climbed up, rung by rung. Her lungs were about to burst. She did not open her eyes or her mouth until she felt a crisp, cool breeze all around her, and then she swallowed a huge gust of air. "*Gaaaaahhh!*"

Light poured into Abigail's eyes as she opened them. Air rushed into her mouth and chest. Removing the clothespin from her nose, she smelled the city again, sawdust, sweat, dirt and mud, smoke and fire, hot metal, ash, and, finally, the rotten egg stench of sulfur. The awful odor made her feel nauseous. Then she jumped when she heard a loud, metallic, rasping noise and then a loud *clang!* Whirling around, she spotted Sergeant Blood. He replaced the manhole cover, trapping the yellow vapor inside the tunnel.

A few men who had been standing next to the manhole coughed, but not nearly as bad as Mr. Makepeace, whose eyes were swollen and red; coughing and wheezing, he kneeled on the ground, placed a handkerchief over his mouth and vomited. Precinct Zero subdued him.

Turning to the building, Abigail nearly fainted with relief when she saw that it had not collapsed. She removed the Intrepid Cap, letting her spectacular red hair spill out. Blinking several times, focusing, she hollered in triumph. A fully repaired Watchtower, disguised in a police uniform, along with several officers from Precinct Zero and several dozen construction workers, held up the massive wooden frame of the building. Other men frantically worked to shore it up from below. Breathing in and out, she relaxed. Even though a dozen men gritted their teeth and lifted with all their might until their faces were red, Abigail smiled giddily, knowing that Watchtower secretly held up the entire structure all by himself.

Then she panicked. *Where did he go? Where?* She searched the top of the building but could not see him. *Father!*

"Abigail?"

Her heart thumped at the sound of his unmistakable voice. She whirled around. Martin stepped forward, a worried look on his face. "Abigail, is that you?"

"*Oh, thank heavens you're all right!*" Abigail rushed forward and embraced him fiercely.

Martin embraced her too, and then he kneeled and gazed into her eyes. He noticed her saddlebag, her Intrepid Cap, her watch, and he shook his head in confusion.

"Abigail. I told you to stay at home. Why are you here?"

"Go on," she heard another familiar voice. "Tell him."

Little Wade, fully healed, descended like an angel from the sky, smiling down at her. He took his place at her side, and, at that moment, Abigail realized they were both completely surrounded by dozens of dirty, sweaty men.

"*What's going on here?*" a nasty voice split through all of the noise.

One man stepped forward out of the crowd. Unlike the workers, who dressed in rough, dusty work clothes and boots, this man wore an expensive, maroon top hat and a matching tailcoat and matching cane and even matching shoes, all of the finest quality. He even wore maroon leather gloves. His golden pocket watch matched his golden spectacles. Somehow, no dust seemed to ever settle on him, and he huffed and sniffed, annoyed. Tall and thin, he turned his nose up at everything, and everyone, around him.

"Mr. Rance..." Martin stood up and removed his hat, bowing his head. All of the men did the same thing. Glaring down his nose through his spectacles at Abigail, her father, the officers of Precinct Zero, and finally, Mr. Makepeace, who continued to cough, retch and wipe his tearing eyes, Mr. Rance rapped his maroon cane down against the sidewalk. Then he spread his thin lips open again as he unleashed his nasty, thorny voice.

"*Well? Can anyone answer my question?*"

Martin struggled to speak. Sergeant Blood also hesitated before he spoke. Little Wade could not reveal himself, so he simply floated beside her, silent. Mr. Makepeace tried to speak, but gagged dryly and stopped.

"I can, sir," Abigail spoke up.

24

GOBSMACKED

As the men waited impatiently, Abigail felt her metal watch *click-click-click*. Little Wade floated at her side. Gulping, clenching her fists, she summoned up the will to speak.

"It all started while I was reading at home. Leaning out my window, I overheard a pair of Longshadows whispering about how they were going to murder me and my father, Martin Reid." She pointed to her father.

"The Longshadows had tried to kidnap me the night before, you see. I managed to get away, so they wanted to make sure I learned a lesson. Anyway, when I discovered these Longshadows conspiring, I could not just stand by and do nothing, so I snuck out of my house and followed them. Sorry, Father. I know you told me to stay home, but you also taught me that I should always try to do something if I could prevent bad things from happening, so one moral principle overruled the other."

Martin gazed at her, dumbstruck.

"Along the way, I sought assistance from some very nice people, including several police officers who happened to be making their rounds. They agreed to help me."

She pointed to Sergeant Blood, who played along, quite impressed with Abigail's storytelling abilities.

"So, working with several police officers, I decided to follow the Longshadows and see what they planned, and that's when I discovered the real threat. Now, I should inform you that a rather nasty brawl erupted between the Longshadows and the Wild Cards at a theater not far from here earlier this morning. Well, that happened because the Longshadows were following me and crossed into Wild Card territory. I didn't mean to start a scuffle between them, but when two groups of unpleasant people get together, I don't think they're going to sit down for tea and crumpets."

Everyone laughed.

Encouraged, Abigail went on. "So, anyway, the brawl between the Longshadows and the Wild Cards quickly spread throughout the city. That obviously threatened to cause problems for the rest of the underworld, so organized crime called in that man." She pointed to Mr. Makepeace. "They hired him to set things right for them, and that meant doing what the Longshadows had failed to do: murder my father, kidnap me, kill me if necessary, whatever would make the problem go away."

All of the men, many of them fathers themselves, grumbled. Even Mr. Rance, who Abigail could tell was not the nicest of people, glared at Mr. Makepeace.

"You...tried to murder a...little girl?" Mr. Rance looked at him in disbelief.

Mr. Makepeace, still kneeling, coughed, and then he spat on the ground.

Everyone turned back to Abigail.

Mr. Rance inquired, "How did you find him?"

"Well, I requested help from the police. So together, we followed the gangs to their meeting place, a warehouse, where Mr. Makepeace, the Longshadows, Wild Cards, and all of the other gangs all plotted together to kill me. One of those gangs included a man I nicknamed Mr. Goldsmoke, a dangerous man who wears a mask and concocts toxic chemicals to hurt his enemies. Specifically, he uses acids to inflict damage and uses yellow sulfur gas to drive people off...hence 'Goldsmoke' seemed an appropriate moniker."

"I think I know who that is," one of the workers exclaimed.

"I think I do, too. He's a member of the old Bottled Spiders gang," another man added. "He's a 'orrible man, truly 'orrible."

Abigail continued, "Well, the police interrupted the meeting. There was a great battle in the warehouse, absolute pandemonium. In the end, the New York Police Department prevailed and arrested most of the ruffians. Unfortunately, Mr. Makepeace escaped and raced back here to kill my father."

All around Mr. Makepeace, the crowd booed.

"I managed to catch up to him in the sewer tunnel, where he attempted to murder me with a knife."

Sergeant Blood, who had disarmed Mr. Makepeace, held up Mr. Skinner's long, fearsome knife. The crowd grunted.

"How did you stop him?" Martin asked, still completely dumbfounded.

"Well, it's quite simple, really," Abigail explained. "During the scuffle between the police and all of the gangs, Mr. Goldsmoke used his yellow sulfur gas against several police officers. I saw that it choked the throat and inflamed the eyes, but it did not kill or seep through the skin. During the battle, Mr. Goldsmoke, unfortunately, escaped capture, but not before he dropped his bag of chemicals, which contained several of his grenades. I managed to get my hands on the bag."

All of the men murmured, impressed. Abigail went on.

"Well, I figured that Mr. Goldsmoke would be very well organized with his chemical weapons because they are so dangerous. From his discarded bag, I managed to confiscate a grenade that looked the same as the ones he had used during the battle, so I trusted that this particular one would perform the exact same function, a reasonable conclusion, I think."

Everyone listened, completely rapt.

"So I followed Mr. Makepeace back here to the construction site; however, I could not find him anywhere despite surveying the entire scene. Then I found that this particular manhole was partially uncovered, which led me to believe that Mr. Makepeace had lowered himself down into the sewers. I surmised, correctly, that he planned to use some of Mr. Goldsmoke's acid to weaken the foundation of the building while my father worked way up top. He could bring it down, kill my father, and make it all look like an accident. No one would notice the pungent smell of the acid because there would be so much wreckage and death from the collapsed building. No one would ever know that a murder had taken place, and if he used the sewers, then no one would see him perform the dastardly deed. No one would ever know that he was ever here."

"He could've killed us!" one of the workers exclaimed.

"How much damage has the foundation suffered? Speak!" Mr. Rance demanded, very concerned.

"We're not sure. We've managed to shore it up, Mr. Rance! Those officers showed up just in the nick of time, especially that tall one. He's as strong as a giant, that one."

Abigail smiled and winked at her father, who still stood there, astonished. "Father, I'm going to use a word that I've been wanting to use for quite some time. You look *gobsmacked*."

Rance barked orders. "I want men down in the sewers immediately to repair the damage and replace the foundations. Work overtime if you must. Whatever it takes. Whatever it costs! Now!"

"Yes, Mr. Rance!"

Immediately, several men went to work, gathering the necessary supplies and tools.

"Please continue, young lady." Mr. Rance leaned forward, interested.

"So back to the manhole, he left it partially open, not only because it was quite heavy to move, but also because it would be far easier to get out again the way he came in if he chose to do so."

"You followed him...down there?" Martin pointed to the sewer.

"I did," Abigail replied and then turned to the rest of the crowd, who continued to listen. "So when I went spelunking down in the sewers, I knew I needed to stop him and drive him back up to the surface. Well,

I'm just a little girl. I don't possess any weapons like a pistol or a knife. I wouldn't really know how to use them anyway; however, as I mentioned earlier, I did scavenge one of Mr. Goldsmoke's grenades from the battle in the warehouse. So I reasoned that if I popped the gas, the stink and general unpleasantness it caused would force Mr. Makepeace to leave the tunnels immediately. I assumed that he originally planned to escape deep into the sewers, but I calculated that, if I used the gas, he would panic and would likely escape the same way he came in. Better to do that than risk getting lost in the sewers while inhaling the toxic gas. It seemed like an astute calculation. It worked."

"Very shrewd," Mr. Rance complimented her.

Two men re-opened the manhole, removing the metal cover, releasing a yellow cloud. They coughed.

"The vapor should have mostly dissipated by now," Abigail advised them. "Nevertheless, beware of the pungent odor."

"Be careful!" Mr. Rance ordered his men.

"You will find a string that I tied to the ladder," Abigail counseled them. "I tied the other end to the door that leads straight to the foundation. Use it to guide you."

The workers thanked her and descended into the tunnels. One of them yelled. "There's a little bit of yellow gas down here, but it's not too bad!"

"I found the string! Very helpful. Thank you!" a second voice echoed up from the manhole.

"You're welcome!" Abigail called down to them.

Martin shook his head, amazed.

"How did you manage to get out of there without succumbing to the poison yourself?" Mr. Rance pressed her for details.

Abigail pulled out her metal watch, *click-click-clicking*.

"Well, first I pinched my nose with a clothespin, ensuring that no toxins would enter through my nasal cavity. Once that was done, I thought that if I kept my eyes closed and held my breath, I should be all right. So I held the watch in one hand to keep track of how much time I could hold my breath. With my other hand, I guided myself back by pulling on the string that I brought with me and that your men are currently using now. Anyway, while I guided myself out of the vapor-filled tunnels, I could feel the clicks of my watch counting off the seconds."

She cast a sidelong glance at Little Wade, who shook his head in amazement, a look of immeasurable pride on his face.

"A...very good friend of mine told me that because I'm only thirteen years old, I only need to be brave for thirteen seconds at a time. Being down in that poisonous tunnel, I listened and counted as the watch ticked. Well, it turns out that I can hold my breath in poison gas for quite a bit longer than thirteen clicks of a clock, so...I suppose that makes me braver than I thought." Abigail eyed Little Wade. "I think my friend already knew that. I think he knew that all along, but he wanted me to learn it for myself, and I did."

Little Wade winked at her. All of the men stood there, mouths agape.

"So, in conclusion, gentlemen, I apologize sincerely if I smell like sewage and rotten eggs. My shoes splashed around in fetid water and my hair and clothing have been infused with sulfur residue from Mr. Goldsmoke's grenade. I hope it does not irritate your eyes and nostrils too much, and I hope that this story has not irritated your ears."

Silence.

At first, Abigail blushed, embarrassed. "Did...I do something wrong?" she asked, nervously.

Spontaneously, the men burst out into applause, and Abigail blushed again, even redder this time. She curtsied. Only Mr. Rance did not applaud. Fixing both of his hands firmly on his maroon cane, he turned to Martin.

"This your little girl?"

"Yes, sir, she is."

"What's your name, carpenter?" Mr. Rance looked at him quizzically.

"Martin, sir. Martin Reid."

"And I'm Abigail Reid," she declared, reaching out and taking her father's hand.

"Quite the warrior," Mr. Rance complimented Martin.

One of the workers popped his head out of the manhole.

"Mr. Rance! We can definitely salvage it. One of the joiners got eaten through, but we can easily replace it. As for the rest, it's whole. A bit of cracking on one of the crossbeams, but it's not too bad. Whatever she did, it saved the whole foundation."

"It's simple science," Abigail interjected. "For every yellow vial of acid that Mr. Goldsmoke concocts, he always carries an equivalent vial of a green base that neutralizes the acid. It's obviously a safety measure. I observed Mr. Goldsmoke using one of the green bottles during the battle to stop his acid from melting through one of his allies (it's a long story). I decided to filch one of those bottles from the bag along with the grenade, so when Mr. Makepeace tossed the acid onto the wood, I tossed the base. I shut my eyes to protect myself from the gas, and that threw off my aim, so I'm sorry for that. I think I managed to negate at least some of the damage."

"No need to apologize, Abigail Reid. If you had not done that, the damage would be a thousand times worse," Mr. Rance observed, and then he turned to Mr. Makepeace, who still knelt on the ground next to a puddle of his own barf. Pulling out a handkerchief and holding it in front of his nose, Mr. Rance scowled at Mr. Makepeace with utter contempt.

"You cowardly little worm," Mr. Rance sneered at Mr. Makepeace. *"Get him out of here!"*

The officers of Precinct Zero bound Mr. Makepeace and then lifted him off the ground. Before they dragged him away, Mr. Makepeace managed to draw closer to Abigail and smile one last time.

"Remember what I told you, girl," he whispered. "If you want peace in this city, someone has to burn."

"Yes," she admitted. "Today, it's you."

Mr. Makepeace frowned, not quite expecting that. Then he gulped when two officers of Precinct Zero dragged him toward the police omnibus. The officers promptly locked him inside and transported him away to prison.

"Well, that was rather exciting, wasn't it?" Mr. Rance briefly removed his maroon top hat and wiped his brow with his handkerchief before resetting his hat on his head. "All right, everyone, back to work."

The crowd dispersed and the men returned to their jobs, bustling about the construction site, resuming their sawing, hammering, shoveling, grunting, and yelling.

While most of the officers of Precinct Zero cleared out, Watchtower, still in disguise, stood close by. To relieve him, the men had placed multiple wood beams to support the frame, which had stabilized. Little Wade hovered next to Watchtower. They both appeared relaxed and satisfied; the crisis had ended and the danger had passed.

"Mr. Rance," Martin requested quietly, sheepishly. "Would you mind if I leave to walk my daughter home?"

"Certainly not," Mr. Rance peered down his nose at Abigail. "Walk her home."

"Thank you, sir."

"Don't come back."

"What?"

"I'm sorry, Martin," Mr. Rance sniffed. "I'm afraid I must dismiss you."

25

WORKING MEN

"You're...firing me?" Martin Reid's mouth dropped open.

"What?" Abigail was equally surprised.

Mr. Rance sniffed irritably as if the very question offended him. There were still more than a few workers standing nearby. Many of the men gasped.

"Of course, I'm firing you. Look at all of the chaos you've caused here. The frame's nearly collapsed. We nearly lost the top two levels."

"No, we didn't," Martin objected, defending himself. "My daughter prevented the foundation from being destroyed, and we shored up the frame. Look, it's still standing strong. That oversized copper helped prop it up. He just saved us weeks of work."

"Maybe we should hire *him* instead," Mr. Rance snickered, glancing over at Watchtower, who balled up his fists and was tempted to bonk Mr. Rance on the head. Little Wade stopped him.

"Please, Mr. Rance," Martin pleaded. "Everything worked out in the end."

"Yes, things worked out at great expense. Your fellow workers will need to spend hours down in the sewers, replacing that foundation. That's hours of expensive, hazardous labor. All of this nonsense has already cost me a significant amount of money."

"Please, Mr. Rance, I need the work. I'll work a double shift, triple."

"He's a good worker, sir," one of the other men chimed in.

"Tremendously talented carpenter. We could really use him," another one mentioned. Mr. Rance waved the other workers away as if they were annoying flies. They bowed their heads and went back to work.

"I don't know what you did to anger the Longshadows, but whatever you did, you brought your problems here, and that could have hurt or killed any one of these men, including me. It's your fault that scoundrel came here."

At this point, Abigail could not keep silent. "Wait, you're punishing my father because the Longshadows wanted to kill him and kidnap me?" Incredulous, Abigail fumed. "That makes no sense whatsoever."

Mr. Rance glared at her, annoyed. "I don't want any trouble. I'm responsible for this site, and the people paying for all of this don't care for any attention from the Longshadows or anyone else. They don't like...interruptions or inconveniences."

"Interruptions? Inconveniences? Did you not see what just happened? I told you that many of the Longshadows have been arrested. They won't trouble anyone now."

"I'm not going to argue with a child. Right now, both of you represent an expensive distraction. I've made my final decision. Martin, collect your tools and leave the premises immediately."

"You can't do that!" Abigail roared.

"Oh, I can't, why not?" Mr. Rance sneered.

"She did not mean it, sir," Martin tried to intercede.

"I did mean it. Every word! My father's the best carpenter on this whole site. You're going to miss him when he's gone."

"The moment your father leaves this site there will be ten men lining up to take his spot. Now, get out of here and take your problems with you!"

"You'll regret this!" Abigail yelled.

"Abigail, please be quiet!" Martin hushed her.

"Better teach your daughter some manners, Martin," Mr. Rance chuckled. "She's brave all right, but she needs to know her place. You need to know yours, and it's not here, not now."

With a huff, Mr. Rance tipped his hat and turned his back. Tapping his cane loudly on the ground as if cracking a whip, he snapped his fingers snobbishly and he roared at the other men. "*Back to work! Double time it!*"

Abigail watched as dozens of burly men snapped to attention and scrambled around the worksite.

"What a terrible, awful man." Abigail gritted her teeth. "I'm going to give him a piece of my mind." She stormed forward.

"Abigail stop!" Martin pulled her back forcefully. "You're only making things worse! Just stop! *Stop!*"

Abigail saw the desperate look on her father's face.

"Please, Abigail...don't make the situation any worse."

"I am...I'm sorry. I didn't know. It's just...it doesn't make any sense at all. Why are you obligated to be so polite to him when he treats you like a dog. Worse than a dog, like dirt?"

"Mr. Rance commands great respect among the wealthy and workers alike. He runs many sites like these. I don't know when I might need work from him again. You're making things worse, not better."

"It's ridiculous. You're the best carpenter here. You should be designing and building the whole thing."

"Abigail, listen to me," Martin knelt down, gripped his daughter's shoulders, and gazed deeply into her eyes. "I haven't lived in this city for very long. I'm new here. It takes time for people to get to know me."

"It's not fair."

"I know it isn't. I'm just happy you're safe. Let's go home."

Walking hand in hand, Martin and Abigail headed home. Abigail talked the whole way back, telling him the entire story (well, mostly). She told him about the sympathetic police officers that provided her with the map and the schedule and how she felt so much safer and happier even after just one morning. She also told him about Brooke. "We tried to rescue her, but she sacrificed herself to save four other children, and me." Abigail followed up by assuring her father that Brooke was likely to be rescued soon. In response, Martin offered to visit Mr. Adams in the hospital as soon as he could.

Of course, Abigail left out several key elements: Little Wade, Watchtower, ghosts, mysterious men in black disappearing through portals into other worlds. While Martin grunted in response, Abigail occasionally glanced over her shoulder and spotted Little Wade following them (at a polite distance).

First, Abigail and Martin stopped by the Peculiarly Positive Shop, where Professor Obradór and company rumbled up to the door until they all practically overflowed out of it. Warmly and loudly, they introduced themselves to Martin, explained that they were the ones who gifted Abigail the saddlebag, and they assured Martin that they would be delighted to help his daughter in any way possible.

As they walked along, heading home, "Nice people, eh?" Abigail teased her father.

"Nice...yes," Martin agreed. "Awfully strange...but yes...I get a good feeling, but Abigail, I need to ask you...who gave you that watch?"

"Mr. Singh. Let's go see him right now. He wants to meet you."

Martin Reid suddenly realized that they were standing in front of Saran Singh's Exotic Imports and Exports.

"I'm supposed to walk you home," he remarked, "but you were leading me instead."

"Better start getting used to that." Abigail winked.

Ever polite, Mr. Singh appeared at the entrance to his shop.

"You must be Martin Reid." Mr. Singh saluted him.

"I am," Martin answered cautiously, a little suspicious at first.

"Very pleased to meet you, sir." Singh extended his hand in friendship.

Martin took it reluctantly, surprised to find a man with a grip as firm as his own.

"I understand your daughter seeks safe passage to school and back home again. She has been reaching out to her neighbors to assist her in this venture."

"That's right," Martin answered, guarded.

"Well, you may consider me an ally. I believe I am already marked on Abigail's map."

"It's all right, Father. He's a friend." She squeezed her father's hand.

"May I present my daughters, Sati and Trisha." Two adorable Sikh girls shyly appeared behind their father's legs and waved.

"You are also raising daughters, Mr. Singh, so you know what it's like."

"I do. There is nothing I would not do for my precious ones, Mr. Reid."

"Still...this watch. You just gave it to Abigail?" Martin eyed him suspiciously.

"No, I consider it a trade in exchange for this."

Saran Singh opened his hand and presented Abigail's lucky chess piece, the queen.

Martin shot a disapproving glance at Abigail. "I made that for you as a gift."

"I am returning it to you." Saran Singh extended his hand. "It served its purpose, proof of your great skill. You can return the watch at any time. However, I believe your daughter has become quite attached to it."

Martin cautiously took back the chess piece. "What do you get out of this, Mr. Singh?"

"We both benefit. Your daughter described you as an eminently talented carpenter, Mr. Reid. Would you be interested in discussing selling your wares at my shop?"

"I...I would."

"We can split the proceeds, a reasonable percentage for me as the distributor, the rest for you. I can provide clients who would very much appreciate handmade goods. They will pay quite handsomely. It will not substitute for a whole job, but it will provide you income, and your hours will be flexible. It would be a shame to deny the world your talent."

Abigail squeezed his hand enthusiastically.

"I'll...I'll...uh...I'll stop by tomorrow with more samples. We can discuss what you would like me to make for you, but...I won't be able to make anything large. I don't operate or possess a shop of my own. I did up in the country, but not anymore."

"Indeed, you will need proper facilities. If only there were someone who could provide it for you." He winked at Abigail, and then they all heard a loud *ding ding ding*. "Right on time." Saran Singh pointed to someone, or something, behind them.

Turning around, Abigail craned her neck upward. In front of her stood the strangest bicycle that she had ever seen. The front wheel was enormous, at least ten times the size of the back wheel, which was tiny in comparison. Not only did the bike appear distorted, but it also stood astonishingly tall. Perched on top of the bizarre bicycle, a plump little man with a stovepipe hat and a mustache so broad that it looked like a second pair of bicycle handlebars sat comfortably. He swung out a metal kickstand to stabilize his strange vehicle. Balanced on his seat, this rotund individual addressed them in a voice that sounded like a tuba. "Greetings, fellow denizens of New York!"

"What are you riding?" Abigail inquired.

"It's called a Penny Farthing!" The squat man with the handlebar mustache tipped his hat. "It's an antique, well, sort of. They were all the rage twenty years ago, but they have sadly fallen out of fashion." He gestured to himself to point out that he was a dwarfish man. "However, as a person of diminutive stature, I find them particularly practical. I enjoy the view from up here."

"As a person of diminutive stature myself, I can relate," Abigail replied.

"Begging your pardon, sir," Martin interrupted, "but...who are you?"

"Are you Martin Reid?"

"Who's asking?"

"Martin Reid, the carpenter?"

"That's right."

The short, plump man on the Penny Farthing bicycle smiled.

"Greetings, Martin Reid. Tom Archer. Pleased to make your acquaintance." He then extended his hand, which clutched a business card. Martin reached up, took it, and examined it.

"Archer's Woodworks…Fine Carpentry and Furnishings," Martin read it out loud and looked up, a flash of hope in his eyes.

Mr. Archer smiled. "That's correct, Mr. Reid. Archer's Woodworks supplies the finest products to clients all over the city of New York. This morning, my friend Mr. Singh showed me a sample of your work."

"That's just…that's just a tiny little thing." Martin adopted a slightly defensive, humble tone. "I can do better."

Mr. Archer gently put up his hand.

"I know excellent craftsmanship when I see it, Mr. Reid. If you're capable of carving that fine, intricate detail on something so small and delicate, then I've no doubt you can do anything I need you to do. I've been in this business for a long time, and I'm an excellent judge of talent. I want you to come work for me."

"Work…for you? You're hiring?"

"Oh yes. We've got back orders piling up for furniture. Additionally, in a few years, this city will commence construction on an incredibly vast, sophisticated, subterranean rapid transit system. They're going to call it The Subway."

"The Subway?"

"Yes, they're taking inspiration from the London Underground. In a few years, there will be construction sites all over, and those sites will require wood scaffolding to support the workers. My firm just snagged a very lucrative contract with the city. It's at least a decade of steady, paying work. I'm going to need somebody like you."

"My father works wizardry with all kinds of wood. He built our whole house in Tarrytown!" Abigail jumped up and down.

"I don't doubt it," Mr. Archer laughed. "Your delightful daughter enchants, Mr. Reid."

"She means everything to me, sir, which means I must provide for her. Begging your pardon, Mr. Archer, but might I inquire as to the pay and hours?"

"You'll find the pay stable and fair, the hours reasonable, eight in the morning to about six in the evening with a full hour for lunch and rest. After hours, if you wish to work on your own projects, you can use company facilities. We can come to some sort of arrangement regarding what goods or works of art you wish to produce using my workshop. I will require that I receive a reasonable percentage of whatever you manage to sell. Does that sound fair to you?"

"It does. So far."

"He'll require a contract," Abigail interjected, and then she winked at her father. "Please don't misunderstand, Mr. Archer, you seem to be a fine and amiable man, but I've been taught to always secure professional promises in writing."

"I agree entirely," Mr. Archer smiled and produced a bunch of papers from his overstuffed coat pocket. "I brought your contract with me. One moment, please."

Mr. Archer sifted through the papers, chose one, and handed it to Abigail. "It's in here somewhere. Hold this, please, Abigail."

Mr. Archer continued to rummage through his pockets. Curious, Abigail unfolded the paper Mr. Archer gave to her. She saw a childlike drawing, the unmistakable image of Little Wade and Watchtower. Gasping, Abigail quickly glanced up to Mr. Archer, who winked at her.

"Ah! Here it is. EMPLOYMENT AGREEMENT FOR MARTIN REID."

Mr. Archer unfurled the contract and handed it to Martin, who took it and scrutinized it.

"Do you mind if I take it home with me so I can look it over?"

"Please do. I think you'll find everything in order."

"If a gentleman considers himself as good as his word, then he shall have no problem writing it down and being bound to it," Abigail repeated Little Wade's exact words. "A good friend told me that."

"What a coincidence," Mr. Archer replied, laughing. "A good friend told me the very same thing when I was a boy."

Folding up the contract and sliding it into his pocket, concealing his excitement, Martin cleared his throat. "I'd...uh...like to take a look at your shop before I say yes."

"I think that's a capital idea. Stop by tomorrow morning after church, get a good look at our facility, and meet some of your fellows. On Sabbath I allow my carpenters to use the workshop for their own projects, so you'll meet your fellow artists. I know the Lord says not to work on the Sabbath, but, as far as I'm concerned, it's not technically work if you're doing what you love. It's not work if it's art. So it's the perfect time to visit. You'll find the address on the card. We'll work something out. If it's amenable to you, then you start first thing Monday."

"Yes, sir."

"Please don't call me 'sir,'" Mr. Archer shook his head. "I'm not better than you. I just own a better bicycle. Mr. Archer will suffice."

"I'll come by tomorrow, Mr. Archer, after church."

"Excellent. Tomorrow. I look forward to it. Well, I better be off." Mr. Archer tipped his hat. "Tons of work to do. So very nice meeting you, Abigail."

Abigail returned Mr. Archer's Little Wade and Watchtower contract. "You carry this with you?"

"Just a little something that I take with me wherever I go. It reminds me that it's good business to be good to people."

On cue, Little Wade, arms crossed, a satisfied look on his face, materialized next to Abigail. Mr. Archer winked at Little Wade. "Always good to see you." Retracting his kickstand, *ding-ding-dinging* his bell, Mr. Archer, pedaling excitedly with his little legs, raced away on his most unusual, lopsided bike. The instant Mr. Archer left, Martin immediately pulled out the contract from his pocket and read it excitedly, peering closely at the words. While watching him, Abigail whispered to Little Wade.

"Did you just secure my father a new job?" Abigail palpitated with excitement.

"No, you did." Little Wade smiled. "The opportunity to connect the right people will define the next century. We just placed two people together that should meet. Now the future rests with them."

Martin finished reading the contract.

"Father? Are you all right? Will it help?"

"Yes," Martin nodded, excited, tears forming in his eyes, which he quickly wiped away. "He'll pay me well, not quite everything I'm making now, but it's one job, not three. The hours and work will be much better, and...if you don't mind my being around more—"

"I think that sounds perfect." Abigail smiled brightly.

Martin turned and extended his hand to Mr. Singh, who shook it firmly.

"Thank you, Mr. Singh, for putting me in touch with Mr. Archer, but especially for helping my daughter." Visibly moved, Martin's voice softened.

"You are a good man, Martin Reid. You will find that many good people live in this city, and we all want the same thing, a better place for our children."

26

THE LONGEST SHADOW

Finally, Abigail and Martin made it home. Still talking, talking, talking, Abigail climbed up the ladder into the attic. Martin followed her and closed the hatch.

"So as you can see, I met with the Peculiarly Positive Shop, but that got me wondering...if there is a Positive Shop, does that mean that somewhere there is a Negative Shop? Is it peculiar? Or perhaps it's—"

The instant they were alone, Martin embraced his daughter fiercely. Tears welled up in his eyes. She stopped talking.

"I almost lost you." Martin hugged her like a bear. "Twice, I almost lost you."

Abigail's eyes welled up, too. "I couldn't let them hurt you. I'll never let anyone hurt you."

"I'm supposed to say that." Martin broke the embrace and paced around the apartment. Then he slumped down on his bed and hung his head. "I'm supposed to keep you safe, not the other way around."

At that moment, Little Wade politely poked his head in through the wall, careful not to interrupt them. Abigail saw Little Wade and smiled, and then she crossed over to her father and placed her hand on his shoulder.

"You're supposed to be a good man who tries his best," Abigail comforted him. "That's what you are. That's what you've always been."

"Abigail," Martin began. She could tell he struggled to say what he was about to say. "I'm...I'm sorry about earlier today. I've been thinking...about what you suggested to me early this morning. You wanted to walk around the neighborhood and talk to people to see if they would help you. I didn't listen. Now I believe...I *know* you're right. We need to solve this problem, but if we wait until tomorrow, we'll be wasting time. I just hope you know that if anything ever happened to you..." His voice trailed off.

"I know." She gently reached out and touched his face.

"You showed me how brave and tough you can be."

"I had help." She stole a wink at Little Wade, who floated in the corner.

"So...given that...I think...yes...you can definitely take a stroll around the neighborhood and talk to more people, but please be careful."

"I will. The streets are much safer today than yesterday."

"That's true, but that's not the point. You were right, Abigail, and I was wrong. This morning when we spoke, you made a good point, and I didn't listen. Despite whatever happened today, the gangs will return. They always do. Monday will come, and this problem won't go away unless we solve it now. Cooping you up here won't accomplish that. You're a smart girl. You've got a good head on your shoulders. I don't like it, but I'll allow it. Investigate today, but don't go into anyone's house. Don't go inside where a door can close behind you, and you do this only during daylight. At sundown, you come straight home, and, whoever you speak to today, I want to meet with them tomorrow. Do you understand? You're not to stay anywhere behind closed doors unless I look the proprietors in the eye first and approve them, like those strange people at that Positive Shop place or Mr. Singh. Do you understand?"

"Yes, Father."

"Every time you walk away from me," Martin confessed, "every time you turn a corner and disappear, every time you pass out of my sight, I'm terrified that I will never see you again, or that you will come back…different. I'm afraid that something will hurt you, change you, and I will miss it. There will be so many moments where I know you will suffer, and I will wish that I could have been there."

"I will disappear, but I will come back, Father, and when I come back, I will be a little stronger every time."

Sadly, Martin stroked her red hair. "You're not even the same girl that you were yesterday or this morning. You're not a mouse anymore, are you?"

"I'm something better, something far more dangerous."

"I love you, Abigail."

"I love you too, Papa."

They hugged warmly. After a few moments, Martin raised himself up slowly, achingly. "Time to go back to work."

"Can't you rest?"

He shook his head. "No. We need the money."

"Mr. Rance fired you. You have the rest of the day free. Stay here with me. Oooooh…we can walk around the neighborhood and find more allies together!"

Martin shook his head.

"I must work, Abigail, as long as I still have hours left in the day. I can rest tomorrow."

"Where will you go?"

Martin hesitated.

"I'll go…I'll go over to the docks on Jackson."

Little Wade reacted, visibly concerned.

Abigail shook her head sadly.

"No, Papa, please no."

"They always need people. I can pick up a shift."

"No, Papa, please. You work there too much already. They make you lift heavy things. It hurts your back. You get so tired. Every time you come back injured in some way. It's dangerous."

"I won't be the only one there, and it pays very well for a day's work."

"That's because it's not safe. Your bosses know it's not safe."

"We need the money, Abigail!" Martin, frustrated, snapped at her. "What do you want me to say? What would you have me do? Mr. Rance fired me and will likely never hire me again."

"But what about Mr. Archer's offer?"

"Mr. Archer's offer might not work out. I can't let the rest of this day go to waste. I must find more work. The bosses at the docks know me. I need to stay in their good graces. If I work extra today, I can accomplish that."

"This…is all my fault."

"No, it's not your fault."

"Yes, it is. I'm the reason you lost your job, a job that you wanted."

"You're just a girl who wants to go to school. I don't blame you. I blame the gangs that caused all of this. You saved my life, Abigail."

"I just wanted to do something good for you, and now it's gone all wrong."

"No, it hasn't," Martin consoled her. "I'm so proud of you, Abigail. You have become so much braver and stronger than I ever could have hoped. Having you for a daughter has been, and is, the most important, most wonderful thing in my whole life. Nothing else matters."

"I'm lucky to have a father like you."

"We're both lucky," he laughed bitterly, "but we're also poor, and I must go."

Martin got up to leave, but Abigail reached out and clutched his hand. She squeezed it tight. "Promise me you will take care of yourself. Promise me you will be safe, and that you will come straight back here once you complete your task."

"I was about to say the same thing to you," Martin laughed.

Abigail embraced her father. "I don't want you to go."

"I'll be all right," Martin comforted her. "It's just for this afternoon."

Little Wade, floating nearby, whispered gently.

"He will be safe. We have people at the docks."

The words reassured her, but the relaxed look on Little Wade's face made Abigail immediately feel even better. She squeezed her father.

"You're so much like her, like your mother." He held back tears. "It's glorious."

"I miss her every day," Abigail cried.

"I miss her, too."

"Will this ever get easier? Will it ever hurt less?"

"I don't know," Martin answered. He pulled away from his daughter and let out a deep, painful sigh.

"Your mother...is so proud of you. She smiles down on us from Heaven. I'll see you soon." Already exhausted, Martin Reid exited through the hatch, shut it behind him, and sadly climbed down the ladder.

Wiping away her tears, Abigail crossed to the window and opened it. Waiting a minute, looking down onto the alley, she watched her father exit their house. Tired, Martin limped down the street on his way to work at the docks.

"Will Mr. Archer's job work out for him?"

"He gave your father a contract, Abigail," Little Wade assured her. "Mr. Archer will honor it. Watchtower and I gave you a contract, too. We offered to assist your father, and we intend to make good on that promise. Workers deserve dignity. Your father has forgotten what it means to hope. It frightens him to think that his situation might actually improve. By the end of the week, when he realizes that Mr. Archer means everything he says, your father will smile again."

Abigail reached into her pocket and pulled out Night Owl Nell's silver coin. "I wanted to give him this, so he could rest today. It's worth more than a day's work."

"Save that coin for another time, Abigail. Night Owl Nell gave that to you for emergencies. There will be other hard days. You know this to be true."

Clutching the coin in her hand, Abigail watched her father disappear into the crowd. Then she turned away from the window, but just before she closed it, a folded paper in the shape of a bird zipped into the attic from outside.

"What?" Abigail glanced at it strangely. "Is this from Watchtower? I didn't see him down there."

"No, it's not. Wait..."

Little Wade darted outside.

Abigail, intrigued, perked up, walked toward the paper bird, and stooped down to pick it up. Suddenly, Little Wade melted back through the wall and screamed.

"Don't touch it!"

Startled, she refrained from handling it. "I don't understand. Didn't Watchtower throw it in?"

"He's not here. He's still at the construction site aiding in the recovery. Shut the window. Now. Stay out of sight." Little Wade urged her.

Doing as he asked, shutting the window, Abigail felt a chill. "Then...who threw it?"

"If it's who I think it is...do not touch it with your bare hands."

"Is it...poisoned?"

"I'd put on your rubber gloves."

Quickly, Abigail fished them out of her saddlebag and stretched them over her hands until they snapped snug.

"Go on, Abigail." Little Wade's voice trembled.

"You're afraid," Abigail observed, surprised.

"Yes, and you should be, too."

Slowly, carefully, Abigail knelt down and picked up the paper bird. She delicately unfolded it, revealing a letter.

She read it out loud.

Dear Little Wade and Watchtower (and Client),

Congratulations! No doubt, you are currently celebrating the arrest of Mr. Makepeace, a critically important member of organized crime in this city. In addition, you have successfully apprehended and detained many members of the Longshadows, Wild Cards, and several other gangs. That is precisely what I wanted to happen.

With Mr. Makepeace gone, and many senior members of New York's criminal syndicates out of the picture, thanks to your heroics, the nefarious elements in the city will look to someone else to unite them and keep the peace: Me.

Then again, I've always been here, haven't I? We've been playing this game of ours for decades, almost as long as you've been a spirit.

You'll never beat me, Little Wade. For every move you make, I make two. As you read this letter, my men are committing a range of offenses. Your Precinct Zero, severely weakened from today's battle, can do nothing to stop my plans, nor can any of your officers or agents save the children I intend to kidnap and enslave for my own purposes.

Finally, this last section is addressed to Little Wade and Watchtower's newest client, the spirited young lady with spectacular red hair. My men tried to kidnap you last night. You think you were saved, but you are now in even greater danger.

No doubt, you think Little Wade and Watchtower are magnificent.

You think they cannot fail. Wrong. They can, and they have.

Ask them about the clients they have lost along the way.

I don't mean the ones that died. When Little Wade sat you down and presented his contract, he undoubtedly neglected to mention us. When I say "us," I mean the Clients that lived and suffered because Little Wade and Watchtower let us down.

We number in the hundreds. Over the years, we found each other, and we formed a gang of our own. We call ourselves The Believers. We used to believe in Little Wade and Watchtower. Now, we believe in ourselves.

I am their leader. Ask them about me.

Then fire them immediately.

If you do, I will spare you. I give you my word as a gentleman.

If not, then I will see you very soon, and I regret to say that you will find the circumstances most unpleasant.

Sincerely Yours,
Henry Lobe

Abigail folded up the letter very slowly. Even though she knew her rubber gloves protected her, she handled the poisoned piece of paper extremely carefully, as if she held a razor blade in her hand. She brooded. A million questions sprang up in her mind, but one towered above all of the rest.

"Who is Henry Lobe?"

A minute of total silence passed before Little Wade spoke. Abigail had never seen him so terribly sad.

"I told you, Abigail, although Watchtower and I approach every client with the best of intentions, and we always make our best effort...we do not always succeed. Henry Lobe was our first failure. Our enemies took him from us, and he has tormented us ever since."

"He's the leader of the Longshadows, isn't he?"

"Yes, Henry has become one of the most powerful criminals in the city. He took over the gang after Watchtower and I defeated their original leader. Under Henry, the gang has become even more powerful and dangerous. He ordered your kidnapping."

"So he chose to be a criminal."

"Did he? Watchtower and I...we promised to protect him. Instead, we let him slip into the hands of the horrific man who...made him... what he is now."

"Surely, you don't blame yourself for what Henry Lobe has become."

"We do, and we will never forgive ourselves. The longest shadow, Abigail, is guilt."

"That's utterly ridiculous!" Abigail fumed.

"He suffered terribly because we failed him," Little Wade contradicted her.

"Are you actually defending him?" Abigail continued to fume until she burned bright red. "People suffer every day. You don't see them choosing to lead vicious gangs and hurl creepy messages through the windows of young girls. Decades have passed, plenty of time for him to have done something productive with his life. He has chosen to be a sinister villain all on his own."

"I understand him, Abigail. I understand all of these criminals.

Henry Lobe, Mr. Makepeace, all of these terrible men. When I look at them, I see me."

"That's positively preposterous. How can you possibly even consider such a notion? You're practically an angel."

"When I look at them, I see me for one simple reason, Abigail. Inside every evil man with a hard heart and a cynical, bitter soul; inside every man who hurts other men; inside every man who hurts women and children; inside every single one of those men, deep down, is a sweet, innocent, little boy who died too soon."

"Listen to me." Abigail looked her friend straight in the eye. "You are nothing like these terrible men. Because you possess great power, you take the whole world on your shoulders. You obligate yourself to save all the children in this city, but you can't save everyone. Men like Henry Lobe are not worth your time, or mine for that matter."

Abigail held up the letter.

"On that note, literally, we should take this to the police immediately. It's rather incriminating."

"Look again."

She unfolded the note again and saw that the writing on the paper had vanished!

"It's called Single Ink. You can only read it once."

"Well then..." Abigail refolded Henry Lobe's letter, lit a candle, reopened her window, and burned the letter, which crumpled into acrid smoke that slithered out into the sky. "I hereby reject Henry Lobe's suggestion to fire you. I'm no fool. He will never honor his peace offering. He means to torment me no matter what I decide, so that's that. Any enemy of yours, by the transitive property, becomes one of mine."

"Thank you, Abigail, for your kind words," Little Wade replied dejectedly, "but we've never defeated him. Even today, we fell short. We had Brooke Adams within our reach, but we failed her, and you."

Abigail desperately wanted to reach out and touch him, to comfort him, but she could not.

"You didn't fail. No one else in this city cared about Brooke's disappearance. She became just another number, another statistic until you and Watchtower intervened. We saved four other children today, children who will be spending tonight with their families for the first time in weeks or months. You gave them hope. You've given me hope."

"You give us hope too, Abigail." Little Wade smiled sadly. "Watchtower and I, we do what we can, but we collided with our own limitations today. Watchtower and I nearly perished. We won today only because of you. *You* took down Mr. Makepeace. You were...astonishing."

She blushed. "Well, a new friend of mine, in fact, one of the best friends I have ever had, once told me in this very room that surprise is one of the most beautiful things that can bloom in this world."

"I said I was astonished," Little Wade gently corrected her, "not surprised."

Blushing, embarrassed, Abigail giggled. "It's all thanks to you. You showed me what I could be, what New York could be for me. I know it's just a glimpse. I felt so lost before, but now I feel like I can do anything I set my mind to. You showed me that."

"You just needed a little push. Anyone could have done what I did." Little Wade replied bitterly. "I'll never speak for Watchtower, but I know that I'm not that great."

"This is more than the humility of a gentleman," Abigail observed. "After all you have accomplished, why are you so down on yourself?"

"Because I don't know who murdered me."

This stunned Abigail into absolute silence.

Little Wade whispered painfully, tears forming in his eyes. "I don't even know *why*."

After a long silence, Abigail, shaking her head, finally spoke.

"That's...why you've been a ghost for so long," Abigail guessed. "You can't cross over until you find out."

Nodding his head, he sighed deeply, sadly, painfully. "It's been so many years, whoever did this to me is probably long dead by now. Every case we take, every villain we defeat, I keep wondering if we will stumble upon some answer around the corner. You and your father are not alone, Abigail. Watchtower and I also know what it's like to be afraid to hope."

"Mr. Makepeace knows something, doesn't he?"

"Watchtower and I both think so, and now he's in custody, thanks to you. You're not only going to use the Secret Passage of Hope, Abigail, to cut through all of the shadows and grime of this city. You are part of it, and you have been a most pleasant stop."

"I want to hug you so badly it hurts." Abigail's eyes teared up. "I wish I could. You're an absolute gentleman."

"Warner." Little Wade smiled. "My last name is Warner."

"So pleased to meet you, Wade Warner."

"Don't forget the Little."

"Nonsense." Abigail shook her head. "Wade Warner, to me, you are larger than life."

"I told you that one day this city will be the greatest in the world." Little Wade gazed out her round window. "It will be because of its children, because of people like you."

"Henry Lobe knows who murdered you, doesn't he?"

"Most certainly. He taunts me every year...riddles, puzzles, jokes. He knows, and it's his sweet revenge to keep that secret from me, but if Mr. Makepeace can offer something—"

Abigail snatched up her saddlebag. "Then let's get back to work. The Secret Passage of Hope must be completed! Henry Lobe plots against us. We must strike at him before he strikes at us. Let's continue the adventure! I just need to change clothes...again."

"Understand, Abigail, that the Longshadows will not take this lying down. Henry Lobe will send an assassin to destroy you."

"Like Mr. Makepeace?"

"Worse. Much worse."

Abigail quieted down.

"Aren't the Longshadows gone now? We damaged them very badly today."

"Unfortunately not. It will take more than today to fully defeat the Longshadows. Watchtower and I plan to permanently cripple the gang. Still, even if we succeed, we cannot destroy evil forever, Abigail.

We can only defeat it for a time. Now, with the Longshadows badly weakened in this neighborhood, we possess an opening. Now we can build your Secret Passage of Hope." He gestured to her clicking watch. "The Great Gang Trap bought us time."

"What about my father?"

"Your father will be safe for the time being. He's among friends, and our agents will watch him closely. The Longshadows won't dare attack him now, but you will be out there, exposed. They consider you the real problem, Abigail, the real threat. They will focus their efforts on you."

"I'm just a girl who wants an education," Abigail beamed, "but I suppose that terrifies them more than anything."

"It does. You don't have to be a ghost to haunt people."

"Oooooooooh, I like that." Abigail grinned excitedly. "I like that very much...but wait, does that mean I must abide by the Laws of Haunting?"

Little Wade laughed proudly. "No, Abigail, you are very much alive. You are free."

"Well, this free young lady wants to continue the adventure. I am your client, and I wish to continue this great game of chess. Together, we make our next move!"

"You're certainly not a mouse anymore, Abigail Reid." Little Wade then raised his hands and conjured up another map of the Lower East Side. "As I mentioned earlier this morning, many different ethnic groups call this neighborhood home: Irish, Italians, Jews, Chinese, Hungarians, Germans, Russians, Indians, Africans, Spanish. Each one of these tightly knit communities is united by language and culture. Unfortunately, years ago, the Longshadows divided this neighborhood, and they sowed discord by doing something very clever, Abigail. Using their sneakiest burglars, they stole important artifacts from every one of these populations. Worse, they made it seem as if the different communities stole from each other!"

"That's horrible but brilliant."

"I agree, fiendishly clever. As a result, all of these different groups no longer trust each other, nor do they trust the police to rectify the situation. If we wish to build your secret passage, if we plan to ask that people open their hearts and their doors to you, we must give them a reason to believe in people again, to trust people."

"So we must steal every artifact back," Abigail interjected, becoming very excited, "and return everything."

"Yes. Luckily for us, the Longshadows arrogantly locked away all of these artifacts in one place, somewhere hidden in the neighborhood. At this hideout, they can admire all of the precious items they have stolen from people over the years. It's called the Thieves' Museum."

Abigail practically jumped up and down. She could barely contain herself. "We're going to give the items back to the people and inspire the neighborhood! What a brilliant plan!"

"There exists one obstacle," Little Wade cautioned her.

"What?" she asked, somewhat deflated.

"No one knows where the Thieves' Museum is…but…"

"You know."

Little Wade smiled slyly. "We know it's located somewhere in the Lower East Side, but we need your help to locate it. So what do you say, Abigail Reid? Would you like to do a bit of good and help us break into the Thieves' Museum? Unusual, I know, that we're asking you to help us commit a robbery, but we intend to steal things already stolen, so we consider it really more of a counter-robbery, and Precinct Zero will be involved, but I really ought to be responsible and warn you that it will be danger—"

Before he could complete his sentence, Abigail enthusiastically roared. Her voice carried upwards toward the ceiling and the sky beyond, rattling the world.

"*I consent!*"

COMING SOON!

ACKNOWLEDGMENTS

This novel would not have been possible without my friends, family, and partners without whose support I would have been unable to bring this dream to life. The list is too long to be included here, but they know who they are.

There are three people that deserve special recognition. A few years ago, after a particularly bad day I lay my head down on my pillow to try to sleep. That night I dreamed of a floating, ghostly boy and a metal giant with the face of a gaslight wearing a suit and top hat. As I dreamed, they marched through the black city of my nightmare, banishing the dark. Between them walked a little girl with fiery red hair, like a burning rose. I didn't know how or why, but I felt an immense sense of Hope.

When I woke up, I started writing.

ABOUT THE AUTHOR

Sean March is the creator and author of Little Wade and Watchtower.

Born and raised in New York City, Sean attended Elementary and Middle School in Manhattan and spent his childhood on the streets of the Lower East Side. He can vividly recall a fateful night when, running home late from school, he was accosted by members of a local gang. Two mysterious strangers came to his aid, chased off the gang members, walked him home, and then bid him good night. Sean's one regret was that, in all of the excitement, he completely forgot to ask his rescuers their names. This series is dedicated to them, and to any child who is having a hard time and is seeking inspiration.

An avid reader of history, Sean lives with his family, which includes two adorable pugs.

This is his first novel.

Made in the USA
Middletown, DE
14 November 2020